A House in the Land of Shinar

BERNADETTE MILLER

ARCHWAY
PUBLISHING

Archway Publishing books may be ordered through booksellers or by contacting:

Archway Publishing
1663 Liberty Drive
Bloomington, IN 47403
www.archwaypublishing.com
844-669-3957

Because of the dynamic nature of the Internet, any web addresses or links contained in this book may have changed since publication and may no longer be valid. The views expressed in this work are solely those of the author and do not necessarily reflect the views of the publisher, and the publisher hereby disclaims any responsibility for them.

Modified photo of cobblestoned road by Thomasz Kuran aka Meteor 2017 (https://commons.wikimedia.org/wiki/File:Guzow-Oryszew Road-cm 04.jpg), https://CreativeCommons.org/licenses/by-Sa/3.

Scripture taken from the King James version of the Bible.

ISBN: 978-1-4808-8443-4 (sc)
ISBN: 978-1-4808-8444-1 (hc)
ISBN: 978-1-4808-8445-8 (e)

Library of Congress Control Number: 2020901100

Print information available on the last page.

Archway Publishing rev. date: 01/15/2021

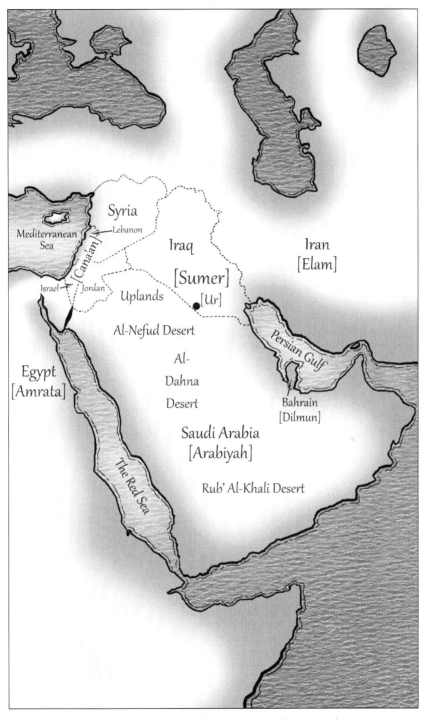

The Land of Shinar (Sumer in southern Iraq),
and surrounding area, c.3500 B.C.

"And it came to pass, as they journeyed from the east
that they found a plain in the land of Shinar;
and they dwelt there."

–*The Bible*, Genesis, Chapter 11, Verse 2

INTRODUCTION

OVER FIVE THOUSAND YEARS AGO, long before there were Jews, Christians, Muslims, and the *Bible*, a tiny, non-Arab country in southern Iraq called Sumer (the land of Shinar) accomplished amazing things. Perhaps their most astonishing accomplishment was how their mythological stories somehow became linked to the *Old Testament*.

While the Middle East consisted mainly of primitive Bedouin Arabs living in desert tents, the sophisticated Sumerians built cities with paved streets, and homes whose whitewashed walls glittered under the hot sun. Their ziggurat, a mud-brick building complex, soared some sixty feet toward the sky. Never content with simply overcoming the impossible, the incredible Sumerians also created kingship, a bicameral congress, and an organized army. Among their many other innovations, they developed the arch, dome, and wheel, and went on to create calendars, clocks, and trial by jury. Schools and libraries were established. They created an early form of banking that included Letters of Credit. Even more surprising for such an ancient period, the Sumerians' preoccupation with wealth and prestige resembled our own.

All this wizardry took about three-thousand years, ending in 2004 B.C. Then, like a puff of smoke, the Sumerians were gone, conquered by an Arabic people called Amorites. Fortunately, Sumerian scribes preserved their culture by writing their history on mud-brick tablets, including the naughty escapades of their gods and goddesses.

Dr. Andre Parrot, a director of the Mari Archaeological Expedition in Iraq, wrote in his book, *Nineveh and the Old Testament*, that biblical stories like, "The Garden of Eden," "Adam and Eve," and "The Great Flood," probably originated in Sumer. A distinguished archaeologist who discovered the Sumerian graves, Sir Leonard Woolley, described in his book, *The Sumerians*, their major city-state called Ur. Several millennia later, *The Old Testament* mentioned Ur as Abraham's city.

Probably the most revealing is *The Sumerians* by Professor Samuel Noah Kramer, who spent thirty years translating the tablets. Sumerian scribes scornfully described their "vulgar Arabi" neighbors, assuring readers, present and future, that the Sumerians, deeply prejudiced about foreigners, weren't Arabs.

It's therefore ironic that a crude Bedouin, whose itinerant tribe perhaps worshipped an imaginary bull-god, heard the Sumerians' mythological stories while bartering his wool in Sumer. He might have believed that the stories were real, assuming deeper meanings by a culture superior to his own primitive religion. Perhaps he then transformed the stories' plots to conform to his tribal beliefs, and thus created the roots of a new religion, Judaism, that culminated in a profound work of art, the *Bible*.

Although *A House in the Land of Shinar* is fiction, the possibility that encounters between Bedouin Arabs and Sumerian citizens might have led to the beginning of Judaism is based on archaeological evidence. However, the time period in the novel has been compressed to spread events over several generations rather than several millennia.

Bernadette Miller

CHAPTER 1

July, 3500 B.C., Arabiyah
(Al-Dahna Desert in central Saudi Arabia)

AT DUSK, DREADING THE WEEKLY WORSHIP, Tiras said good-bye to Milcah, one of his three wives, and kissed her cheek. Then, turning in her black tent warmed by a glowing copper lantern, he smiled at his adorable, five-year-old daughter, Shallah, who was tugging at his robes beneath his open sheepskin cloak. "Baba, baba, baba," she murmured, using the affectionate term for father. He scooped her up in her robe, and felt her tiny heart beating against his chest while she kissed his closed eyes.

"I must go, my darling Shallah," he finally whispered and set her back on the carpet. He continued smiling as she watched him tug out a shawl from a storage sack hanging against the tent wall, wind the shawl into a turban as protection against the nocturnal cold, and then fasten his cloak's toggles. Milcah handed him the prayer rug. He tucked it under an arm, his beard-framed smile changing to a frown. "I'll be back after the ceremony," he said grimly to Milcah, who nodded in response.

Outside, Tiras rushed to join his father, Mashech, the tribal sheikh, and their Bedouin kinsmen who had already passed Milcah's tent and were headed toward the camp's boundary marked by a row of bushy-headed tamarisk trees. As the robed men trudged past dozing flocks of sheep, goats, and donkeys, their thick woven socks and leather sandals cushioning the hard, pebbly sand, Tiras sought reassurance in the soaring limestone cliffs and the high reddish dunes opposite that provided some protection from warring tribes. In the far distance, the Al-Ubiyah Oasis beckoned with its palm-fringed lake and lush pasture under the graying sky. The peaceful surroundings seemed to say, "Do not worry, Tiras. It's safe here." But he knew better.

Like Tiras, each of his scowling kinsmen clutched a rolled-up prayer rug under their arm. Some also carried a sack of butchered goat meat that stained their sheepskin cloaks over robes already soiled with food particles and animal saliva. Others held unlit copper lanterns. The men complained about the worship ceremony, whispered lest their bull-god, Martu, overheard and punished them. Only their priest, Abu-Summu, could interpret the bull-god's wishes and issue his harsh judgements. Tiras remembered how just last week, a boy of nine, had been bound in ropes on the altar and beaten until his naked flesh was raked with gaping wounds.

As usual, Abu-Summu had directed the tribe's Council of Elders to carry out the punishment, meant to discipline the child's father for questioning Martu's motives. The Elders, a group of senior, male Bedouins elected by the tribe, acted as judge and jury to hear tribal violations—except when the case involved the priest. After the punishment, the weeping father had daubed his son's wounds with a woven cloth soaked in date wine to ward off evil spirits and then wrapped his whimpering child in a blanket. His kinsmen had murmured condolences as they headed back toward their black tents peppering the sand. They swung their copper lanterns lit from the ceremonial fire, illuminating a path through the desert darkness.

"How can we prevent Martu from punishing more children in this horrible way?" one man finally whispered.

Bernadette Miller

"We must be careful not to offend Abu-Summu," another man warned.

Others stared grimly at the reddish sand dunes as they recalled the revulsion of past punishments.

"You can't know what it's like until it happens to you," the father of the tortured child added, his beard damp from tears as he stroked his son's arm.

"But if we protest," another man said, "we see how Abu-Summu punishes us. Do we want to watch more children beaten?"

"We must find a way to soften our god's demands," Tiras said. "I've tried challenging the priest, but nothing has changed."

"It's too dangerous," Mashech, his father, added. Bitten by a jackal during a hunt, Mashech limped with his cane fashioned from a stout tree branch as his free arm clutched a prayer rug. "Before I became the sheikh," he continued, "remember how I complained to Abu-Summu? Then, my daughter, Mariah, was beaten and died soon afterwards of a sickness. All we can do is wait for our priest to grow old. Even he can't prevent his own death."

"That must be so," the others responded with dejected nods as they dispersed into their tents. Their lanterns flickered out in the darkness.

No, that can't be so, Tiras promised himself. As the sheikh's son, he would find a way to challenge their fierce bull-god.

Meanwhile, though, the men had to listen to their priest.

೮೦ ೮೪

With increased scowls, the Bedouins knelt on their prayer rugs, and stared, rigid with expectation, at their priest, Abu-Summu, with his long black beard and fierce dark eyes. He'd already piled up stones to form the altar, a cube three feet high, topped by a wooden ledge that featured the twin, silver horns representing Martu. Beyond the altar, a crackling bonfire of tamarisk branches, aided by the wind god, Al-Qais, showered sparks upward toward the sky, home of the twinkling star goddesses and Martu, their bull-god, who dwelt among them.

Tiras turned from the altar, his thoughts focused on his dangerous mission. So many children had been punished to satisfy Martu's insatiable demands. He constantly worried, like his kinsmen, about protecting his three children. *I must do something,* he thought. *But if I continue challenging Martu, the priest will punish my entire family.* His uncle had complained and was banished to the wilderness with his wives and children, a death sentence without the tribe's protection. Tiras shook his head in sorrow at the memory of how the priest had destroyed his uncle's family and so many others as well.

Now it was time to try a new tactic. Instead of challenging the priest, he would appeal to his kinsmen. The outnumbered priest must heed the tribesmen's wishes. He couldn't punish all of them. Tiras nodded to himself and turned toward Abu-Summu standing before the altar. He needed the right moment.

It was obvious that Abu-Summu was growing old and might not last much longer. He looked gaunt and shriveled beneath his cloak and robes. His bearded cheeks were hollow like empty lake beds. He stared at the silver horns glittering in the light from Il-Lah, the moon god, and chanted a warning in his high-pitched voice to the surrounding *shetans* and *jinns,* the unseen imps associated with evil spirits.

The tribesmen talked about their animals, the food they produced, and their family relationships concerning births and forthcoming marriages. Then, as usual, they recounted ancestral stories that had been passed down through generations. Tiras groaned when Abu-Summu recalled how his great-grandfather's grandfather, a priest called Shem, summoned the arrival of their bull-god.

"Let's remember the terrible sickness that had destroyed half our tribe," the priest reminded the silent men. He spread his thin arms beneath his cloak as if to embrace the listeners. "How my ancestor, Shem, dreamed of a powerful bull named Martu that promised good

Bernadette Miller

health. So we began worshipping Martu who favored my ancestors, and now me, his humble servant, with his requests. Let's thank our generous bull-god for prosperity." He paused a moment.

He's considering what to say next, Tiras thought, but he stayed silent, too.

"Oh, my kinsmen, we must honor him with unwavering devotion," the priest implored them. "Otherwise, we're doomed to hardship. Great Martu has spoken."

The tribesmen murmured, "Yes," in unison as their heads bent in submission toward their rugs.

Abu-Summu gathered the horns from the altar as preparation for the final ritual.

This was his chance, Tiras decided. He jumped up and turned to the cowering men. "Why must we always fear Martu?" he called out. "Why doesn't he inspire us with hope? Can't you see, my kinsmen, that we can't live forever with fear?"

Abu-Summu's indignant face reddened with anger. He swiveled toward the meddler. "Tiras," he shouted, "since boyhood you have challenged my wisdom and authority! As I keep reminding you, Martu expects absolute loyalty or he'll abandon us to the jinns. That's a tragedy I've struggled all my life to avoid, just like my wise ancestors. Be wary of antagonizing our powerful bull-god!"

"Listen to him, Tiras!" a council Elder shouted.

Other tribesmen shouted their agreement.

Tiras shook his head. *Was he going to fail so quickly and easily?* He turned toward the men cowering on their rugs. "But why must we suffer for the slightest sin? Isn't it better to challenge the priest than to punish our children?"

The tribesmen began arguing among themselves. One yelled, "Do you want Martu to ruin us? Is that your hope for our future?"

Others yelled more warnings.

Tiras hesitated. How could he convince them? He must keep trying, he assured himself.

Mashech, helped by Tiras, struggled to rise with his injured leg. He turned to the priest and said with feigned, utmost pleasantness, "Dear Abu-Summu, we all know that since he was a child, Tiras has questioned everything. But he won't challenge Martu again." He smiled at Tiras. "Isn't that so, my son?"

"Yes, baba," Tiras replied. Despite being a grown man, he couldn't disagree with his father, the sheikh, before the tribesmen. Still, his body stiffened with anger at the priest admonishing him.

Abu-Summu nodded as if soothed by the sheikh's reprimand of his rebellious son. He turned toward the tribesmen. "Tonight marks the beginning of a new moon-cycle," he said. "Those of you whose turn it is, bring your share of goat meat to stain the altar with blood. After Tiras's insults, Martu will welcome your offerings."

Several men jumped up and crowded around the altar to unload their sacks of butchered meat. Each shouted, "Here's my portion!"

Tiras's favorite cousin, Ruach, rose and said, "I forgot." Husky Ruach, his eyes downcast before the priest, added, "My eldest son was ill and needed my attention. I'll bring twice as much next time."

Irritated at Ruach's neglect, Abu-Summu pointed a bony finger at him. "To pacify our god for your disregard, your youngest son shall be flogged. The great Martu has spoken!"

Ruach stared at the sand. "Flog me instead. My little son is innocent."

"But the lesson is stronger when your son is flogged," Abu-Summu declared. "Don't further anger our god by denying him."

Enraged that Ruach's obedient son would be battered for his father's minor sin, Tiras exclaimed without considering the possible danger, "Why must Martu always demand that an innocent child be harmed? It's unjust! Any of us would gladly take the child's place."

Abu-Summu's face pinched in fury. He swiveled toward Tiras. "Over many years, I have warned you and warned you! I tried to forgive your dishonoring our generous bull-god out of respect for your

Bernadette Miller

father, the sheikh. But my warnings have fallen on deaf ears! Tiras, you've exhausted my patience. Only punishment will convince you!"

The priest stared upward at the star goddesses. "Martu hungers for Shallah. Bring your daughter to be punished. Great Martu has spoken."

Stunned, Tiras paled beneath his beard. He glanced at his father who was shaking his head, also unprepared for this outcome.

"Bring her now!" Abu-Summu shrieked. "Or you and your family shall be banished to the wilderness and probably devoured by *Lotan*, the serpent god!"

"Son, you must do this for our family," Mashech said with a faltering voice. "You know how much I love Shallah. But we dare not risk Martu's revenge."

"Tiras, listen to the sheikh!" a tribesman shouted in panic. "Or who knows what else Martu will demand."

Tiras stared at the priest and mentally scolded himself for endangering his family. Why hadn't he realized what might happen from his reckless behavior? "You're asking me to do something evil," he finally said with a shaky voice, hoping by some miracle to dissuade the tribe's tormentor and spare his beloved daughter.

As if calmed by finally punishing the troublemaker, the priest replied gently, "No, Tiras, it isn't evil to appease Martu's fury. We must beg him to forgive your insults." His gaze shifted upward. He called out, his voice pleading. "Oh, great Martu, pardon our troubled kinsman, Tiras. As atonement, he offers his only daughter for punishment."

The priest's hands curled up and down before the crackling bonfire. "Come to us, adored god."

Intent on the priest's eerie gestures and the bonfire's angry sparks, Tiras thought he saw Martu descending from the star-studded sky to hover above the altar. He had envisioned the god so many times that this vision seemed particularly vivid and frightening. His stomach tightened at observing the reddened eyes, flared nostrils, and hooves pawing the air which were just as awesome as the priest had described them. The bull's massive face nodded as if satisfied by the forthcoming punishment.

Tiras shook his head to dispel the image and fight off his cowardice. He should refuse the priest. Refuse Martu. Save his daughter! Then, he reminded himself that if he disobeyed Abu-Summu, his entire family would be banished. He faced a horrible dilemma: save his daughter from flogging or save his family from banishment and certain death.

His stomach began heaving as he walked slowly from the bonfire, as if even his bowels protested the evil deed.

Inside Milcah's tent, Shallah ran toward him. "Baba!"

He stroked her face and told Milcah in a voice drained of its usual force, "Martu demands Shallah's blood."

"No!" Milcah shrieked. "Don't take our daughter!" In the lantern's light, plump Milcah grabbed Shallah and held her close against her bosom.

Shallah began whimpering at the shouting and confusion. "I want baba," she cried, squirming in her mother's arms.

Tiras blinked back tears. "I must take her to the priest," he told his wife. "Do you want Martu to attack us with disease? Or have us banished from the tribe? I can't allow my entire family to die." He stretched forward to grab Shallah.

"No!" Milcah backed against the tent as the child squirmed to free herself so she could run to her father.

"You know that I don't want my innocent daughter punished," Tiras said, his cheeks damp. "Abu-Summu forces me." He tugged and suddenly pulled the little girl toward him and lifted her against his cloak.

Shallah put her arms around Tiras's neck and whispered in his ear, "Baba, why is everyone crying?"

Milcah flailed her empty arms, her robe stretched tight across her thick waist. "No, my husband, don't do this horrible thing! Give her back to me!"

Bernadette Miller

"You know how much I love Shallah. But what can I do? If I refuse our bull-god, our family might be destroyed. What choice do we have?"

"Have Abu-Summu kill me instead but don't punish our child!"

Tiras bit his lip. "I'd gladly sacrifice myself but not my entire family."

Reluctantly he turned from his wailing wife as she trailed behind him, imploring him not to carry their daughter back to the altar.

Shallah began crying and whispered, "Baba, have I done something bad?"

He shook his head and clasped her to his chest. "Shallah, I love you more than you'll ever know, but I must..." His voice choked up. He couldn't speak.

Back at the altar, he approached Abu-Summu, and handed him Shallah who squirmed in the priest's embrace.

"No! I want baba!"

"Ah, the challenger finally obeys Martu," Abu-Summu said and grasped the child in his arms as she continued shouting, her robes flying about.

"No! No!" Shallah beat the priest's chest. "I want baba! Let me go! Let me go!" She began kicking the frowning priest.

Abu-Summu held her writhing body atop the stone altar while she continued kicking and screaming. Several of the Council Elders helped the priest remove the child's robe and restrain her so they could secure her with ropes that dug into her flesh. Struggling in vain to free herself from the ropes, she kept crying, "Baba!"

Milcah rushed to the altar, shouting, "This is wrong! My daughter doesn't deserve this!"

An Elder wrapped his arms about Milcah to detain her. Others, using tree branches as clubs, began swatting the naked girl writhing on the altar, but gently out of respect for her grandfather, the sheikh.

"Hit her harder!" the priest shouted. "Tiras must atone for continuously insulting our devoted protector. Harder! Harder!

He must understand the consequences of criticizing our beloved bull-god!"

Desperate to obey their priest and avoid punishment themselves, the Elders struck Shallah with renewed force.

"Baba!" the girl cried out to Tiras when the clubs struck her, ripping open the tender flesh. Like so many other children, she screamed in anguish while blood began dripping downward in rivulets over the stone altar. To Tiras it seemed to last forever. Her cries suddenly grew feeble. Then, an eerie silence engulfed the desert. The tamarisk trees stood motionless in the moonlight as if in bereavement. The Elders gazed in horror at the altar where Shallah lay there with her throat smashed from a heavy club. Her dark eyes remained open, staring at nothing.

"She's dead!" Milcah screamed and collapsed, sobbing, against the bloodied sand, near her daughter's inert body atop the altar. She raised a fist toward the Elders. "You killed my poor, innocent girl!"

"Martu welcomes our sacrifice," Abu-Summu declared.

But some tribesmen, recoiling in horror, shouted, "It was a mistake!"

"Yes, a mistake!" other shouted, their bodies trembling.

Tiras's stomach heaved. His darling little girl was dead? Brutally murdered? No, that wasn't possible. He clenched his hands into fists at his helplessness and stumbled toward the altar. For several minutes he gazed down at his dead daughter, unable to grasp the shock of her suffering and his loss. Then, he stumbled from the ritual place to vomit behind a tree. When he returned to his prayer rug, he buried his tear-stained face in upturned palms so Abu-Summu wouldn't mock his grief. He'd never forget how he'd abandoned dear Shallah and now feared for his two young sons. They depended on him for survival, not being tortured and perhaps dying in such a horrible way merely to satisfy a cruel bull-god.

What could he do to avenge his daughter's death? Tiras wiped his wet beard with the hem of his robes. Perhaps this terrible scene had shaken the men's faith in their embittered priest and his insistence for human torture. And perhaps the priest was wrong about Martu's commands. If so, a father must bear a dreadful guilt as long as he lives, but how to determine if the priest were wrong? Confused, he looked up.

Abu-summu's cloaked figure stood with uplifted arms that twisted toward the altar. His silhouette swayed before the bonfire's leaping flames against the darkened desert. Even the moon god had fled the unjust scene. "Oh, great Martu, let us appease your wrath with our precious offering. Don't abandon us because of our ignorant ways. Let your mercy guide us again to good health and fertile pastures. I beg you to forgive our faults."

"Yes!" the tribesmen shouted in unison, bending their heads toward their rugs in submission.

৪০ ০৪

Tiras buried his daughter that night to avoid attracting wild animals seeking prey. Because Milcah wasn't allowed to witness the burial of her child who'd been punished to atone for the father's guilt, she was sent alone to her tent to grieve her lost daughter. But cousin Ruach and other close family members joined Tiras in digging a pit at the encampment's boundary beneath a tamarisk tree. Shallah, wearing her robe and turban, was laid to rest in the tiny pit and covered with sand. Ruach outlined stones at the head of the grave and more at the foot to indicate a burial, and Tiras piled her few clothes atop the grave for needy travelers.

After the burial, Tiras returned to Milcah's tent to console her. Instead, she screamed at him as he opened the tent flap and entered the mag'ad, the front area for dining, chatting, and entertaining visitors.

"Get out!" She pointed an accusing, stubby finger at him. "Get out! You allowed our beloved daughter to be murdered. I never want to see you again!"

"But I, too, am grieving," Tiras said, trying to vindicate himself from the terrible burden that he knew would haunt him for the rest of his days. He would carry that image of his beloved daughter slaughtered to satisfy the tribe's bull-god while he stood by, trapped in fear of the god's retribution for intervening.

"Out!" Milcah shouted again. She grabbed an empty copper kettle and pointed it toward him as a weapon. He began backing away on the carpet, toward the tent flap, proving to himself once again his cowardice. "And don't come back!" Milcah shrieked while Tiras hastily backed outside and headed for the tent of his first and favorite wife, Na'amah.

After he tugged open the flap to her tent, Na'amah set aside her weaving and, unlike Milcah, rose with a smile. "My beloved husband. I'm so glad to see you."

He looked at his beautiful, first wife. As always, he admired her deep-set dark eyes outlined with kohl, a beauty supplement, and the thick braid dangling against the pink shawl and black robes, and thought once again, how he wished she were his only wife.

She paused at noting the tears dampening his beard and said anxiously, "What happened?"

Tiras squatted on a cushion and began sobbing despite himself while Na'amah squatted on a cushion beside him. He held his head in his hands and explained the sacrifice, ending with, "It's my fault that I allowed my precious daughter to be murdered. How could I have sat by and said nothing?"

Na'amah learned toward him and put her arms about his shoulders. "It wasn't your fault, Tiras. You saved our family from destruction." She kissed his forehead and added gently, "Rest, husband. I'll serve supper."

He nodded and they silently shared a bowl of rice with meat drippings, followed by yoghurt and dates. He gulped goat's milk to

Bernadette Miller

wash down his food, and leaned back, wishing with all his heart that he could bring back his daughter.

Na'amah placed her hand on his arm. "Tiras, please stay with me again," she whispered. "Don't go to another."

"I can't keep breaking my wedding vows." He paused. "Milcah won't allow me into her tent since Shallah died. And I haven't visited Abada and little Canah for half a moon-cycle. Abada warned me that our son is headstrong. He needs my advice and discipline. Otherwise, he might do something bad when he grows up and the tribe will turn against him."

Tiras paused, noting a glint in Na'amah's dark eyes. He hated to refuse his first love and again remembered their wedding night that had held such passion. It seemed like only yesterday instead of nine years ago when he was fourteen, that Na'amah's belly had refused to bloom with child. So, the Council of Elders persuaded him to wed again, insisting that more children increased the tribe's power and were necessary during old age. Following their orders, he wed his second wife, Milcah, and then again a third wife, Abada. He'd loved all his children, innocents who depended on him for survival, but Na'amah's announcement of carrying Rimush was the happiest day of his life. Unfortunately, she remained jealous of his other wives, but that seemed a minor problem now at this terrible time of losing Shallah.

"All right, I'll stay with you tonight," he relented, despite himself, hoping his favorite wife could lessen his grief over his beloved daughter's murder. Na'amah's smile warmed him. After dinner, he found some relief from his torment about Shallah by playing with his youngest child, three-year-old, curly-haired Rimush. He smiled at his son shouting with glee as he chased after the stuffed goatskin ball that Tiras threw across the tent carpet.

That night, the couple swept aside the qata, the tent's dividing curtain, and entered the maharama, the women's section in back, where Rimush was already asleep in his rolled up rug. Tiras drew his wife into an embrace to kiss her sweet lips but he couldn't make love.

As the naked pair lay over the conjugal rug, Na'amah stroked his face, a breast touching his chest. "Tiras, since Shallah died, you're losing interest in my body. Don't you love me anymore? Are your other wives more appealing?" She waited for an answer. Her dark eyes narrowed. "Tell me. I must know."

"I still love you," he whispered, "but I can't... Not tonight." He sought words to explain his shame at his cowardice about Shallah, but could find none.

Na'amah rose, frowning. "Then maybe you'd better see Abada," she said. "I have no right to interfere with your manly duties." She curled up in another rug.

Tiras, exhausted, closed his eyes and was about to fall asleep when Na'amah snuggled beside him under the rug, her arm curved about his shoulder. Now he was aroused and soon their bodies were one.

Early the next morning, his third wife, Abada, swept aside the qata and stood silhouetted against the dawn goddess's pink attire slanting between the tent's weave. Careful not to awaken Na'amah who slept peacefully, Tiras followed Abada outside the tent.

She paused, staring at him with her alluring heavy-lidded eyes and an intriguing mole beside her full lips. "So, you spend all your nights with your first wife while the third lies in wait for nothing."

"Sorry." Tiras shrugged. "I'll try to visit more often."

"Visit? Like a distant cousin?" Her fists on her hips, Abada glared at him. "I'm your wife! I don't need an invitation. What happened to the two nights chosen for me?"

Na'amah appeared outside. She yawned. "Abada, why are you stirring up all this commotion? And at such a sad time for him after losing his daughter. He'll see you soon."

Abada exclaimed, "You greasy bladder of shit! You're not his only wife. We should work together to make Tiras happy, the way other wives do. Instead, you want to keep him all to yourself. Your jealousy will destroy this family!"

"Kelbeh!" Na'amah shot back. "All you think about is lovemaking? Our husband fulfills his obligations among us whenever he can. I'm surprised he can find your kisich under all that blubber."

"Shlicke!" Abada wagged a finger. "Mashech will hear of this! Don't think you can become Tiras's only wife. My son needs his father's attention."

"Tell Mashech or the entire family if you like!" Na'amah said. "I'm the one my husband loves. He married you and Milcah only because the Elders insisted on it. So leave us alone!"

Face flushed, Tiras raised a hand to silence them. "Enough! I'll be with you tonight," he told Abada. "I'll talk to Canah then. Go back to your tent." He watched her shake a fist at Na'amah and then stride across the sand to her nearby tent.

Before he could reproach Na'amah, her hands cupped his scowling face. "I shouldn't have persuaded you to stay with me last night. It's my fault."

He couldn't help but smile at her concern and followed her inside the tent where she served breakfast, stuffing him with bread-cakes, yoghurt, goat cheese, and wild honey. He silently scolded his weakness. As usual he'd yielded to her wishes and ignored his responsibilities. He treated Abada unfairly. He sighed about his squabbling wives. Despite his well-meaning intentions, he knew that he could be content with just Na'amah, if that were possible.

ଔଔ

For two moon-cycles, long after Shallah's burial, Tiras lay sleepless at night. He kept reproaching himself as he lay upon his wives' conjugal rugs. He remembered his daughter's dimpled cheeks and trusting smile, and how she had struggled to talk and then walk while she put one wobbly foot after the other. How he'd beamed with pride when she ran across the sand to catch the stuffed goatskin ball and shouted triumphantly, "Baba, I got it!"

He kept asking himself, why had he been so cowardly, not protesting more to Abu-Summu about his daughter's savage death? How could he have silently watched Shallah's suffering? Her horrible death was as much his fault as the priest's. He'd remained frozen on his prayer rug, as if drunk with date wine, unable to shout his objections, fearful of any new demands by the terrifying priest.

I'm a coward, Tiras whispered to himself one night while still seeking personal forgiveness. Beside him, Na'amah slept peacefully. He gazed at the copper lantern's softly glowing embers beneath the hanging storage sacks, as if the light might show him a way to forgiveness. But there was none.

Finally, he tugged at his portion of the rug to avoid awakening Na'amah, rose, and swept aside the tent's dividing curtain to enter the mag'ad, the visitor's area. With narrowed eyes and trembling lips, he strode across the carpet and squatted before the open tent flap, his hands curled into fists. He reminded himself that suffering wasn't his alone. The entire tribe suffered because of their bull-god's cruelty.

Perhaps it was time to seek a new tribal god! So what if Martu sought revenge. Why hadn't the bull-god conquered the neighboring tribes' chief gods as Abu-Summu had predicted? Maybe Martu's power was limited. If so, a more potent god could topple him, which would be a well-deserved punishment. The bull-god should treat worshippers with respect instead of slashing at their hearts!

Tiras stared at the reddish dunes spreading like waves of blood across the horizon as he pondered his new mission. But where to find such a powerful god? And if he found one, how could he persuade it to conquer Martu and protect the tribe from Abu-Summu, their vicious priest?

Bernadette Miller

CHAPTER 2

August, 3517 B.C., Arabiyah

WHEN HE WAS SIX, TIRAS enjoyed riding a donkey by himself. His mother, Zabaia, had tied him between storage sacks that first time. He clutched the reins, kicked his sandals against the donkey's fat belly, and called out in his most commanding voice, "Eeyah!" The donkey galloped across the pebbly sand.

His mother shouted from behind, "No, Tiras! Don't urge the donkey faster!"

He giggled and let the donkey run while a breeze ruffled his robes.

When the Abram tribe stopped to set up camp about a mile from the Al-Ubiyah oasis, his mother scolded him as she untied him. "Didn't I warn you about making the donkey go faster? You must listen to what I say or you'll be killed." She paused. "The poor donkey will be worn out, running with heavy storage sacks."

"Yes, oomah," Tiras replied, using the affectionate term for mama. He stifled a grin that might invite another frown, but he knew he would still urge the donkey to run.

"Oh, my son. So young, with such a strong will." Zabaia hugged him against her bosom. Then, holding him at arm's length, she pushed aside his robe and fingered the fig-shaped birthmark on his left shoulder. "A sign of importance! Someday if you set your mind to it you'll accomplish great feats."

"What feats?"

She shook her head. "I can't talk more. I must set up our tent."

Tiras nodded and watched his mother unload poles from her donkeys. She unwrapped a black goat hair tent made of woven panels sewn together with large copper needles. As she spread the tent on the sand, he approached her, saying, "Oomah, let me help."

"You're too young," she replied and pounded a pole into the sand with a mallet fashioned from a tree trunk.

"I'm little but strong," Tiras said, pouting. He raised his arms under his robe and displayed his muscles.

Zabaia laughed. "Yes, very strong. I'll remember that when you grow up and say you're too tired to help." As she lifted one end of the tent, Tiras tried to raise an edge. "All right, son," she relented. "But don't pull on it."

He held the edge tightly, his muscles aching. He pressed his lips together to avoid crying out from the effort.

She stretched the tent over the poles. "Step back!" she ordered Tiras. She lifted and pushed, grunting from the hard work. The tent with its multi-peaked roof rested securely on the poles and draped over the sides. Using the knotted, tension ropes, she began attaching the tent's edge to the poles.

Tiras reached up to help by grabbing at the tent.

She said sharply, "No, Tiras, don't touch that! It's dangerous."

He stepped back. How long would she treat him like a baby? He couldn't stand it.

"The tent could unloosen and hurt you," she explained.

"Then let's kill the bad tent!" he declared. "And it won't hurt anybody."

"I don't want to destroy it," she said, attaching more ropes. "I own the tent so everything you see here is my responsibility."

Bernadette Miller

"Why?"

She finished attaching the last rope. "Because in case of separation we'll know who gets what."

"What's separation?"

She began unloading rugs and cushions from the storage sacks stacked on the sand. "Separation is when I say to Mashech, I don't want to be your wife anymore. Don't enter my tent again."

"Why would you say that? Don't you love baba?"

"I do love him. I'm not asking for a separation. I'm just trying to explain..." She sighed. "So many questions." Inside the tent, she spread a large carpet over the sand. Tiras set a cushion on the carpet as she'd instructed. Oomah bent down and hugged him. "You're a good boy," she said. "But you want to know everything at once. Be patient. You'll learn it all when you're grown."

Nodding, he nestled against her bosom and decided to continue asking questions. He refused to be treated like a baby! He closed his eyes and pictured the delicious supper his mother would prepare that evening.

Later, he watched her squat at the outside hearth to bake bread-cakes. His stomach rumbled with expectation. Over the shallow pit filled with glowing embers, Zabaia placed large stones and covered them with a copper plate. She stirred flour into water from a goatskin sack and shaped the kneaded dough into cakes dimpled with dates that she baked on the plate. Soon, the bread-cakes exuded a sweet smell. He was about to ask if he could have one—he couldn't wait!— when he saw his father approaching.

A silver, six-pointed star on a beaded chain glinted against Machech's robe as he bent to kiss Zabaia's cheek. "Salaam 'alaykum, Zabaia," he said.

She looked up and smiled. 'Alaykum salaam, Mashech." With wooden tongs, she overturned the bread-cakes sizzling on the copper plate.

Before Tiras could beg for one, his father picked him up in his miniature robes. He swung him around and set him down gently. "Now, my little man, I'm the new sheikh, the tribal chief," he said. "Just elected by the Council of Elders. Do you know what happens to bad little boys who don't obey their parents and the priest? They're eaten by dragons!"

Tiras shivered. "And little boys who do obey?"

"Ah, they're given dates and milk and honey and hugged."

Tiras gazed up at his tall father looming over him. "Someday, I'll kill a dragon."

His father's bearded cheeks widened into a grin. He shook his head. His black braids flew about his shoulders. "Only if you obey your parents. Otherwise, you won't live long enough." From his robe pocket he withdrew a six-pointed star on a miniature chain necklace that resembled his own. "Your mother made this amulet for you from silver at the oasis. You'll get longer ones as you grow older." He placed the necklace around Tiras's neck. "The six-pointed star has been our tribal symbol for generations. In olden times, our hunters wore such an amulet and killed dragons, earning honor for the tribe. Just grasp the amulet and it will always protect you."

"Now I can kill dragons," Tiras said, smiling as he stroked the amulet. He paused. "Baba, have you ever seen a dragon?"

"No. But stories about them have been handed down for generations."

"Where are they?" Tiras asked. "Why don't we see them?"

"Well, most of them probably went to the netherworld below the sand to eat bad people."

Tiras shivered again. "Don't the dragons have bread-cakes and milk?"

Mashech chuckled. "You ask too many questions, son."

"But, why—"

"Enough! Soon you'll enjoy your mother's supper. Now, I must leave. I'm staying tonight with my second wife and children."

Tiras nodded but wished baba would stay with him and his

mother. He was sad every time baba left their tent to attend his flock of sheep and goats, go hunting, or visit another wife.

Later, when Il-Lah spread his golden fingers across the dark desert, Zabaia set on the tent's carpet two copper lanterns containing lighted pellets of dried gazelle dung that exuded the sweet fragrance of thyme and chamomile, which was the gazelle's food. The tent walls shimmered. She wrapped Tiras in a warm sheepskin rug lined with wool to ward off the night's coldness.

Too excited about the dragons to sleep, he watched oomah squat on the carpet and spin wool, her twin braids shiny in the light from the lanterns. Her right palm twirled a spindle while her left palm guided the fleece streaming from a tree branch beneath her left arm. She sang a lullaby about a lost lamb bleating for its mother.

Tiras stared at the tent wall and tried to picture a dragon. Were they as tall as baba? he thought. Did they fly through the air? Or did they run along the sand? He grasped his magic amulet and pictured fighting a dragon when he was a man. The beast was as big as a mountain, breathing fire from a huge mouth with sharp teeth. Long claws seemed poised to grasp him as he climbed upward on its belly. The long, scaly tongue flickered with sparks. Unafraid, he unsheathed his dagger and drove it into the dragon's heart past his scales. A great roar echoed through the desert as the dragon died.

Tiras looked down at the dead and defeated dragon. He had won! He was a great fighter! The vision faded though and he wondered if there really were dragons?

Zabaia stopped singing. "Go to sleep, little one," she called out. "Tomorrow we'll help shear the sheep. And you'll be tired."

"I'm thinking about my amulet. What do dragons look like? Where do they come from? Have you ever seen one? Why do they eat bad little boys?"

She burst out laughing. "Always so many questions. You'll wear us out."

"Oomah, why can't you and baba tell me what a dragon looks

like? Why do people believe in them if nobody knows what they look like? Were the dragons made up? Is Martu made up?"

"Tiras, I've heard about dragons since I was a child. So they must be real! Someday you'll learn all the answers to your questions and become a great sheikh. Meanwhile, obey me, your baba, and Abu-Summu, our priest. Especially obey Martu. He must be real! Abu-Summu warns us that our watchful bull-god sees everything. You must obey Martu or we'll lose another child, like Mariah." Eyes dampening, she turned away. "Now, shhh, little one. Go to sleep!" She bent over the twirling spindle.

He closed his eyes but remained awake. *When I grow up, I'll kill a dragon. Then, the tribesmen will tell stories about me like the ones they tell near the bonfire.*

ꙮ ꙮ

Tiras looked forward to learning more from Loban, his eldest and favorite brother. Loban had a bulky body, bald head, and two wives, but no children. He taught him survival skills, such as finding water in the desert after a drought by squeezing certain plants that held moisture. At the age of ten, it was time Tiras knew these things.

One day, Loban hung a storage sack of Tiras's clothing on one of the upright branches of a tamarisk shrub, its remaining branches spraying the sand. "We'll get the sack on our return," he explained. "So we don't wear out the donkeys."

Tiras looked up at the sack and pouted. "Suppose other children take it? I don't want to give them my robes and turbans."

Loban put his warm hands on Tiras's shoulders. "Our code forbids claiming personal items. Your clothes are safe."

Tiras nodded with relief. Loban reached down and tickled Tiras in his arm pits. "Are you so tiny you can't help anyone else?"

"Stop! Stop!" Tiras squealed. He bent over and laughed so hard tears ran down his face.

Loban hugged Tiras. "I love you, little brother."

"I love you, too, big brother," Tiras whispered, his arms encircling the older man's broad shoulders.

At suppertime, Tiras wanted to eat with Loban, but his mother said, "Not this evening. Your father will join us."

Tiras nodded, smiling. He felt special when his father joined him and his mother instead of choosing one of his other three wives.

In the mag'ad, the tent's front area, Mashech emptied his bowl of meat and rose with a solemn expression. 'Son, it's time to worship our beloved bull-god, Martu."

"Why are you afraid of Martu?" Tiras asked, rising.

"He's everywhere," his father whispered. He helped Tiras don a sheepskin cloak from a storage sack hanging against the tent wall. "Martu's constantly watching. He could destroy us."

"I'll be careful," Tiras promised as he tugged on the cloak, though he wasn't sure what it was he shouldn't do.

Zabaia swept aside the dividing curtain that concealed the woman's area, and kissed them good-bye.

Mashech smiled at her, and then whispered to Tiras, "Don't say anything evil about our bull-god. Somehow Martu finds out and punishes us."

Tiras nodded, but he wondered why everyone warned him that Martu was everywhere when he'd never seen the bull-god, only the altar horns. Over and over they told him to obey the priest or Martu would punish them. So, why hadn't he seen the bull-god? Was Martu real?

᠗᠙ᚳᚸ

One afternoon when Tiras was twelve, the Abram tribe encamped again near the Al-Ubiyah oasis in the Al-Dahna desert. As his tribe passed the village entrance with its palms and bushes, he gazed in awe, as usual, at the adobe houses and shops clustered along the alleys' pebbled streets. He wondered what secrets the villagers hid from visitors. Did they have strange animals? Maybe dragons?

From a stall lining an alleyway, Al-Halwa's thick bars made from sesame butter and honey beckoned with their sweet candy smells. His mother tugged at his elbow to move on. In the shops, his family bartered their wool and woven items in exchange for flour, rice, dates, copper pots, bowls, daggers, and glittering lapis lazuli and carnelian gemstones to fashion into jewelry for bartering or to wear at celebrations.

Afterwards, they enjoyed themselves at the lake, and then ate at a cafe built of limestone and owned by non-Bedouin Arabs who lived in the village. Other Bedouin tribes occasionally visited the café along with the locals, and over the years Tiras had learned words from several tribal tongues. Visiting the café felt like a festival with his family eating meat stew, drinking date wine, and chatting with the strangers. Musicians played familiar melodies until late evening when everyone returned to their tents.

೮ೞ

One afternoon, instead of joining the others at the lake, Loban had gained permission for Tiras to explore the oasis. Instead, Loban led him to another café at the far end of the oasis visited by the locals. There, for the first time, Tiras saw a nearly-naked dancing woman. He'd been enjoying a bowl of Al-Halwa and a cup of goat's milk when the musicians began playing. The beaded curtains parted at the rear. A pretty woman entered. He stared at her round face and beaded shirt that barely covered her large breasts. Her finely-woven pants gathered at her ankles. Kohl outlined her dark, almond-shaped eyes. A headpiece with dangling blue beads crowned her long black hair. She danced, clicking something on her fingers as she undulated to the lively music. Guests shouted and tossed coins into a basket that was passed around. Tiras's stomach tingled pleasantly, with his zibbinu rising. Lately, he'd begun fondling his penis harder and harder until one night he gasped with pleasure when a sticky glob erupted over his belly. Then he had thought with anxiety, *Oh, no, Martu punished me. He broke it!*

Guilt kept him silent over his possible sin. Later, he realized Martu couldn't have broken his zibbinu. Otherwise, it wouldn't continue pleasing him. Confused, he finally confided in Loban in the cafe.

"It's okay," Loban said, smiling. "I started at your age. There's nothing wrong. When you get married, you won't need to." He paused, stroked his beard, and said, "Someday you'll learn to enjoy a woman. Kiss her lips. Caress her softness. Then, stick your zibbinu inside her."

Tiras grinned. It sounded like fun.

Loban leaned across the scarred wood table and whispered with narrowed eyes, "Tiras, don't mention I brought you here."

"Is being here sinful?" Tiras asked. He couldn't stop staring at the dancing woman. He wished he could put his zibbinu inside her and discover what it felt like.

"Well, not quite a sin..." Loban's voice trailed off. He sipped his date wine and added, "Let's just say that twelve years old is time to see something of the world."

"I like it very much," Tiras said, proud at being considered almost grown up at twelve. "As long as dragons don't punish us."

Loban frowned. "I'm more worried about our priest finding out. I'm tired of—" He paused as the pretty dancer approached him.

"Would you like to dance with me?"

"No, he can't," Tiras explained. "He'll be eaten by dragons as punishment."

"What!" The woman burst into laughter. She turned to the room full of admiring men. "These ignorant Bedouins," she called out. "All they know is sheep and goats and sleeping on the ground."

Loban jumped up. There was a loud smack as he struck her

across the face. "Sharmata! Don't think you're free to insult us." The smack was so hard that the woman lost her balance. She grabbed at a table and slid onto the slatted floor.

Some village men quickly surrounded Loban. An older man with a gray beard and black robe snarled, "Ibn haram! Don't suppose you animals are free to call our women whores and strike them." He pulled out his belt dagger and lunged toward Loban who tried to twist sideways, but the stranger stabbed him in the chest. Loban collapsed onto the floor against a table. He clutched his blood-stained chest. Wine splashed over the table and pooled on the floor.

"Tiras, run to baba!" Loban gasped. He closed his eyes and remained still.

"Catch him!" a man shouted as Tiras bolted from the room.

Tiras ran as fast as possible through the alleys to find his father. He glanced back a couple of times but no one was pursuing him. *Oh, Loban, please don't die,* he prayed. *I love you. It's all my fault about the dragons.*"

He found his father swimming at the lake and related what had happened. By the time the tribesmen donned their robes and hurried to the village, the café was closed. The furious men peered through the windows. The tables were lined against the wall, with the benches stacked. The blood had been washed away. Loban's body had disappeared.

Mashech rushed to the nearest house to learn of his son's whereabouts. He pounded at the wooden door, but nobody answered. Tribal members pounded at other doors. The houses were dark. The villagers must have left, taking Loban's body with them.

"There'll be bloody war here," Mashech muttered. "Bloody war from the Abram tribe."

Mashech kept his word. The following morning, before Al-Uzza, the dawn goddess, tinted the sky, his tribesmen stormed into the houses at Al-Ubiyah, smashing down the wooden doors. The villagers awoke to see men with daggers and swords bent over their beds, hacking at them as they tried to flee. The women and children, screaming in terror, fell on their knees beside their beds.

"Please, don't kill us," a woman begged, just before a sword pierced her heart.

The village men who escaped the initial blows crawled toward their weapons stashed beneath the beds. It was too late. Half asleep, they stumbled about in the feeble light from a small window only to feel in their back a blade's fatal thrust. Mashech had ordered his men to kill everyone. Even the babies. The hands and clothes of every tribesman dripped with blood as the men exacted their vengeance.

As an adolescent, Tiras had been spared from fighting with other tribes. He witnessed the carnage anyway as the villagers, their clothes bloody, staggered outside and fell into the dirt. He watched for a while and then stumbled to the village entrance where he vomited his breakfast into the bushes. He wiped his face with a robe sleeve and reproached himself for his childishness.

Twelve is almost a man! Men don't vomit at such sights. I've seen killings—animals slaughtered. But his limbs trembled. *Dear Loban,* he thought, *I'll never see you again. All because of what I said about the dragons.* He sank among the bushes and beat his chest. *I'm sorry, Loban! I'm so sorry!*

His father finally found him. "Come, son," he said and pulled up Tiras by the arm.

Accompanying baba back to camp followed by their kinsmen, Tiras walked with an unsteady gait. He rubbed at his tear-streaked face to remove evidence of his weakness.

His father tried to comfort him over Loban's death. "We can't bring your brother back. But we wreaked vengeance against those who murdered him."

Tiras looked up at his father and blubbered, despite himself, "But, baba, I saw the man who killed Loban. Old. Gray beard. Black robe. Why didn't we kill just him?"

"Because he destroyed my son's body and then hid among the

villagers. So we killed the villagers. Tribal justice demands we protect each other. If we don't, who will? Blood calls for blood. An eye for an eye. Remember this lesson." His father paused. "It's Martu's will. Abu-Summu will explain."

But back at their camp that night, Abu-Summu didn't explain why the entire village was punished for one man's sin. "Justice has been done as demanded by Martu," he declared.

The tribesmen agreed. The slain man's spirit could rest in peace. They bent on their prayer rugs and stared at the sand in full obedience.

Tiras felt compelled to speak. To the astonishment of the much older tribesmen, he said, "That doesn't seem fair. We should have killed just the bad man who killed Loban. The others were innocent."

Abu-Summu stared at Tiras. "Only a child and already a challenger," he said. "Stirring up our tribesmen against Martu! You must mind our god's wishes, or Martu might require a sacrifice. Perhaps a brother."

Tiras's father shivered beside him. Reluctant to bring shame upon baba and the tribe, Tiras said, "I...won't question...Martu again." He was glad at pleasing his father and placating the priest, but questions remained. Someday, he promised himself, he would find the answers. Then he'll share the truth with his kinsmen and they'll listen.

After the ceremony, still feeling guilty about Loban's death and the villagers destroyed in retribution, Tiras returned to his mother's tent. He couldn't understand why the tribe was so terrified of Martu when he'd never seen him. Later, rolled up in his rug prepared to sleep, he finally envisioned the bull-god.

As the tribesmen had often described, Martu descended from the sky with flared nostrils and burning eyes. His huge hooves pawed the air. "Obey me, Tiras!" he ordered in a deep voice. "Or I'll kill you and your entire family!"

"I will!" Tiras cried out in terror. "Always. Please. Don't hurt my family."

Bernadette Miller

Martu snorted. "That's up to you. Obey Abu-Summu. Or suffer the fate of your sister Mariah."

"But Mariah was innocent! Why did you—"

"Again, you question me! Stop! Or you shall pay dearly."

Before Tiras could answer, the bull-god disappeared. He awoke under his rug and shook with fright as he glanced about the tent bathed in Il-Lah's light. Nearby, his mother snored gently. To avoid awakening her, he tiptoed past the qata and squatted on the carpet in the mag'ad, where he gazed past the open tent flap at a distant reddish dune. He'd finally seen Martu, he thought, if only in a dream. And he'd angered him with questions. Abu-Summu must be right, he thought. We can't disobey our god. Only our priest knows what Martu wants.

He'd better be careful, he thought, rising. Martu might hurt his family again, like poor Loban. Then, he thought how unjust it seemed to punish so many villagers because of one bad man. He shook his head in confusion, crept back to his rug, and pulled it around him. Tired, he rolled over, but before sleeping, he offered one last prayer to Martu not to harm his family. Who knew what possible revenge Martu planned for a worshipper's doubts!

CHAPTER 3

September, 3500 B.C., Arabiyah
(Al-Nefud Desert in northern Saudi Arabia)

TWO MOON-CYCLES AFTER HIS DAUGHTER'S sacrifice, Tiras's tribe bypassed their last stop in the Nefud, the Al-Gaffah Oasis, because the lake had dried up. Instead, the Council of Elders agreed to encamp farther east at the Al-Mawf Oasis. In the popular oasis café, other tribesmen discussed the nearby country of Sumer, a small land squeezed between Arabiyah and the country of Elam farther east.

Tiras, eating with his kinsmen, set down his bowl of rice and meat to listen. Perhaps the newcomers would reveal something useful about the Sumerian gods. They agreed that Sumer was a great country, even greater than Amrata.

"Greater than Amrata!" Tiras exclaimed, his curiosity aroused. "I've heard that Amrata is the greatest country of all."

An elderly Bedouin turned toward Tiras. "Amrata has only the Nile River," he said. "But Sumer has two rivers, the Tigris and Euphrates. Their main city, Ur, is near the Euphrates, and the biggest city I've ever seen for bartering. The mud-brick wall is enormous with a bronze double-gate decorated with carved figures. Many different tribesmen crowd the wide boulevard to trade at the large bazaar and marvel at the fine houses. It's worthwhile just seeing the Sumerians with their strange clothes and hearing their unknown tongue."

Another younger man with a scarred face complained, "The round-trip takes half a moon-cycle, not enough time to meet the good-looking women." He sighed and added, "I'd like to pat their pale skin and tiny ass." The other men laughed and Tiras joined them.

A fat man joked that everything else in Ur was big, like him. "Big roads. Big houses. A big tower that disappears into the cloud god."

Tiras leaned forward. "Please tell me about the magic tower."

The Bedouin wiped goat meat from his beard. "It's behind a wall with a garden and gate. So tall it touches the sky god. Many visitors speak in different tongues. Might be a shrine." He paused and added, "Their gods are strange."

"How so?"

"The Sumerians don't worship animals like we do. Instead, they have statues that look like people. Smiling mouths. Gentle eyes. Their gods don't ask for human sacrifice."

A younger Bedouin joined the conversation. "The Sumerian gods are too weak for the desert. Our tribal god is strong like thunder and lightning."

Tiras listened intently, his eyes squinting in surprise. The Sumerian gods were smiling? Gentle? No human sacrifice? How had the Sumerians learned to attract such sympathetic gods? While his tribesmen discussed bartering in Ur, he decided that, with baba's permission, he would accompany them and discover the Sumerians' secret. If Ur were as great as these men claimed, perhaps he could find another god to overthrow vicious Martu. He planned to ask his father that evening.

ಬಿ ಚಿ

When Il-Lah rose above the horizon to greet the star goddesses and light the darkening sky, Mashech limped across the sand with his cane. He approached the tent of Tiras's first and favorite wife, Na'amah. Resting in the mag'ad, Tiras jumped up to greet his father bending beneath the opened tent flap. Na'amah was busy behind the qata. Helped by Tiras, baba sank on a cushion, his robes draped around his extended legs.

"Thank you, my son," he said and opened his cloak.

Tiras sat with drawn-up knees on a cushion. "Baba, I want to journey with some tribesmen to Sumer. We heard that their city Ur is good for bartering. The round trip takes only a half moon-cycle. I respectfully request your permission."

Mashech rubbed his injured leg beneath the robe. "Only a few men? I can't allow it. You might be hurt by a wild animal, just as I was. Or worse."

Tiras tugged at his beard. "I may be skinny, unlike cousin Ruach, but my muscles are strong. I can survive the journey. Besides, the tribesmen could help."

"My only remaining child!" Mashech shook his head, his gray plaits tossing about his shoulders. "Too dangerous."

Tiras pulled up his robe to cover his nearly hairless chest. If only he'd been built like husky Ruach, he thought. A tough ram instead of a dainty ewe. Then perhaps his father would show more faith in his skills. He didn't answer. After all, obedience was expected from the sheikh's son.

∞ ♋

Disappointed at not visiting Ur, Tiras watched his kinsmen leaving. As protection against the blistering sun goddess, Al-Lat, he'd rewound his shawl into a turban about his head and face, exposing only his eyes. From his vantage point atop a flat rock, he sighed deeply as the tribesmen, shouting among themselves, led their donkeys laden with baskets of wool toward the distant Al-Ubiyah Oasis. He clenched a fist. He'll persuade baba to let him go alone.

Otherwise—and his heart raced at the thought—he'll disobey the sheikh and go anyway.

ଞୠ

Each afternoon while a nephew tended his flock, Tiras climbed the rock in anticipation of his tribesmen returning. They finally appeared one day. They waved back at him as they guided their overloaded donkeys toward the camp. He scoffed at their baskets stuffed with Sumerian goods. Learning how to attract a compassionate god was more valuable than trading wool for bowls and jugs!

He clambered down and rushed to his cousin, Ruach. "Salaam 'alaykum," he greeted Ruach.

"'Alaykum salaam," Ruach responded with his gruff voice.

The men embraced.

"Come to Na'amah's tent," Tiras pleaded. "I'm eager to learn about the Sumerians."

"I should see my wives first," Ruach said. He studied Tiras and smiled. "Well, all right. Let me unload my basket. I have a Sumerian-crafted gift for you."

"You're a loyal friend as well as kinsman," Tiras replied, eager to hear about the mysterious Sumerians. When his cousin soon reappeared, Tiras beamed his thanks at the copper bowl with painted scenes balanced on a pedestal. He sighed with admiration as he filled the bowl with dates. While Ruach, grunting, sat cross-legged on a cushion, Tiras politely turned aside to fart, and then cleaned clay cups by spitting into them and wiping them dry with his robe sleeve. He set cups of goat's milk beside the dates and sat with drawn-up knees on his cushion.

The men ate with their right hands, avoiding their unclean hands used to relieve themselves. Tiras glanced outside. Apparently the bull-god was busy elsewhere. "Please tell me about Ur," he said. "Did you hear about their gods?"

Ruach thought for a moment. "Nothing about their gods. But I saw a wondrous sight, a very tall tower that reached to the sky."

"Reached to the sky!" Tiras echoed in amazement. "And what else did you see?"

"Well, something strange after bartering my wool at the bazaar." Ruach paused, drank some goat's milk, and smiled at Tiras who leaned forward eagerly to catch every word. "The bazaar," Ruach continued, "is a large square with tempting smells, savory meat turning on skewers, and hanging baskets of sweet Al-Halwa. There's a strong, pungent smell from huge vats where Sumerians turn animal hides into a soft material with different colors that they sell on rugs. So many merchants with so much goods! I never saw a bazaar that big. The sides are lined with stalls but the back row is where I traded my wool for rice and other necessities and the gift I gave you. Then, I had some time to look around and admire the tiny soapstone statues, eating utensils, carved platters, pretty painted pots with tubes for pouring, and..." He paused to sip goat's milk.

"Yes?" Tiras urged. "Please tell me about the strange thing that you saw."

Ruach nodded. "Well, as I was leaving Ur, leading my donkey toward the city gate at the end of the wide boulevard lined with palm trees, four Sumerian warriors approached. They rode on the backside of an animal that had three heads decorated with feathers. The animal moved swiftly and kicked up so much dust it was hard to tell what it was. I never saw anything like it. I thought it must be a dragon. Its sides were protected by wood painted with pictures. One warrior guided the heads with long whips. I quickly dragged my donkey behind a palm tree and barely caught a glimpse of it, or I might have been crushed." He paused and loosened his robe, revealing his thick chest hairs.

"A dragon!" Tiras could scarcely breathe for excitement. He paused. "Are you sure?"

Ruach shrugged. "We've all heard about dragons. What else could it be?"

Bernadette Miller

"Go on," Tiras coaxed. Perhaps the Sumerians' success with their gods arose from taming violent beasts.

Ruach leaned forward. His arm muscles bulged beneath his robe. "Sumerian dragons have numerous, peculiar feet. The front ones look like animal legs but the back ones are round and roll like a ball. They create sparks against the stone streets. I never saw any animal like that. But the strong dragon could easily crush anyone daring to stand in its path." He reached over to eat another date.

Tiras's jaw dropped in surprise. If he could slay one of those dragons, he thought, he'd gain enough power to win another god's respect. "I must visit Ur!" he exclaimed.

"No, you mustn't," Na'amah said, appearing from behind the qata. She guided a boy of six. "Please, husband, I couldn't bear it if you didn't return. And our darling son needs his father's guidance. Remember, you promised to teach him how to hunt next year. How will we survive without food?"

"I won't die," Tiras said and gazed at his wife. But he remembered that there was one child, Shallah, he'd never see again.

Curly-haired Rimush put his arms around Tiras's neck and whispered, "I love you, baba."

Tiras covered his son's thin cheeks with kisses and thought about Ur, how he might learn to conquer Martu. Filled with hope, he played with Rimush, tickling his ribs. He grinned as Rimush bent over with giggles.

Na'amah said with trembling lips, "Tiras, if you disobey your father, who knows what the priest will demand—maybe Rimush." She bowed her head in anxiety, anticipating the possible nightmare.

Deep in thought, Tiras reproached himself. Was it right to make his beloved so unhappy? Again, he heard Shallah's screams. To honor her memory he mustn't cling to cowardice. He gazed upward at Na'amah. "I can't stay ignorant to avoid possible danger," he said. "If Ur offers a better life, I'll bring that knowledge back to the tribe."

Na'amah, straightening, stared down at him in disbelief. "Even if it kills you?"

Tiras fell silent, unsure how to appease her. He couldn't reveal his plans to overthrow Martu without alarming his wife and possibly alerting the bull-god to his mission. He rose to embrace her. "Someday you'll understand why I must journey there."

She shook her head at his stubbornness and led Rimush behind the qata for his evening meal. Tiras and Ruach hugged good-bye and Tiras watched his cousin cross the desert to his tent. *Ruach has seen Ur,* Tiras thought, *but I could not.*

୫୦ଓଷ

One evening, while Na'amah crooned Rimush to sleep behind the qata, Mashech opened the tent flap. Helped by Tiras, he sat, refused the dates, and stared in cold silence. Finally, he said, "Son, since childhood you've stubbornly followed your own path. You deliberately antagonize our priest by challenging our revered Martu. And now I hear that you plan to visit Sumer alone, ignoring my wishes and our wise Elders' warning about traveling away from the tribe's protection. I'm afraid you won't live to old age. Surely as a father you know I must protect you. After losing five children, I couldn't bear to lose the last one."

Pained at disobeying his father, Tiras leaned forward. "Baba, I love you and don't want to disobey you. But my dear daughter, Shallah, died a most horrible death. Suppose I learn in Ur how to prevent it? Suppose we never have to watch another child scream in agony?"

"Yes, our god's demands are hard," Mashech whispered. "But we must obey the priest."

"Not if there's a better way in Ur," Tiras blurted. His voice dropped to a whisper. "I've heard that the Sumerians don't have human sacrifices. I can't sacrifice another child. Next time it might be Rimush. Don't force me to fear for my two sons."

Mashech said softly, "I understand your grief about Shallah. But how can you cross the desert without the tribe's protection? What

Bernadette Miller

about sudden sandstorms? Flash floods? Attacks by wild animals? Warring tribes? Roaming bandits? Surely you realize how hard it would be for me if something happened..." His voice trailed off. The men fell silent.

Tiras nodded and turned away with a grimace. Why must his father continually remind him that he needed safeguarding like a fragile woman? Just because he was short and thin, not tall and rugged like Ruach. He swallowed his annoyance and reproached himself. His father worried about him.

Mashech's face sagged as he set down the Sumerian bowl of dates. "If I don't permit your leaving," he said with trembling voice, "you'll hate me. So I give permission most reluctantly. It's a long time away from the tribe."

Tiras leaned over to kiss his father's cheek. "Thank you, dear baba. You've granted a wish next to my heart." *At last*, he exulted, *I'll see mysterious Ur and learn about their gods!*

Baba's graying brows furrowed with anxiety. "You know that we leave within two moon-cycles for the Uplands," he said. "If you don't come back in time..." He turned away as if unable to bear the thought of losing his remaining child. A date slipped from his fingers onto the soiled carpet.

"I'll be back in time," Tiras said. He picked up the date and handed it to his father. "The journey will go well. I'll just follow the caravan trail past Al-Mawf Lake and return that way. Like our kinsmen on their recent journey."

The men embraced. Mashech said hoarsely, "May the gods preserve you, my son, and bring you back safely."

"And may the gods preserve you, dear baba." Tiras watched his father limp outside. His enthusiasm dissolved into uneasiness. Baba was already past forty winters. His face, darkened to a chestnut brown from the scorching desert sun, was deeply creased. Some yellowing teeth were missing. Suppose something happened while he was in Ur? He shook his head. It was important to discover how to replace Martu and save his remaining two children.

Later that evening, Ruach entered Na'amah's tent and told Tiras, "I wish I could go with you, but an evil jinn attacked my third son. I can't leave him and his mother. It would destroy Mashech if he lost you."

"I can defend myself!" Tiras retorted in irritation. "Because I'm lean doesn't mean I'm frail. Because I lack chest hair doesn't mean I'm afraid. My body is strong. Like my will. I'll survive."

Ruach bent to embrace Tiras. He whispered, "I'm sorry for doubting you. Go to Ur. Satisfy your dreams." Tiras hugged him back and Ruach said, "You know we'll always be close friends. That will never change."

"I love you," Tiras said.

"I love you as much," Ruach said. They embraced again.

After his cousin left, Tiras tried not to worry, but he spent a restless night beneath the conjugal rug, rising and returning, wondering if the trip were worth the anxiety he caused his family.

When Tiras awoke, Al-Uzza greeted the sky god with her crimson hue. He left sleeping Na'amah, quickly devoured some bread-cakes, and stepped outside to find Na'al, his donkey whom he'd raised from a foal. The large gray-colored male stood almost five feet with huge white shaggy legs and a white belly. He grazed at clumps of grass behind Na'amah's tent.

Tiras patted the coarse mane and Na'al brayed his welcome. To avert a jinn's evil eye, Tiras tied a string of blue beads around an ear. In the woven knapsack to be tied around his back, he had packed a sheepskin cloak, a rug for sleeping, and a wooden slingshot with leather thong. He loaded Na'al with two baskets of wool and a basket of provisions: goatskin water bags, lumps of pressed dates, balls of hard goat cheese, baked bread-cakes that Na'amah had prepared the previous evening, and lizard skin sacks holding liquid butter.

Tiras pinched his lips at the morning fog shrouding the distant Al-Mawf Lake. He remembered Abu-Summu's explanation for the fog. All the gods banded together like an egg until they agreed to separate themselves and form the world. Suppose today that the gods decided not to separate, punishing him for defying the priest? He shook his head. It was a risk he must face for his children's sake.

Patches of land began appearing. Raucous sea birds swooped over the lake. The gods had separated!

Relieved, he finished tying the baskets that Na'amah had woven from thick desert roots, and he gazed at the caravan trail that stretched before him like a beckoning finger. He was finally going to Ur! he thought with a grin. His journey was worthwhile. If he returned with a new, caring god to defeat Martu, and no more children were sacrificed, the tribe would welcome him with hugs and kisses and a big celebration. He'd save his children and the tribe like the brave Bedouins of olden days.

The packing finished, Tiras led his donkey toward the oasis lake. He glanced back at the tents speckling the sand. The women prepared their outdoor hearths for meals while small children played nearby. Soon, the lake, tents, hearths, tribe, flocks, and every familiar scene disappeared from view. Ahead, a landscape of yellow and reddish sand spread toward the horizon, punctuated by abal bushes, acacia trees, and large dunes along the caravan trail. For the first time in his life, he was alone in the desert with its potential dangers and nobody to help him.

He remembered the terrifying sandstorm when, much younger and not yet a man, he had lost his brother, Doloch, and he fell into a reverie afraid of the same misfortune.

ఠుఁ

The storm had arrived without warning. It tossed sand, dust, stones and debris high into the air and the temperature had dropped sharply. The gale-force wind blew across the Abram tribe's encampment. Their tents swayed. Zabaia rushed outside and shouted to her older sons, both widowers, to help refasten a tension rope. It had loosened with a loud snap, exposing the mag'ad to the harsh weather.

He had held onto a pole to keep from falling in the fierce wind. He shouted, "Oomah, can I help?"

"No! Stay in the maharama!" his mother shouted. "You're too young for men's work!"

Tiras clenched his fists, feeling humiliated, and thought, Stay in the women's area. Like a baby! Skinny although almost fourteen, he still hated being treated like a child. As the wind whistled through the tent, he held down his head, reached for the poles, and groped his way past the qata. He stood behind the dividing curtain and pushed aside one end so he could see outside, shielding his face from the biting sand.

Zabaia rewound her turban tightly about her head and face. She screamed instructions to her grown sons against the howling wind. "It's starting to rain, so maybe the storm won't last long! Shargu, hold down the pole in the sand. Doloch, fasten that rope!"

While the storm god splashed torrents upon the camp, slim Doloch pulled at the tension rope coiled on the wet sand. Finally, he shouted, "Oomah, I can't see what I'm doing! I can't hold on much longer. We need baba!"

"He's helping his youngest wife! She can't manage by herself with a small child!"

"Then let's ask our other brothers! Oomah, I can't–" Doloch suddenly pitched forward. The knotted rope curled about his legs like a monstrous lizard, trapping him. Face buried in the sand, he struggled to push himself up. The storm pelted him with dust and stones. His body disappeared beneath the wet rubble piling on top of him. His movements ceased.

"Oh, Martu, please save him!" Zabaia ran to her fallen son, her robe soaked. "Shargu, help your brother!"

Short and stocky, Tiras's second-oldest brother, Shargu, had been born deaf and mute, but he'd often played with him. Pummeled by the sandstorm's fierce wind, Shargu stared at his mother bent anxiously over the mound covering Doloch.

Tiras rushed outside to help.

His mother yelled at him, "Go back to the maharama! You'll be injured!"

Bernadette Miller

But Tiras shook his head, determined to help no matter what oomah said. He fought to keep his balance in the wind and downpour. Shargu pointed at the mound covering Doloch and made whimpering sounds. Zabaia nodded. The trio tore at the sand and debris. Their roughened hands bled. After several hours, they managed to free Doloch's legs from the tension rope. Shargu fastened the rope onto a pole.

"Doloch! Doloch!" Zabaia cried out when the storm finally passed and the wind subsided. She and Shargu dragged Doloch's body inside the tent. They laid him on the rug. Frantically they brushed away remaining debris with Tiras's help. Doloch wasn't breathing.

"Tiras, hurry, get Abu-Summu. He'll know how to treat Doloch."

This time, he obeyed her instructions. He ran from the tent and soon reappeared with Abu-Summu who examined Doloch. The priest shook his head. "My kinsmen, nothing more can be done for him. He's past help. He's suffocated."

"No!" Zabaia dropped to her knees. She pulled her dead son over her lap. "This isn't fair! My sweet son has done nothing to anger Martu. He can't die!" She cradled Doloch's body in her arms and moaned with pain at her loss.

Abu-Summu nodded and said, "It's always sad to lose a child but Martu has spoken. We must calm his anger. Prepare a goat for sacrifice. I'll find Mashech."

After he left, Zabaia cradled her dead son in her arms. "Another one, another one," she kept repeating.

Mashech soon appeared. His recently-broken leg was wrapped in cloths beneath his robe. He leaned on his cane fashioned from a stout tree branch. "We lost Doloch?" he asked solemnly, his eyes dampening. Zabaia nodded, her face wet with tears.

Mashech turned to Shargu staring at his father. "Son, we must prepare Doloch for his eternal journey. Your brothers and Ruach will help with the burial."

With great sadness, Tiras envisioned his mother still cradling her dead *son, and his family's grief when they buried Doloch several hours later. Then, Shargu died a year later, bitten by a scorpion.*

Another brother gone, Tiras thought as his mind returned to his current situation. He trembled. Was it his turn now, traveling alone in the desert to the far city of Ur?

⅒⅓

Na'al brayed softly, yanking Tiras from his reverie. He reminded himself that he wasn't alone, not while he still had Na'al. He grasped the six-pointed star worn around his neck. The magic amulet would protect him from danger.

In the slight breeze, he leaned forward on his donkey and stroked the bristled ears. Na'al brayed in acknowledgement, and Tiras focused on his journey. Although the landscape remained constant, he knew that the wind god, Al-Qais, blew from east to west in the Nefud. Occasionally, he rested the donkey by trudging beside him. After a couple of hours, they paused to eat. Na'al feasted on the abal bushes. Tiras sat beneath an acacia and enjoyed goat cheese with butter and dates from his sack of provisions. He drank sparingly from a goatskin bag that smelled and tasted of goat. He had to preserve the precious water as much as possible or he might die of thirst before it rained again. His left hand rested on the copper dagger in his leather belt pouch. The Walla tribe, he knew, would challenge a solitary traveler crossing their land without their permission, and no tribute of several sheep. But Tiras had reasoned that, traveling alone, he couldn't slow down his journey by caring for more animals until paying tribute.

His father had explained why the Abram tribesmen must always pay a tribute.

"Many generations ago," baba had said, "tribes arriving in Arabiyah claimed vast portions of the desert and built wells for their flocks. If we pay a tribute, we can cross their land and use their

Bernadette Miller

wells. But if we try to cross and don't pay, the tribe will fight us to the death."

He gazed at the distant oasis as if seeing beyond the horizon. "Someday, son, we'll have our own land. Filled with sparkling lakes and lush pastures of wildflowers and honeycombs."

Tiras scanned the desert as he walked beside Na'al. His kinsmen had often discussed wanting their own desert land, but where? His Amorite ancestor, Abrahamu, had left his native Ugarit to marry a cousin in Arabiyah, but all the land within the migration routes had already been claimed by other tribes. He shook his head. He'd better focus on his journey which could be dangerous, instead of dwelling on the past.

One evening, at twilight, he built a campfire near an acacia tree and rested against Na'al. He felt content, warmed by his donkey and the campfire. Across the sky, Al-Lat teased Il-Lah by flaunting her coral, rose, and scarlet apparel. Tiras sighed in wonder at the beautiful sun goddess. Finally, her farewell colors radiated across the distant horizon. She slipped below to yield to her moon lover, and the gods embraced. The world turned gray except for the glowing fire. It grew chilly and he donned his sheepskin cloak from the knapsack.

"Yes, the desert can be cruel but beautiful," he murmured to Na'al. "But Martu, who rules our lives, dwells not in the desert but in the sky." He gazed upward toward the star goddesses.

From among a cluster, Martu seemed to glower with red eyes and stomping hooves. "Tiras, you feel safe away from my altar," he imagined Martu complaining. "No matter what you do or where you go, I'll discover your betrayal. So beware or I'll destroy you and your family. I have spoken!"

Tiras bowed his head in apparent devotion and thought hard. The bull-god mustn't discover the quest to replace him. "I don't want to abandon you!" he cried out, dropping to his knees and hoping he was convincing. He spoke to the sky as if Martu hovered over him.

"My kinsmen beg for your mercy. We beg you not to demand more than we can give."

He prostrated himself, trying to convince Martu of his continued devotion. The moon god suddenly hid behind a cloud and Martu disappeared. Again, Tiras heard Shallah's pitiful cries for help. Would he never stop remembering? "Martu," he cried out again to the star-studded sky, "please give me a signal that you understand my people's plight."

As expected, unfeeling Martu remained silent amid the sparkling stars. Perhaps the bull-god sensed his worshipper's deceit. Tiras rose and stroked the donkey's neck. Someday, he thought, he'll no longer need to implore disdainful Martu. Instead, a new god would hear his pleas and respond with sympathy. Na'al nuzzled his shoulder as if reassuring him that his quest would succeed despite dangers. He squatted near his campfire and marveled at how calmly the trip was going, despite Martu.

Then, a ravenous jackal dared to approach within several feet. The jackal snarled at him, causing Na'al to back toward an acacia and bray in alarm. Tiras fought for calm as he withdrew a slingshot from his knapsack. He fired a stone and hit the jackal in his forehead. It yelped but kept approaching, its jaws wide and its tongue lolling to one side as if already tasting the fresh meat it hungered for. Na'al brayed again in warning as the jackal approached closer. Tiras ignored his pulse quickening and fitted another stone in his slingshot. As the jackal was about to pounce, he fired and hit the animal's right eye. The jackal howled in pain and began backing off, crouching low to the ground. He fired a stone into the left eye. The animal staggered and fell against the sand, writhing in pain. He unsheathed his dagger and quickly slit the furry throat to avoid disobeying the Bedouin code by torturing the animal further.

Exhausted, Tiras sank beside the dying jackal and watched its blood spurt onto the sand. He would have meat for supper but the blood was baram, forbidden. Blood was an animal's life fluid, its spirit, and must be offered as a sacrifice to Martu. He drained the remaining blood and covered it with sand to hide it from animals. Perhaps this show of devotion might pacify the god.

Over the campfire, Tiras roasted the flesh impaled on twigs. He gingerly plucked off hot pieces, shook them to lessen the heat, and ate the savory meat, licking his lips in satisfaction. When the cooked meat grew cold, he packed a small amount in his provision sack and dragged the carcass twenty feet from the campfire. Yellow-headed vultures, buzzards, and blue-black crows joined a pair of hyenas fighting over the kill. Their shrill cries filled the desert.

The next morning, when Al-Uzza brightened the sky, Tiras concluded that Al-Qais must have grown angry at him for letting the jackal suffer. The sky darkened. The wind bit at his face. He tightened his turban about his head to defend himself from the sand.

Na'al brayed at the unwelcome turn of events. Tiras wrapped his arms around his donkey's neck. "It's my fault for upsetting Al-Qais," he whispered. "I should have killed the jackal with my first shot instead of blinding it."

The pair huddled together under a stone outcropping while Al-Qais vented his fury at Tiras's sin. Sand sprayed his exposed neck and crept under his robes, causing his body to itch. He covered his face to shield his eyes, and hugged Na'al with his free arm. The donkey shook himself. His shaggy head drooped in weariness. The wind intensified as they crouched as close to the ground as possible.

Abruptly, Na'al turned his head toward the east and brayed. Tiras patted the coarse mane matted with sand. Again the donkey twisted his head toward the eastern horizon. He brayed loudly.

Tiras shouted, "Something else troubles you, Na'al?" Shielding his face from the wind, he turned in the donkey's direction. Several blurry figures appeared against the distant horizon. Barely visible through the sand, they seemed to be riding toward him.

Walla tribesmen! Tiras's pulse raced. He quickly donned his knapsack, loaded the donkey with the wool and provisions, and led weary Na'al toward a nearby dune. Al-Qais whistled about the pair as they lunged forward against the wind-god's anger and hid behind the dune.

Although the campfire no longer burned, charred embers would reveal recent use. Their tracks in the sand would clearly betray them. The wind subsided. Tiras peered from behind the dune and glanced at the sky with gratitude. Al-Qais wasn't angry but trying to help! The gracious god had buried the campfire and tracks beneath piles of sand.

Na'al brayed again.

Tiras clamped his hand around his donkey's muzzle to keep him quiet. They waited for what seemed forever. Finally, donkeys' hooves resounded louder in the desert stillness. He brushed sand from his face and peered from behind the dune. Three men appeared in the distance, their robes flowing behind them as their donkeys sped toward his hiding place. Tiras huddled against Na'al and waited, hoping the tribesmen wouldn't hear his pounding heart. The stomping of the donkeys' hooves sounded louder.

When the tribesmen arrived, one said with a hoarse voice, "Looks like someone's been using a campfire." The men slid off their animals.

"Yes, I see the outline beneath the sand," another said in a high-pitched tone and made scratching sounds as if digging. "And burnt pieces of meat," he added.

"No tracks, though," said another in a deep voice. "Too damn bad the storm god covered them. Might be the Ghata, snooping around."

Na'al moved restlessly beside Tiras whose heart pumped fast at the danger of being discovered. He stroked Na'al's mane and kept his hand clamped around his muzzle.

"Ghata," the hoarse one agreed. "The bastards will sneak into our camp and burn it down if we don't find them."

"Well, they can't be that far," the deep voice said. "But it's hard to track them after the wind-god covered everything."

"Let's return to camp," the high-pitched one said. "There's a shortcut over those dunes."

"Good idea!" the deep voice said. "The Ghata probably went that way."

Tiras gasped with fear. They'd surely catch him and Na'al behind the dune. His life was over. He'd never get to Ur. Never replace Martu. Never see his beloved family again. They'd weep for him... With his hand still pressed around his donkey's muzzle to keep him quiet, his other hand grasped the six-pointed star around his neck. The magic amulet would save him, just as his father had promised when he was a little boy.

The high-pitched voice said. "In the end, it's quicker to ride straight ahead. Climbing the dunes will slow us down."

The deep voice sighed. "Thanks to the wind god, there's not much to see anyway. We should warn the Council Elders."

There was a shuffling sound as the men mounted their donkeys. Tiras gasped with relief and peeked from behind the dune. The men rode off. He was safe! He thanked Al-Qais for saving his life and continued his journey with Na'al.

৪০ ০৪

Several days later they reached the marshland leading into Sumer's Euphrates River and a small village. Needing rest, Tiras squatted by the road bordering the marshes. He stared at the odd, arch-shaped houses in the water. Made of reeds lashed together, the houses floated on individual islands of land. Fishermen with poles steered basket-shaped boats around the houses.

Refreshed, Tiras mounted his donkey and guided him along the road toward Ur. Soon, the marshes disappeared. Fertile fields lined both sides of the river. Barley, millet, and emmer waved in their furrows as if greeting him.

When he arrived the following morning at Ur, he stopped Na'al and gazed in disbelief at the massive mud-brick wall several miles in circumference enclosing the city. He couldn't have imagined any place that big despite the descriptions he had heard. Nor could he have imagined the gleaming double-gate of decorated bronze that was closed. Tiras continued staring in awe. Oases had no such protection. Desert villagers welcomed travelers.

He finally dismounted and stood several feet from the gate, wondering if there were a secret opening. *Magical Ur!* he exulted. *He would find a way inside. He would barter with his wool and question the merchants about their gods.*

The double-gate suddenly swung open, creaking on its hinges as if inviting Tiras to enter. Beyond the gate, a huge square featured a bazaar, just as cousin Ruach had described. Rugs were heaped with merchandise and stuffed stalls lined the edges, while owners and customers haggled over prices. He hesitated at entering. How could the Sumerians know of his coming? They might be shetans waiting to harm him...or perhaps to welcome him? His heart raced at possible danger. He finally ignored it and led Na'al through the opened gate. Again he hesitated. Now, he would finally learn about their gods, he thought with a sense of accomplishment and hope. He would even try to persuade one to replace spiteful Martu! He stared at the oddly-dressed people who hurried along the boulevard near the bazaar. What marvels and deceptions awaited him in this unusual land?

Bernadette Miller

CHAPTER 4

October, 3500 B.C., Sumer
(Ur, a city-state in southern Iraq)

THE REVERED SCHOLAR AND PHYSICIAN, Mah Ummia, whose real name was Enki, had acquired the honorary title of, "great teacher," after years of privately teaching wealthy students and becoming headmaster at the Edubba. Today, he'd excused himself from his teaching duties to prepare for his daughter's wedding in two days. In preparation, slave girls filled huge alabaster urns along a balcony surrounding the courtyard that was open to the sky. The heady fragrance of red yucca, purple anastatica, and white hawthorn permeated the balcony and bedrooms with their thatched roofs of woven reeds. The aroma drifted down toward the courtyard where bearded musicians draped their shawls about the high-backed chairs and sat, waiting to rehearse.

The bald musicians rested their instruments on the floor, smoothed their ankle-length white pleated skirts, and adjusted their belted money pouch, their chests bare. Male slaves wearing loin cloths bathed the musicians' hands and feet and distributed new sandals. Soon the rhythms of reed flutes, lyres, tambourines, and harps reverberated throughout the house.

Mah Ummia, whose appearance resembled the musicians,

adjusted his multi-colored shawl over his bare shoulder and listened for a while to the rehearsal. "Yes, that's good," he said. "We'll rehearse again." He pointed to a room off the courtyard. "Refresh yourselves. There's bread and beer."

While the kitchen resounded with the musicians' chatter, Mah Ummia's exquisite young daughter, Unanna, hurried down a stairway from the balcony and through an arched entrance to the courtyard. Following the fashion for prosperous ladies, she wore a tight-fitting tufted gown and puffed-out black wig topped by a headdress with dangling beads. Usually she appeared immaculate but now the fifteen-year-old looked disheveled. Her black gown was spotted with stains. Tendrils escaped from her wig. Her face was wet with tears.

"Adda," she implored, "I can't marry Balulum."

Mah Ummia sighed deeply. He stroked his graying beard that reached his chest. "Unanna, my dearest daughter, this wedding must take place. Don't make another scene. I beg you."

"But you know why I can't marry him."

Mah Ummia paled beneath his beard. "Nevertheless, you shall marry him. I've already arranged it with the High Priest. Balulum has supplied the wedding gifts. He already has your dowry. Your future husband will arrive any moment. Together we'll sign the marriage contract on the clay tablets."

"But I don't love Balulum. He's crude. Uneducated. Not like Dumuzi—"

"Unfortunately, Dumuzi is poor, as you know very well," Mah Ummia interrupted. "We've gone over this again and again. Dumuzi probably expects to gamble away your inheritance, like his father. Balulum doesn't need my money. He truly loves you. With Balulum, you'll never grovel in poverty. Nor worse, sell your children into slavery to pay your debts. You will not see Dumuzi again."

Unanna flung out her arms in exasperation. "How can you betroth me to a man who's old and fat? Unsuitable for me in temperament!"

Bernadette Miller

"That's enough!" Mah Ummia daubed at his perspired brow and sat on a musician's chair. Laughter drifted from the kitchen along with the aromas of roast pig, garlic, leeks and mustard, sweet barley cakes, and brewing beer. "I've explained this repeatedly," Mah Ummia continued in a deliberately calm voice. "Even if Dumuzi does love you, it takes many years to develop sufficient skills like mine. He must learn to teach wealthy pupils privately in addition to supervising the Edubba. Meanwhile, he would depend on me for support. A demeaning situation for a husband. I won't explain it again. See to your wedding clothes. Majeena will help." He sighed. "If only your mother were alive to witness her daughter's wedding."

"Ama would die all over again," Unanna interrupted. "Please, adda, don't abandon me to a life of misery. Let me wed the man I love. Or remain a maid. Ama would have wanted me to marry Dumuzi."

He rose to straighten her headdress. "Unanna, your mother wouldn't have wanted your marriage to a pauper. And it's unnatural to remain a maid. Never knowing a man's caresses and tender whispers. You'll learn to love Balulum, as I learned to love Ningal." He paused and tucked the stray tendrils beneath her wig. "My parents also arranged our betrothal. But Ningal and I were happy. Balulum adores you. He's good-natured. Affectionate. Very wealthy. He'll do everything to please you."

"I'll never love that horrid man. Never!" Unanna turned and fled through the courtyard, nearly tripping on the brick-paved floor. She ran up the stairs. Sobs emanated from her bedroom behind the balcony.

Mah Ummia shook his head in frustration, his heart stabbed by his daughter's despair. He knew he must remain firm and not let her surrender to youthful infatuation. He signaled a slave girl to escort the musicians back into the courtyard. The wailing reed flutes seemed to echo the muffled sobs from upstairs. Mah Ummia was about to dismiss them when a male slave appeared. The music stopped. The slave bowed.

"I bear an important message," he murmured.

Sobs continued from upstairs.

"Well, what is the message?" Mah Ummia asked. "I'm in the midst of something important."

"Please, master, it's most urgent. Master Balulum can't come today to sign the marriage tablets. He's been stricken ill. He lies in his bed."

"Stricken ill?" Mah Ummia repeated in surprise. He mused to himself, *Hmm, an unfortunate occurrence. Are our gods trying to warn me against blundering?* He shrugged and turned back to the slave. "Tell your master I'll visit him today."

The slave bowed low, turned, and ran outside. In the courtyard, the sounds of reed flutes still pierced the air. Mah Ummia waved his hand at the musicians. "Come back tomorrow," he ordered. The musicians sauntered toward the entrance. Mah Ummia flinched at hearing their whispers, no doubt gossiping about his daughter. He wouldn't trade his beloved daughter for all the shekels in Sumer.

He'd always nurtured and loved her. Despite his grief over losing his wife, Ningal, in childbirth, he had cradled Unanna's tiny body and caressed her plump cheeks and black curly hair. He remembered his thoughts while looking at his daughter. *Dearest one, you haven't left me. Here is our child, the sweet result of our love.*

Later, Unanna's first babbled words were, "ad-ad-adda." How it gratified him that she tried to speak to him first despite spending much time with her nurse. After a year he encouraged her to walk. In the upstairs nursery adjacent to his bedroom, he held out his arms. "Come to me, dear." Gripping her cloth doll, she struggled, hesitated, and stumbled toward her father. He caught her just before she fell. "I have you, precious one," he said, and she bobbed her head in relief, clinging to his bare arms.

Fear gripped him now. Suppose, caught up in youth's passion, Unanna ran off with Dumuzi? He might never see her again. Like most Sumerian fathers, he'd diligently taught her that happiness meant accumulating assets and valuing success. Still, she would toss aside all his guidance to run off with a poor teacher. He must save Unanna from a life of degradation without driving her away in anger.

He climbed the balcony stairs to check on Unanna, and entered her bedroom. Relieved, he saw her in deep sleep beneath the wool coverlet. Her wig and headdress were heaped on a bedside chair. He whispered, "May our gods protect you."

Now Mah Ummia remembered Balulum's illness. He hurried to his bedroom at the far end of the balcony where he filled his leather pharmaceutical sack, and left the house. Outside, he shielded his eyes from the sun god. Utu seemed angry, glaring down at him. Again, Mah Ummia experienced an uneasy foreboding. Was it possible that despite his best intentions his daughter's betrothal to Balulum displeased the gods? He sighed. It was impossible to know what the gods wanted. But they controlled everything.

Beyond the winding, cobblestone alleys, he reached the broad Ceremonial Boulevard shaded by date palms. He scanned the lofty whitewashed mud-brick houses looming above their surrounding walls. Contentment gradually replaced his unease. This was his beloved Sumer, his own native land. Unlike foreigners who reveled in ignorance, his ancestors had invented many useful things. He glanced along the boulevard. Here lived his closest comrades. Many were former classmates who'd become teachers, merchants, physicians, or scribes. Others had been elected to the Upper House of Nobility in the Bicameral Congress to argue laws and legislation with those in the Lower House of Commoners known as, "the fighting men." Mah Ummia's contentment turned to frowns. Despite his wise ancestors' legacy, how should he deal with his unhappy daughter? His own father had urged him to join the family business but finally yielded to his son's chosen profession. Was he equally harsh with Unanna? He remembered how he had begged his father to allow him to teach.

ဆာ ငာ

Originally, his parents had named him Enki after the god of wisdom. His father, Lugalanni, had expected their only child to complete his studies at the Edubba and then help manage the family's mercantile business. Enki had other dreams. Shortly after his twelfth birthday, he again asked to become a teacher. He fell into a reverie, recalling his conversation with his father.

His father had sighed and offered the same argument now used with Unanna. "You know that beginning teachers are poverty stricken. Again I remind you, how will you support yourself? You wouldn't be able to provide for a wife and children. So they must depend on me. Not the miserable life I foresee for either of us."

"But business matters seem boring," Enki had replied, using a different approach. "Always worrying about who owes and how much." He hoped that perhaps his father would realize his lack of business skills. "I should become a teacher," he continued. "I enjoy learning and passing it on to others. Ama would have approved."

"Boring?" His father scowled. "Our family business has supported us well for many years. Where's your gratitude?" He paused. "Your mother wouldn't have approved. She was too busy spending her time with another man."

They grew silent. Enki bit his lip, remembering his compassionate mother. It was too bad his father had divorced her and married Nanshe, a young woman three years older than he. "My teachers have praised my gift for teaching. I remember everything and can easily explain it. They say I could become a great teacher..." His voice trailed off as his father had shaken his head.

"Only the gods can predict the future. Son, when you join my business, you'll see fascinating sights. Elam. Amrata. Ugarit. Arabiyah. You'll earn enough to be comfortable. Like my father I've been content."

Filled with anxiety, Enki had pondered how to convince his father. One evening, he stared at the wall frescoes of pious Sumerians praying in pearl-paneled temples, and decided that he must convince

Bernadette Miller

his personal god, Lord Enki, his namesake, to help him. He began skipping classes at the Edubba to beseech Lord Enki's help. He bypassed the family chapel, a small room beneath the balcony staircase, and instead visited the god's temple at the Sacred Way.

As Lord Utu bathed the city in sunlight, Enki hurried along alleyways radiating out from the Sacred Way. He crossed the Ceremonial Boulevard and headed toward the complex containing Ur's temples and the king's palace. A high mud-brick wall enclosed the Sacred Way.

Enki pushed past the gate crowded with gawking foreigners, past the garden, and climbed the steep steps up the mud-brick ziggurat that hovered some sixty feet over Ur. Its façade of burnt bricks, set in bitumen, glistened. Three stairways joined a huge gateway at the first terrace beneath two more increasingly smaller terraces. At the top stood a shrine to the father of the gods: Lord An.

On the first terrace, Enki entered Lord Enki's rectangular temple filled with buttresses and columns adorned with geometric designs. He dropped a shekel that clanged in the copper bowl on the offering table. The god's marble statue stood in a wall niche. He gazed at handsome Lord Enki's perfectly-carved face. "Glorious god," he whispered during that first visit, "please let me become a teacher. I'll gladly bathe and feed you, and faithfully worship you all my life."

Still, his father refused to let him follow his dream. Again, Enki visited Lord Enki's temple. This time, he placed a plate of barley cakes on the offering table. Surely the god couldn't resist delicious food and might be tempted into resolving his namesake's predicament. He prostrated himself against the brick floor and looked up at the statue. "Splendid Lord Enki, please let me become a teacher. If you do, I promise to persuade the heathen Arabi to adore you. Please heed my prayer."

He waited for a sign that Lord Enki had responded. Finally, several days later, apparently pleased with his namesake's promise, the god finally heeded by distracting Lugalanni's attention away from his son's ambition. An elderly trusted slave had revealed his young wife's infidelity. Lugalanni punished her by reducing her status to concubine. Then her father began a court case which Enki resolved in his father's favor. He testified truthfully that he'd seen Nanshe meeting her lover in the moonlit garden.

After the mashkim, a legal arbitrator like a bailiff, read the verdict on the courthouse steps, Lugalanni sighed with relief and turned to his son. "You helped win my case and I'm grateful. Lord Enki has blessed me with a clever son. You deserve a reward."

"Please, adda, let me become a teacher."

His father sighed, then nodded grudgingly. He looked at Enki grinning from ear to ear. "But if you change your mind, I demand you join our family business!"

"I will," he had agreed. They never discussed it again.

Mah Ummia followed his chosen profession and became successful, given his current name, and able to afford a comfortable life with a fine, three-bedroom house and garden as well as several slaves. He also studied medicine and observed operations, but his mastery couldn't save his lovely Ningal who left him an infant daughter. Distraught over losing Ningal, he immersed himself in teaching, curing illnesses, and raising his daughter.

When grown, Unanna resembled his deceased wife. She had the same petite figure, creamy complexion, and high cheekbones. Like most Sumerian fathers, he sought a suitor for her whose affluence surpassed his own. After inquiring among friends, he discovered that a bazaar shop owner had the desired financial means and was single again. Mah Ummia decided to meet the owner and possibly arrange a betrothal.

The bazaar filled a large square at the far right of the Ceremonial Boulevard. It bustled with merchants and customers and exuded the musky smell of hides tanned into leather and meat turning on spits. He threaded his way among rugs piled with merchandise: soapstone figurines, clothing, vases, platters, eating utensils, woven carpets and

Bernadette Miller

cushions from Arabiyah. He headed toward the stalls lining the back of the square.

The dirty, foul-smelling Bedouins, hugging their baskets of wool, eyed him suspiciously, probably distrusting a foreigner who spoke their language. Mah Ummia nervously tugged at his graying beard. "Just hear what I have to say," he urged in their language. The Bedouins turned their backs on him and muttered among themselves. He shrugged and left them. He would try again another day.

The jewelry merchant's stall was nearby. He pushed aside the beaded curtain. Inside: necklaces, earrings, pins, bangles, and pearl combs dotted the counters' woven coverlets. Mah Ummia knew the young clerk, Dumuzi, who'd begun teaching at the Edubba and supplemented his meager income with a job at the bazaar.

"I heard that Balulum's wife died four months ago from illness," Mah Ummia mentioned while straightening his multi-colored shawl over his left shoulder. "You probably know him."

Dumuzi added more jewelry to the counters and looked up. "Yes, he's very lonely. Begged everyone to find him another wife. He's a good owner. I have no complaints. He's not refined, but has a kind heart. Very rich. He owns many shops beside this one."

Mah Ummia examined a necklace of carved ivory beads strung amidst blue lapis lazuli. "It so happens that my daughter's ready for marriage," he remarked. "I'm seeking a suitable husband for her."

"Well, Balulum's looking for a wife," Dumuzi said and rose. "Balulum would treat your daughter well. Should I ask him?"

Mah Ummia nodded and studied the necklace.

"That's special jewelry I designed," Dumuzi added, watching his prospective customer. "Unique pieces cost more."

"My daughter appreciates unique things," Mah Ummia replied. He purchased the necklace and arranged to meet Balulum.

When he returned home, Unanna greeted him with a hug and stepped back. Her black gown studded with red carnelian defined her slender figure. She looked regal, especially the black wig topped by an elegant beehive-shaped headdress trimmed with silver hoops. He handed her the necklace.

She studied it for a moment. Her lips curved in a mischievous smile, like her mother. "Oh, it's most attractive. Thank you, adda."

His heart melting with love, Mah Ummia took the necklace to clasp around her slender neck. "My darling daughter, it's time you married. I'm seeking a husband for you."

She frowned when he faced her. "So soon? I'm too young for a husband."

"My dear, you've become a woman. Ready to bear children. After I die, you'll need protection and guidance. Meantime, you need a man's intimacy. Someone who can lavish on you anything you desire."

She remained silent and fingered the necklace. Her bright pink nail paint couldn't surpass her pink-tinted cheeks.

Mah Ummia sighed and reassured himself that when she married an affluent man who adored her, as he did, she'll be content.

😕☃

Following Dumuzi's arrangement, Mah Ummia visited the rich merchant's home among others lining the Ceremonial Boulevard near the bazaar. He gazed up, impressed. The mansion rose four stories above its mud-brick wall. He pushed open the gold-filigreed gate and walked along the paved walk, hugged by a landscaped garden. Beyond the mosaic-inlaid archway, he entered a frescoed courtyard stuffed with furniture. Chair backs were adorned with intertwining flowers or animal heads. A table with clawed feet featured a miniature gem-encrusted harp. Another supported a carved golden ram balanced upright on two legs and caught in a leafy jeweled bush.

Slaves rushed about, attending to duties. One bathed the visitor's hands and feet and tugged on new sandals. Others cleaned the balcony, dusted furniture, swept, and carried baskets of food to the kitchen. Mah Ummia smiled with approval. Balulum must be exceptionally wealthy with such a lavish house and so many slaves. He pictured his daughter married to such a gentleman: supervising the household, hiring workers to redecorate the rooms, landscapers to rearrange the garden, and shopping at the bazaar to buy expensive items. She might entertain influential visitors from the nobility class. His mind raced through possibilities. King Mesanigalanna and his royal sons might attend a sumptuous banquet here in this very house. Unanna's son, his future grandson, could marry a princess. His mind raced with visions of such an exciting prospect!

Balulum, panting for breath, hurried downstairs and entered the courtyard. He smiled at his guest and motioned for him to sit beside a table holding golden bowls of figs and fluted goblets of beer. Five years younger than his guest, stout Balulum sat with his generous belly sagging over his belt. Grunting, he lifted his stomach, scratched his bare chest, and pointed at the refreshments. "Help yourself." He talked at length about his anguish at losing his wife, how all his relatives had died, leaving him the entire family fortune.

"I'm eager to wed my lovely daughter to a kind and wealthy suitor," Mah Ummia explained when Balulum finally grew silent. "She's very intelligent. She can converse on a number of subjects. Being a teacher, I taught her at home and can assure you that her grasp of mathematics is astonishing. It's too bad that girls aren't allowed to enroll at the Edubba, only boys from the merchant class."

Balulum leaned forward. "Ah, now I have hope of regaining my happiness. I have no family, no children. No one close to me." He paused, looked toward the courtyard entrance, and turned to Mah Ummia. "Well, you say she is lovely and exceptionally bright and that's commendable. But I wonder about her figure?"

"She's very slim and well proportioned," Mah Ummia assured him.

"Hmm," Balulum said and gulped some beer. Setting down the goblet, he said, "I don't suppose you would know her size? I mean, if she's very slim, as you say, then I assume her breasts are very small?"

"They're in proportion to her figure." Mah Ummia frowned and then reprimanded himself. After all, his potential son-in-law had a right to question him about such an important matter in a future bride.

"But I wonder also, if it isn't too personal..." He paused and coughed.

"Please, Balulum, I intend being frank with you."

"Well," Balulum gulped more beer and wiped his mouth with a pudgy finger. "That is, may I inquire about your sexual relationship with your wife? Is it satisfactory? I need to know so that I can judge—"

Mah Ummia jumped up from his chair. "Really! My relationship with my deceased wife is too personal. I wouldn't consider discussing that with anyone."

Balulum, grunting, propped himself up by leaning on the side table. He said, "I wouldn't dream of upsetting you. Please, sit, and refresh yourself. Have more beer." He proffered a goblet to his guest.

Mah Ummia shook his head and sat in disgust. Still, he reminded himself that a wedding was a serious business. Balulum had a right to be wary and ask numerous questions, no matter how repulsive.

"Well," Balulum said, smiling at his guest, "if your daughter is as lovely as you say, she'll lack for nothing. I'll make her very happy. Arrange a meeting and I'll decide."

It was arranged for the following week. Although Mah Ummia left the mansion frowning at crude Balulum, he reassured himself that it was a good match for his daughter. He reminded himself that his own prosperity—a sizeable inheritance from his father plus the substantial income as a teacher and physician—couldn't compare with his prospective son-in-law's affluence. Unanna would be adored by one of the wealthiest men in Ur, able to buy anything her heart desired. She would live like a queen, her every whim catered to, and her children might marry royalty!

80 03

Now, his mission was different in visiting Balulum again. Mah

Bernadette Miller

Ummia turned his attention from memories to the present as he entered Ur's wealthiest section where Balulum's mansion soared above the gated wall. Although his prospective son-in-law was ill and needed his help, Mah Ummia paused. He frowned as he fingered his pharmaceutical sack. Unanna vehemently opposed the marriage. But she shouldn't have pledged herself to a poor struggling teacher. It was his parental duty to erase from her heart her impractical love for Dumuzi and turn her affection toward Balulum, her future husband. He worried then that he might be wrong to deny his daughter the man she loved. After all, he had loved his dearest Ningal with all his heart, just as Unanna loved Dumuzi. He shook his head at his uncertainty. If he allowed Unanna to marry Dumuzi, he foresaw for her a life of poverty and misery ahead. She might one day come to hate her father for allowing her to pursue that disastrous path. On the other hand, if she must marry a detested suitor, she would come to hate her father anyway for forcing her into an unhappy marriage. It was so difficult to decide the best course of action!

He shook his head and walked toward the mansion.

CHAPTER 5

August, 3500 B.C., Sumer

U NANNA HAD MET DUMUZI ACCIDENTALLY. After learning about her betrothal to the merchant, Balulum, she'd visited Ur's bazaar as a distraction from an unwanted marriage. She'd never met her betrothed but saw no reason to surrender her pleasant, carefree life. Instead, her father urged her to bear the responsibilities of a wife. At the bazaar, she pushed aside a stall's beaded curtain and stepped inside. The young clerk, busy arranging jewelry on the coverlets, didn't notice her until she spoke.

"Could you make a ring to match my necklace?"

The clerk glanced up. Startled, he recognized the jewelry he'd sold to Mah Ummia for his daughter. He stared at the girl's beauty, overwhelmed by her pink-tinted complexion that matched the pink tufted gown, her glittering headdress, and her tiny waist enclosed by a silver belt.

"Stop staring," she said, her chin uplifted. "You're making me anxious."

"I...I'm sorry...my lady," he stammered, using the polite form of address for the daughter of a renowned teacher. "I was surprised you're wearing the necklace I designed."

"You...designed my necklace?" Unanna looked again at the tall, handsome clerk who looked to be just several years older than she.

Above his tufted skirt, black curls sprayed his bare chest and along his muscular arms. His sprouting beard barely covered his narrow cheeks. His gaze had turned gentle. His thin lips were slightly curved in a smile while his dark eyes focused on her.

"So you're a designer as well as a clerk," she said.

"I'm also a teacher," he declared, "although I'm just beginning my career. That's why I started working here for a few hours."

"A teacher! You must know my father, Mah Ummia, who supervises the Edubba."

"Yes, I admire him greatly." The clerk smiled and introduced himself. "I'm Dumuzi." He paused. "I could make a ring to match your necklace if you return in two weeks."

"I will," she said. They studied each other with interest. "Well, I should return home or my father will worry."

"I look forward to seeing you again, my lady."

"And I look forward to seeing you," Unanna blurted out. She blushed, wondering how she could be so bold with a stranger. He smiled. She smiled back. Their gaze held for a moment.

Nervous but strangely happy, she turned and strolled along the Ceremonial Boulevard. She fingered the necklace which seemed magical. Hadn't it caused the blood to rise to her forehead, her pulse to race most unexpectedly, and her sandaled feet to fly as if winged? "Dumuzi." She repeated his name several times, and sighed. Adda mustn't find out. He'd never allow a poor suitor to court her. How could she persuade him? She pondered various ruses. Despite adamant refusals, he usually yielded. Just last year, bored, she'd wanted to visit her aunt, her mother's sister in Lagash. The scene was still vivid in her mind.

Seated in his courtyard, Mah Ummia had shaken his head. "A young girl traveling to another city by chariot? Accompanied by only two slaves? With possible bandits lurking behind roadside bushes? No. Too dangerous. I can't allow it."

She'd burst into tears. "I never knew my mother," she said standing before him. "Can't I at least visit her sister?" She'd refrained from dabbing at her eyes and smudging the kohl. Looking her best usually helped in getting her way.

He scowled in his chair and looked up at her. "Unanna, my dear, can't you see I'm worried about your safety? Do you want to get killed? My only child."

She smiled and tugged playfully at his beard. "But that's exactly why you shouldn't refuse me, dear adda! Please let me leave, or I'll be grief stricken. You wouldn't want to see me sad...?" Straightening, she burst into tears again and noted his wounded look. But all her ruses had failed. He still refused.

She fled to her room and wept ceaselessly for an hour.

Finally, he relented and reluctantly climbed the stairs. "My dear child," he said upon entering her room. "Your resemblance to my beloved Ningal, whom I still greatly miss, makes it difficult to deny your requests. So, I give my consent."

"Thank you, my wonderful adda!" she gushed and hugged him.

"My beloved daughter," he murmured, smiling.

After he left, she hurriedly had her personal slave girl, Majeena, pack for the trip to Lagash, where she had a wonderful time with Aunt Nidiba. When she returned, her father greeted her at the courtyard archway with a wry, "I love you. But I shouldn't spoil you."

"Adda, you aren't spoiling me. You're just making me happy. As ama would have done." She smiled at his deep sigh and hugged him. "Aunt Nidiba was so kind. She treated me to sweets and introduced me to her delightful neighbors."

Mah Ummia patted his daughter's arm, content that no harm had befallen her. She was still his jewel who deserved a worthwhile suitor. "Yes, my dear," he said, ever the docile father.

ಬಂ ಲ

Now, arriving home from the bazaar, Unanna reproached herself for having assumed that Dumuzi cared about her. He seemed smitten by her beauty. But did he share her sudden longings? She grew torn by doubt and began questioning his motives. His tender gaze might have been prompted by adda's esteemed position. What should she do? Maybe she shouldn't return to the bazaar stall. She wouldn't want to persuade adda to allow Dumuzi's visit and then discover that her suitor's interest lay in her father's affluence. She shook her head. She'll forget about him, she thought.

⁝⁞

The following week, slaves prepared for Balulum's visit to Mah Ummia's house so the betrothed couple could meet. The slaves cleaned, plucked flowers from the garden to fill the balcony urns, and set bowls of honey cakes and goblets of beer on side tables in the courtyard. Music resonated upstairs where Unanna dressed to greet Balulum. Frowning, she glanced at her slave girl.

Majeena had a round face and cropped black hair that lay flat against her forehead. She wore a simple black dress from neck to sandals. Bought at birth from indigent parents and raised by Mah Ummia to be his daughter's future slave, Majeena seemed resigned to her lowly status. She never questioned it, and never disobeyed orders. She helped her mistress struggle into an ankle-length blue gown with a high neckline and long sleeves. As was the fashion, she braided Unanna's waist-long hair and spiraled it upward, tucked under the black wig that puffed out over her shoulders.

Over the wig, she carefully placed the glittering coin-studded headdress with more coins cascading toward Unanna's shoulders. Her golden earrings swayed to and fro when she rose. The special necklace of carved ivory and lapis lazuli designed by Dumuzi adorned her gown.

"You look beautiful, my lady," Majeena whispered.

Unanna frowned. "All this for a man I don't want to meet!"

"Maybe you'll change your mind when you talk with him," Majeena said. Unanna shrugged as her slave tugged on the sandals.

"It's silly to worry. My father usually does what I want and what I want is the handsome boy I met at the bazaar." She bit her lip, remembering her earlier decision to forget about him.

Majeena smiled. "Yes, my lady." She awaited further instructions.

"You're dismissed," Unanna said. She descended the stairs to the courtyard where a male slave approached Mah Ummia.

"My lord, Master Balulum has arrived."

"Show him in," Mah Ummia said. Unanna frowned, her eyes narrowing. Mah Ummia glanced at his daughter. "Don't worry, my dear. He'll take good care of you. In time you'll appreciate a rich, kind man whose only concern is your happiness."

The musicians stationed near the courtyard's whitewashed walls played softly as Mah Ummia introduced the couple.

"Ah, you are lovely," Balulum grunted with a smile. "Just as your father said."

Unanna shifted from one foot to the other.

Silence followed.

"My young daughter's nervous," Mah Ummia said. He gestured toward a pair of high-backed chairs. "Have a seat, Balulum. Rest yourself. Have some refreshments." He motioned to Unanna to sit beside their guest.

Balulum's tufted skirt spread over his chair like a ship's sail. From a belt pouch, he wiped his forehead with a soiled cloth and gulped some beer from a side-table goblet. "I, too, am nervous," he said, replacing the goblet. "Sweating, as usual. Like a hog in heat." He snickered and turned to Mah Ummia. "I'd be honored to wed your daughter." He gulped more beer and placed a pudgy hand over his thick lips to soften his belch.

Unanna flushed. Her lower lip trembled. How could she marry this fat, obnoxious old man who drinks so much beer? Adda must be blind!

Instead of sympathizing with her distress, he said, "Unanna, you aren't replying to our important guest's gracious compliments. You're insulting us both by ignoring him."

Bernadette Miller

"I'm...sorry," Unanna stammered. "You're right...I'm...nervous about marriage."

"Well, that's natural, my dear." Balulum reached for her hands which she promptly clasped in her lap. "But I'm sure our marriage will be blissful."

"Yes, most blissful," Unanna muttered facetiously.

Mah Ummia beamed, encouraged that his daughter was finally responding to her suitor. "I'll arrange a dinner," he said, "so that you two can become better acquainted." He paused, thinking. Maybe he should also invite Dumuzi, a part-time teacher at the Edubba, who also worked part-time for Balulum, and had praised him highly at the bazaar. That might show Unanna that wealthy Balulum, apart from his appearance, had a kind heart and was a worthwhile marriage prospect.

Mah Umma, smiling, looked at Balulum. "I was thinking of inviting your young helper, Dumuzi, who brought you and my daughter together."

"Well, I don't know..." Balulum paused and then chuckled. "Dumuzi is headstrong, and I'm not sure he's worth his salary, meager as it is."

"Really?" Mah Ummia said in politeness. He already knew that Dumuzi had written, without his permission, to some of his pupils' parents, asking for an increase in his wages. He'd reprimanded him, but the boy was stubborn. Still, he must admit that Dumuzi had excellent teaching skills.

Balulum shook his head. "He doesn't know his place. Such impropriety! Definitely not one to succeed in Ur."

Mah Ummia nodded. "But when I was seeking a marriageable prospect for my daughter, Dumuzi spoke very highly of you, and that's why I considered you."

"Spoke highly of me?" Balulum's fleshy cheeks widened into a grin, swelling his double chin beneath the beard. He mused aloud, "Well, if you want to show your gratitude to Dumuzi for his kindness in finding my charming bride, then why not?"

"Balulum, that's very thoughtful of you," Mah Ummia said. "I'll invite Dumuzi, a fine young man who will make a splendid teacher someday."

Despite her former resolve, Unanna's heart began thumping. She'll see Dumuzi again! She tried to appear nonchalant, forcing herself to hide her joy. "Well, I'll leave that up to you," she said dryly as if Dumuzi's visit didn't matter. She glanced at her father and rose, indicating the meeting was over.

Mah Ummia followed his guest to the door. "I'm sure the dinner will go well."

"I'm eager to see your beautiful daughter again," Balulum said, looking back with a smile as he was ushered out by a slave.

හ⊙ᬃ

Each day felt like a year to Unanna until she saw Dumuzi at the dinner party. That evening, when Unanna and Dumuzi met again in her home, a light kindled. They couldn't speak before their hosts, but gazed at each other across the platter-laden table, interrupted by clinking utensils and slaves bustling with food service. Later, when Balulum prepared to leave, he walked outside with Unanna, followed by Mah Ummia and Dumuzi. At the garden gate, Mah Ummia paused to chat briefly with his prospective son-in-law.

Unanna, stepping aside, couldn't help glancing at Dumuzi who waited nearby. He gazed at her steadfastly as if caught by a goddess's magic spell. She watched him walk away with Balulum who chatted excitedly about his future bride, while his clerk, Dumuzi, continually exchanged glances with Unanna.

Longing to be with him, she wondered if she should visit him at the bazaar. Then she wondered if he would try to see her. To her delight, while her father attended an urgent matter at the Edubba, a male servant from the bazaar brought a message.

Wearing a tufted skirt, unlike the loin cloth of slaves, he bowed before Unanna and said, "Mistress, my message is from someone who hired me to give you this ring. He said you'll know who it is and the ring is free, a gift."

Unanna gasped. The ring matched her carved necklace. Her heart fluttered with excitement. "Yes? What's the message?"

"He wishes you to meet him at the bazaar. This evening. Six o'clock. Near the sweets stall."

Unanna caught her breath. Dumuzi! She hesitated. Adda would be angry if he knew but she could calm him. Besides, she couldn't refuse her love. Discouraged, Dumuzi might never try to see her again. She slipped the ring on a finger. It fit perfectly. "Tell him I'll be there," she said and ran upstairs to choose appropriate clothing for her tryst with Dumuzi.

৪৩ ৫৪

That evening, Unanna wore a simple black gown beneath the tufted cloak to conceal her identity from possible onlookers, although by six o'clock the bazaar was usually deserted. Majeena had twisted her long braid upward in a ponytail beneath the hood.

At the nearly empty bazaar, her face partially concealed behind the hood, Unanna approached the sweets stall. With a tremulous heart she stepped gingerly over bits of garbage. She began scolding herself that she was being ungrateful by disobeying her father. Adda loved her. He was rightfully concerned about her future. All that was true, except that she loathed Balulum, a horrible suitor. How could she convince Adda that wealth wasn't the most important thing in life?

At the sweets stall, she saw Dumuzi who waited impatiently. She lifted her hood. Her heart pounded at seeing his smile. His eyes shone with pleasure at seeing her.

"You came to meet me," he said. "My love. Please say that you care about me." He tried to clasp her to his chest.

She pulled away. "I can't see you again. It's hopeless. You know that I'm betrothed to Balulum."

"Oh, may the gods pity me!" He gazed at her with grief. "What a fool I was. I suggested him to your father as a prospective husband. Can you forgive me, sweet Unanna? I had no idea then..." His voice trailed off. Unable to speak, he stared at the ground.

She struggled to deal with her emotional turmoil and scolded herself. She'd betrayed her father by falling in love with a forbidden suitor. Besides, suppose Dumuzi didn't really care about her? Suppose he merely wanted to court the daughter of a prominent teacher just to advance his own ambition?

"How do I know you care about me and not my father's success?" she exclaimed impetuously.

He stared at her in disbelief. "How can you say such a thing!" he burst out. "I love you. From the moment you stepped into the shop." Flustered, he gazed into the distance at the moon god peeking above the horizon. "It's true that your father wouldn't accept me as a suitor because of my lowly station. But I'm working hard to improve. Mah Ummia himself encouraged me to continue teaching. He said that someday I might privately teach wealthy pupils as he does. His very words."

He gazed at Unanna. "You're all I want. I'd love you, even if your father were poor." He paused. "Let's pretend that your father is poor. That you're just a servant and I'm a struggling teacher. Would it matter then?" He returned her smile. "As long as we love each other, our future isn't hopeless. Please give me a chance."

She gazed at him, at his pleading eyes and sincere gaze. He was so sweet, sweeter than anyone she'd ever known. And he loved her. Her heart raced with excitement. He loved her! Then she thought how her recklessness might destroy the only parent who'd always cared for her.

Dumuzi stroked her hand. "Unanna, please say you forgive me for introducing your father to Balulum."

At his touch, her flesh tingled. Flushing, she whispered, "I forgive you."

Bernadette Miller

"Then tell me you'll see me again," he said and ran his hand over her sleeved arm.

She turned away, quivering. "Impossible. My father wouldn't allow me."

"He reached out to embrace her. "Oh, my love. Tell me that you love me, too."

"No, we mustn't." She turned away, agitated, not knowing what to do. She yearned to be in his arms but felt torn about her father. She felt as if she wanted to die.

As if reading her thoughts, he put his arms around her. She tried to pull away. Her strength was no match for his. He pulled her against his muscular chest. She struggled to remain stiff, hoping to discourage him. Instead, it seemed so difficult to deny her feelings, as if her body had become weightless and her thoughts utterly serene. But she suddenly thudded back to earth when she began worrying about upsetting her father who worked so hard to ensure her happiness.

"What can we do?" she asked Dumuzi. "My father's determined I should marry Balulum."

"My sweetheart," Dumuzi murmured and bent to kiss her. She turned her head in protest. "Please let me love you," he pleaded.

Despite her resolve, she yielded to his lips and melted against him. They finally parted, gazing at each other. Here's the man she wanted who wanted her, she thought. Surely, she could persuade her father to cancel her betrothal by making him see how miserable she'd be with Balulum. She needed to stress how she'd rather kill herself than marry that repulsive old shopkeeper! She reminded herself about her victory in visiting Aunt Nidiba and other opportunities. She'll use her charms again and marry wonderful Dumuzi!

"Oh, Dumuzi," she said and grasped his shoulders. She pulled his body against hers. Something hardened against her when they kissed again. Her face flushed as though she were ill. Only Dumuzi could cure her love sickness. She must succeed in persuading adda.

"I'll ask for your hand in marriage," Dumuzi murmured when they separated.

"Not yet or my father will become angry! I need time to change his mind about Balulum." She squeezed Dumuzi's hand. Filled with warmth, she said, "Be patient. He usually lets me do whatever I want, if I'm determined enough."

"I'll just ask," Dumuzi said. He grasped Unanna's hand in his. "If he refuses, I'll devise another plan."

Repressing her qualms, Unanna agreed and they kissed again. She invited Dumuzi to visit the following morning.

❧❧

In the courtyard, unaware of his guest's intentions, Mah Ummia offered Dumuzi refreshments which Majeena set near his chair. Unanna sat beside Dumuzi.

"So, young man," Mah Ummia said, smiling, "what's the purpose of your visit?" He joked, "More jewelry for my daughter?"

Dumuzi, blushing, stammered, "Mah Ummia, I..I..have fallen deeply in love with Unanna. She shares my feelings. I...ask...for her hand in marriage."

"What!" Mah Ummia's face contorted in a scowl. "How would you support her until you established yourself?"

"I could borrow the money," Dumuzi said timidly.

Unanna jumped up and rushed to her father. "Adda, please let us marry."

Mah Ummia raised his hand in silence. He stared at Dumuzi. "How would you repay the twenty-five percent annual interest on the loan?"

Dumuzi, discouraged, stared at the brick floor.

Unanna placed her hand on her father's arm. "Please, adda, let me choose my husband. After all, I have to spend the rest of my life with him. Isn't love important, too?"

"No more!" Mah Ummia said. "My daughter, I have only your welfare at heart. You will marry Balulum. An excellent suitor who can provide for your every comfort. Not a poor teacher who offers poverty and despair. You'll make Balulum a good wife. When you're mature, you'll appreciate the wisdom of my choice."

He turned to Dumuzi. "Young man, don't come here again. Don't make any effort to contact my daughter."

Dumuzi looked dejected as Mah Ummia escorted him outside. He stared ahead with narrowed eyes, his thin lips tightening as if refusing to cry. Mah Ummia returned to the courtyard to find Unanna weeping.

Heartbroken at her engagement to Balulum and deprived of her only love, she fled upstairs to plot her next move. Why marry someone she hated just because everyone in Sumer worshipped shekels? Still, she didn't want to disobey her father whom she loved dearly. What should she do?

ස ශ

Leaving his daughter in despair, Mah Ummia had hurried to the Dublal-makh to pick up the marriage tablets for signing by himself and Balulum. Doubts flooded his heart. Was his decision practical? Afterwards, he relieved his anxiety by visiting Lord Enki's temple at the ziggurat. He gazed up at the god's marble statue in the wall niche. He entreated Lord Enki's guidance.

"I remember arguing with my father the same way," he told Lord Enki. "Adda didn't want me to pursue a teaching profession because of the low payments. The only occupation I cared about." He bent to prostrate himself against the cold, brick-paved floor. "My divine Lord Enki, it's my duty as a father to ensure my daughter's future, not saddle her with a demeaning life. So, should I deprive her of happiness? The kind I shared with her mother? Which path should I follow?"

He raised his head and turned sideways to look at gracious Lord Enki. His neck muscles began twitching. A bad sign, he thought, and stared at the niche. Lord Enki was surely ordering him to plan his daughter's wedding to Balulum or face dire consequences. Unanna shouldn't marry a poor teacher.

He rose, grateful for the god's silent advice, but he couldn't shake off anxiety, uncertain that his decision was wise. Tomorrow, he thought, he would visit a temple prostitute. That would calm him. He dropped a shekel into the bronze offering bowl and smiled gratefully at Lord Enki who seemed to smile back in reassurance. Holding the marriage tablets in his arms, he hurried home.

৪০ ০৪

Now, fortified by his session with Lord Enki, Mah Ummia paused at Balulum's gold-filigreed gate. He frowned. His prospective son-in-law's illness urgently needed his attention. First he must cure his patient. Then he'll decide his daughter's fate. He hurried inside Balulum's courtyard where he waved away the slaves approaching with basins and cloths. He rushed upstairs. Balulum lay deathly-pale beneath the soiled coverlet. His black beard was matted with flecks of dirt. Eyes closed, he moaned with pain.

"I'm here to cure you," Mah Ummia said. He bent over his patient and lifted an eyelid. The eye looked reddened and watery.

Balulum groaned. "Oh, my poor stomach."

"I have a remedy," Mah Ummia said. He untied his pharmaceutical sack and withdrew a gourd. It contained pears and the roots of the manna plant, both pulverized with herbs, and soaked with pear juice. He held up Balulum's head. "Drink this. Vomiting will help."

"Oh, oh, oh," Balulum moaned. His pudgy hands clutched his swollen belly. "Too much beer. Too few barley cakes. I'll die like an old fart. Please, Lord An, god of my parents, don't let me die before my wedding."

"Nonsense!" Mah Ummia said. He pried open Balulum's mouth. "My friend, you need this to save your stomach. Do as I say!" He helped lift Balulum's head from the pillow.

Balulum weakly opened his mouth. He gagged as the liquid charged down his throat. "The cure is worse than the illness," he grumbled. He fell back on his bed. Several minutes later he leaned over the mattress and retched into a large copper basin.

"Good," Mah Ummia said. "But we must postpone the wedding until you've recovered."

Balulum looked up, his ashen face and beard covered with food particles. "Postpone? No! Bring the tablets here. I'll sign. I want to marry your lovely Unanna. I dream about her nightly."

Mah Ummia shook his head. "We must wait until you're fully recovered. For now, my friend, rest. I promise you'll wed my daughter soon enough. I'll return."

"All right. But return with the marriage tablets. The only thing keeping me alive is the hope of wedding your daughter." Balulum leaned over to retch again. "You see?" he gasped, "even in this condition, I think only of her."

"Nevertheless, you need rest," Mah Ummia insisted and retied his leather sack.

Since Balulum was a future relative, Mah Ummia declined his generous offer to pay for a physician's visit: a minna, worth sixty shekels, valued at nearly fifteen pounds of silver. Outside, Mah Ummia headed toward the bazaar near the outer wall to replenish some medicinal herbs in his sack. Along the way, he pondered his distress over Unanna's unhappiness at her betrothal to Balulum despite his wealth. How to resolve the dilemma? He sighed deeply. It was his fatherly duty to find a proper suitor for his daughter. Then, he considered his other choice. If, only three days before her wedding, he yielded to her heartfelt pleas and dissolved her betrothal to Balulum, she would still refuse any suitor other than impoverished Dumuzi who was unacceptable. He shook his head in confusion as he arrived at the bazaar.

At a stall, Mah Ummia refilled his sack and paid the owner. Suddenly, a four-wheeled chariot drawn by three wild asses hurtled along the boulevard, kicking up dust. Warriors wearing leather skirts and helmets rode in the chariot, their spears thrust forward. Citizens, shouting, scurried out of the way. Mah Ummia noticed a Bedouin wearing filthy robes and a turban waiting near the bronze, double-gate with his donkey. Despite the crowd clearing a path around him, the bedraggled Bedouin remained frozen, his dark eyes wide with amazement as if he'd never seen a chariot.

Suddenly the Bedouin clutched his amulet necklace, withdrew his dagger, and stepped directly in front of the chariot.

Impulsively, Mah Ummia ran forward to save the berserk man from getting killed. The chariot rumbled toward the bronze double-gate. A warrior's whip urged the asses to increase their speed. Hoping to save the man from severe injury by the swiftly-approaching chariot, Mah Ummia, using all his strength, yanked him away just as the chariot sped past them and through the open gate. He silently prayed to Lord Enki to let the man live. But why, he wondered with amazement, would anyone deliberately risk his life to step before a speeding chariot?

CHAPTER 6

October, 3500 B.C., Sumer

T IRAS HUDDLED WITH HIS DONKEY near the bronze double-gate. Mesmerized by the large city, he stood gaping at the oddly-dressed Sumerians hurrying along the palm-shaded avenue. To his right, enormous houses rising above mud-brick walls discouraged unwanted visitors. To his left, a crowded bazaar beckoned with tempting aromas from baskets of cinnamon sweets. He debated bartering some wool for a sweet.

Suddenly a dragon carrying warriors on its back hurtled toward the gate. Dust was flying. The Sumerians ran to make way. His heart racing, Tiras glimpsed through the dusty haze the dragon's three heads and painted wood armor. Its round feet struck sparks against the stone paving, just as his cousin Ruach had described.

Tiras unsheathed his belt dagger. Here, he thought, was an opportunity to prove his courage and impress a Sumerian god to replace Martu. With his left hand he grasped the magic amulet hanging about his neck, ignored his pounding heart, took a deep breath, and stepped forward. He would slay the onrushing dragon by stabbing at its necks.

Screams arose from the crowd. Someone frantically pulled him away, but not before the dragon bit his leg. The intense heat, swirling dust, and pain overpowered him. He fainted, his dagger tumbling to the ground.

Tiras lay dazed for a while against the paved street. Confused, he opened his eyes. He was still alive! The mighty bull-god, Martu, hadn't dealt the supreme punishment for his earlier questioning. He touched his throbbing calf. The savage dragon had bitten into the bone. The wound swelled, purpled by venom. He sat up slowly. Excruciating pain shot through his body. Na'al brayed loudly as if voicing his concern.

A Sumerian man, wearing a long, white skirt with pleated hem, bent over him.

Struggling with pain, Tiras stared up at the old man who looked past forty winters. He studied his bald head and lengthy gray beard, the bare and wrinkled chest, and his pale brown eyes. The Sumerian gently disentangled his multi-colored shawl twisted against Tiras's robe and draped it over his left shoulder.

Weak and dizzy, Tiras raised a fist at the possible shaman. Be careful, he warned himself. The Old One might be casting a dangerous spell! Groaning with pain, he picked up his dagger and pointed it toward the stranger.

The Sumerian, straightening, cried out, "My people mean you no harm. I saved your life."

Tiras shivered before the omnipotent shaman. How could the Sumerian know Bedouin words?

"I'm a physician and can treat your wounded leg," the Sumerian said.

Tiras reminded himself that the Old One might have useful magic. His help shouldn't be ignored. He slid his dagger inside his belt pouch, grasped the extended hand, and rose unsteadily. His arm outstretched over his donkey, he limped beside his benefactor. The Sumerian with his leather sack smiled at citizens respectfully giving way. Despite the pain, Tiras noted people's disdain of him. Some even held their noses as if he smelled bad!

Bernadette Miller

"I'm called Mah Ummia," the Old One told Tiras in his Bedouin tongue. "In Sumerian it means Great Teacher. You look surprised at my speaking your language. I learned it in our school called the Edubba. We have dictionaries of foreign languages written on clay tablets."

He paused as Tiras's jaw dropped in astonishment and then smiled. His mouth was filled with white teeth despite his age. "Are you in Ur to barter your wool like other Bedouins?"

"Yes. But also to learn about your gods. But—" Tiras hesitated. He had to be careful what he said about Martu and his brutality. Who knew, he thought, where Martu might be lurking about and listening?

Mah Ummia beamed at learning of Tiras's desires. "After I treat your wound, I'll explain everything, if you wish."

"I'm most interested in learning," Tiras gasped, grimacing from the agonizing pain. "I hunger for knowledge of the world."

"Hunger for knowledge?" Mah Ummia nodded with satisfaction. "I'm also a teacher. I'd enjoy an eager pupil. Of course, at no cost to you." At last, after all these years since his childhood promise, he'd found a Bedouin who wanted to leave his primitive ways. What a pleasure it would be to teach him.

Despite the intense pain, Tiras smiled at his sudden luck. He would learn all about the Sumerian gods and return to his tribe with the new knowledge. Suddenly, another dragon charged down the street. The helmeted warriors focused on the bronze gate, their long spears pointed forward. Dust sprayed the street as the vicious animal approached. Tiras turned away, feeling faint again in the heat and dust.

"Don't you fear the dragons?" he panted as Mah Ummia urged him toward a house's mud-brick wall. Na'al tossed his head and brayed at being shoved against the wall. The dragon dashed by with no one bitten. Tiras sighed in relief.

"Dragons?" Mah Ummia replied. "No, my friend, they're chariots we make that transport people and merchandise. They're used in battle, too. Chariots aren't harmful. Unless you step in front of them."

"Why are their back feet round?"

"They're not feet. They're called wheels. Something my people invented. The animals pulling the chariot are onagers, related to donkeys."

Tiras nodded. "I have much to learn."

The pair proceeded along the broad avenue. To divert his companion's attention from his pain, Mah Ummia explained, "Our king and dignitaries use this Ceremonial Boulevard for celebrations. Most important is the Akitu, the New Year holiday, starting next week. Our revered king, Mesanigalanna, as the bridegroom, represents Lord Dumuzi, our vegetation god. The High Priestess, as the bride, represents Lady Inanna, our goddess of love."

"You have many gods!" Tiras exclaimed, marveling that the first Sumerian he'd met talked about his gods.

"And there's the Sacred Way." Mah Ummia paused before a cluster of buildings surrounded by a high mud-brick wall. "It contains temples and other important buildings."

Temples! Tiras stared up in amazement at one building that loomed so high it seemed to touch the sky. A wooden gate entwined with carved flowers enclosed the huge complex. Beyond the opened gate, he glimpsed a jasmine garden. The crowd at the gate chattered in different tongues. The tall building must be the magic tower Ruach had described.

"Please tell me about the tower," Tiras implored.

"It's called a ziggurat. Foreigners are welcome to visit but not to worship in our temples. The gate to the entrance is called in Sumerian: Babu-Ilu, Gate of God. That translates in your language as Bab-El."

The Tower of Bab-El. Tiras paused to remember and pass it on to his tribe. It was much grander than Martu's simple stone altar. Maybe that's why Martu was so demanding. Tiras smiled to himself despite his aching leg. He'd just arrived in Ur and already learned a lot.

Mah Ummia added, "When you're well we can explore the area if you wish."

"I'd like that," Tiras said enthusiastically, trying not to wince at his continuing pain.

Mah Ummia smiled and guided him along narrow, winding alleys with cobblestoned streets that radiated from the boulevard. He pointed at the two-story, flat-roofed, and windowless houses flanking an alley, their whitewashed walls shimmering in the sunshine. "The baked bricks for our houses come from mud from our bountiful river, the Euphrates," he said. "To secure the bricks in place, we use bitumen, a kind of tar, also dug from our river which offers many treasures."

He finally stopped before a house with an opened wooden door. A husky man wearing a loincloth and sandals strode along the pebbled walk, past the palm hovering over a grassy yard and small flower beds that lined the white picket fence. He bowed low to Mah Ummia, and unlatched the metal gate. He led Tiras's donkey along the pebbled walk surrounding the house and beyond to a backyard shed with other animals. Na'al brayed his protest at being separated from Tiras, who stared after him with a frown.

"Your donkey will be well cared for," Mah Ummia assured him. He grasped his guest's elbow and helped him inside the house. In the large courtyard with whitewashed walls, Tiras slumped with fatigue in a high-backed chair with a cane seat. His host disappeared through one of the arches surrounding the courtyard and soon returned with a leather sack and a pitcher of cold water that he set on a side table. Tiras immediately drained the cupful and two more.

"Another?" Mah Ummia asked.

Tiras shook his head. Mah Ummia pushed aside the robe and rubbed the injured leg with vegetable oil. While his leg bone was being reset, Tiras clamped his mouth shut to stifle screams at the unbearable hurt and shut his eyes. He dared not cry out though he felt his eyes watering. Mah Ummia might think him weak like a woman.

"Fortunately, the bone is fractured, not broken," Mah Ummia said. "But you're still young. I can help it to heal." He showed Tiras how to make a poultice. Using a terracotta bowl and utensil, he mashed dried herbal roots, added beer, and mixed the ingredients. He spread the paste in a soft woolen cloth that he tied to Tiras's leg. To protect the bone from further injury, he fashioned a cast from wood strips and bound it with reeds about the injured leg. Finished, he lifted his steepled hands toward the sky and chanted a prayer in Sumerian.

"Oh, Ninisinna, divine goddess of medicine, help me to repair this poor man's injury. Spare him from much suffering, and let his leg become as new."

As Tiras gazed with concern at his host's weird chanting in a tongue he didn't understand, a regal-looking young woman entered the courtyard. She wore a carved necklace over her black gown. Her puffed-out black wig emphasized her creamy, pink-tinted cheeks. Metallic threads from a golden headdress shaded her eyes outlined with kohl. Her jeweled earrings swayed to and fro as she hurried toward Mah Ummia. She stopped short at seeing Tiras, glanced at him with contempt, and then conversed with Mah Ummia in that same unfamiliar tongue Mah Ummia had spoken earlier. He listened to the strangers' conversation, bewildered at hearing strange-sounding words he didn't understand.

Startled, Unanna asked her father, "Why is this filthy Bedouin in our house? He smells terrible. And what happened to Balulum?"

Her voice trailed off as Mah Ummia held up a hand. "Unanna, I saved this man's life. He suffered a severe accident. He's now our guest. Don't insult me by insulting our guest. As for Balulum, he's too ill to sign the marriage contract." Mah Ummia paused for a moment at Unanna's intense look of relief. "Hmm, perhaps the gods are displeased with this marriage," he added, stroking his beard.

"Perhaps I should reconsider your wedding. I'm undecided. I must weigh the possible consequences."

"Oh, adda, thank you!" Unanna rushed to kiss his cheek.

"Don't thank me. I said I might reconsider. But I doubt I'll change my mind."

Smiling nevertheless, she turned to Tiras. "You brought me good luck so I welcome you to my father's house. May the gods favor you."

"This is Unanna, my daughter," Mah Ummia said to Tiras in his familiar language and translated her words.

Tiras returned her smile. "And may the gods favor you, as well," he replied.

Mah Ummia nodded his approval at his guest's response and translated his words into Sumerian. "Daughter, tell Majeena to prepare an extra meal for our guest."

When his host turned toward him, Tiras said, "I understand you don't want payment for teaching me. But how can I return your kindness? Undischarged obligations bring dishonor to my tribe, the Abram."

Mah Ummia responded, "Teaching you my religion will fulfill my promise to my family's personal god, Lord Enki. The powerful god helped me to become a teacher which my father always objected to." He paused. "Like the Bedu, the Sumerian word for your people, we Sumerians also worship many gods. But here is where we differ. Each Bedu tribe selects a special god to defend and protect the entire tribe. But each Sumerian family selects its own personal god as protector. My family chose Lord Enki, god of wisdom."

Tiras rejoiced that he would finally learn about their gods. "Please tell me why people exist."

Mah Ummia nodded. "That story has been handed down from ancient times on our clay tablets." At Tiras's puzzled expression, he said, "Well, I'll explain the tablets later." He paused and continued, "Lady Nammu, the goddess of the primeval sea, asked her son, Lord Enki, to create servants for them. Lord Enki advised her to fashion clay in his image. She did so, helped by Nin-ti, Lady of the Ribs, also known as the birth goddess. So, the two goddesses created the first man, a new-born babe. The gods created us in their image to serve them after we die."

Tiras nodded, thinking how the birth goddess, also called the rib goddess, shaped a baby from clay. He smiled at the seemingly-logical explanation. "So your people were made in a god's image," he said. "Your gods are very clever. Animals couldn't serve them the way people can."

He paused and asked Mah Ummia, "Why hasn't our tribal god, Martu, told my tribe these things? Perhaps our bull-god fears the discovery. Then he'll no longer be worshipped—" After speaking so boldly, Tiras stopped and silently warned himself. Better not deliberately antagonize Martu, he thought.

A pretty girl entered. Tiras stared at her round face, cropped black hair, and large breasts. Her dark eyes focused on the floor. She looked about fifteen, the same age as the royal-looking girl, but she wore an unadorned black dress from her neck to her sandals.

Mah Ummia issued instructions to her in Sumerian, and then turned back to Tiras. "My daughter's personal slave will bathe you before our evening meal," he said.

"Slave?" Tiras said, surprised. Like his kinsmen, Tiras disapproved of slavery. It seemed unjust to grant people and animals the same status. He simply nodded at Mah Ummia, not wishing to upset his kind host. "Where do the slaves come from?"

"Special agents at the bazaar buy babies from indigent parents," Mah Ummia replied. "Conquered people also become slaves. Such as the Elamites and other tribes from the mountains east of Sumer. Slaves are used mostly as servants. Some as concubines, a practice I've condemned. Like other property, we take good care of our slaves. They're clothed. Well fed. Their medical needs are attended to."

The slave girl bowed low to Mah Ummia and his guest. Tiras smiled at her. She started to smile, and hesitated, looking uncertain. "What's her name?" Tiras asked Mah Ummia.

Bernadette Miller

"Dumu Majeena. Dumu means unmarried, a maid. But you may call her Majeena."

Majeena, on hearing her name, blushed at being discussed and turned away.

"Majeena," Tiras repeated softly. Despite himself, he continued staring at her. A man with three wives shouldn't show interest in a maid, he reminded himself.

Suddenly, he remembered the sandstorm where his brother Doloch died. And his mother's bitter reproach afterward about his pursuing young tribeswomen before being wed. She and Mashech were looking for potential brides for him as soon as he turned fourteen. Soon he had married Na'amah and had never regretted it.

☯☯

Tiras, startled in his reverie, heard Mah Ummia shove back his chair that scraped against the brick floor.

"Come, I'll help you upstairs to your bath," his host said.

Tiras stared at him. "A bath? With water? Here?" With his heavy leg cast, he leaned awkwardly on the old man.

They climbed a stairway to the balcony. He bit his lip to repress crying out from his painful leg. "Water's scarce in the desert," he gasped. "Occasionally, we swim in an oasis lake, thanks to the lake goddess. Almost as enjoyable as love-making! And we clean our teeth with the araq twig. It has sharp points."

"We bathe in water daily," Mah Ummia said. His lips curved in an amused smile. "We use soap for our bodies. Herbal paste for our teeth."

He confused Tiras even more by remarking, "Our plumbing diverts water from the river into our homes."

Tiras stared, amazed at the Sumerians' magical powers. How could they command water to do their bidding? Do their gods offer this blessing?

"I'll teach you everything so you'll understand," Mah Ummia

said. "Stay until your leg is well enough for travel." He waved an arm at his guest's protest. "Otherwise, you'll become crippled."

Like baba, Tiras thought. His poor father's injury had rapidly aged him. He frowned, thinking ahead. Soon, his tribe will leave the Nefud Desert. If he didn't return in time, he'd have to travel alone to the Uplands where it might take a moon-cycle to find them. Still, he must allow his wound to heal or become crippled. Besides, the wise Sumerian had important knowledge that he craved.

Tiras nodded and leaned on his host's free arm. He limped upstairs and along the balcony. "Mah Ummia, I deeply appreciate your help, and willingness to teach me."

"For a Bedu, you're surprisingly eager to learn," Mah Ummia said. "I wish more of my pupils copied you."

They entered a tiled room. Tiras gawked at the bronze tub and pipes that spurted water. Sumerian magic! He turned to Majeena waiting nearby with scrub brush and towels. Exhausted but curious at being washed by a woman he didn't know, he sat on a high-backed chair, helped by Mah Ummia.

After his host left, the slave girl stripped off Tiras's robes. Blushing despite himself, he watched her scrub grime from his naked body with an oily substance. She avoided his left shoulder's fig-shaped birthmark. He enjoyed the lather and her hands touching his bare skin but her caressing touch disturbed him. Flushed with embarrassment by his rising zibbinu, he glanced up at her dark eyes, full lips, and black hair flattened against her head like a cap. Her large breasts loomed over him.

Despite Abu-Summu's demanding faithfulness to one's wives, other women always excited him. He loved his wives, especially Na'amah, and tried to obey tribal codes. Perhaps powerful Martu was merely testing the tribe when he demanded faithfulness. A man's arousal at seeing a pretty girl was nearly uncontrollable.

Majeena smiled shyly while continuing the sponge bath. Finished, she dried his body and wrapped him in an ankle-length, white skirt with pleated hem, his chest bare like Sumerian men. She wrapped her arm around him and helped him downstairs to the kitchen off the courtyard. As a distraction from his interest in the slave girl, Tiras scanned the beehive oven resting on a tall base of mud bricks. He admired the copper pots hanging along a wall, and the copper platters and gold goblets stacked on opposite shelves. Oasis shops never displayed so much.

Mah Ummia entered and sat beside Tiras at the long wooden table. Another slave girl brought Tiras's filled platter. He shoved it toward Mah Ummia, expecting to share. The old man shook his head and soon bent over his own platter. Surprised, Tiras stared at his baked fish with olives, barley cakes, figs, and the nearby goblet of beer. It was too much for one man while many went hungry, he thought, feeling guilt. Ravenous, he shrugged and ate with his right hand. The food would be wasted if he didn't eat it.

"No, my friend, there's a cleaner way." Mah Ummia handed him silver utensils, some with scoops and others with teeth. He demonstrated their use.

Tiras struggled to maneuver the clumsy utensils. He put them down in disgust. "I'm hungry. This will take too long."

Mah Ummia patiently showed Tiras by way of example.

Tiras watched for a while, struggled again, and then grinned with pride as if he'd lived in Sumer for many moon-cycles while eating with utensils.

"You're an apt pupil," Mah Ummia said, surprised.

When the meal ended, he issued instructions to the slave girl waiting against the wall. She carefully scraped the leftovers into bowls. He turned to Tiras. "We don't believe in wasting food. We conserve as much as possible."

"I agree," Tiras said. "But the desert can be brutal. We'd rather roast a whole goat and starve later rather than watch a guest go hungry. If asked, we'd help any traveler with shelter, food, and protection for three days and nights. But it's impolite to question his purpose for travel. We might ask about his homeland and gossip about other tribes. Our camps are isolated. So we crave the latest news."

"Ah, but that's where you and I differ," Mah Ummia said. "We believe that a man should live within his means. Not squander a goat simply to impress a guest."

"My people don't consider it squandering." Tiras paused and reproached himself. It was rude to argue with his host who'd shown such generosity.

"Come, I'll take you to your room," Mah Ummia said. "You need rest."

Tiras leaned on his host's free arm, limped upstairs, and along the balcony. He stuffed his fist into his mouth to avoid crying out from the pain. Mah Ummia pushed aside the curtained doorway of a bedroom. Inside, Tiras gazed in wonder at the wall panels of pearl mosaics. Chiseled Sumerian figures with widened eyes stared at him. Others knelt in prayer in a temple. Majeena followed them and smiled shyly at Tiras.

"She'll help you," Mah Ummia said and left him alone with the slave girl.

Tiras held Majeena's sturdy arm, and limped to the bed with its carved headboard. She helped him remove the skirt and clothed him in a simple white robe. He sank into a comfortable straw mattress and pulled the wool coverlets over him. The Sumerians like luxury, he thought, watching Majeena leave. Perhaps their gods are gentle because of soft city life. That's why they don't demand sacrifice. But in the ruthless desert could a Sumerian god protect his tribe?

CHAPTER 7

October, 3500 B.C., Sumer

TIRAS'S LESSONS WITH MAH UMMIA began upstairs while the invalid rested in bed, his body propped against the headboard, letting his outstretched leg heal under the wooden cast.

Mah Ummia welcomed the distraction. Frustrated by his daughter's unhappiness and his inability to resolve it, he again postponed the wedding. He still felt that she should marry Balulum, an excellent provider, but detested forcing her to marry against her will. Unanna had wept continuously, refusing consolation unless he agreed to her marriage with Dumuzi.

She finally complained to her father, "How can you expect me to marry such a repulsive man? I despise him."

Mah Ummia stared at her, aghast. She despised Balulum? Such a marriage must prove disastrous. "I'll think it over," he reluctantly told her. She rushed with gratitude to kiss his cheek. "I haven't decided," he warned her. "I'm just considering it." He sighed in bewilderment, wondering how he could possibly consider granting her a life of poverty with Dumuzi. Still, her hopeful smile warmed him.

He waited a few weeks to develop an excuse for delaying the marriage. Finally, he visited his prospective son-in-law and said,

"My dear Balulum, my young daughter isn't ready for marriage due to her youth and innocence. She's being prepared. You need patience."

"Of course. I understand," Balulum said and added, "Have more beer, Mah Ummia." He proffered a goblet toward his guest.

Mah Ummia took a few sips to please his guest and left, satisfied he'd temporarily postponed the problem.

But two weeks later, the prospective groom sent a slave to inquire about setting another wedding date. "My master wishes to know when he can sign the marriage tablets."

Mah Ummia sighed. "Tell your master that marriage with my daughter will happen as soon as she approves. I'm certain I can convince her."

He felt satisfied that in time he could resolve his problem with his daughter. Meanwhile, a challenging diversion awaited: teaching the primitive Bedouin his religion and thus fulfilling his youthful vow to Lord Enki. That first day, he told Tiras that he must promise to teach the Sumerian religion to his tribe.

"I agree," Tiras said, rejoicing that at last he would find a worthwhile god to replace the spiteful Martu.

෯ ෬

Despite his aching calf, Tiras's life seemed pleasant now with a comfortable bed, delicious food, a pretty slave girl to wait on him, a wise Sumerian to explain their religion, and no more squabbling wives. Strangely enough, Martu hadn't punished his defiance. Perhaps the bull-god hesitated angering the Sumerian gods, thereby inviting his own destruction.

Each day, Mah Ummia sat at his guest's bedside to relate stories about the Sumerian gods. Tiras marveled at the abundance of water in Sumer and the miracles the Sumerian gods performed. Like parents, they could be patient and understanding, but they punished

Bernadette Miller

disobedience. Mah Ummia said that stories about their gods had been handed down for generations on clay tablets.

"Lord An, father of our gods, created the world by his Divine Word," Mah Ummia explained one afternoon. He uttered his wishes and it was so."

"The Divine Word," Tiras repeated, awed. "Our tribal priest, Abu-Summu, interprets our bull-god's wishes."

"Ah, but how can a dumb beast exert more authority than our gods who look like us?"

Tiras hesitated as he digested this meaning and then nodded in agreement.

Mah Ummia continued. "Lord An fashioned the world from a ball of chaos surrounded by a primeval sea. Then he separated the land from the water. We Sumerians are our gods' chosen people. They taught us how to advance our culture while others remain ignorant and struggling to survive. Surely our gods smile upon their chosen people."

"Your gods' chosen people," Tiras echoed, awed again. "Yes, they clearly love you. But why?"

Mah Ummia paused, surprised at his guest's astuteness. His lips curved in a wistful smile. "It's beyond man's knowledge to know the gods' intent." He rose, adding, "I must leave you. I'm busy with my teaching duties at the Edubba."

Tiras nodded but felt disappointment. Except for Majeena bringing him food, he was alone most of the time and beginning to feel bored. He looked forward to more lessons with Mah Ummia who finally appeared after supper.

The teacher drew up a chair beside Tiras's bed and explained about schools. "Tribes like yours teach by example," he said. "Sumerians pass on information that's written on our ancient clay tablets. We also teach special professions. Legal. Medical. Engineering. Literature. And many more. Learning in Sumer is given much respect."

Tiras, feeling stupid, tried to grapple with the information but the unfamiliarity eluded him. Perhaps a visit to the school and actually seeing the teachers and pupils might help his understanding all the strange things in Sumer. He could tell from Mah Ummia's expression that his guest wasn't sure he understood everything.

"I'd like to visit your Edubba," Tiras said finally.

"Yes, I can arrange that when you're recovered," Mah Ummia said. "But let's continue about my gods. A high priestess who'd pledged celibacy bore a son on our river bank. To hide her sin, she put her baby in a basket, sealed the lid with tar, and slipped the basket into the river, certain the boy would drown. But a fisherman found the basket and raised the baby as his own. The baby grew up to become an important leader."

Tiras nodded but thought how terrible it was that a mother tried to drown her child. Thankfully, someone saved it. He memorized the story so he could repeat it to his tribe.

"I know little about our desert gods," he said, his voice quavering. "Except for the human sacrifice to Martu. I can't forget my tiny daughter's horrible suffering when our priest forced me to sacrifice her by having her whipped. I fear for my other children."

Mah Ummia sighed deeply. "That's terrible. We Sumerians are highly civilized. We'd never permit such atrocities. He studied his pupil. "Why didn't you reject that evil?"

Tiras's face burned in shame. "I longed to but dared not. As a child, I didn't believe in Martu. But after many moon-cycles of watching the priest describe Martu's power, gesturing wildly with his hands before the blazing altar, my heart finally caught on fire. I saw Martu in a dream and shivered at his terrifying presence. After that, I saw him a lot, and not just in dreams." Tiras paused. "If only I could find a god to replace vicious Martu. Please tell me more."

Mah Ummia replied, "Unlike animals, Sumerian gods can reason like men. That's why they're merciful."

"Your gods are merciful." Tiras stared incredulously at the old man with his bald head and lengthy gray beard.

Bernadette Miller

Mah Ummia sighed. "All my teaching is like a drop of water in the river. Here's another story you should know that shows our gods' power. Once, a human mocked Lady Inanna, goddess of love. As punishment, she sent devastating rain for six days and nights that flooded the entire world. Fortunately, Lord Enki, the god of wisdom, felt pity. He advised the virtuous king of Shuruppak, Ziusudra, to build a large boat. King Ziusudra loaded the boat with animal pairs so their seed wouldn't perish. The boat finally landed at Mt. Nisir, far north, beyond the cities of Bab-Ilim and Kish. From there the population flourished again."

Another interesting story, Tiras thought. Although their gods punished wrongdoers, they showed pity for suffering worshippers. Unlike Martu!

"I crave knowledge like sheep seeking pasture," he told Mah Ummia, despite deep misgivings that Martu would still discover his betrayal. "Please tell me more."

"Gladly," Mah Ummia replied. "But it's late. Majeena is ready to bathe you." He rose and left after issuing instructions to the slave girl.

Majeena nodded and helped Tiras, limping, to the bath. When she stripped off his robe and helped him to sit, his manhood again demanded attention although he still yearned for his favorite wife and their son. His body's hunger couldn't be denied, he reasoned silently. Since his journey to Ur, no woman wrapped her legs about him, or even kissed him.

Majeena lathered him with the oily white substance. She spoke, but he didn't understand. Nervously she pointed at herself. "Majeena." Then she pointed at him and raised her dark brows questioningly.

"Tiras," he said, delighted at her attempting conversation.

"Tiras," she echoed.

At her saying his name, pleasure flooded him. His arms prickled with bumps.

"Tiras," she repeated and began scrubbing his chest. "Tiras," she said several times.

"Majeena," he said and repeated it several times. He enjoyed her wet hands touching his bare skin.

Again she pointed at him and said, "Lu."

"No. Tiras."

Her head bobbed in agreement. "Lu," she repeated, pointing at him. She patted her breasts. "Munus."

"Ah, man and woman," Tiras said, his eyes lighting up in understanding. He repeated the words in Sumerian.

Nodding, she scrubbed a leg. She paused, and then pointed at the tub's water. "Ab," she said. Her gaze focused on his erection. She said, without blushing, "luabgal." He flushed and turned away. If only he could explain that in this situation he couldn't help being aroused. He turned toward her. "Luabgal," he said and sighed. The pair gazed at each other and burst into laughter. They laughed heartily for a while. It was the first time he'd laughed since arriving in Ur.

When she finished scrubbing him, she rinsed and dried him with cloths. She wrapped him in a soft robe. When he stood, she spoke again in Sumerian, indicating he should lean on her sturdy arm. His body tingled. Smiling, she maneuvered him to his bed. He watched her leave, wishing she would spend the night. But wasn't it best that she leave? Surely, his host wouldn't approve her staying with him. Before falling asleep, he repeated Majeena's name. His hand satisfied his erection. He dreamed that they kissed and made love. But then he reminded himself about his quest to replace Martu. The lessons with Mah Ummia were far more important than his feelings for a slave girl.

80 03

Mah Ummia welcomed the digression from the troubles with his daughter. During a session, he handed Tiras a clay tablet with strange markings. "They're symbols representing words," he explained. "It's called writing. Something we invented long ago. I'll teach you our

Bernadette Miller

language. Simple words are combined to form longer words. Dub means clay tablet. Sar means to write. Therefore, a dubsar is a scribe, a writer of tablets. And 'e' means house. And 'ba' means of. So, e-dub-ba means House of Tablets where I teach."

Tiras nodded and fingered the tablet's markings. "Dubsar," he repeated. "Edubba. Writing." More Sumerian magic! Nothing like the tongues Tiras had learned during childhood.

Seizing every opportunity, he practiced with Mah Ummia and Majeena, delighted to chat with her, however clumsily. When alone, he repeated each word numerous times so that he learned quickly. First he spoke in phrases, and then simple sentences. He began acquiring grammar and vocabulary. To help his progress, Majeena at first spoke slowly and distinctly and used gestures as if he'd been born deaf and mute, like his brother Shargu. After three moon-cycles, he could converse, although he occasionally stumbled, forgetting a word's meaning.

Mah Ummia, astonished by his guest's unexpected aptitude, exclaimed, "I've never had such a smart pupil!"

Tiras beamed with pride.

Curious about his host's people, so different from all that was familiar to him, Tiras asked numerous questions. "What do you call your land, in Sumerian?"

"Ki-en-gir," Mah Ummia replied. "In your language, it means Land of the Civilized Lords. We call ourselves sag-gigga. Black heads. Not like the people south of Amrata who have black skin. As you can see, our skin is fair, though our hair and eyes are dark."

One morning, Tiras asked in Sumerian, "Were your people always here?"

Mah Ummia spoke slowly, pausing occasionally to translate from Sumerian to Tiras's tongue. "According to our history, we arrived several millennia ago, before the Great Flood. Some think our people originated in Elam, a country to our east. Perhaps our ancestors called themselves black heads to distinguish themselves from most Elamites with blond heads. But others argue our origin might have been farther east. Perhaps the Indus Valley, but certainly not west in Arabiyah. We've never lived among your tribes."

He looked at Tiras listening intently. "You're highly intelligent," he said.

"Thank you," Tiras said. "Learning gives me great pleasure. I enjoy the stories and the opportunity to speak in your native tongue."

⁞

Thrilled by his acquired knowledge despite the gaps in understanding, Tiras began disregarding Majeena's extra attention, her sighs and shy smiles when she bathed him or clothed him for sleep. He reasoned that it wasn't right for the unmarried slave, a virgin, to expect a foreigner with three wives to lie down with her. She finally stopped trying to entice him. As before, she simply attended to his bodily needs, but he still wanted her.

After four moon-cycles, Tiras's leg bone had nearly healed. In the courtyard, Mah Ummia gently removed the wooden cast and lay the strips on the paved floor. "Would you like to visit our ziggurat?" he said as he bandaged the wound with a fresh poultice. "You seem well enough to walk."

"Yes, I'd like that," Tiras replied. It would be a welcome distraction from forbidden thoughts of making love with Majeena and thereby betraying his host's trust.

To prepare him for his walk, Majeena removed his night shirt and tugged on his desert robes that she'd scrubbed with essence of anastatica, an overwhelming, sweet fragrance. She avoided looking at him directly. He did the same, but also politely refrained from holding his nose at the unbearable smell to avoid offending her.

Outside, Tiras limped with his cane beside Mah Ummia. He admired Ur, a colorful city crowded with alleyways, shops, and houses scented by gardens.

"Ur measures about four miles in length and a mile wide within

Bernadette Miller

the mud-brick wall," Mah Ummia explained. "Canals supply water to our fields and plumbing for our homes."

Tiras nodded. The Sumerians were amazingly clever, able to command water, but his people were also clever to survive the harsh desert.

The pair reached the ziggurat's gate, the Bab-El, crowded with foreign visitors who chattered in many tongues while staring up at the soaring tower. Tiras scanned the crowd: black people from the south of Amrata and sun-browned tribesmen, such as the Amorites, Midianites, and Phoenicians, who clutched their stained robes, adjusted their turbans, and chatted among themselves. He suddenly longed for home. If only he could see his family. He was about to tell Mah Ummia that he'd like to talk with some of the desert tribesmen. They might know the latest gossip about his tribe. Where were they? Who were betrothed? Who had wed? Who gave birth? Who had died?

Before Tiras could ask, Mah Ummia said, "Let's go up." Tiras nodded. He disliked disagreeing with his kind host. Mah Ummia gently grasped Tiras's elbow and guided him through the gate and past the garden. Again, Tiras gawked up in amazement at the three terraces and topmost shrine that stretched to the sky god. He cautiously placed his cane on each steep, narrow step. At the first terrace, Mah Ummia suggested they rest. Panting, Tiras gratefully sank onto the brick floor amidst trees and buttresses.

"The three terraces symbolize the world's three divisions," Mah Ummia said as Tiras glanced about. "The netherworld, the Earth, and the dwelling place of the gods. The topmost shrine belongs to Lord An, father of our gods."

Tiras nodded thoughtfully. He remembered Mah Ummia explaining how Lord An impregnated his wife, Nin-Kursag, Lady of the Mountain, the Sumerians' earth mother, who gave birth to the others. But how could only two Sumerian gods, Lord An and Nin- Kursag, produce all the other gods while the fierce bull-god,

Martu, produced none? Was Martu impotent? Was he less powerful and therefore couldn't reproduce? It was a difficult question and dangerous. He looked about cautiously, but Martu didn't appear. Nor had he since Tiras's arrival in Sumer.

Relieved, Tiras turned toward an adjoining temple beyond the trees. "What else is in the Sacred Way?"

"It's vast," Mah Ummia said. "Besides the temples, there's the king's palace, storehouses for religious offerings, workers' dwellings, and the Dublal-makh, the courthouse inside the great temple." At Tiras's puzzled look, Mah Ummia added, "The courthouse is where people who violate our written laws are judged. We don't have dungeons as punishment. Instead, wealthy citizens are reduced to poverty. Far more horrible. Criminal slaves and the criminal poor are banished."

Tiras frowned at the mention of slaves. His kinsmen wouldn't tolerate the idea. Fortunately, Sumerian slaves could escape their life of servitude, but only by becoming criminals or buying their freedom. He kept his thoughts to himself.

Mah Ummia helped Tiras to rise. "On this level we'll visit the temple of my family's personal god, revered Lord Enki."

In the god's shrine, Tiras gazed in admiration at the niche displaying a beautifully-carved marble god, handsome Lord Enki with his perfect face. "Come," Mah Ummia said. He helped Tiras descend the steep steps from the terrace. In the ziggurat's basement, they entered a large courtyard called the Ga-makh, the great storehouse, where worshippers waited with their offerings in a pandemonium of noise: mooing cattle, bleating sheep and goats, braying donkeys, and squawking birds, amidst sacks of offerings stacked against the mud-brick walls. Scribes examined and weighed everything, while others handed out receipts on clay tablets and made duplicates for the temple archives.

Outside the courtyard, Mah Ummia pointed to a temple across the corridor. "That's the priests' living quarters. But the most interesting part of the temple, the dwelling I visit most often is for the temple prostitutes. It cools my blood."

Tiras wrinkled his nose in disgust. "My tribesmen scorn prostitutes. They're unclean and wicked."

"In Sumer, temple prostitution is an honorable profession," Mah Ummia replied as he helped Tiras up the ramp and back onto the Sacred Way. "Each priestess married to a god fulfills her mystical marriage vows by having intercourse with worshippers. I'm taking you to a priestess of the second caste, the Sal-Me. They're concubines of our moon god, Lord Nanna, and his wife."

He led Tiras to a long blank wall fronting the Sacred Way and said, "All devout worshippers know about this particular temple for Lord Nanna." At the end of the wall, he helped Tiras walk around bushes and underbrush. Beyond a garden, they entered a small square building and passed through the lobby. Duplicate chambers lined a winding passage in a maze of long, vaulted rooms that confused Tiras. He stared, wondering how anyone could find his way through the maze.

Mah Ummia didn't seem confused. He walked determinedly along several corridors and finally paused before a curtained doorway. He turned to Tiras. "I've already arranged your tryst and paid the donation," he whispered. "Go inside. Enjoy yourself. I'll also visit a priestess." He pointed to the end of the corridor. "We'll meet there later."

Tiras nodded instead of protesting his disapproval of prostitutes. At least he could satisfy his sexual frustrations. His cane swept aside the curtains and he limped into the room, puzzled that priestesses lay down with worshippers. Why would a Sumerian god prefer a woman instead of a divine goddess? He scanned the carved bed, wool coverlets, and ornamented rugs and cushions, probably woven by a desert tribe like the Abram. His manhood rose when he saw a priestess sitting on a chair.

"Welcome," the priestess said in Sumerian. She turned about on her chair. Naked under a sheer muslin dress, she revealed an ample bosom and stocky build. Her graying black hair flowed down her stooped back.

Tiras hesitated, unsure what to do next.

She gestured for him to undress. "Don't be afraid," she said, smiling, and revealing yellowing teeth. "You'll enjoy yourself."

Surprised by her advanced age and unappealing appearance, he leaned his cane against the wall and fumbled with his robe while she undressed. "Let me help you," she said, and startled Tiras by swiftly disrobing him. "Come, you aren't a child. Don't worry about your leg wound. I'll satisfy you. And so satisfy my Lord Nanna."

Naked, Tiras lay on the bed. The priestess, smiling, straddled his thighs. To his shame, his manhood wilted. Despite her efforts at massaging his zibbinu, he couldn't revive his earlier excitement. All his resolutions had proven futile. He wanted innocent Majeena, not a temple whore.

"So, you don't desire a priestess," she said, shrugging. She dismounted and dressed. "Go back to your desert, Bedu," she said with scorn.

He joined Mah Ummia in the corridor, shame still burning Tiras's cheeks. "Thank you," he said with a smile of gratitude, without revealing his impotence. Despite himself, he thought how easy it would be to lie secretly with Majeena and steal her virginity. He couldn't afford to buy her, but he still wanted her. No, it wasn't right to betray his kind host's friendship and generosity. Once a female slave's virginity was gone, the price for her plummeted.

As they walked along Ur's winding alleyways toward home, Mah Ummia, asked, "Did you enjoy yourself with the priestess?"

"Yes," Tiras assured him. "It went well."

He hated lying, but thought that was better than upsetting his host. Mah Umma would wonder greatly why he had failed. Perhaps it was Martu after all who had softened his suddenly stricken zibbinu?

After supper, despite his sexual longings, Tiras enjoyed the stories

Majeena told him about the Sumerian gods. One story in particular lingered in his memory while she bathed him.

"Somewhere in the Great Gulf, the earth mother, Nin-Kursag, created an eternal paradise for the gods called Dilmun. It bloomed with divine plants, lush grassland, fragrant roses, and date palms. She created it solely for the gods' enjoyment. In Dilmun they could refresh themselves to avoid sickness, aging, and death."

"A paradise for the gods so they will never die!" Tiras exclaimed. "How enchanting!" He must share with his kinsmen this enthralling vision. Why shouldn't such a paradise also exist for Bedouins? How truly wonderful that death might not be the end, but a fresh beginning.

He said, "Majeena, how do you know these stories?"

Seated beside his chair, she dipped her brush into the tub. "My master taught them to everyone in our household. Would you like to hear more?"

"Yes, please!" Tiras touched her hand. His flesh tingled at the touch. He looked away, and then then back at Majeena who stared at him. She bent and scrubbed his arms while relating a story about Lord Enki, god of wisdom.

"One morning, Lord Enki was relaxing in Dilmun. He became so starved he ate parts of a divine tree. This infuriated our earth mother. She had created the trees as eternal comfort for the gods. Swearing revenge, she caused poor Lord Enki such indigestion he lay near death. Finally she took pity and called on Nin-ti, Lady of the Ribs. Nin-ti is also known as the birth goddess, Lady Who Brings Life. She healed Lord Enki by replacing his ribs."

Tiras's forehead wrinkled in thought. A sick god was cured by a goddess called the Lady Who Brings Life, who replaced his ribs. Although many of the stories, like this one, seemed interesting and sometimes amusing, what did they mean? When he repeats the stories to his tribe, they'll ask many questions. He should ponder their significance beforehand.

"Did you understand what I said?" Majeena asked due to his long silence.

He smiled at her. "Do you ever wish you weren't a slave?"

She looked startled, her dark eyes widening. "No, I never think such things. Slavery's my natural condition. Like being born a woman with dull black hair." She paused and added sheepishly, "That's why I keep it short." She dried him with cloths and wrapped him in a robe.

He stood and ruffled her hair. It felt silky. "I like your hair!" He returned her smile. "Bedouins don't have slaves," he said slowly, seeking the appropriate words and occasionally stumbling. "We're all born equal. But children must obey their parents, even after they're grown. And obey the sheikh, our leader. Also, we can't disagree with our priest."

She pursed her full lips. "Rich Sumerians, like Mah Ummia, own slaves. That's our way. I can't change it. But tell me more about your people."

"With pleasure!" He leaned on her arm as they walked along the balcony to his bedroom. "My tribe, the Abram, descended from a Bedouin called Abrahamu many past cycles. Each bayt...tent... stands for a family. Blood-related families unite to form a clan. Clans unite to form a tribe."

Majeena helped him onto his bed and motioned for him to continue.

"Sometimes, during special pasture seasons," he continued, watching her adjust the coverlets, "two or three blood-related families unite to form a 'dar'. The 'dars' migrate together and will defend themselves, even against other blood relatives, if necessary. We worship many gods, but our chief tribal god is a bull, Martu. Our priest, Abu-Summu, interprets Martu's wishes."

Tiras paused. He began trembling at the memory of Shallah. "Martu demanded my darling little daughter to be beaten badly to atone for my questioning him and she died." He paused, trembling at the memory. "I didn't dare disobey. Or I'd be struck down by our fierce god. Or worse, my family would be driven from the tribe."

Majeena stared, her jaw slack in horror. "Has anyone ever disobeyed Martu and not been struck down or driven away?"

Now it was Tiras's turn to stare. "My tribe can't arouse Martu's anger by disobedience! Look what happened when a Sumerian man mocked your Lady Inanna and she punished your people with the Great Flood. Only Lord Enki's pity saved the world from destruction." Tiras's voice dropped to a whisper. "It's dangerous to challenge a god. I'm trying to find a Sumerian one to replace Martu, but he mustn't find out. He's probably busy now in the desert. Otherwise, if he discovers my quest, he'll kill me."

"Our gods are much kinder," Majeena said.

Tiras nodded. "The desert is much harsher than your soft life here. There, a drought could last for many moon-cycles. Wadis—I mean, lakes—dry out. The sand becomes cracked. There's only goat cheese to eat. Finally, Martu sends rain. The pasture returns. And we survive."

He gazed at the wall mosaics and added softly, "A truly benevolent god could provide our own desert land filled with fertile oases, wild honeycombs, and the milk of many goats." He leaned against the headboard, folded his arms across his belly, and gazed at her. "Please sit with me a while, Majeena. Tell me more about your gods." He moved to one side to make room.

She sat at the foot of the bed and told him several stories about Lady Inanna. Their hot-headed goddess of love, it seemed, had never-ending adventures pleasing to her worshippers. "Our gods are different from your bull-god," she concluded. "They make mistakes, like people."

He nodded. Suddenly tired, he tried to repress a yawn so Majeena wouldn't think him bored by her stories. But she misunderstood. Blushing at perhaps overstaying her welcome, she rose hastily and said, "Well, it's getting late. We can continue tomorrow."

Tiras grudgingly nodded. He longed for her to stay, but dared not seduce her. After she left, he repeated her stories. Then he debated his feelings for her that couldn't be denied. How to lie with her and not betray Mah Ummia? To take her virginity would insult his benevolent host. Not having her frustrated him and surely the girl. Martu would respond to his infidelity with reprisals, never understanding. The conflict was unfair. Sometimes a man needed satisfaction regardless of the cost.

He decided to discourage any inappropriate behavior with Majeena, despite her sighs and stares. Finally, as before, she simply attended to his needs. He assumed that she was finally convinced he no longer cared for her.

Bernadette Miller

CHAPTER 8

February, 3499 B.C., Sumer

FOUR MOON-CYCLES SINCE HIS ARRIVAL, Tiras awaited dinner with the family while Majeena prepared to bathe him, having assembled scrub brushes and fresh cloths. Clean water sloshed in the tub. He noted that her hands were unsteady. When he smiled at her, she looked away. His face flushed. She gently disrobed him, averting her gaze from his naked body and piercing stare.

"Majeena," he whispered, "don't be shy. You know I desire you."

Startled by his admission, she stared at him in surprise. He embraced her and they kissed. He pressed her yielding body against him.

"I'll come to your room after dinner," she whispered.

৪০ ৫৪

All through the evening meal, Tired could think only of finally making love with Majeena. But he forced himself to respond to the family's questions about his condition. Were they anxious for him to be on his way, he wondered? They had been so gracious and wonderful so far.

Bidding everyone a good night, and refusing help to ascend the stairs, he used his cane and made it to his room. Moments later, Majeena noiselessly entered, almost like a shadow.

When they lay together on the bed's coverlets, joy flooded Tiras. He caressed Majeena's warm skin and kissed her lips. Their tongues explored each other's mouths. He fondled her breasts. They covered each other's bodies with kisses and vowed to keep their trysts secret. He lay on his back and helped her to straddle him, carefully avoiding his wounded leg. He swelled inside her and they moved against each other in a growing frenzy. With satisfaction he heard her soft moans until he lay back, gasping with relief.

Afterward, they rested quietly against each other. He stared at the ceiling and worried that Mah Ummia might discover his betrayal. What could he reply to his benevolent host? The bed covers bore droplets of blood. Majeena was no longer a maid. No man would pay for her freedom to marry her. Nor would his family accept a wife from a faraway land who spoke in an unfamiliar tongue and followed unknown traditions.

೮ಂಣ

Tiras still missed his family and often thought about them. Still, he remained in Mah Ummia's house, unwilling to leave although he could walk normally without a cane. Despite wrestling with his guilt, he continued his lovemaking with Majeena.

Finally, he told his host at breakfast, "I shouldn't impose on your generosity any longer. My leg is healed. I have no reason to linger here."

Mah Ummia waved his arm in protest. "Stay as long as you wish, Tiras. It's my pleasure to have you as my guest and teach you."

Tiras was quite aware that he was seen as a distraction from his host's dilemma. Unanna, he knew, kept pressing her father to approve her marriage with Dumuzi while the prospective bridegroom, Balulum, continued demanding a reason for the wedding's delay.

Still, Tiras nodded with relief at his host's generosity. His present life seemed pleasant, unlike the desert's harsh burdens.

But later, in his bedroom, he began debating his own dilemma. He felt stabs of guilt when he thought of his beloved wife, Na'amah, and their son, Rimush. How much had his son grown during all this time? Remorse clung like a blister on his contentment. He belonged with his tribe and to share his new knowledge. It was wrong to continue imposing on Mah Ummia's generosity and betraying his host, but how could he give up those exciting nights with Majeena, all that savory food, and the important lessons about their gods that he could use to replace Martu? The more he learned, the better.

Once, in his bedroom, he leaned against the headboard and thought hard about a solution. He had betrayed the rule of hospitality by continuing his nightly trysts with the slave girl, knowing that he had no right to take her maidenhead unless his host had offered it. Should he do the honorable thing and confess to Mah Ummia? He shook his head. That might further burden the teacher who was trying to resolve his own problems about his daughter's suitor. It might be wiser to let his secret remain buried. Tiras stared at the Sumerian wall frescoes. He'd linger here just a little longer, he decided, to avoid being crippled like his father. Then he'd return to his beloved family.

He usually stayed in his room after supper. He rested, reliving Mah Ummia's stories about their gods and anticipating his later meeting with Majeena. Then, since he couldn't help overhearing his hosts' arguments echoing from the courtyard, he began to squat on the balcony, peer down through the wooden railing, and watch the drama with Mah Ummia and Unanna. She continually pleaded to marry Dumuzi who had won her affection. Tiras realized he shouldn't take sides in a family matter, but it was too bad she was being forced to marry someone she hated. On the other hand, his tribe also arranged marriages and they usually worked out well.

Na'amah was proof. After all, most parents loved their children and probably knew from experience what was best for them.

℘CB

One evening, Unanna jumped up from her chair and said, "Adda, you promised to reconsider my betrothal to Dumuzi. Do you intend to break your promise?"

"Unanna, don't use that tone with me. I'm not subject to your orders. You must obey me. Don't make me drive you from my home to have peace of mind."

"I'm sorry to cause you anxiety. But can't you see I don't want to live without Dumuzi? He's my life. My dearest love—"

"You're still young," Mah Ummia interrupted. "How many loves have you had to compare him with?"

She bit her lip and remained silent. Tears coursed down her cheeks. She withdrew a cloth from her dress and daubed at her eyes.

Mah Ummia sighed deeply. "I'm still debating the problem," he said with a gentle smile and left her sitting in the courtyard.

Unanna clenched her fists as twilight bathed her in shadows. Slaves lit the lanterns hanging against the whitewashed walls. She remained fixed in her chair as if unwilling to rise.

Tiras left the balcony and walked back to his room. His stomach was pleasantly full with a delicious dinner of lamb, pomegranates, and honey cakes. He'd enjoyed Majeena giving him his sponge bath and telling stories about her gods. Now he eagerly awaited her nightly visit. She soon swept aside the doorway curtains. Whispering and giggling in the dark, they stripped and climbed onto his bed.

Suddenly, a slave entered, holding a lit lantern. Unanna followed, her eyes blazing with anger. The slave hung the lantern on a wall hook and left when Unanna waved him away. Tiras and Majeena, still naked, sprang apart on the bed.

Bernadette Miller

"What's going on here?" Unanna said. "Majeena, get up at once and put on your clothes. Tiras, how dare you lay with her!"

"We aren't hurting anyone," Tiras muttered as he struggled off the bed and pulled on his night shirt. Majeena hastily tugged on her dress.

Unanna turned to Majeena. "Go to your room."

In the shadows, Majeena's dark eyes widened in fear. "Mistress, please don't tell the master. Please don't punish me. I love Tiras. I can't help it—"

"Leave now!" Unanna ordered.

Tiras turned away, as Majeena slinked out of the room. He felt terrible at having deceived Mah Ummia and now the additional shame of being caught. Unanna would surely tell her father that their guest had stolen their slave girl's virginity. "I'm...sorry..." he said, trying to lighten the burden of his guilt.

"That's good," Unanna replied, distracted. She sat on a nearby chair and indicated he should sit on the bed.

He climbed awkwardly onto the bed's edge and leaned forward. His heart began beating fast as he anticipated the deserved punishment. He would surely be thrown out of Mah Ummia's house in disgrace. Perhaps it was just as well. He'd overstayed his visit when he should have returned to his family. Still, he would hate for Mah Ummia to learn of his deception. He owed his host a great debt and he had repaid it with treachery. He waited to hear his almost certain fate.

Unanna surprised him with a smile. "You know if I tell my father, he would have nothing more to do with you. Your pleasant stay here would end." She paused at Tiras's sad nod. "But suppose you help me resolve a difficult situation. Then, I might consider helping you in turn."

"What help do you need, my lady?" Tiras said, wondering what severe bargain she wanted to make and if he could comply.

"Persuade my father to let me marry Dumuzi," she said.

Tiras paled. "How can I do that, my lady? I have no experience in such matters."

Unanna nodded impatiently. "That doesn't matter. My father told me that he promised to take you to the Edubba tomorrow. While there you must try to persuade him." She paused and bit her lip in annoyance. "For some reason, he likes you. He thinks you're very intelligent for a Bedu, and he'd listen to you. Just make sure your opinion is favorable to my cause."

"Maybe I can't convince him?" Tiras said with narrowed eyes.

"Well, you know the alternative," Unanna said. She paused and added, "It won't be as difficult as you imagine. Just tell him that you're certain Dumuzi will become a successful teacher and able to support me. And that marriage with Balulum would be a terrible mistake because I despise him. You'll succeed in this. Then I'll forget I saw you in bed with Majeena. Can't you at least try?"

Tiras silently debated her arguments with deep concern. He had little choice: either do as she asked or be denounced in disgrace. After all, her cause was worthwhile. Why shouldn't she marry the man she loved? He'd fallen in love with Na'amah. Surely, Mah Ummia's daughter deserved the same opportunity. Besides, not obeying her demands would result in an embarrassing situation for him and hurtful to Mah Ummia whom he respected and owed so much.

"Well, I'll try to convince him," Tiras said finally.

"Splendid!" Unanna rose.

"But if I do, let me continue with Majeena."

Unanna paused at the curtained doorway and remained silent for a moment. Finally, she said, "You're lucky I won't reveal your betrayal to my father. All right, you can continue with Majeena, but only if you succeed on my behalf. Then, you'll earn my deepest gratitude. I'll even invite you to my wedding."

Tiras nodded and watched her leave. He remained on his bed, shaken by the unexpected turn of events.

Bernadette Miller

CHAPTER 9

February, 3499 B.C., Sumer

WHILE TIRAS ACCOMPANIED MAH UMMIA to the Edubba, along the Sacred Way, he pondered his current problem. Several moon-cycles past, he'd requested a visit to the Edubba to gain more knowledge about the Sumerian religion, but now how could he persuade Mah Ummia to allow his daughter to marry the man she loved, Dumuzi? He shook his head. Failure meant dismissal and disgrace.

The pair soon arrived at a whitewashed building with a curtained doorway. The corridor and side rooms, open to the sky god, echoed with pupils' chanting.

Mah Ummia ushered his guest through the curtains and into a corridor. "Here, I'm the headmaster. Or, as they like to call me, School Father." He frowned and added, "Dumuzi is the assistant headmaster, known as Big Brother. The first room on our right is for beginners." He paused with Tiras outside the arched doorway. They peered inside.

Seven-year-old boys filled the rows of mud-brick benches. Clothed like Sumerian men, the boys wore ankle-length tufted wool skirts with their narrow chests and shoulders bare. They sat stiffly at their wooden desks and focused on the teacher.

Mah Ummia exchanged a cool smile with Dumuzi who resumed teaching.

Dumuzi picked up a lump of wet clay. "Pupils, watch closely. I'll show you how to prepare a tablet for writing. First, wash the clay like this one. Then shape the clay into a small square cushion like this. With your second finger, divide the cushion into four squares as I'm doing. Now you can write on it." He picked up a reed stylus, wedge-shaped at one end, and carefully incised cuneiform signs across each square. He held up the tablet for the pupils to see. "Our sun god will kindly dry the tablets," he concluded. "But afterward we must harden the tablets in an oven to make sure they don't break."

As Dumuzi continued teaching, Tiras whispered to Mah Ummia, "No girls?"

Mah Ummia whispered back, "It takes many years to learn to read and write our language. Unfortunately girls can't concentrate for the time required. Though Unanna might—" He broke off abruptly and continued. "Women receive a limited education from their fathers. Mainly religion."

"My tribesmen don't consider our women stupid," Tiras said softly. "My mother, Zabaia, was clever like my wives. They could set up a tent in the desert. Make an oven in the sand..." He fell silent, hating to disagree with his kind host. Then, as he recalled the tribe, he remembered his daughter's sacrifice. Shallah was a clever child who might have become a clever woman, like Zabaia. He tried to lessen the pain by turning his attention to his present dilemma about Unanna.

"Your daughter is exceptionally smart," he whispered. "I'm sure she could make wise decisions."

"She's gifted," Mah Ummia agreed, "but girls can't attend school. Only boys. The wealthiest hire private tutors such as myself. The poor study trades. Carpentry. Sculpting. Jewelry making. And so on."

Several pupils, spotting the visitors, shouted, "Hello!" They began shoving for a better view. A burly man with heavy jowls hurried along the corridor. His bare, sagging breasts swayed from side to side. He clutched a reed switch and moved surprisingly fast despite the long skirt.

"Who's that?" Tiras asked, alarmed, as he stepped aside. Surely the man wouldn't beat these young boys.

Mah Ummia sighed. "The Special Proctor. Unfortunately, youths often become rowdy. There's much to learn. Discipline must be strictly enforced."

A student shouted "Hello! Hello!" at the visitors.

"Be quiet!" the Special Proctor yelled and thwacked his back.

Tiras winced, imagining the pain felt by one so young. There must be a kinder way to control the students. Besides, where was the harm of greeting visitors?

The boy being beaten began sobbing. "Stop crying!" the Special Proctor yelled and hit him again. The student stifled his sobs. He bent his head low over his desk and covered his face to hide his whimpering. Red welts appeared on his naked back.

Other boys shouted in sympathy for the one being beaten. "Stop hitting him! It's unfair! He's just welcoming the visitors! He didn't insult the teacher!"

"Be quiet so Big Brother can teach!" the Special Proctor yelled again, his face reddened with rage. He ran about, beating students until the room grew eerily quiet. Dumuzi, his lips tightened in disapproval at the Special Proctor's cruelty, resumed teaching. Noise erupted from another classroom. The Special Proctor hurried outside to the corridor, his switch clutched in his fist. Dumuzi and the young students sighed with relief.

Tiras shook his head. Learning was useful, he thought, but he wouldn't want to be beaten. From another classroom, the Special Proctor shouted, "Quiet!" Sobs erupted followed by more thwacks of the switch. Tiras glanced toward the corridor. The Special Proctor seemed to enjoy hurting people...like Abu-Summu. He shuddered at remembering Shallah's horrible death. Why did some men enjoy torturing others? And why did people endure it? Wasn't it better to resist them? Why not revolt? Join together and turn on the torturer like Martu.

Then, he thought, as he often did, that Martu might destroy the tribe in revenge. Who can defeat a god? Tiras's stomach tightened as he dwelt on his tribe's predicament. To divert his thoughts from his sudden tension, he again turned toward his problem with Unanna.

"I like Dumuzi," he whispered. "He seems like a nice fellow who sincerely loves your daughter. I'm sure he'd work hard to make her happy."

Mah Ummia frowned. "I admire him greatly as a talented teacher. But he offers my daughter only poverty and despair."

Dumuzi called upon a pupil to recite yesterday's lesson.

"Tu-ta-ti, nu-na-ni, bu-ba-bi..." The young pupil read from his tablet, repeating Sumerian grammar.

"Come," Mah Ummia said to Tiras. "I'll show you the advanced classes."

They strolled along the corridor. Mah Ummia smiled at Tiras's wide-eyed gaze as they entered a classroom with older boys. He whispered, "Here, we teach mathematics, the study of numbers." Tiras, bewildered, stared up at him. Mah Ummia held up five fingers, then two, then seven. "Five and two equals seven," he said. "Simple arithmetic. Mathematics requires much more learning."

"Oh," Tiras said, delighted at understanding a new thing. "Numbers. Yes. Like three sheep and two goats. Five."

Mah Ummia nodded and led him inside the classroom. They chose an available bench near the rear. The pupils, excited by the visitors, began twisting about to see them until the teacher said, "Be quiet and focus on your studies! Or I'll call the Special Proctor." The class quieted and the teaching resumed.

After several minutes, Mah Ummia rose and led Tiras outside. He paused in the corridor and briefly summarized some of the school's courses: architecture, agriculture, law, and engineering.

Bernadette Miller

Tiras listened carefully but much of it refused to enter his overworked head. "I can't remember any of that," he said. "I must be stupid."

"No, my young friend. Your mind is trying to grasp too much in a short time. But now you understand how much there is to learn."

"You've already taught me so much," Tiras replied as they headed toward another class room. He returned Mah Ummia's smile. "But I wonder why you feel that Dumuzi will always be poor? Besides teaching here, couldn't he also teach privately someday, as you do?"

Mah Ummia nodded. "That could take many years. He might be quite old by then."

"I don't understand," Tiras said as they lingered outside the literature class. "You told me that you began teaching privately when you were young and earned enough shekels for a comfortable life, besides the generous inheritance from your father. Isn't Dumuzi's teaching good enough to follow the same path?"

"He's an excellent teacher! Very much like me at that age."

Tiras nodded with satisfaction.

"But I also have a serious problem with Balulum," Mah Ummia continued in a whisper. "He's already accepted the dowry. He's waiting to sign the marriage tablets prepared by the Sanga, the high priest, that are waiting at my home. It's true I'm wealthy. But Balulum is far wealthier. If I annul the marriage, he could drag me into court. Even though he never signed the tablets, he could drain me of shekels because of my broken promise."

"Maybe Unanna could assist you in this," Tiras said.

"How?"

"Well, Unanna could tell Balulum that she changed her mind about the wedding." Tiras paused, pleased at having Mah Ummia's full attention. "She could insist that she's too young and wants to wait five years. Meanwhile, it isn't fair for such a nice fellow as Balulum to remain alone for such a long time, deprived of a wife's comforting caresses. Therefore, he should seek the loving wife he deserves."

Mah Ummia nodded. "That's a possibility," he said after a while. "I'll think about it."

Tiras smiled with satisfaction. "If you follow this plan, your daughter could then marry Dumuzi after a respectful period. When Balulum protests, explain that your daughter fell in love after the postponement of the wedding with Balulum. It just happened. It wasn't planned. Why then would Balulum still want a wife who loved another? Your daughter's happiness is your chief concern."

"That's a clever approach," Mah Ummia said thoughtfully as he guided Tiras into the literature class. "I'll think about it."

They sat on a crowded bench. Again, the pupils twisted about to see the visitors until the teacher said, "Be quiet or I'll summon the Special Proctor."

The class quieted and the teaching resumed.

After several minutes, Mah Ummia leaned toward Tiras and whispered, "The pupils read aloud from the clay tablets. Epics, hymns, fables, essays, poetry, and lamentations."

Tiras found one lamentation particularly moving. It dealt with a righteous man who suffered through no fault of his own. At the end, Lord Enki, unlike Martu, stopped the suffering man's weeping and restored his happiness although Tiras couldn't understand how. But was it fair that a good, pious man who worked hard all his life must suffer for no reason?

He rose and accompanied Mah Ummia to the corridor's last room. Again, they hesitated outside the door.

"Theology," Mah Ummia said. "Our most important class. Only older boys could understand the great debt we owe our magnificent gods for creating us."

Tiras beamed. Their gods—at last!

"Most of these young men will become priests," Mah Ummia

whispered beside Tiras on the bench. He waved at the teacher to continue.

Fascinated, Tiras leaned forward as the teacher explained the gods. The man was short and slender like a boy with hairless arms and chest. His dark eyes shone with enthusiasm. He walked with a mincing gait beneath the tufted skirt. Surprised, Tiras stared at the teacher. Never had he seen a man so unmanly, more closely resembling a girl.

"First, our chief god, Father An," the teacher said with a high-pitched voice. "He and Nin-Kursag, our sweet earth mother, created the others." He pointed to the tablets on the students' desks. "All the divine children are listed there. Beloved Lord Enki, god of wisdom, who created Earth. Our generous Lord Enlil, god of the air. Nin-Ti, Lady of the Ribs and birth goddess, who helped create the first man. At the bottom of the list are the Annunaki, Father An's youngest children, who disobeyed him when grown. As punishment, the Annunaki sprouted wings and must forever carry the dead to the netherworld. The first human-like beings with wings."

Another pupil raised his hand and was given permission to speak. "Where is the netherworld? Why do we go there?"

The teacher said seriously, "When we die we must repay the gods for the wonderful enjoyment of life given us. The netherworld lies beneath the soil. There in that dim gray world, as shades of our former selves, we gratefully serve our gods forever."

Tiras felt uncomfortable. He tugged thoughtfully at his beard. Dead people remained forever in the netherworld to serve the gods? It sounded dark and dreary whether a person had been good or bad. Surely a good person deserved something pleasant. He smiled when he remembered Majeena's story about a paradise called Dilmun. He shook his head. That lovely place was reserved for the gods.

After another half-hour, Mah Ummia whispered to Tiras, "Time to leave. I think you've seen enough."

As they stepped outside into the sun god's waning glare, Tiras said, "That last teacher was strange."

Mah Ummia sighed. "He prefers men to women."

"Men to women?" Tiras repeated, confused, and stopped walking. "You mean making love?"

Mah Ummia nodded.

"But how can they... I mean, what do they..." Tiras's voice trailed off. He gazed at Mah Ummia for the answer.

"Such as you might do with a woman. Except from the rear. It's called sodomy."

"What!" Tiras exclaimed, horrified. "That's wickedness."

"No, my friend, that's how the gods made them. Many are good and gentle. They don't harm anyone." He motioned to Tiras to resume walking.

"But it's wrong! Your people should banish them—"

"You fear what you don't understand," Mah Ummia interrupted. "There are quite a few such men in Ur. Their personalities vary. Some are smart like the teacher. Others stupid. Some feminine. Others masculine."

"But aren't you afraid to have them teach young men? Suppose all those pupils become like the teacher—"

"Some might," Mah Ummia interrupted again. "Others won't. When grown, they will decide for themselves. It makes no difference. As long as the man can teach well."

"My tribesmen are loving and affectionate," Tiras said, confused. "They hug and kiss each other. But if a man behaved like that theology teacher, the tribe would kill him."

Mah Ummia frowned. "Our theology teacher is highly regarded. From a wealthy family with an irreproachable reputation. As long as he shows no public display—any affectionate display in public we regard as inappropriate—we take no interest in his preferences." He looked up, shading his eyes from Utu's mellowing heat. "But now my stomach is teaching me it's almost time for dinner. We must hurry. I still have duties to perform."

Bernadette Miller

He paused and rested his hand on Tiras's shoulder. "I'll consider your suggestions about my daughter. You're very wise for your years and station in life. Of course, my chief concern should be her happiness. But I'm known as a man of my word. I don't wish to betray Balulum's trust and ruin my reputation which Sumerians hold dear. After patiently waiting for months, Balulum deserves his bride."

Tiras nodded, feeling defeated. Once Unanna finds out his quest to help her had failed, she'll surely tell her father who will then throw him from his house in disgrace. How can he persuade Mah Ummia without angering his generous host?

CHAPTER 10

February, 3499 B.C., Sumer

THE FOLLOWING EVENING, UNANNA APPEARED again in Tiras's room, preceded by a slave girl with a lit lantern that she hung on a wall hook. She waved the slave girl away with an imperious command and sat on the cane-bottomed chair nearby. "So, did you convince my father as we'd discussed?"

Perched on the bed's edge, Tiras shook his head. "I don't know, my lady. I tried my best. He said he would consider my suggestions."

"Not good enough!" She pointed a finger at him. "You know the penalty for failure."

"Yes." Tiras looked away and tried to think up a solution to his problem. He turned toward her. "Of course, if you reveal my trysts with Majeena, you will also reveal that you kept it secret from your father. I wonder if he will see that as a betrayal."

Unanna looked at Tiras in astonishment. "You're quite clever for a Bedouin. Too clever. Perhaps I've been wrong about you."

"Besides, it isn't over," Tiras continued in a soft voice, hoping to allow more time to make his case. "Your father said he'll consider my suggestions. He didn't refuse. So there's still hope."

Unanna rose and looked thoughtfully at the unwanted guest.

"You might be right. Let's wait to see if my father changes his mind about Balulum. I'll keep quiet for a little longer."

She turned and left abruptly, leaving Tiras to ponder a solution if Mah Ummia insisted on his daughter marrying Balulum. What else could he say to convince his benefactor? He shuddered as he pictured Mah Ummia's slaves pushing him and his donkey beyond the garden gate and throwing his belongings after him in the alleyway. No, he couldn't let that happen! He would find a way to preserve his dignity and avoid shame.

∞∞

For several days, Tiras listened to Mah Ummia's stories about the Sumerian gods, his goal about replacing Martu almost forgotten in his new dilemma with Unanna. He still devoured the abundant meals Mah Ummia provided. He still spent early evenings on the balcony, watching the slaves sweeping the courtyard brick floor, washing the plastered walls, and hurrying back and forth from the kitchen with buckets and scrub brushes. He continued to worry about his benefactor's reaction to his guest's betrayal. Yet, he continued his nightly trysts with Majeena.

∞∞

Meanwhile, Mah Ummia had his own dilemma to resolve and pondered it after dinner while sitting in the fragrant garden. Occasionally, he gazed from the velvety grass and flower beds lining the fence and turned toward the palm frond waving above him and the twittering birds, perhaps whispering about his daughter and her sweetheart, Dumuzi. He kept asking himself if it was honorable after many months to deny Balulum the bride he'd been promised. If he followed Tiras' advice, he would be betraying his potential son-in-law and damaging his own reputation. Conversely, he knew that his beloved daughter would never be happy with Balulum whom she despised. Then, was it honorable to deny his daughter her right to happiness?

୧୦ଓଃ

Tiras finally decided to approach Mah Ummia and try to settle the problem that was eating at his contentment. One evening, he joined Mah Ummia in the garden and sat beside him on the wooden bench.

His benefactor smiled at him. "Well, my friend, I've given much thought to our conversation at the Edubba. And I've decided to agree to my daughter's marriage with Dumuzi. Of course, as you so wisely said, my chief concern should be her happiness. With my help, Dumuzi should advance rapidly in his profession and soon teach privately as I do. He is, after all, quite talented." Mah Ummia sighed and added, "I'll also consider your suggestions on how to deal with Balulum."

Elated, Tiras said, beaming, "A wise choice. I'm sure you will never regret it."

Later, before Tiras could reveal his success to Unanna and savor his triumph, her father advised her of the good news in the courtyard. Fresh from his bath with Majeena, he listened from the balcony.

Mah Ummia told Unanna, "I've been thinking about your unhappiness over Balulum. Suppose I agree to your marriage with Dumuzi. Despite his lack of money, would you swear to love, obey him, and be faithful? Would you work like a servant to conserve shekels?"

"I'd do anything!" Unanna jumped up to kiss his cheek.

"Just a moment. I must think clearly." He patted her arm and remained silent for a while. Then he said, as if to himself, "I'll be offending Balulum. For months he patiently waited for a bride. Now I must tell him he won't have a bride, after all."

Bernadette Miller

Unanna's deep sigh filled the courtyard. "Balulum is quite experienced in these matters. He'll soon find another young woman to satisfy his lust."

Mah Ummia stared at her. "You don't sound like a maid. Have you lain with Dumuzi?"

She shook her head in amazement. "Of course not. How could you ask such a thing? I expect to consummate my marriage after the wedding celebration. Like any respectable bride."

"Ah, that's good." Mah Ummia rose. "Well, then, your marriage to Dumuzi is settled."

"Oh, adda!" Unanna threw her arms around his neck and kissed his cheek. "Thank you, thank you, thank you."

He smiled at her enthusiasm and hugged her. His brow furrowed with concern. "I must attend to many matters after this turn of events. Especially advising poor Balulum."

In due course, Mah Ummia sent his slave to notify the former prospective son-in-law that his marriage had been annulled. He kept at home the unsigned, duplicate marriage tablets from the Dublal-makh that had been prepared for Balulum, and he returned to the Dublal-makh the new tablets signed by Unanna and Dumuzi. Then he awaited with dread Balulum's reaction.

೮೦ ೮೮

The overjoyed couple spent their time gazing at each other during dinners or on long walks, no longer forced to hide their feelings. Once again, a wedding feast was prepared. The musicians were summoned for rehearsal. The courtyard resounded with lively music. Slaves cleaned, cooked, and replaced fresh flowers in the balcony urns and the courtyard vases on side tables. Savory aromas drifted from the kitchen. A whole pig was roasted on a spit in the beehive oven.

Mah Ummia tried not to worry about Balulum whom he hadn't

heard from for two weeks. Then, the day before the wedding, Balulum staggered into the courtyard, past the slaves rushing to detain him.

Mah Ummia hurried toward Balulum, hoping to appease his anger.

Balulum was drunk. He stared about the courtyard, his eyes bloodshot. His torn, tufted skirt was speckled with dirt. A grimy, wrinkled shawl partly covered his dirty chest. He pointed at Tiras, seated with the family awaiting lunch. "There lies the root of all my misfortune!" he shouted. "I can only assume it's that savage Bedouin's fault. Before his arrival, my happiness was assured with my lovely bride. Now I'm robbed of all I hold dear. No one to soothe my disappointments. Remove sadness with sweetly-whispered compliments. Or hold me lovingly after a miserable day!"

He spat in Tiras's direction and shouted a stream of Sumerian curses that Tiras didn't understand since no one had taught him such vulgarities.

Tiras looked in bewilderment at Mah Ummia, whose face had reddened in embarrassment and shame as he listened to his impolite guest. His host probably blamed himself for breaking his promise, Tiras thought, but he knew the fault was his. He'd taken advantage of his kind benefactor by convincing him that Dumuzi was the best suitor.

When Balulum paused to catch his breath, Tiras said in perfect Sumerian, "I'm sorry if I caused you grief. I'll leave as soon as possible."

Balulum stared at him.

"Now, sir," Mah Ummia said finally, his eyes narrowed in anger, "my daughter opposed this marriage long before Tiras's arrival. He's my guest. I can't allow such inhospitality. I must insist you leave my house at once."

"You'll forfeit the entire dowry! Not one shekel will I return!"

Mah Ummia deliberately appeared indifferent to calming the jilted suitor. "That's acceptable under the circumstances. But again

I insist you leave." He beckoned to several male slaves waiting near the courtyard entrance for further commands.

Balulum shook a fist. "Your betrayal has infuriated the gods! Grave misfortune will arrive at your doorstep. I'll start a lawsuit and demand your entire fortune. Your household will be scattered to the wind. You'll be cast down and spat upon, the lowest beggar at the bazaar. None of our gods will save you. I'm going to the Dublal-makh to plot your ruin!"

"Your case would fail," Mah Ummia replied calmly. "I still have the unsigned tablets. You have no written proof."

"I'll have my revenge," Balulum snarled, his face scarlet with rage. "You'll bitterly regret your broken promise!"

At Mah Ummia's gesture, male slaves surrounded Balulum. They began pushing him outside the house and toward the gate. He shouted, "I'm going. Leave me alone! I curse you all!"

To everyone's relief, Balulum hurried outside, toward the Sacred Way and undoubtedly the courthouse.

Mah Ummia wiped his perspiring brow.

His daughter ran to him. "I've caused you such unhappiness. Please forgive me." She wept on his shoulder.

He gently lifted her chin. "No, child, it's I who beg forgiveness. I betrothed you to a drunken animal. We're well rid of Balulum. Stop crying and be happy with Dumuzi. Have you forgotten that tomorrow is your wedding day?"

Smiling, she looked at her father, a tear lingering on her cheek. "Yes, I'll be joined to my beloved forever." She hugged him and ran upstairs. "I'll eat later," she called out gaily.

As their meal resumed, Mah Ummia explained to Tiras about the preparation and expense of fighting Balulum's lawsuit. "The High Priest could testify about the betrothal, along with slaves. Balulum surpasses me in wealth. He could ruin me financially by dragging out the case. Of course, my main concern is my child's happiness. As you so wisely reminded me."

Tiras filled with guilt at possibly causing his kind host such sorrow. He had stolen his teacher's valuable time with religious teaching, used a female slave to satisfy his desires, and then persuaded his host to jeopardize himself financially so that his guest could continue sleeping with the slave girl.

"I don't wish to anger Balulum further," Tiras said. "Or be forced to testify against you whom I hold dear."

Mah Ummia shook his head. "You've been an exemplary guest and pupil. I've taken great pleasure in teaching you. Don't leave yet. You shouldn't miss the wedding."

Tiras agreed but felt uncomfortable about secretly lying with Majeena. He couldn't give her up. How could he resolve his dilemma?

That night, after Majeena left him in his bedroom, he had a disturbing dream. Martu punished his adultery by fastening Majeena to his hip. They wandered about for a lifetime. He never saw his family again. He awoke with thudding heart, his face wet with perspiration. It was an ominous warning. What did the dream foretell? Should he take Majeena with him and try to comfort her at his family's rejection? Or should he leave her in Ur to be thrown from her master's house and turned into a beggar, or worse, scorned as a harlot?

Despite Tiras's misgivings, the wedding festivities helped to distract him. Thanks to the gods, the day was lovely with a temperate climate. Above the open courtyard, wispy clouds floated against the sky. Slaves placed more chairs near side tables. Silver platters offered roast pig, boiled beef, and grilled fish, saffron barley, vegetables, and baked bread. Copper bowls provided honey cakes and fruit: dates, grapes, and plums. Fluted goblets tempted guests with beer or date wine.

Seated near the musicians along the wall, Tiras gaped at the food, enough for several tribal weddings. He watched wide-eyed as invited guests filled the courtyard chairs around the walls and the corner musicians played lilting melodies on reed flutes, lyres, tambourines, and harps. The celebration lasted several days. As special entertainment, barefoot young women wearing white gowns with braided reed sashes danced. The guests applauded, shouting for more.

Finally, Unanna entered, looking radiant. She strolled around the courtyard so the guests could admire her white gown with filigreed gold neckline and cuffs and her headdress of white netting dotted with tiny roses. Then, the bridegroom guided his new bride in their stately wedding dance while the guests exclaimed and applauded.

∞ ℭ

Tiras bowed his head, remembering his own wedding. Na'amah had been just as lovely. Their wedding reappeared vividly as if the gods were reminding him of his obligations. He hadn't wanted to marry. When he'd reached fourteen, his parents had arranged a marriage with a young girl from another tribe. He'd resented it. Why tie himself down with the duties of marriage and children when he could satisfy his manhood being single? Brooding about his unwanted betrothal to an unknown girl, he'd sought a distraction.

He recalled how one evening he had secretly visited a religious ceremony held in a small oasis village near his tribe's camp. His eyes widened in wonder as he gazed at the horde crowding the village square. A priest led the chanting to their serpent-god, Ca'adus, protector of good health. The congregants shouted to Ca'adus to preserve them from sickness. Tiras nodded. Maybe he should add his pleas to keep him single. More gods could aid his cause. Of course, Martu would punish him for worshipping another, but why had Martu punished his kind brothers and his innocent sister, Mariah? The bull-god's baffling anger seemed knowable only to the priest.

Near the crowd's fringe, a beautiful young girl stood with high cheekbones and bow-shaped lips. Her small hand clutched an embroidered pink shawl draped about her slender shoulders. Her deep-set dark eyes outlined with kohl focused upon the priest's sermon. Tiras threaded his way through the maze of listeners. He finally stood beside the girl. His pulse raced with excitement. When she turned and gazed at him, he was delighted by her warm smile and even, white teeth.

He whispered, "Walk with me a while to chat by the lake."

"I can't. My mother will miss me."

"We'll simply talk," he urged.

She scanned the crowd and pointed to a stout woman near the priest. "That's my mother. She'll be angry if I leave with a boy. Our camp is nearby. We came for the ceremony because Ca'adus is our tribal god."

Tiras took her soft hand in his. "I want to know you. Let's go for a walk. Just for a few moments so we can talk."

She glanced at her mother. Then she pointed to a brawny man in the crowd's midst. "That's my father. If he finds out I've been with a boy..."

"No. You'll remain a maid. I promise." He gazed at her pleadingly.

He braced as she studied his intense black eyes. Finally, she relented. "Well, just a little while."

While they walked for a few minutes in the chilly night air, he debated how to kiss her. The girl drew her shawl about her face. He put his arm around her, but at her frown he removed it. They sat on a flat rock near the lake. He watched the lake goddess flirt with the moon god by sending ripples across the lake. Il-lah responded by dancing his light against the ripples. In the distance an eagle swooped down upon a rabbit hurrying toward its burrow and carried the squealing rabbit upward in its talons. It seemed like a good omen. Perhaps the girl would soon yield to him. He decided on simple friendliness.

"I'm Tiras from the Abram tribe," he said. "My father is Sheikh Mashech. My mother is Zabaia. Tell me your name and family."

"You're Tiras? From the Abram tribe?" She began giggling.

Bernadette Miller

Disconcerted by her unexpected reaction, he said, "Why are you laughing? Are my name and tribe so ridiculous?"

She giggled harder and clapped a hand across her mouth. "That's amazing," she said finally. "I'm Na'amah."

"What!" He stared at her. "The same Na'amah betrothed to me by our parents?"

She grinned. "The very same."

Stunned but joyful, Tiras said, "Well, this is an unexpected pleasure. I'm happy you'll be my bride. You're lovely and sweet. I'll take care of you always." He embraced her and they kissed. She was tender. Her lips lingered on his. Afterwards, she clung to him, whispering, "I'm so glad you're my betrothed."

To Tiras's surprise, he'd willingly wed Na'amah in a ceremony attended by both their tribes. On that eventful day, the jubilant couple stood before their new home, under the tent flap held open with poles and knotted ropes. Mashech formally introduced the bride to the groom. Then, Tiras lifted his bride's shawl that covered her face, and kissed her. The couple, still stunned by their wedding, nodded modestly at the clapping audience. Behind them, the guests could see the bride's handiwork: rugs, cushions, storage sacks, and weaving materials. Behind the tent was the bride's dowry: a small flock of sheep and goats.

Mashech and Zabaia, beaming with pride, watched the couple, holding hands under the open tent flap, as they drank wine from the same clay cup. Na'amah, laughing, accidentally dropped the cup. Wine spilled over the rug. She put her hand to her mouth in dismay.

"A bad omen!" the priest shouted. "Your future looks dark."

Mashech disregarded Abu-Summu's warning. He called out, "My children, hear my blessing. Step on the cup and smash it. To prove to yourselves that your happiness will survive all obstacles."

Na'amah stomped on the cup, followed by Tiras. The others cheered as pieces flew about. Abu-Summu, pouting, remained silent. The guests ignored the priest's gloomy countenance and enjoyed the feast spread on rugs before Zabaia's tent. Eating communal style, they sampled her stewed lamb, along with dried yoghurt sprinkled with pine nuts, and rice from the oasis mixed with goat cheese. They gobbled the pancakes with sheep's milk butter and honey. Jugs of goat's milk or date wine quenched their thirst.

Musicians gathered. One plucked an oud. Another shook a tambourine. A third shook a rattle. Two men drummed on overturned copper kettles. Several tribesmen jumped up to dance, forming a circle. They clapped above their heads and moved their bodies rhythmically to and fro. The women, seated, began clapping and sang the verses. Then the children sang with their high-pitched voices. The desert resounded with joyful celebration. Soon, Al-Lat greeted her moon lover. Their union spilled shadows over the hushed tribe. The musicians stopped playing. Everyone drifted to their tents.

Tiras gazed at his bride as they helped the family gather the emptied plates and roll up the rugs. Finished, they held hands and entered her tent whose knotted ropes crossed those of Zabaia's, indicating a united household. Na'amah swept aside one end of the qata and entered the women's area. Soon, the couple lay naked on the conjugal rug. Eager to savor his wife's love-making, Tiras no longer mourned the loss of his single status. He caressed his bride's small breasts and flat belly and encouraged her to stroke his zibbinu. She touched it hesitantly while he nodded, smiling. Their tongues explored each other's mouths. His bride looked down in alarm at his swollen zibbinu.

She whispered, "What are you going to do to me?"

"Don't be afraid," he said softly. "I won't hurt you."

She tried to smile. Stroking her body, he slowly entered her. He wrapped her legs around his hips and kissed her lips. They locked in an embrace. Gaining confidence, she gripped his shoulders hard. They rocked back and forth, panting. Blood droplets stained the rug. Finally, his body spent with pleasure, he lay down beside her

Bernadette Miller

to rest. He had never felt so peaceful. At last he had sweet Na'amah for his own.

"I love you," she finally gasped when they parted. She rolled over and looked at him with shiny eyes. "I was afraid," she confessed shyly. Then she smiled. "Maybe we could do it again?"

He smiled at her. "I love you, too. Just give me a few minutes to rest. We can do it as often as you like." They made love for a couple of hours and finally separated to sleep.

After that, the nights flowed one into the other, each sweeter than the next as the years sped by.

℘ ℂ

Now, at Unanna's wedding, Tiras again heard the desert musicians playing at his own wedding, again he felt Na'amah's lips on his, and how she'd wrapped her legs about him, urgently welcoming him inside her. The memory still left him breathless. He glanced about the Sumerian courtyard, the guests eating and drinking, and reproached himself. It was dishonorable to abandon his adored wife and son, preferring instead a stranger's hospitality and another woman's lovemaking. His leg was completely healed. He had postponed his return long enough.

He told his host at breakfast he would leave the following day. "My family surely misses me. Thank you, dear Mah Ummia, for your generosity and kindness."

"Tiras, you've been one of my best pupils," Mah Ummia said. "It's been my pleasure to know you. I'll accompany you to the city gate." He paused. "However, you're welcome to stay."

Tiras shook his head. "I must return to my family. But thank you again for all you've done for me."

That night, Tiras kept his last tryst with Majeena. "Tomorrow, I'm going home to my tribe," he told her. "But I'll return for you as soon as possible," he added to soothe her pain at his departure.

"Why don't you take me with you?" she pleaded, sitting on Tiras's bed. "I can cook and clean and—"

"Majeena," he interrupted, "the desert is harsh compared with your soft life here. You couldn't survive without my tribe's help. I must prepare them to accept a foreigner. Then I'll return for you."

She turned away, quivering. "You'll never return. Once you're in the arms of your loved ones, you'll forget about me. You won't attempt such a dangerous journey again. Not for a slave girl."

"Ah, you're wrong," Tiras said and sat beside her. He wiped the tears slipping down her cheeks. "I will return to Ur. As soon as I can."

She shook her head.

"One more kiss," he urged. He cradled her face in his hands and drew her to him.

"Take me with you," she whispered. "I won't be a burden."

"My beloved, I can't..." He kissed her soft lips and held her against him. He felt her beating heart.

She lifted his arms from her body and pulled away from his embrace. "You don't love me." She began crying again. "Because I'm a slave."

"No, that isn't true!" Tiras again tried to embrace her but she eluded his grasp. "I do love you," he said, trying to reassure her. "But I have obligations to my tribe."

"Obligations," she repeated. "And none to me?" Before he could respond, she continued. "I'll never forget you, Tiras. Never. If you say you'll come back for me...I'll believe you."

"I'll come back," he said.

Her eyes glowed. "Swear by our gods?"

"I swear," he said, filled with doubts about returning. He thought it was horrible to lie, to be untrue to himself. Still, what else could he do? She yearned for his promise although they both knew he might never keep it. He didn't want to keep hurting her.

"Then one last kiss," she said and they embraced.

He expected to say good-bye to her the following morning, but

Bernadette Miller

she didn't appear at breakfast. "She's not well," Unanna explained to Tiras and ordered the slave to pass more food to her guest. Tiras felt disappointed at Majeena's absence. He reasoned that she was probably too hurt to say good-bye. Perhaps it was best. A loving glance might reveal to Mah Ummia their secret trysts.

Upstairs, Tiras repacked his knapsack with his warm sheepskin cloak, Mah Ummia's sleeping blanket, a slingshot, and food, and pondered his journey home. Again, he must survive the desert alone, a long trek without the tribe's protection. He stared at the pearl-paneled wall. "I'll find my tribe," he told the chiseled worshippers with staring eyes. "I'll explain about your gods. How your people built the great city of Ur without Martu's help!"

Tiras looked about and smiled in relief. Martu didn't appear! As usual, he must be busy in the desert. In the courtyard, Tiras exchanged farewells with Unanna and Dumuzi who'd been living with Mah Ummia since their wedding. Because Sumerians didn't embrace publicly, he refrained from hugging his hosts.

Mah Ummia accompanied Tiras and his laden donkey to Ur's outer wall. Tiras felt excited then about teaching his tribe the Sumerian religion, despite the revenge he expected from Abu-Summu and Martu. He must offer his kinsmen this great gift.

Mah Ummia paused at the bronze double-gate. "Where is your tribe now?"

"In winter they usually migrate within the Upland Steppes. North of the Nefud Desert. The Ghata tribe claims the Upland pastures. Other tribes must pay a tribute of several sheep to cross the Ghatas' land."

Mah Ummia nodded thoughtfully. "The closest place to the Uplands would be Bab-Ilim in the North, inhabited by Arabi city-dwellers, not Sumerians." He handed Tiras two leather pouches. "These shekels came from the sale of the wool you brought to Ur. I added more. The funds will help you survive until you find your tribe. Travel north, following the river until you reach Bab-Ilim.

From there, the desert crossing is shorter to the Uplands and less dangerous."

He watched Tiras tie the pouches around his waist beneath the robe. "Remember these Sumerian cities," Mah Ummia said. "Larsa. Erech. Shuruppak, and Nippur. Then, Bab-Ilim."

Tiras repeated the names several times. "I'll remember," he said. "Thank you again for your many kindnesses and generous hospitality. May the gods preserve you, Mah Ummia."

"And you, my friend," Mah Ummia said. "I'll miss your company."

The pair exchanged smiles. Mah Ummia walked toward the Ceremonial Boulevard. Tiras's face sagged at parting from his kind teacher. They might never meet again. Turning, he patted Na'al's mane. Na'al raised his head and brayed loudly as if complaining about Tiras's absence.

"I'm sorry for neglecting you," Tiras apologized to Na'al. He took the reins and walked beside his donkey. "But so many adventures, I had no time." He swiveled to look back at the grand Ceremonial Boulevard and bazaar: the fascinating sights and smells, the walled city of Ur where he'd learned so much. He would miss Mah Ummia!

On the dusty road crowded now with travelers, Tiras continued walking and glancing back at Ur receding on the horizon, carving it in his memory. How the Sumerian gods had created their loyal worshippers from clay and bestowed upon them so much: the wheel, writing, schools, jury trials. ... But how to tell his tribe about those gods? Surely Martu would grow jealous and demand terrible retribution. Dare he risk his family's life to help his people?

Bernadette Miller

CHAPTER 11

March, 3499 B.C., Arabiyah
(Al-Nefud Desert in northern Saudi Arabia)

ANXIOUS TO SEE HIS FAMILY, Tiras headed across the Nefud to his tribe's last-known camp near the Al-Mawf Oasis. As he'd feared, his kinsmen were absent. Distraught, he scanned the hard red sand with clumps of vegetation, and the distant sand dunes. He reminded himself that during the last six moon-cycles, his kinsmen must have sought fresh pastures and were now in the Uplands. Disappointed, he traveled back to Sumer and headed north along the Euphrates River toward the city of Larsa as Mah Ummia had advised.

During his journey, Tiras remembered those fascinating but baffling Sumerian stories. As he rode past the river, he repeated them aloud, hoping to find answers to his quest for a new god. Near Larsa he built a small campfire behind thickets. While Na'al nibbled on grass, he leaned against a palm to eat dried beef with olives and plums. He thought about the Sumerians making strange signs on clay tablets that could speak words, and how they rode on swift wood chariots—not dragons! He could hardly wait to tell cousin Ruach. And what about their laws that taught people how to behave? If only he could find a god to replace Martu and convince the tribe to accept Him.

The next morning he arrived in Larsa where he bought supplies. It was smaller than Ur. Sumerian men with their long, pleated skirts and draped shawls ignored his smile in greeting. He'd forgotten about their scorn of Bedouins, claiming that they ate raw meat and didn't bury their dead.

We do cook our meat and bury our dead! Tiras thought as he walked beside Na'al. The donkey's hooves echoed against the alleys' cobblestones. Tiras shook his head in anger, remembering the insulting remarks. *The Sumerians are smart but they value riches and comfort*, he thought, trying to balance his criticism. *They turn people into slaves. Like animals.*

Na'al brayed as if ignored. Tiras stroked the donkey's bristled ears while thinking, "But we survive our hard life because we love each other deeply. We value freedom and equality, not slavery." His heart beat fast then, knowing that soon he would be home.

Instead of cobblestones beneath his sandals, he would feel sand. Instead of whitewashed houses, he would see towering dunes and limestone peaks. Instead of sleeping in a Sumerian bedroom, he could open a tent flap and admire the glittering star goddesses who seemed so close he could almost reach up and touch them. Even better, he could hug his children and Na'amah. He imagined her lips on his, her body pressing against him. Why had he waited so long to return home? But there was one child, Shallah, he would never hug again.

He led Na'al back toward the main road, his spirit heavy then with remembrance of his young daughter. He scanned an alley lined with houses and shops. Not all Sumerians are greedy, he reminded himself. And what about generous Mah Ummia? May he live a long, fruitful life, protected by Lord Enki, a shrewd god who helped turn marshland into fertile fields. But what about Majeena? he thought then. Will Martu punish me for abandoning her?

Hoping to relieve his guilt by diverting his attention, Tiras glanced about. "Several times I compared Martu poorly with the

Sumerian gods," he whispered to Na'al so that Martu wouldn't overhear. "Maybe our bull-god fears those gods so he dares not act against them! Maybe Mah Ummia's personal God, Lord Enki, protects me." Holding his donkey's reins, Tiras closed his eyes, and lowered his head in submission. "Please, Lord Enki," he whispered, "tell me if you protect me." He waited a few moments. Unhappily, Lord Enki was absent.

He reasoned that maybe Lord Enki, smarter than Martu, was biding his time. Although the Sumerian gods look like sympathetic people, not frightening like a bull, they appear only as statues. Do those gods ever leave their statues?

That evening, Tiras settled between Larsa and Erech. Scrub brush screened his campfire from curious travelers. Sleeping on Mah Ummia's warm blanket reminded him of the Old One's stories. Although enjoyable, they seemed to lack purpose, but then why did the Sumerians eagerly relate them and preserve them on clay tablets?

When Tiras reached Erech a week later, he bought more supplies in the city's bazaar. After eating, he squatted beside his campfire outside of the city and thought about his family. If only he could see them now. In the pebbly sand, he traced his favorite son's outline with a callused finger. Once when Rimush was sick, he'd cooled his body with water he needed himself. During the cold nights, he warmed Rimush's chilled limbs with his own. He never expected to play again with his sick son. Then a miracle happened, and Rimush recovered. He'd thanked Martu. But not now.

He looked about and remembered Majeena's doubts. Despite all the insults, the bull-god remained surprisingly silent, as she had suggested. Perhaps Martu feared the Sumerian gods. The tribe should learn about his cowardice! That would fuel their courage to refuse his vicious demands.

Tiras turned from the campfire and scanned the planted fields across the road that stretched between Erech and Shuruppak. He shook his head in bewilderment. If all that were true, how should he approach those in his tribe who resisted change? There was another challenge: which Sumerian god could replace Martu?

Tiras gazed upward at a billowing cloud, and tried to determine how to find that god. The answer eluded him. He waited, shivering at the possible return of the threatening bull with his flared nostrils and pawing hooves. The land was silent. The bushes behind him remained motionless. The date palms nearby seemed frozen in their stillness. No birds soared overhead.

He remembered Shallah's agonized screams during the worship. How could he be so cowardly, he thought, surrendering his dear innocent daughter to the spiteful priest and Martu? How could he not protest, thereby helping in her murder?

His head bent, he began sobbing uncontrollably, his shoulders shaking. "Shallah, please forgive me," he cried out, feeling as if a heavy stone lay on his heart. "If only you could come back, even once. If only I could see you again to beg your forgiveness!"

Suddenly, Al-Qais, the wind god, blew against the bushes. The palm fronds shivered. The dying campfire spurted embers. Tiras stared at the cloud shredding against the sky. Then, just as quickly the wind died. Everything was still again. It must be a sign that something important would happen!

He imagined then a little girl silhouetted against the cloud remnants. Shallah! She'd come back to ease his despair, just as he'd begged her to! He stared at the cloud wisps hovering above but saw instead his dead daughter's ghost descending with wings flapping about her shoulders, reminding him of the stories about the Annunaki, the Sumerian gods who could fly like birds because of their wings. A sense of relief, almost lightheartedness, washed over him. He hadn't lost his daughter, after all! He saw her as clearly as he'd seen Martu. But perhaps she'd returned to accuse him.

Shaking, he whispered, "Dear child, can you forgive me?" He'd meant to be calm for her sake. Instead, he burst into sobs again. "I'm so sorry I caused you such pain. I should have fought the priest."

Bernadette Miller

"No, baba, please don't cry," he heard her say. Gently, she lowered her little body until her tiny, sandaled feet nearly touched the grass. She folded her wings against her body and drew near him as he squatted by the campfire. While he gazed in surprise, her finger wiped away his tears. Her touch like a gentle breeze by Al-Qais.

He focused on a nearby date palm but saw instead Shallah's misty-white face, plaits, robe, and wings that he would expect of any being from beyond the world, although she also looked as he remembered her at age five with the same warm brown eyes, the same dimpled cheeks and trusting smile. But her speech, despite the childish lisp, sounded older, like a grown woman.

"I know you couldn't protect me from Abu-Summu," she said. "Nobody could."

He started to rise. She motioned for him to remain squatting beside his campfire. Slowly she lowered herself beside him but didn't touch him. She hovered beside him, like a miniature ghost squatting on her haunches, her misty robe's hem puddled around her feet.

"Baba, how will you tell the tribe about the Sumerian gods?"

Tiras shook his head. "I don't understand their stories. But they must be important. The Sumerians wrote them on tablets—" He stopped. How would his little girl understand about tablets and writing?

She smiled. "Yes, baba, I know all about the tablets. Go on, please."

He stared at her, surprised at her knowledge at such a tender age. She came from beyond the grave. She probably knew much more than he. The important thing was that she'd arrived to help him. Despite her age. Despite all the hurt he'd given her. She could forgive, but Martu couldn't.

"I never blamed you," Shallah said. "I blamed Martu." He glanced about cautiously. "Baba, don't worry about Martu. He's cowering behind a cloud god. He's hoping to avoid injury by the Sumerian gods."

"I suspected it. But I feared..." Tiras paused and stared at the campfire. He reached for a loose branch, added it to the fire, and watched the flames crackle. The sparks flew upward. The warmth engulfed him. He turned toward his little girl, half-expecting her to disappear. Relieved, he imagined her still squatting beside him.

"Go on, baba. How will you tell the tribe?"

"We're simple folk, unlike the wise Sumerians," he said, gazing at his beloved daughter. "We can't understand stories about other gods whose lives seem amusing but foolish."

Shallah nodded. "Weren't those stories created for the Sumerians? Maybe they hold secret meanings only those people understand. Try to discover the meanings. Then you can adapt them to our way of life so the tribe will accept them."

He smiled at her wisdom despite her tender youth. "Will you keep me company on my journey home?" he asked although he had no right to expect her help after his dreadful treatment of her.

"I'll stay with you as long as you need me."

"My darling." He reached out to touch her but felt only air. Still, he saw her clearly: The brown eyes in a white, misty face. The white braids, robe, and wings. The way she cocked her head at him. That trusting smile. But she could dissolve like the cloud god.

"Are you real, Shallah?"

"If you want me to be. But you can't touch me. My body is different now."

He nodded, delighted to have her company whether she was real or not. He offered her cooked meat and figs from his basket of provisions. She assured him she didn't need food. When he lay down that night to sleep, she hovered by his side and promised to awaken him should Martu appear.

She was still there the next day and they traveled toward Shuruppak. His daughter floated beside him while he rode Na'al. Encouraged by her presence, he pondered how to convince his tribe to accept a new tribal god, and which one? The Sumerians had so many. There's Lord Enlil, god of the air, Lord Enki, god of wisdom, Lord Utu, the sun god, Lord An, father of the gods, and many more. None seemed suitable for his tribe.

Near Shuruppak, Tiras rested in a meadow with mimosa trees, lush green grass, and pretty little flowers that resembled a heavenly glade like the Sumerian paradise, Dilmun. He inhaled the fragrant air and questioned Shallah squatting nearby. "If the Abram tribe accepted a powerful new god, couldn't such a god create the world solely by his divine word? Command the sky to separate from Earth and it is so?"

She nodded. "A powerful god could do anything."

Tiras paused, thinking. "And wouldn't a merciful god offer us a soothing paradise, like this tranquil meadow, to reward the righteous? Not like the Sumerian paradise for their gods alone." He looked about and sighed with satisfaction. "Our new God might call our paradise by the Sumerian word for meadow: Eden. For here in Eden my heart is nourished and calmed."

Shallah smiled in agreement. He leaned against a mimosa, utterly content for the moment.

Later, traveling to Nippur, he turned toward Shallah who floated beside his donkey. "I can't decide which Sumerian god could replace Martu?" He looked at her thoughtfully. Finally, he said, "Our new god, though powerful, must act like a father, filled with love for his children, unlike Martu, a savage beast. A kind father would never demand sacrifice. But he should be strong enough to conquer brutal Martu."

Shallah replied, "Well, why not a new Bedouin god?"

Tiras thought for a moment. His wise daughter was right. His tribe needed a god fit for them, not the Sumerians! "What should I call Him?"

"How about simply El? Our word for god."

Tiras smiled. "Yes! Our desert god is so forceful He needs no other name. "El is our new tribal God," he whispered to Shallah. He paused, half-expecting Martu's vengeance, still reluctant to believe that his tribe's chief god for so many generations could be conquered. Again nothing happened. He finally became convinced and eagerly began probing Mah Ummia's stories.

"Don't you see, Shallah? The Sumerians must be right that their gods created man in their image. Men are much wiser than beasts. So, El can't be an animal, like a bull, pawing the earth. Our new God must look like us!"

She smiled with her approval. He closed his eyes. When he reopened them and looked upward at a cloud drifting by, he imagined a wondrous, man-like figure riding atop it, propelled by fire.

Sure enough, El looked as familiar as any Bedouin. His skin was brown from the sun. His eyes were dark and His beard black. He wore a white turban and a white robe from neck to ankles. His feet were clad in sandals. Encircled by a radiant light, El skimmed the sky as He rode by on His cloud. Tiras, awed, described the scene to Shallah who listened intently.

"Look, Shallah, there He is! Do you see Him?"

"Yes, yes, I do see Him. Please tell me more."

Inspired, Tiras burst out, "El, resembling a man, wouldn't eat children. Only animals. He would occupy a tall tower in villages, like the Sumerian Bab-El, where He speaks in many tongues so all can understand Him. But in the desert, He travels on a cloud propelled by fire. Do you still see Him, Shallah?"

"Yes, baba. I see Him clearly."

Tiras, consumed by his revelation and the image revealed to him, felt doubly reassured by Shallah, floating by his side. Looking upward, he thought he saw El following overhead as if to protect them from possible danger. Now that he had his new God's guidance, Tiras regarded his former god, Martu, as impotent, unable to hurt anyone.

Encamped near Bab-Ilim, he remembered the Sumerian story about Lady Nammu, mother of Lord Enki. How she and Nin-ti, the Rib and Birth Goddess, fashioned the first man from clay. He

Bernadette Miller

told Shallah hovering nearby, "Didn't I once discover a dead gazelle, hidden in thickets? His flesh had rotted in the desert, leaving nothing but bones and dust. Where was its flesh? So, El must have fashioned it from dust. Not clay as the Sumerians claimed. And El would call His creation, Adham, the first man."

Shallah nodded. "Then, like a loving father, wouldn't El place Adham, in a beautiful place? Maybe Eden, the oasis paradise."

"Exactly!" Tiras agreed. "But in the Sumerian story, Lord Enki ate a forbidden plant there. Lady Kursag punished him by causing severe indigestion. Poor Lord Enki lay near death. Finally, Nin-ti healed him by replacing his ribs. Nin-ti, Lady of the Ribs...also known as the birth goddess, Lady Who Brings Life."

Tiras looked at Shallah waiting patiently while he wrestled meaning from the story about Enki's ribs. He said thoughtfully, "Lady Who Brings Life translates as Evewah, the birth goddess, because she could bear children. "Suppose," he said slowly, "Adham cried not from indigestion but loneliness? El, pitying his creation, might have fashioned from Adham's rib a woman to be his companion and called her Evewah."

Again, Tiras paused and said, "But sorrow must have struck Adham and Evewah. Man no longer dwells in Eden."

"Well, perhaps Adham, like Lord Enki, also ate from a forbidden plant," Shallah suggested. "But not just any plant. An important one."

"The Tree of Knowledge that I've always hungered for!" he exclaimed.

The pair smiled at each other.

As Tiras continued his journey with his daughter at his side, he reshaped the Sumerian stories to suit his tribe. He turned to Shallah one afternoon and said, "What is man's goal? It must be the best path to achieving happiness. And how can man find that path? By obeying El's instructions to pursue an ethical life!" He smiled at his daughter in triumph. Her eyes shone at his new-found insights.

Then, fear gripped Tiras's heart. Suppose, despite his best efforts, the tribe rejected the new God? Suppose Abu-Summu destroyed Tiras's family as punishment? He shook his head at his cowardice and thought, "*Our vicious bull-god mustn't claim more children. El will protect me because my cause is just. Evil can't win against courage and determination.*

He knew that evil often won. So, he reminded himself how his ancestors had risked their lives to establish a home in a new land, Arabiyah. He, too, will risk his life to save his children and his tribe.

CHAPTER 12

February, 3499 B.C., Sumer

AFTER LEAVING TIRAS AT THE CITY GATE, Mah Ummia had hurried home to prepare lessons for his affluent pupils. Parents had sent their slaves, requesting an answer to his neglect. He assured them that he had a religious responsibility. They'd be notified when instructions would resume. He had no regrets. His youthful pledge to blessed Lord Enki had been fulfilled by teaching a simple Bedouin his religion.

As Mah Umma approached his garden gate, he saw Balulum waiting beside his chariot. Balulum staggered toward Mah Ummia. His daughter's former suitor was drunk again! His shawl was torn, his tufted skirt was spotted with stains, and his hairy chest was grimy.

"So, the father of my stolen bride arrives at last!" Balulum sneered. "Now perhaps you can explain why you broke your promise!"

Mah Ummia waited patiently for Balulum to arrive at his side. "You're in no condition to talk," he said calmly, watching Balulum grab the garden gate for support.

Balulum's face flushed; his thick lips seemed to swell with rage. He squinted at Mah Ummia. "I'm in the perfect condition to talk! The gods have already cursed you for your foul deed. Now I'll finish it for them!" He tossed aside his shawl. It floated for a moment, landed on the fence, and became impaled on a pointed post. He tugged at his dagger in his belt sheath. "I warned you I'd have my revenge!"

Alarmed, Mah Ummia stretched out an arm to stop him. "Please, Balulum, you're drunk. You don't know what you're doing."

In one swift motion, Balulum lunged at Mah Ummia with his drawn dagger. Mah Ummia fought to cross his arms in defense, encumbered by his shawl. "I can explain. My daughter refused to marry you—"

"Refused?" Balulum snarled. "A weak excuse! A daughter must obey her father's commands." A rough hand grasped Mah Ummia's throat. "Your teaching is over. All your hopes for Unanna will die with you. Just like my hopes of marrying your daughter whom you promised me. Die. Just as you killed my future!"

He repeatedly stabbed Mah Ummia in the chest.

Blood spurted across Mah Ummia's chest and shawl as he sank to the ground. He gasped, "You're insane and _____" But no other words came from him as his eyes froze and his face hardened into a death mask.

"Adda!" Unanna screamed. She rushed from the house, horrified. She shouted at slaves to help. They chased after Balulum, but his chariot was already beyond their reach. The slaves carried Mah Ummia's body inside the courtyard and upstairs to his room at the end of the balcony. Unanna, sobbing uncontrollably, shouted for a physician to be summoned.

"His spirit has already departed," Majeena said softly, trying to console Unanna.

Unanna flung her arms over her father's bloodied chest. "Oh, adda, it's my fault you've left us." For several hours she sat beside his bed, her gown stained with his blood, overcome with grief. Trembling, she recovered sufficiently to ask a slave to inform Dumuzi.

When the slave returned, he bowed low in Mah Ummia's bedroom and told Unanna, "Master said to tell you that he's going first to the Dublal-makh to charge Balulum with murder, and then he'll return to help with the burial."

Unanna nodded and rested her head against her father's bloody chest.

When Dumuzi arrived, he embraced his wife and said, "The officials sent two slaves to Balulum's house before he could escape. They found him huddled on his bedroom floor, eyes wild, as if seeing drunken visions. They dragged him along The Sacred Way to the courthouse. He'll stay there until the trial."

Unanna stared at him, her dark eyes still blurry with grief. She couldn't accept her father's horrible death. He was a good man. He didn't deserve this fate.

 හ ගි

The next day, they attended the funeral. Hidden beneath the courtyard stairs was the family chapel and hidden beneath that was the brick-lined family tomb. Tremulous beside her husband, Unanna watched slaves pry open a portion of the chapel's paved floor and then open the tomb door. A slave, carrying a broom, descended a ladder and swept the tomb's latest decedents into a corner. Older skeletons were removed to be disposed of with the rubbish. Two slaves carried Mah Ummia's corpse wrapped in clean linen over his skirt and shawl. They carefully lowered his body down the ladder. In the tomb they laid him on his side on the floor.

Sanga, the High Priest, peered down into the tomb and offered a prayer to the family's personal god. He said with uplifted arms, "Blessed Lord Enki, let our beloved teacher have a pleasant journey to the netherworld."

He continued entreating Lord Enki as slaves placed a cup of water and two clay vessels containing food against Mah Ummia's side for his journey to the underworld. Unanna, struggling to stifle her sobs before the slaves, buried her face against her husband as the tomb opening was resealed with bricks.

Dumuzi took her hand and led her upstairs to their bedroom. "Rest, dearest," he said. "I'll send food to you later."

"No, I'm not hungry. I can't bear what happened to dear adda."

"Please rest. It hurts me to see you so unhappy." He stroked her face. "Balulum will be punished. Even if I have to do it myself."

80 CR

Unaware of his teacher's murder, Tiras continued his journey to find his tribe. He encamped one evening near Bab-Ilim before entering the Nefud desert. In the cold nocturnal air, he wrapped his sheepskin cloak about his shoulders and stared, deep in thought, at his dying campfire. The ghost of his dead daughter, Shallah, squatted nearby. He turned to her and described the Annunaki as he had been taught by Mah Ummia.

"They were children of Lord An, who had grown into adults and were punished for their sins."

"What kind of sins?" Shallah asked.

He hesitated, embarrassed at telling her stories she probably shouldn't hear at her young age. "What's important," he said finally, "is that Lord An was so angry, he gave the Annunaki wings and commanded them to carry the dead to the netherworld. The first humans with wings. But why is this important?"

"Well, what does it have to do with El?" Shallah asked.

Tiras gazed thoughtfully at the moonlit sky, El's resting place. "Maybe, like Lord An, our new God wants His children to value honor," he said softly. "The truest path toward happiness. So, tribesmen should face justice: a Day of Reckoning. Then, winged messenger gods would carry the virtuous upward to the Oasis of Eden. But they'll carry the wicked downward to the netherworld."

Shallah shook her head. "The Sumerian netherworld is where good and bad people alike are sent to serve the gods. But bad people shouldn't serve the gods. Wouldn't closeness to such divine beings seem a blessing? Not a curse?"

"Of course, the place for the wicked should be fierce!" Tiras replied. "Sinners roasting forever in a fiery netherworld. Jahannam!"

His daughter nodded and he elaborated about Jahannam, hell, until dawn's welcoming colors sprayed the sky. Tiras glanced about, surprised. He'd spent all night uncovering the significance of the Sumerian stories. Gratefully, he turned to Shallah still hovering beside him. "The dawn above still lights our path, but the Bedouin goddess, Al-Uzza, no longer exists! Do you understand, Shallah? Our divine El is supreme above all other gods. He conquered them. It's sinful now to worship those gods for they're false. For how could any other god compare with El? Soon, I'll tell my kinsmen about Him."

Fear again grabbed Tiras's heart at the thought of challenging the priest, Abu-Summu. But only El offered hope of sparing their loved ones from Martu's unreasonable demands. Unseen now, the Bedouin god probably rested above the sky.

After breakfast, tired but determined, Tiras mounted his donkey. He turned to Shallah. "Come, my darling, let's continue our journey." She floated beside him as they advanced some miles along the road. Shading his eyes, he finally saw a city wall ahead. "That must be Bab-Ilim," he told her.

The pair passed through the city gate. At the bazaar, he bought gifts for his family and chatted with several Arab merchants whose tongues he understood. He finally noticed the mud-brick houses lining the alleys. He'd become so absorbed with his new mission, he'd scarcely paid attention to the towns visited for the first time.

Suddenly he thought he saw Majeena standing before him. In place of her water basin, tears flowed down her cheeks. His heart lurched at his deserting her—shameful behavior. He gazed upward and explained to El, "I couldn't help it. Majeena would hamper my journey and never be accepted by my family."

He trembled. Despite his excuse, El might punish him for abandoning Majeena.

Shallah said, "Baba, have you forgotten that Sumerian proverb about telling me what you have found?"

Tiras smiled at his daughter's sympathy. "Yes, I found much more in Sumer than I lost." But someday, he thought, he would seek Majeena in Ur and they would regain their happiness. Soothed by the memory of the promise he was uncertain he could keep, he and his daughter left Bab-Ilim.

As he traveled north through the Nefud Desert toward the Uplands, he continued adapting the Sumerian stories to present them to his tribe. Despite his lingering fear of Abu-Summu, he anticipated offering his tribe the new religion. At first, they might fiercely oppose it, but he prayed that in time, his kinsmen would accept this vision of a happier future with a kinder god.

North of the Nefud, Tiras saw no people and few animals, except occasionally bustards, a type of bird, feeding on red caterpillars. One morning, to his delight, he spotted the Uplands Steppe stretching to the far horizons. The tribe should be encamped somewhere in the Uplands. He was almost home. Eagerly, he scanned the lush green hills and valleys dotted with grazing sheep and goats, the air bathed in the sweet fragrance of thyme and chamomile. A lark's joyous song encouraged him to loudly sing a tribal melody. Na'al brayed in accompaniment.

As Tiras walked with his daughter who floated beside him and his donkey, he looked up at the sky toward the Nameless One, and thought, *Thank you, dear El, for sending me this pleasurable day and my daughter's companionship.*

The noise, however, had attracted a small group of tribesmen riding their war donkeys down a nearby hill. Reaching the plateau, the tribesmen urged their donkeys onward. The donkeys, decorated with ostrich feathers, kicked up sand as they sped toward Tiras.

Bernadette Miller

He couldn't outride them. He halted Na'al. A hand lingered on his dagger. Shallah had left him, now when he needed her most.

The tribal sheikh approached Tiras with a drawn spear made of bamboo. It's oval-shaped copper head, pointed at Tiras, could surely kill him. The sheikh's muscular shoulders bulged beneath his robe as he observed the intruder. His dark eyes glowered beneath his turban. His thick brows were knitted together. He balanced the spear against his arm and stared at Tiras who dropped his dagger in a show of good will.

"See how a lone jackal dares to cross the grounds of the noble Ghata tribe," the sheikh said. "You entered our land without our permission. I'll kill you where you stand."

"Wait!" Tiras pleaded. "I've become separated from my tribe, the Abram. I'm lost." His pulse quickened but his face remained passive as he struggled to appear calm. "Every winter my family pays tribute to the Ghata for permission to graze at your oases. I beg forgiveness for crossing your dirah without that permission."

He paused as the sheikh pointed his spear toward him. Na'al brayed in alarm. He stroked the frightened animal's neck.

"Why should we believe you?" the sheikh sneered. "You could be a scout for the Walla, our sworn enemies. A group of them also pretended innocence. Weary travelers from the Nefud seeking shelter. Then, during the night, they knifed some of our loved ones in the back, like cowards, and fled with our possessions."

"I'm not a scout!" Tiras exclaimed. "I'm only seeking my family. I plead dakhil—protection in the sight of Ba'al Hadad!"

Having employed the Bedouin oath by calling upon the Ghata's tribal god, Tiras prostrated himself, his turban bent low toward the sand. This time-honored ritual couldn't be ignored.

"You're an honorable Bedouin," the sheikh observed. "Calling upon protection from my god. I'll let you live. Rise. My scouts will guide you to the Abram's camp."

"Salaam 'alaykum," Tiras said politely in farewell, his body still quivering from near death.

"'Alaykum salaam," the sheikh responded. He raised his spear as a signal. The tribesmen wheeled about on their donkeys and rode off toward the eastern horizon except for two Ghata scouts.

Riding Na'al, Tiras wished Shallah would return. Disappointed, he stared at the distant hillside dotted with flowers. She comes when it pleases her, he thought. But the sheikh had spared him, and his mind was set on his new god. Perhaps her mission was finished?

The scouts left Tiras at his tribe's camp. Filled with relief, he scanned the black tents. Home! Then he looked upward toward the sky that concealed El. He ignored his fear of the priest's likely punishment, the sudden throbbing in his ears that echoed his pounding heart. Instead, he raised his arms and prayed aloud. "Oh, mighty El, with Your help, I will show my courage. My kinsmen will reject Martu and all other gods. They'll accept only You. Then my kinsmen will rejoice with a feast at my gift."

∞ ∞

In Ur, with her husband's help, Unanna was able to face each day without a tear-stained face while mourning Mah Ummia. Instead, a kind of hardness replaced her grief. "I want justice!" she demanded of Dumuzi. "I want to see Balulum's head decorating a pole for murdering my father!"

Dumuzi patted her arm. "Dearest, a judge assured me that our father's vicious murderer will receive the harshest penalty possible. What could be worse than reducing the rich merchant to poverty?"

Unanna shuddered. "Yes. Poverty would be fitting."

∞ ∞

Jurors heard the trial in the Dublal-makh inside the great temple at The Sacred Way. Unanna testified along with the slaves and won the case. As usual, the mashkim read the verdict outside on the courthouse steps at the base of the ziggurat. He cleared his throat and spoke in a loud voice while reading from the clay tablet. "Henceforth, Lord Balulum will be stripped of his merchant status. His house, land, and all his shekels belong now to Ur. His shops will close. Letters of Credit will be annulled. Lady Unanna will receive half of the murderer's shekels as compensation for her loss. The balance will pay Balulum's creditors. Any remaining shekels will be donated to Lord Enki's temple."

Ironically, the once rich merchant would be forced to beg for his bread at the bazaar, the very future he'd predicted for Mah Ummia.

Some of Ur's populace gathered about and shivered at the awful punishment of Balulum. The mashkim glanced down at the convicted killer, bound in ropes, and continued reading. "Citizens, look upon this miserable man. A successful merchant turned murderer. From now on, he'll be a lowly beggar. Grateful for a morsel of bread. So heed my warning. Live a moral life. Or you, too, will end up like this man."

Balulum glanced about in bewilderment as if all memory of his foul deed had vanished and he couldn't understand the punishment.

›‹℃

Walking home, Unanna leaned on Dumuzi's arm for support. Afterward, she stayed in her room, crying. She silently picked at her food. Several weeks passed. Persuaded by her husband's coaxing, she began relaxing with him evenings in the garden. After two months, hoping to end her nightmares, Unanna resumed her former activities: inviting guests for small dinners, planning menus, and supervising the slaves. For the first time since her father's death, she shopped at the bazaar and stopped short near the sweets stall where she saw Balulum squatting in the garbage-strewn dirt. Barefoot, he wore tattered robes. His once-heavy body had shrunken.

He extended a basket, his arm infested with sores. In a hoarse voice, he muttered, "Shekels, I beg of you. Please, give me shekels for bread." With reddened eyes and cheeks, he stared past Unanna as if he didn't recognize her.

She turned away, her satisfaction mingled with disgust at his condition, and hurried home. During dinner, she agreed with her husband that they had obtained justice. "But I still can't bear it that my father died so brutally. I pray to Lord Enki his death wasn't in vain."

Dumuzi nodded. "Mah Ummia taught most of Ur's outstanding citizens. He even devoted time to educating an uncivilized Bedouin. Your father's life could never be in vain."

"Nevertheless, amidst all our grief," Unanna said with downcast eyes, "I suffer mornings with nausea and vomiting. Why do the gods mock us?"

CHAPTER 13

March, 3499 B.C., Arabiyah
(The Uplands in northern Saudi Arabia)

T IRAS FINALLY REACHED HIS TRIBE'S camp in the Arabiyah Uplands that straddled the land north of the Nefud Desert. After the Ghata scouts left, Tiras led Na'al over the flat sand toward his tribe's black tents. The sun dipped below the low hills outlining the horizon. In the dimming light, herdsmen returned with their flocks from the oasis pasture. Children played outside their mothers' tents. The women cooked spicy stew on their outdoor hearths.

To Tiras, after wandering so long, saffron and cardamom had never seemed so fragrant, and the children's shouts never so melodious. Filled with happiness, he scanned the encampment. Na'amah's tent was pitched somewhere among the fifty. Leading Na'al, he walked about, calling out, "Na'amah! I'm home!" Gradually the tribe gathered and stared at Tiras as if he were a ghost.

"It's Tiras," some tribesmen began whispering among themselves in disbelief.

"Tiras, Tiras," echoed through the crowd.

"He's here!" Cousin Ruach shouted. "He didn't die!"

Na'amah rushed to him. "Oh, my husband." She covered his face with kisses.

"Dearest Na'amah." He held her in his arms for a deep kiss. His hands caressed her back.

Tiras's two sons yelled, "Baba!" and joined the tableau forming in the desert with Tiras in the center. "Yes, I'm back!" he shouted, trying to hug everyone.

Mashech approached. The crowd parted, making a path for the sheikh. He limped with his cane toward his son. They embraced. "We thought you were dead," Mashech said. "I was certain I'd lost you." Tears welled up in his eyes.

"Baba, please forgive me for my long absence. I had an injury in Ur—" He paused as a gasp erupted from his family. "A chariot injured my leg," Tiras explained. "Fortunately, a kind Sumerian tended my wound. I stayed in his house for four moon-cycles. The Sumerian cured my wound with poultices and bound my leg in a cast."

His kinsmen stared at Tiras, uncomprehending. Abu-Summu, the priest, scowled at the scrawny man with his straggly beard and tired eyes. He pointed a finger at Tiras. "You disobeyed your father's wishes. You ignored your family's warning. Finally you return, speaking of things to confuse us. Martu will punish your defiance."

Despite Abu-Summu's warnings, Tiras beamed at finally being home, and turned to the tribe. "Let's count our blessings that we're together again."

The priest's face darkened with anger. He muttered, "So, now that you've journeyed to Ur, you think my words are of no consequence. We shall see."

He strode to his tent. Tiras ignored his departure.

Ruach rushed to Tiras. After they embraced, Ruach shouted to the crowd, "Let's celebrate my cousin's return with a feast! Let's rejoice that he didn't die as we believed."

The tribe agreed. Tiras's two children tugged at his robe. He reached down and scooped up his favorite son, Rimush, who was heavier than he remembered. "You've grown during my absence. You're almost a little man."

"They said I'd never see you again, baba," Rimush whispered. His arms clung around Tiras's neck. "They said you were sleeping under the sand. But I knew you loved me and would come back."

"Yes, my son, you were right," Tiras said. He pressed the quivering body against his heart. "I'll never leave you again." He set down Rimush and bent to kiss his oldest son, Canah. The boys hugged him, shouting, "Baba, we missed you! Please stay with us!"

"I will!" he reassured them.

Exhausted after his long journey, Tiras felt he needed rest. He led Na'al to a patch of grass outside Na'amah's tent. He stroked the donkey's mane before unstrapping the loaded baskets. Na'al brayed softly in response and grazed on vegetation. Tiras brought the baskets inside Na'amah's tent while she prepared supper at the outside hearth. Exhausted, he curled up in his rug for a nap.

Before falling asleep, he envisioned introducing Majeena to his family. He sighed with regret, knowing it was impossible to bring her here. She couldn't speak the language, nor adapt to the unfamiliar customs. Na'amah would be angry at seeing a new wife, just as she'd been jealous of his other two wives. Majeena wouldn't be happy. Despite her slave condition, she belonged in Ur where Unanna and Mah Ummia treated her well. Majeena was beautiful. Someday, she would find another lover and marry. But will El forgive him for abandoning her after declaring his love?

He closed his eyes and promptly fell asleep. He dreamed about his youth. His sturdy mother held him in her arms. The dream soon dissolved to Ur where he saw again the whitewashed houses with gardens, the winding alleys and spacious boulevard, the soaring Tower of Bab-El at the Sacred Way, the Sumerian gods, and the new Bedouin god he would offer his tribe. El would love His chosen people, as the Sumerian gods loved theirs.

Abu-Summu, of course, would challenge these revelations and

seek vengeance. Tiras trembled in his sleep. *Be a man*, he reminded himself and awakened. *"I'll persuade the Abram to accept El Who loves us as we love our children."*

That evening while Rimush slept behind the dividing curtain, Tiras enjoyed his supper of bread-cakes and rice with fat drippings. Na'amah explained that the food had come from Ruach who had helped her during Tiras's absence. He nodded. "I owe my cousin a great deal," he said. "I must do all I can for him."

After their meal, Tiras rose and withdrew from the loaded baskets several copper jars of Sumerian beer and other gifts for his family bought with Mah Ummia's shekels. He handed Na'amah an ivory necklace of Sumerian scenes, designed by Dumuzi. It was similar to the one Dumuzi had given his wife.

Na'amah stared at it. "Who are these odd people with their strange clothes?" she asked, fingering the necklace. "Why are the men's chests bare?" She shook her head in bewilderment at Tiras's descriptions. He gave her gold filigree earrings and wound a gold-threaded belt around her waist. "These gifts are too beautiful for me," she protested.

He nuzzled her neck. "Na'amah, don't you know you've always been the most beautiful woman in my life."

"Oh, Tiras, I burned for your love. Like the sun god yearns for the sand."

He held her in his arms and kissed her welcoming lips. They undressed and lay down. He caressed her breasts and belly and was quickly engorged. He slid inside her. Her arms and legs gripped him tightly. They rocked back and forth until the explosive release when both gasped and fell back on the rug. How could he have remained absent from her all those months? He had nearly forgotten how much he loved her. For over an hour they made love and finally lay side by side, naked hips and thighs touching. Her hand caressed his face and slid over his body as if to reassure herself he wasn't a dream.

The following day, delighted to have her husband back, Na'amah

Bernadette Miller

helped the women prepare for the evening's welcoming banquet. She roasted a whole goat in her sand oven. In a pit lined with stones, the top open, she built a blazing fire. When the fire burned down, she placed stones over the glowing embers and the cleaned goat on the stones. Larger stones were placed across the opening. She sealed it with a thick layer of mud. It took two hours to cook the goat, plenty of time for Tiras to visit his father's tent after returning with his flock. He gave the old man an embroidered white robe, purchased in Sumer.

"I'll wear the new robe to the banquet," Mashech promised. He stared uncertainly at a copper carving.

Tiras explained, beaming, "This gift reproduces the Tower of Bab-El in Ur."

Mashech's eyebrows raised in puzzlement at his son's enthusiasm.

"The Tower is so tall, it touches the sky god," Tiras said, groping for a way to convey the Sumerian ziggurat's immensity. "Visitors come from around the world, speaking in many tongues."

Mashech nodded, uncomprehending, and patted the copper carving.

Tiras smiled and left, planning to give his two other wives bracelets of ivory and silver, along with alabaster figurines with wide, staring eyes.

Milcah, his third wife, refused the gift, and stammered, "We're— no longer—married. Because of—Shallah's sacrifice—and then your long absence, I—separated from you. I'm content with my new husband, a cousin."

Stunned, Tiras stared at her for a while. He silently left to find his second wife, Abada, whose excuse was similar. In her tent, Abada said coldly, "Tiras, I couldn't wait any longer. I was sure you were dead and I needed a husband. So I separated from you and married another."

Tiras left Abada without saying a word, trying to deal with his trip's consequences. He sought his two sons playing outside Na'amah's tent. Grateful he hadn't lost them, he gave them miniature donkeys carved from wood. They squealed with delight, "Baba, baba," and promptly waged a mock fight with their donkeys. They settled it when Rimush paused and announced with a smile, "I won."

Canah, his older brother, scowled and returned to Abada's tent.

That night, the tribe celebrated Tiras's homecoming after his long absence. They feasted on Na'amah's bowls of goat meat with rice and yoghurt. The other women contributed bread-cakes, wild honey, figs, dates, and date wine. As before, musicians played and tribesmen jumped up to dance. They formed a circle, clapped above their hands, and swayed rhythmically to and fro. Kneeling on their rugs, the women chanted the verses and clapped to the rhythm. Finally, the children's high-pitched voices pierced the desert air with the melodies everyone knew by heart.

When the festivities ended, the plates and cups gathered, the rugs rolled up, and the revelers retired for the evening, Tiras joined Na'amah in her tent. He held Rimush on his lap and sipped a final cup of wine before Na'amah led her yawning son to bed. Later, when Tiras lay beside his wife under the warm rug, she confessed that she'd refused to marry Ruach who had guarded Tiras's flock during his absence.

Her voice wavered. "Believing you were dead..." She paused and continued, "The Council of Elders insisted I choose a husband, your cousin Ruach, for protection. I've spent all these past months fighting the Council. The Elders threatened to strip away our flock if I didn't wed. Only your father and Ruach sided with me. Ruach sympathized with my distress. He told the Council he refused to wed a reluctant widow. He would wait until...until I accepted your death. And now...now you're here, at last."

Tiras embraced his faithful wife. "Dearest love, please forgive me. And I bless cousin Ruach for his understanding. I'll never leave you again. I promise."

Na'amah, smiling with joy, soon fell asleep, her face serene in

Bernadette Miller

the moonlight. Tiras, leaning on an elbow, reproached himself for staying that long in Ur. He shouldn't have caused his beloved wife such sorrow. He lay back, his arms folded beneath his head, and stared at the tent ceiling as he relived the day.

His concerns soon shifted to the next evening. Fear replaced excitement. He pictured tomorrow evening and how Abu-Summu would try to summon dread with Martu's stern warnings. This time the priest would fail, Tiras reminded himself, because he could offer a powerful new god, El, who'd conquered all the other gods. El would help him find the right words to subdue the priest. He would place all his trust in El. Evil Martu would be destroyed.

CHAPTER 14

March, 3499 B.C., Arabiyah

THE FOLLOWING NIGHT, THE ABRAM tribesmen stared at the altar horns glittering in the moonlight. Tiras watched the bonfire roar, casting shadows on the priest's face and his gnarled hands curling up and down like demon claws. It raised shivers along Tiras's spine. Amidst the dome of stars hanging over the cold desert, the moon hid, as if afraid, behind clouds. He clutched his sheepskin cloak about him, seeking warmth and courage. Suppose Martu really were supreme, as the priest insisted? No! He must remain resolute.

The priest pointed at Tiras. "Here is one who thinks himself beyond Martu's reach. Challenging our great god with his questions. Oh, tribesman, search your heart, as Martu searches. Ask if in any way you've again offended our god."

Despite his resolve, Tiras faltered. Dare he defy Martu and invite banishment for his family or risk sacrificing one of his sons? He scanned his kinsmen cowering with bowed heads on their prayer rugs. They should be freed from their bull-god's cruelty.

"We've done nothing to arouse Martu's anger!" he shouted, surprised by his own fervor.

Bernadette Miller

The tribesmen murmured in agreement, but their heads remained bowed as if even this acknowledgment could incite tragedy.

The priest grimaced at Tiras's challenge to his authority. "Nothing? Since childhood you have repeatedly defied me. You see nothing wrong with your behavior?"

"No!" Tiras replied. "In Ur, I learned about the merciful Sumerian gods. They don't demand human sacrifice. They're kind and loving as a father to his children."

He waited, his skin prickling in anticipation of Martu's retribution. None came. Martu must be hiding behind a star, he thought, not from the Sumerian gods but probably from El! He watched the tribesmen gazing downward at the sand in frightened submission. They needed his help!

Tiras jumped up. "Listen, my kinsmen! There's a God more powerful than Martu! A God who conquered all others. But He offers hope, not desperation."

Stunned, the trembling tribesmen awaited Martu's inevitable swift and dreadful response. The bull-god didn't appear. Silence reigned over the desert.

Abu-Summu, outraged by Tiras's challenge to Martu, shouted, "For this impiety, Martu demands your son, Rimush, as sacrifice. The great Martu has spoken!"

"I refuse to offer him because he's innocent!"

The worshippers raised their heads to gape in astonishment at Tiras. Nobody had ever dared to refuse the priest. Abu-Summu, also astonished, repeated his demand. "Will you surrender the child to appease our bull-god's mounting fury?"

Pale but determined, Tiras stood mute near the bonfire. Its flames licked up like hungry tongues for his favorite child. Martu's inertia finally stopped his quivering. Courage renewed, he shouted, "I've seen another God! And spoken with Him! A powerful, loving God Who created us in His image. We shall be His chosen people—the first to recognize Him!"

Furious, the priest said, "For this blasphemy, Tiras must be sacrificed. Or Martu will strike everyone—"

"Let us hear what my son has to say!" Mashech interrupted.

"What can he know?" an Elder asked. "Martu has been our tribal god for generations. Tiras will destroy us!"

Ruach called out, "We must listen if Tiras offers hope!"

"No!" a tribesman shouted. "We'll all die because of his stupidity!"

They continued arguing, torn between horror of the old god and the promise of something better—uncertain what to believe.

Abu-Summu stepped forward and spread his arms toward the altar. "Kinsmen, hear me! Don't forsake the bull-god of our ancestors. Pasture lands will wither. Our flocks will diminish, unable to give birth. The tribe will sicken and die from the jinns." He turned toward Tiras. "I must stop you from enraging Martu or our tribe will be destroyed. All because of foolishness you learned in Ur." He swiveled toward the worshippers. "Our bull-god demands Tiras's sacrifice. The great Martu has spoken!"

Tiras fought to maintain his courage. Blood rushed to his head. He began shaking. He reminded himself of his urgent mission. Ignoring his terror, he addressed the tribesmen. "The Sumerian religion isn't foolishness! Their gods love them. They treat them with respect. Answer their prayers and ask for little in return. Not like Martu who demands our children and gives nothing back! Kinsmen, don't let our priest persuade you otherwise with his lies."

The scowling priest turned to Tiras. "So, after one lone journey you're wiser than I am, the priest who has led our tribe. Wiser than the sheikh. Wiser than the Council of Elders. You're so wise that you know what Martu wants and doesn't want. "

Abu-Summu glared at Tiras, his taut face wreathed with hatred. "Only I, your priest, know what Martu wants! That's my duty. It's been my ancestors' duty as far back as my great grandfather's grandfather." He shook a finger at Tiras. "You'll pay the price for your disrespect!" He closed his eyes, looked upward toward the sky, and said, "Martu demands sacrifice for this outrage. You and your entire family! They'll all atone for their kinsman's recklessness."

He scanned the worshippers who were cringing on their rugs. "Kill this dangerous sinner! Kill him before our enraged bull-god destroys our tribe!"

A tribesman, livid, jumped to his feet. "Kill Tiras!"

Others shouted, "Before we're all killed!"

"Feed his entire family to Martu!"

"Let them writhe on the pyre! Begging our god's forgiveness!"

"Come forward," the priest said. He beckoned the men with raised fists to approach Tiras. "We must prove our love to Martu," he urged them. "Our impatient bull is watching us."

The tribesmen began crowding around Tiras. He stood with lips tightened in determination, his heart pounding in his ears. El will protect me, he told himself.

Abu-Summu pointed at Tiras. "See how the heretic challenges Martu. And us, his own kinsmen. Strike him! Kill him! Our beloved Martu will devour the traitors. Let us pray that our bull-god forgives us for this terrible betrayal."

"Wait!" Mashech said. He struggled to rise, helped by Tiras, determined to control his panic. With pleading eyes, Mashech scanned the threatening crowd. "Twice my son crossed the desert alone and survived. He became injured but lived among strangers who cured him. He must be favored by this unknown god. Don't obey our priest who has brought us so such suffering. My son offers a choice. At least hear his message."

The tribesmen hesitated.

"No! Don't listen to them!" Abu-Summu shrieked.

The men glanced with widened eyes from the priest to Tiras, and then toward the shiny horns on the altar.

"They invent lies to deceive us!" Abu-Summu screamed. "There's no such god! Only Martu who rages at our uncertainty!"

Ruach rushed to Tiras and Mashech and stood proudly beside

them. "The priest seeks to control us," he said, his jaw muscles twitching in fear. "Who knows what Martu wants? We only know what the priest wants!"

The tribesmen pivoted toward Abu-Summu. He glowered with rage, his face contorted, and his body shaking. "Because only my ancestors and I understand Martu's demands! Do you dare to discard this learning? Risk having our powerful bull-god crush us?"

Mashech bent toward Tiras. "Son," he whispered, "call upon your God. Let Him know our despair. Beg Him to guide us."

Tiras pondered a moment, wondering how to persuade the tribe to replace vicious Martu? He looked up at the sky and whispered, "El, please help us."

As if from afar, he thought he heard El whisper back, *"Don't be afraid. I am with you."* The tribe didn't hear El since Tiras thought that only he heard Him. They continued glaring at him with raised fists. Encouraged by the new god, he swallowed his fear and stood with arms uplifted toward the sky.

"Martu, I call upon you to defend your power! If you're still our fierce tribal god, stop hiding behind a star. Strike me down dead! Now! Or we'll reject you forever."

The men hushed in disbelief at Tiras's audacity. They gazed upward and waited. But Tiras stood with a defiant expression. Minutes passed. The nervous tribesmen began murmuring among themselves. "Martu will kill us all! Why does Tiras risk our lives?"

Exasperated, Tiras strode to the altar's ledge. He hurled the silver horns onto the sand. He shouted, "Look, Martu, see how I despise you! See how I laugh at your weakness! See how I discard your horns like rubbish. If you're still potent, kill me. Now!"

A gasp rippled through the crowd. Shocked by Tiras's extreme condemnation of Martu, the tribesmen were suddenly mute. They stared in anxiety at the naked ledge stripped of the sacred horns, and held their breaths, waiting for their bull-god to strike Tiras dead and then the entire tribe. Except for the crackling bonfire, the desert's

Bernadette Miller

silence embraced the men staring up at the jeweled night sky. More time passed in the tense silence.

"But, look, Martu doesn't appear," one tribesman dared to murmur.

"He doesn't punish," another said in wonder.

"Our bull-god is speechless," a third added in bewilderment.

"Because we've abandoned him," Abu-Summu insisted. He gathered up the horns from the sand and held them against his chest. "Martu will punish all of you!" he screamed, his face reddened. "You'll witness his revenge!"

Tiras shook his head in disgust at the raging priest who had murdered his cherished daughter. He turned to the tribesmen. "Martu has been conquered by El!"

Shocked by the unexpected events, the bewildered men swiveled toward Tiras. He stepped before the altar. "Rejoice, my kinsmen! Never again will Martu demand our children! Like a loving father, El will care for us and protect us if we pledge our loyalty solely to Him."

Beyond the stone altar that had nearly fed Martu's hunger, Tiras gazed upward at the sky and El's home. If only El would appear and reassure him that he was right.

Then, as if fulfilling his own summons, Tiras envisioned the revered figure hovering like a ghostly Bedouin above the altar. Entranced, he lifted his arms toward his reassuring vision who filled him with peace, not hate.

The men fell silent, watching Tiras's radiant face. They scanned the sky, seeking the appearance of a god, but saw no one.

"There is no supreme god but Martu!" the priest yelled.

Tiras focused on the confused worshippers, and then cried out with his voice booming in the desert. "Oh, my kinsmen, I have spoken with merciful El. He'll answer our troubled prayers with love. Don't deny El who pities our torments. Cast aside all other gods for they have been defeated. El alone rules us."

The men sank onto on their rugs, dumbstruck by Tiras's vision and his thunderous voice that was so confident, as if emanating the unknown being's power. They waited in uncertainty, gazing expectantly at the night sky, wondering if the unknown god would indeed rid them of Martu. They waited, but nothing happened.

"You see?" Abu-Summu sneered. "Tiras's god is terrified of Martu! He can't help you."

The tribesmen began muttering among themselves, unsure what to believe. They were afraid to reject Martu for the new god who might be impotent.

"But Martu doesn't punish us," Tiras said. "A sign that his power is gone."

'No!" the priest shrieked and picked up the horns from the sand. "Martu bides his time, that's all."

"Bides his time?" Tiras said and shrugged. "Your god is terrified of the new God. El has conquered him."

He turned toward the tribesmen shivering on their rugs, unsure whom to believe. Finally they raised their heads to gaze at Tiras, waiting for him to speak.

"Listen, my kinsmen!" Tiras said, his arms spread out beneath his cloak. "Powerful El created the world by His Divine Word. In the beginning, El said let there be a paradise and an earth. So He separated the waters above the sky from the waters below the sky, and He called that place above the sky, paradise. Then El said, Let the waters under paradise be directed to their appropriate place. And He called those waters, rivers, and the dry land, earth. And when El saw what He had done, He smiled, and said, that is good."

From far away, Tiras envisioned Martu groaning with pain, beaten by El. The once-mighty bull staggered from behind his protective star. Bellowing with anger and fear, blood spurting from wounds, he began plummeting toward Earth, snorting and pawing the air to resist his fate. A large fiery crater opened up in the desert. The bull toppled into it, far down into the netherworld. The crater sealed shut. The flat sand reappeared, speckled with acacias and abal bushes. Flower-dotted hills again outlined the distant horizons.

Bernadette Miller

Elated by his new vision, Tiras continued, "When El defeated Martu, he cast him down into the netherworld, a horrible place called Jahannam that blazes like a gigantic fire. There, the defeated bull walks upright, like a man, but still retains his horns, tail, and hooves. His task is to burn sinners through eternity."

Tiras paused. The bull god's responsibilities had changed. He needed a different name.

"After defeating Martu," Tiras continued, "El humiliated his enemy by calling him Be'elsebub, like our former tribal god. But El showed mercy. He gave Be'elsebub limited power as Satan, a prince of evil spirits."

The tribesmen leaned forward, listening thoughtfully. Tiras, encouraged, added, "As a Satan, Be'elsebub must obey El's commands. After our death, on Judgment Day, El will decide our fate. For we'll all be judged on whether we have lived a moral life." He paused again, waiting for the tribesmen's reactions to his explanation. Would they accept it?

The men stared into space as if thinking. Their silence seemed ominous. Then, Ruach shouted, "Martu's been defeated! Tiras speaks the truth!"

A second shouted, "His powerful god has overcome Martu!"

A third raised his arms to the sky. "Thank you, merciful El!"

"Never again will cruel Martu demand our children," a fourth said softly, as if unable to fully comprehend the subduing of their despised god.

"A miracle!" Ruach shouted.

"A miracle!" others agreed and jumped up in jubilation. Joining hands they began dancing around the bonfire. "At last we're free of Martu! We're free! Free!"

Tiras scanned the ecstatic faces lit by the fire. Exultation filled him. It was as though El had given him prophetic visions to enthrall the tribe. Smiling, he motioned his kinsmen to sit. Eagerly they knelt on their prayer rugs and waited for Tiras to continue. He explained how El had created man from dust, making his creation in El's own Bedouin image, and calling him Adham, the first man. He explained how the first woman, Evewah, had been created from one of Adham's ribs.

"Tell us more!" the tribesmen shouted.

"El placed his creations in a paradise called Eden. The most magnificent oasis. It overflows with fragrant flowers, mimosas, and tasty fruits."

A tribesman called out, "Where is the Oasis of Eden?"

Tiras pointed toward the twinkling windows of El's heavenly home. "There, high up in the sky. So that El can see everything we do. But He can hear our prayers and pleas for help. No longer are the twinkling lights the star goddesses. They're the windows of El's magnificent home in Eden. "

Another tribesman called out, "How come people no longer live there?"

"Because Adham ate from the Tree of Knowledge," Tiras explained to his eager listeners. "Eating from this special tree was forbidden so that El's creations wouldn't uncover His secrets and spoil them."

A tribesman asked, "But why did Adham disobey El and eat something forbidden?"

Tiras paused a moment, thinking, and remembered how he'd envisioned the story with Shallah's help. He described how Adham and Evewah ate the forbidden fig because of the serpent, Lotan, and so were banished from the paradise of Eden. "Like a dutiful father, El disciplined his creations," Tiras concluded. "We must always follow His instructions. He knows what's best for us."

The men whispered among themselves, amazed and captivated by the explanation. They nodded at Tiras to continue. They ignored the priest scowling by the stone altar.

"Hear me, my kinsmen," Tiras continued. "If we live a moral life, El promises eternity in His peaceful Oasis of Eden. Messenger

Bernadette Miller

gods with wings will fly the righteous there. But dead sinners will be flown down to Jahannam, the fiery netherworld, where Be'elsebub will burn them forever."

"Tiras, tell us more," Ruach begged.

"Yes, more!" others shouted.

It had grown late. Soon the moon would greet the horizon. Tiras said, "Tomorrow I'll continue explaining. Now it's time to rest with our wives and children."

Abu-Summu, as if awakening from slumber, shrieked, "Martu hasn't fallen into the netherworld! He'll punish all of you for your blasphemy. Raise havoc with your loved ones! Your wives and children will sicken and die! You'll see! Martu has spoken!"

Tiras shook his head at the priest. He said gently, "El guides me in all I tell you. He speaks through me."

Ruach rose. "Let's rejoice that El defeated vicious Martu. Tomorrow we'll hear more about merciful, El Who will never abandon us as long as we're faithful to Him."

The men gathered up their rugs and made their way back to their tents. They chatted excitedly about the new God offered by Tiras.

Abu-Summu stumbled over the sand, the horns cradled in his arms, his face flushed with anger. "Martu will return!" he shouted before entering his tent. "You'll see!"

CHAPTER 15

May, 3499 B.C., Arabiyah
(The Uplands in northern Saudi Arabia)

ALL DAY WHILE TENDING HIS flock, and many hours at night while Na'amah lay asleep, Tiras continued adapting the Sumerian stories for his tribe. Once, while squatting in the ma'gad, he stared through the open tent flap and recalled a Sumerian poem about a man who suffered despite living a blameless life. Tiras agreed it was unjust, but couldn't find any significance for his tribe.

"Shallah, I need you," he said. "Please come to me." Now that he had El's help, he wasn't sure whether his daughter would appear. Suddenly he imagined her slipping down toward his tent. He beamed with satisfaction.

"I heard you, baba," she said, hovering beside him. "I know what the poem means."

"Yes?"

"El is testing mankind to discover if a good man remains loyal even when facing hardship."

"Ah, that must be the answer," Tiras replied. Shallah was so wise. "Suppose a man who knew good fortune most of his life suddenly suffers. Should he then turn against his Creator?"

"No," she said. "In gratitude for the gift of life, he must abide by the fate the Creator gives him."

Tiras nodded. With Shallah's help, he would finally uncover all of the meanings that flowed from El through the Sumerian stories, like the Great Flood.

He pondered its significance one afternoon as he rested on a flat rock with his shepherd's crook. Shallah appeared and he related how Inanna, the Sumerian goddess of love, was mocked by a human. Furious, she caused the Euphrates and Tigris rivers to overflow and flood the Earth. Only worthy King Ziusudra and his family were saved by building an ark shared by pairs of animals.

When he finished, Shallah replied slowly, "Maybe our God would flood the Earth as reprisal for man's wickedness."

"Exactly!" Tiras said, satisfied that his faith in his daughter hadn't been misplaced. "But instead of the Sumerian King Ziusudra," he said, continuing to fashion the answer to suit the tribe, "our God would save a pious tribesman, No'amah. Men, women, and animals would again flourish on Earth. That way, El's creation wouldn't be entirely destroyed."

Shallah nodded.

He focused on his daughter floating beside him. "Maybe, my darling, you can help me understand justice. When I was a child, our tribe murdered everyone at Al-Ubiyah Oasis because one person there murdered my brother Loban. Was that fair punishment? According to the Sumerians, a sly human gardener once crept upon Lady Inanna who lay asleep in a garden. Awakening, she discovered the blood from her maiden head and grew furious. Unable to find the rapist, she punished Sumer with plagues. Wells dripped blood over the palm groves. Violent storms battered the flowering fields. A horde of locusts overran the land."

He finished with a sigh and looked at Shallah.

"Like a father, El must discipline his disobedient children," she reminded him. "But He reserves severe punishment, such as plagues, for only the worst crimes."

"Ah, that must be so!" Again pleased by his daughter's helpful response, he thanked her and rose. "Now I must prepare another sermon for the tribe."

ೞ ೪

During the following moon-cycles, Tiras described to his kinsmen the story of the Great Flood. He explained how El once sent horrific plagues to sicken unredeemable sinners. "That's why we must obey Him," he continuously warned his wide-eyed listeners. And he reminded them that if they avoided evil deeds, like human sacrifice, they'd be richly rewarded with long life, prosperity, and an afterlife in Eden.

Abu-Summu, as usual, disputed Tiras's sermons. During a pause, he shouted, "Insulting Martu is evil! Denying his great power is more evil! Our jealous bull-god will take revenge. He'll crush all of you. Great Martu has spoken!"

The worshippers, irritated by Abu-Summu's intermittent threats, frowned and motioned for Tiras to continue. Since Martu hadn't harmed them, the priest's warnings had become tiresome. Fascinated by Tiras's unusual stories, the men insisted on hearing his sermons.

But Tiras became troubled at preaching about good and evil. After all, hadn't he abandoned sweet Majeena in Sumer after swearing he'd return for her? He kept reproaching himself. Even though a moral path was best for his kinsmen, how could he persuade them to follow it after he himself had sinned?

One night, just before dawn, he decided to trust in El's commands on how to atone for his sin. El would guide him and the way would be clear.

During many sermons, Tiras ignored the priest's ranting and repeated that El was the only true God Who loved them, like a caring father. Naturally, he emphasized, El expects obedience and loyalty in return. He hoped his kinsmen's terror of the bull-god would fade into vague memory, and be replaced with gratitude and love for their benevolent El.

৪০ C৪

Abu-Summu wasn't alone in refusing to accept Tiras's mutinous idea. Na'amah brooded that her son might still feed a blazing pyre. In her mind she kept picturing her beloved child screaming in agony while she wept at her helplessness. Finally, she approached Tiras during supper while Rimush played on the carpet. The boy dragged his wooden donkey bought by his father in Sumer.

"How can you be certain that El is powerful enough to replace Martu?" Na'amah asked. "Don't you feel Abu-Summu's rage which grows daily? He'll find a way to convince the tribe to sacrifice our son. Please, husband—"

"Na'amah, have faith in me," Tiras interrupted. He put down the bowl of rice with meat drippings. "I've spoken with El. I've witnessed His greatness. I'm certain He'll deliver us from vicious Martu."

"So you no longer care how I appeal to you?" she burst out, her voice rising in hysteria. "You stubbornly defy a powerful god bent on punishing us. Martu will devour our beloved Rimush, my only child." She burst out sobbing.

The little boy stopped playing and ran to his mother. "Oomah! oomah!" She bent to kiss his cheek.

Tiras leaned over and hugged his son. "Na'amah, please don't cry for Rimush. He won't satisfy Martu's appetite. I promise."

Rimush grabbed his father's arm. "Baba, please don't let Martu eat me," he wailed.

Na'amah lifted her head, her eyes damp, and turned to Tiras. "Can't you see what's happening? Our son is terrified. How can we promise him our protection? After our marriage I forsook my own god, Ca'adus, to worship Martu. Now, once again, I'm asked to exchange gods."

Tiras gathered his wife and son in his arms. "Martu, a beast, could never love you and Rimush like El, who created us in His own image. Unlike Martu, El doesn't punish slight offenses. Only vile ones."

But Na'amah, unable to conquer her panic, continually urged Tiras to yield to Abu-Summu and renounce El.

She finally followed him outside the tent one morning as he was leaving for the pasture, and put her hand on his arm. "Dearest husband, I want to believe you," she implored. "Every day, while tending chores, I try to convince myself that El is stronger than Martu. But how can I believe in your God, knowing our priest's determination to get revenge for rejecting Martu?" She picked up Rimush and held him in her arms. "Our son's life is at risk! Can't you see that?"

The little boy, shivering, turned to his father. "Baba, I don't want to be eaten," he whispered.

"No, my son." Tiras wiped away the tears cascading down Rimush's cheeks. He looked at his wife. "Na'amah, I'm offering you both a far better life. If only you could see how our happiness depends on denouncing Martu and worshipping El. How important this is for Rimush's future."

Still unconvinced about El, she sought Martu's help. While Tiras tended to his animals at the pasture and Rimush took his late afternoon nap inside the tent, Na'amah turned her gaze from the outdoor hearth and anxiously scanned the pale blue sky. Although she'd never seen the bull-god, she was certain he existed. Before Tiras began preaching about El, male visitors had often discussed Martu in hushed tones, warning each other to be careful not to offend their chief benefactor or suffer severe punishment. They'd also mentioned that Martu occasionally rested behind a cloud god.

"Oh, Martu," she prayed aloud as she gazed upward at a cloud, "please don't turn from us because of my husband's recklessness. I beg you to make him realize his folly and return his affection toward you. Please don't injure my dear family."

Each day she prayed to Martu without Tiras's knowledge, while still pleading with him to believe again in the bull-god.

Bernadette Miller

"Martu isn't our champion but a proven enemy!" he continually warned her. "We must never worship him again!"

Finally she appealed to Mashech, who replied, "I sympathize with your anxiety about Rimush, but you don't understand my son's mission." He bent to cuddle the curly-haired boy gazing up at him. "Tiras's speeches have inspired our tribe. He promised deliverance from a horrifying god who caused great misery among us. How can we close our ears to his urgent message? Na'amah, future generations will relate how Tiras became a great hero. Don't discourage him."

She sank onto a cushion, put her hands on her eyes, and burst into sobs. "So you, too, are blind to the horrible tragedy awaiting our family. What can I do to prevent it? Martu won't respond to my pleading. Tiras has turned our jealous bull-god away from us."

"Martu has never responded to our pleading," Mashech said softly. "But our new God will."

Na'amah continued beseeching Tiras to stop worshipping El and insulting Martu. Finally, Tiras reached out one evening to cup her face in his hands and said, "Without your faith, dear wife, I shall surely stumble and lose my way. How can I continue preaching when my beloved scorns my ideas? Should I again submit to Martu? A vicious god content only with hate and revenge for the slightest offense? Please believe in me. Like our kinsmen."

She sighed and bowed her head in resignation. "Tiras, you always had a rebellious spirit. The only tribesman who dared challenge our priest. Maybe that's why I love you." She paused and took his hands in hers. "Forgive me," she said gently. "I've ceased being a good wife. If the entire tribe can stifle their fears and accept El, why not the one closest to you?"

She smiled then to show her acquiescence and wrapped her arms about him. But her body quivered against his as if she still doubted El and had yielded only to please him. Later that night, they slept wrapped in each other's arms, at peace with their love. But Tiras knew that while the tribe slumbered in tranquility, Abu-Summu was awake, seething with rage, and planning revenge.

CHAPTER 16

WHILE THE TRIBE MIGRATED IN search of pastureland, Tiras continued preaching at the weekly ceremony. The spellbound tribesmen remained enraptured by his stories. Ecstatic at their acceptance of the new God, Tiras ignored Abu-Summu glowering by the altar. He hoped that the priest would tire of ranting and in time accept El as the tribe's true God.

Occasionally, Abu-Summu interrupted with comments like, "Martu will have his revenge! You'll see!"

Finally, during one ceremony, Ruach shouted back, "Martu can't strike our Tiras. The jealous bull-god is in Jahannam. Busy awaiting the wicked."

"That is so!" Mashech shouted in agreement.

"Martu bides his time," the priest retorted. "Our furious bull-god will strike down Tiras and the entire tribe for this blasphemy. Martu has spoken!"

Exasperated, Tiras said, "Evil Martu will never hurt us again! He demanded our children's lives but gave nothing in return. El conquered him."

"Conquered!" a tribesman repeated.

"Never again will we cringe in terror!" another shouted.

"Then, let's praise El because He loves us," a third called out.

They began chanting their loyalty, led by Tiras who gazed upward at El's home in the sky. The tribesmen demonstrated their allegiance differently to break with the past. Kneeling, they no longer bent their heads against their rugs in submission. Now, they rapidly bent their heads back and forth to show agreement with their new God's commands.

Later that night, sleeping beside his wife, Tiras had an ominous dream. Canah, his son with his former second wife, was dragged by a wolf behind a sand dune and eaten. Abada screamed it was Tiras's fault they had lost their little boy. Martu snatched the gift of a son that had been denied him. In the dream, Na'amah again grew anxious for Rimush. She begged Tiras to stop preaching about El. He refused. He awoke, his heart racing.

Dawn was slipping through the tent's weave. Na'amah lay peacefully beside him wrapped in their conjugal rug. Her forehead was smooth, free from worry. He pulled aside the rug and sat up, trying to understand his dream. Should he revert back to Martu or suffer the consequences? He shook his head, his jaw clenched in determination, convinced again that El will help overcome his lingering terror.

୫୦ ୧୫

Tiras continued preaching with renewed fervor. During one ceremony, when he paused, Mashech called out, "Son, how can we keep worshipping something nameless? El, meaning God, is not a name. Please tell us His name."

Tiras hesitated. Naming El might unclothe His mystery and diminish His grandeur, but the tribe needed a specific name to hold sacred. "I will reveal it," Tiras said, "when El reveals it to me. But afterwards tell only your children and grandchildren. Never except for very good reason utter the name aloud. That would be blasphemy." He paused. "Be patient. Our beloved El knows what's best for us."

The next afternoon, Tiras scrambled upon a tall rock. He looked skyward and cried out, "El, please tell me Your name so I can tell my kinsmen."

Arms upraised, he gazed at the cloud floating overhead. A cool breeze caressed his cheek. As if from a great distance he imagined a voice thundering from above.

"*I am that I am,*" El said.

Tiras nodded in awe, hesitant to prod El for further information, but he needed an explanation for the tribe. "Can't you reveal Your name to me?" he pleaded. "Our tribe adores You. But they insist on knowing Your name."

"*Then think on it,*" the voice thundered. "*You will arrive at an answer.*"

"I will think about it," Tiras promised, his heart racing.

Afterwards, he wrestled with possible names but couldn't decide. The name should be of the desert, like El. The Cana'ans had many gods: Moloch, god of fire, Sydyk, god of justice, Yam, god of the river, and Yarikh, the moon god. The list went on and on, as did the gods of the Amratis. Which name should he choose? He'd promised El and his tribesmen to uncover the secret.

ஐ௸

One morning, before breakfast, Tiras's former second wife suddenly opened the tent flap. Abada's heavy-lidded eyes looked wild. "Our son is gravely ill. We don't know what's wrong. Come to him."

Tiras and the mother rushed to her tent. Abada's husband watched as Tiras squatted beside his eldest son lying on a rug. Canah's skin had turned cherry red. The boy breathed with shallow gasps. His tiny heart beat rapidly. Tiras anxiously studied his son. A jinn must have invaded the once-sturdy body, draining away his life.

He couldn't expect the priest's help. Abu-Summu would sneer that Martu had his revenge at last.

Horror slashed at Tiras's heart. Martu had struck his family in revenge, just as Na'amah feared. He shook his head. No! The bull-god was in Jahannam, punishing dead sinners.

Tremulous with worry, Tiras bent over Canah. The child's breath exuded the smell of bitter almonds—poison! Somehow Abu-Summu had managed to poison his son, perhaps offering him food with finely-mashed almond pits.

He turned to Abada who was shivering with worry. "Remove his clothes," he said. "Place cool cloths on the boy's face. And feed him something sweet, like honey."

From behind the qata, she produced a goatskin of precious water. She dripped a few drops on a clean rag, wrung it out, and placed the compress on the boy's hot forehead. He moaned. His chest rose and fell with short breaths. Abada removed his clothes. His entire body was flushed. She rushed behind the qata to find a goatskin of honey. With her finger she smeared the honey inside the boy's mouth.

"Swallow," she said. He lay still with closed eyes. With her other hand, she pried open his eyes. "Canah, eat the honey."

He struggled to obey, his tiny jaws grinding at the food. "Oomah," he gasped. "I can't."

"Yes, you can. Swallow it!"

Canah swallowed and Tiras took the boy's limp hand. "You will heal, my son. El will drive out the evil spirit that possesses you. Listen to my voice. You will recover." He prayed silently. *Blessed El, please cure my son, I beseech You.*

He turned to Abada. "Keep feeding him more honey," he said, and left for the pasture. He soon returned with a basket of special herbs. He sprinkled some atop the honey, left the rest with Abada, and silently thanked Mah Ummia who'd taught him the art of healing.

He then headed toward Na'amah's tent, where he told her, his voice shaky, "My son was poisoned."

"So, Martu finally got his revenge," she said, looking up from the outdoor hearth where she baked bread-cakes. "He sickened your son, Canah, Now he'll come after Rimush." She buried her face in her hands and began crying. Rimush stopped playing nearby and ran to his father.

"Baba, will Martu eat me?" he said, shuddering.

"He won't!" Tiras held out his arms to the boy who snuggled against him. He turned to his wife. "Martu didn't poison Canah." Anger gnawed at his heart; Tiras tried to restrain it by stroking Rimush's curls. "He lacks any power to punish me for my supposed impiety. Canah was poisoned by mashed almond pits in his food. I'm convinced of it."

"Are you certain that Martu isn't guilty?" she asked, squatting near the blazing hearth.

When he nodded, she paused and stared up at the cloud gods. "Then what can we do about the priest? He'll always find ways to harm us." The smell of burning bread-cakes caught her attention. With wooden tongs, she transferred the cakes, blackened at the edges, from the glowing copper plate to clay bowls resting on the sand. The acrid smell lingered.

"How can we save our family?" Her brows furrowed in anxiety.

"Abu-Summu will harm anyone who opposes him," Tiras replied. "Only his banishment can save our tribe. But such a harsh sentence must come from our kinsmen, not me, their temporary priest. I'll discuss it with Ruach."

The following evening, while returning to camp with their flock, Tiras told his cousin what had happened.

As they tramped over the flat sand dotted with clumps of vegetation, Ruach's face darkened with anger. "Abu-Summu is guilty!" he shouted amidst the din of bleating sheep and baaing goats. "We should punish him!" He waved a fist. "I could kill him with my bare hands!"

"No," Tiras said. "Banishment is better. Let El decide whether Abu-Summu and his family should survive in the wilderness."

"I'll suggest it after worship," Ruach said, still scowling.

Tiras nodded and returned to Na'amah's tent. That night, lying

Bernadette Miller

beneath the rug with his wife, he rose, as usual, to squat at the tent flap and gaze upward at El's heavenly home. Again, he pleaded with El to cure Canah. Then, resting his bearded chin on upturned hands, he pondered a possible name for El to satisfy his kinsmen.

The hallowed name, or at least a part of it, should suggest benevolence—the opposite of Martu! The Amrati had a gentle moon god, Yah, who would inspire hope, but a tribal god also needed power. Otherwise, how could He crush all the other gods? Wait, he'd forgotten Wah, the Cana'ans' strong storm god. They formed a potent pair to increase El's influence. But maybe Yahwah sounded like childish babbling?

During the next ceremony, Tiras promised to reveal El's name. His hesitation seemed an eternity to the tribe. Finally, he said, "The name of our new god is... Yahweh."

Awed, the tribesmen whispered the name among themselves. "Yahweh... Yahweh is our god."

"But when speaking aloud," Tiras warned, "He is called El. Never reveal His real name to outsiders." He held out the six-pointed star around his neck. "Our tribal symbol will be El's symbol to show that we are His chosen people!"

Mashech called out, "As His chosen people, we'll confirm His existence by the six-pointed star!"

The others nodded solemnly. A tribesman yelled, "Let's thank El that Abu-Summu's threats no longer terrorize us!"

Tiras exchanged a glance with Ruach to remind him of their chat about the priest who clutched the bull horns.

"Banish Abu-Summu to the wilderness!" Ruach shouted. "He should be punished for his savage deeds, murdering our beloved children. He even tried to poison Canah with mashed almond pits."

The others agreed. "Banishment!" they yelled in unison.

The tribesmen jumped up. They rushed toward the former priest. He ran toward his tent, still clutching the horns, scurrying away like a desert rat. They laughed at the exiled priest and shouted after him.

"Abu-Summu, pack your tent!"

"Take your wives and children to the wilderness."

"Never threaten us again."

"Leave us in peace!"

Tiras watched with satisfaction. The tribe's fears had finally been vanquished, along with their priest.

He then told them the story of a holy tower called Bab-El. "It's surrounded by a fragrant garden and wooden gate entwined with carved flowers and rises to the sky. From the holy tower, El speaks to worshippers in different tongues so all might understand Him."

"Ah," the tribesmen said in awe and leaned forward to catch more of the wondrous tale.

"Can anyone see this tower?" Ruach asked.

Tiras nodded. "Yes, in the Sumerian city of Ur. But don't worry, my kinsmen. El is everywhere, most often in the desert. From our simple stone altar, He hears our prayers and pleas and will answer them."

It had grown late. The moon was half-way across the sky. Tiras ended his sermon by reminding the worshippers, "Obey only El. Do not worship other gods for they are false."

"We will obey only El!" the tribesmen echoed in unison.

As Tiras doused the bonfire with sand, the worshippers rose and chatted excitedly among themselves about Tiras's stories, El's secret name, and the priest's banishment. Finally, they gathered up their prayer rugs and began leaving.

Ruach spotted Abu-Summu riding a laden donkey away from the camp. His family trailed behind him with their donkeys. Ruach pointed at the travelers as they passed beyond the bonfire and shouted, "Abu-Summu, you're banished forever! Never dare to threaten us again!"

The priest turned toward the worshippers and glared at them. "I'll never stop seeking Martu, the only god I've ever known," he called out stubbornly. "I'm certain that someday the bull-god will reward my faithfulness by returning to protect me and my family." He spurred his donkey on and waved at his family to follow.

The tribesmen smiled in triumph as their former priest, provider of boundless misery, rode across the sand in disgrace. Behind him, children on donkeys rode with downcast eyes. Black-robed women with pinched lips walked beside them.

So, Tiras thought with satisfaction, his tribe's evil priest had finally been banished, but would the tribe approve his taking Abu-Summu's place? It was a big responsibility. If the tribe suffered, he'd be blamed. Still, only he could lead the tribe to El, their true god.

൪൪

When Mashech passed away in his sleep, Tiras, mourning his loss, was afraid that the tribesmen would think this was the work of Martu. But he convinced them that it was Mashech's old age that permitted him to die peacefully.

Several evenings later, an Elder stooped to enter Na'amah's tent during supper and said, "Tiras, the Council wishes you to appear at our meeting."

Tiras nodded, hopeful it was good news. He immediately accompanied the Elder to the large tent in the midst of the encampment. Inside, the new sheikh rose, having been elected since Mashech's passing. The sheikh motioned Tiras to stand before the Council squatting in a semi-circle.

"We've elected you our new priest as well as medicine healer," the sheikh said. "Your cousin Ruach and the husbands of your former wives will help to tend your flock to free you for your new duties."

Tiras beamed his gratitude: elected both the new priest and medicine healer! "I won't disappoint your trust in me," he said and returned to Na'amah's tent with the joyful news.

൪൪

Afterwards, he worked hard to justify the tribe's faith in him. He gathered herbs for the sick, prepared sermons for worship, and constructed a new stone altar for the weekly ceremony which now would involve only worship and not floggings or sacrifices. He also found time every evening to visit his sick son, Canah. Despite the boy's lingering illness, Tiras felt confident that El would respond to his pleas. Canah's strong, muscular body would be cured.

Finally, as if in answer to his prayers, Tiras rejoiced one day at seeing Canah sitting upright on the rug. The boy ate yoghurt. Still weak, he slowly set down his bowl with a slight shiver. His reddened cheeks had become tanned again.

He smiled at Tiras. "Baba, I think the evil spirit has gone."

Tiras rushed to embrace the boy. "El has cured you." He glanced at his former wife and her husband. "Remember how our El cured my son. Pray only to Him."

They smiled with gratitude and replied in unison, "We will."

ಬಌ

During the tribe's migrations, Tiras continued gathering herbs and experimenting with potions. Admiration grew for his cures, a sign that El had sanctioned him. But most important to Tiras was his devotion to El and his debt to the Sumerians for their wise ideas. He decided to name the ceremonial altar: the Ark.

"Like that ship that protected No'amah during the Great Flood," he told the tribe during a sermon. "Our Ark will protect us against the flood of foreign gods. A wooden ledge will span the cube's top. Atop the ledge, I'll place El's sacred symbol, the six-pointed star. My favorite donkey, Na'al, will transport the sacred ledge from pasture to pasture."

Despite the tribesmen's acceptance of the new religion, Tiras worried how to prove to them that they were indeed El's chosen people. One night, alone after a sermon, he squatted beside the altar

Bernadette Miller

and bowed his head in prayer. *El, please send a sign that the Abram tribe has been chosen by You.* In the desert, so quiet that he could hear his heart beating, he envisioned the answer suddenly thundering down upon him from an unseen but powerful presence:

"I shall test the Abram with a pledge in the form of a covenant. Their agreement to the covenant shall prove their loyalty to me. Then, I shall reward them, my chosen people, with their deepest desire—their own desert land. No longer will they pay tribute to others. The Promised Land will abound with lush pastures, fruits of every description, plenty of animals to hunt, and an endless supply of goat's milk and wild honey."

"A covenant," Tiras marveled. His breath caught in his throat. "Our own land of milk and honey," he added and smiled in wonder. The covenant was exactly what the tribe needed, he thought. Although the pious tribesmen remained loyal to El, doubts must linger as with any religion, but El knew what was best for them. The Promised Land! He closed his eyes and saw it vividly. Plentiful oases with sparkling lakes and lush pastures, palms dripping with sweet dates, tamarisk trees heavy with wild honeycombs, and the flocks surging in numbers. Surely in their own Promised Land the tribe would prosper.

Excited about the forthcoming covenant, Tiras repeated El's promise to the tribe. "Then, when we consent to the covenant," he explained, "El will provide our own desert land. A flourishing valley, overflowing with goat's milk and wild honey. Never again must we pay tribute to others! In that Promised Land our tribe shall increase by vast numbers. Our one true God shall bless us, His chosen people. We'll enjoy good health, long life, and prosperity."

Transfixed in rapt attention on their prayer rugs, the Abram tribesmen shouted, "We shall obey El! And teach our descendants to obey! El has chosen us! We eagerly await the covenant."

CHAPTER 17

April, 3499 B.C., Sumer

IN UR, UNANNA HAD BEGUN complaining of nausea and vomiting. Dumuzi fetched the midwife who washed her hands in beer, reached under the bed coverlet to probe inside Unanna's womb, and confirmed her first pregnancy. Upon the discovery, Unanna wanted to convert her father's former bedroom into a nursery. She circled the room one morning, debating where to put a cradle.

"Adda would have wanted this," she told her husband who watched from the curtained doorway. "His spirit will guard our child from the demon galas. Those horrible ghosts of the unburied dead will never harm our son."

"Let's choose a name," Dumuzi said.

Unanna laughed. "That isn't difficult. It's Enki. Like adda's birth name."

"And if it's a girl?"

Unanna flinched. "No. It will be a boy. His spirit moves inside me." She paused and said softly, "My father died because of me. I can't replace him, but I can name my son after him."

"Whatever pleases you, beloved."

"For dinner, perhaps fish stewed with garlic? And yoghurt with figs?"

"That's fine."

"But no beer. You're drinking too much."

"I'll drink water."

"Good." She left to find Majeena to supervise the meal preparation.

&)(&

Dumuzi sat on the edge of Mah Ummia's bed. He pressed his hand against his bare chest. For the past several months he'd felt occasional stabbing pain in his chest. He'd secretly visited the physician tending Unanna's pregnancy. The physician agreed not to burden her with additional concerns. Neither potions nor poultices helped. Unable to discover the cause of Dumuzi's illness, the physician prescribed beer to ease the pain and advised his patient to entreat his personal god for a cure.

Upon rising and before retiring to bed, Dumuzi prayed in the small chapel beneath the staircase. Kneeling on a cushion, he cleansed his body with oil and gulped beer from a copper cup. He placed his god's statuette in the wall niche, bowed, and chanted supplications. Still, the pain persisted, but Dumuzi didn't want to worry Unanna. She happily purchased nursery furniture and ordered the slaves to weave baby dresses. Surely his illness would disappear as mysteriously as it had appeared, he reasoned. If not, they could worry about it after their child's birth. Meanwhile, he should discover what had angered Lord Enlil, god of the air. Perhaps Lord Enlil was jealous that he'd begun favoring Lord Enki, god of wisdom, his wife's personal god.

He tried to reassure Lord Enlil that he remained the god's faithful servant. He bent before the wall niche. *Dear Lord Enlil,* he silently prayed, *I must show favor to my wife's personal god. But inside my heart, my allegiance belongs to you. I beg you not to forsake me.* To make sure the god didn't doubt his sincerity, he donated food and personal belongings to the chapel, such as, leather sandals, a woven shawl, and a gold dagger.

Unfortunately, Unanna discovered him one day begging Lord Enlil to heed his prayers. Pausing in the doorway, she confronted her husband. Her dark eyes glared with rage. Her hands rested on broadened hips. "Dumuzi, why are you deliberately provoking me? You know that Lord Enki has been my family's god for generations. Should I invite his revenge by appealing to another god? Should we bring catastrophe upon our home?"

Dumuzi, still on his knees, was confounded by the turn of events. He stammered, "I...I had no intention...of upsetting you. Please... calm yourself. Henceforth, I'll pray only to Lord Enki. The matter should be of no consequence. It's...already forgotten."

Calmed, she approached him and he rose to embrace her. "Ah, you're a sweet husband, Dumuzi," she murmured in his arms. "You always try to make me happy."

He sighed. "My life's mission."

After his attempts at appeasing Lord Enlil ceased, Dumuzi's pain subsided. He concluded that his wife had been correct. He shouldn't have returned to Lord Enlil whose concern for him had fled. As Unanna's pregnancy grew, Dumuzi became more attentive. He temporarily excused himself from teaching at the Edubba to care for his distracted wife who seemed to need him every moment. During the day she had strange urges. A slave found her wandering outside with nobody to help her. She would hold her swollen belly as though she couldn't comprehend why she'd lost her youthful figure. She craved unusual foods, such as: fresh dates stewed with garlic, or apples baked with sea brine.

She ordered Majeena, "Sleep on a straw mattress outside my bedroom door in case I have sudden needs."

"Yes, mistress," Majeena said. Having gained considerable weight herself, she found it awkward to sleep on the floor mattress and preferred a bed. Nevertheless, after the lit lanterns were extinguished and the night god clothed the house in his dark mantle, she lay down on the mattress with effort. In the morning, she rose, grunting, as she grabbed at the plastered wall for balance.

At first, her weight had caused no alarm, simply curiosity as to why she'd developed all that fat. Unanna shrugged it away. She was probably overeating to compensate for worry about the responsibility of rearing her mistress's child.

After another month, the slave's condition became plain. She was pregnant.

Unanna was indignant, immediately aware that Tiras had to be the father. "So your lover, Tiras, betrayed you."

Majeena stared at the courtyard's brick-paved floor. "I'm not sure, mistress."

Unanna's finger stabbed the air. "You've lain with so many men, you don't know the father?"

"No...only one."

"Then it must have been Tiras!"

Majeena pouted. She refused to confirm the culprit. She stared in stubborn determination at the floor.

"Majeena, tell us," Unanna urged. "You won't be punished."

Tears clustered on Majeena's cheeks. "I still love him. I can't say his name."

Unanna's heart was moved. "Majeena, we'll take care of you and the baby. But we must know the truth. If it's Tiras, as I'm sure it is, we won't punish you. It would be impossible to find him in the desert and bring him back for trial. I promise that your secret will be safe with us. It's Tiras, isn't it?"

Majeena hesitated. She finally whispered so low they could barely hear her. "Yes."

Unanna flew into a rage. Her fist jabbed the air. "That damned desert rat! After all that my adored father did for him. First, Tiras stole your virginity. Then, he impregnated you and abandoned you. If given the opportunity, I'd strangle the accursed man!"

"But, mistress, you said my secret would be safe—"

"Yes, yes, of course," Unanna interrupted impatiently. "You may stay here and raise the child. But remember, it will be a slave like yourself. When it grows up, it must do our bidding. It will never lack for food, clothing, or shelter."

Majeena burst out sobbing. "Mistress, I'm grateful for your generosity. I'm sorry for causing trouble. Please forgive me." She kissed the hem of Unanna's dress.

Unanna bent and patted Majeena's head. "That's enough. Stop crying. You and your child are safe here. But if Tiras ever tries to see you again, tell us immediately."

"Yes, mistress," Majeena said, although she had no such intention. She left to supervise the menu according to Unanna's wishes.

Unanna pressed her hand against her forehead and sank onto a chair. She wearied from the stress about Majeena's pregnancy.

Dumuzi, ignoring his own sudden pain, rushed to his wife's side. "Are you ill? Can I get you anything?"

"No, don't worry." Unanna relaxed in his arms. She pressed his hand against her swollen stomach. "Feel our son kicking inside me."

He kissed her cheek. "A fine boy it will be. Exactly what you want." Then, without warning, he collapsed on the floor. His bearded face was deathly pale.

She screamed for Majeena who came running, lumbering along as fast as possible despite her added weight. "Hurry!" Unanna said. "Send for the physician. My husband's sick."

At Majeena's orders, slaves rushed to the inert Dumuzi. One ran to fetch the physician. Two slaves carried him upstairs to the conjugal bed, followed by Unanna. He didn't move.

"Dumuzi, what's wrong?" Seated by the bed, Unanna touched his face. It looked drained of blood as if by the demon galas. "Dumuzi, can you hear me?" She prayed to Lord Enki, hoping to revive her husband, and finally to Lord Enlil. She reproached herself for forcing

Bernadette Miller

Dumuzi to switch his loyalty. Perhaps Lord Enlil had crushed Dumuzi in a jealous rage. Her entreaties to both gods came too late.

After examining Dumuzi, it took only a moment for the physician to declare with a grave expression, "I'm sorry. Your husband is dead. He's been ill for months but I wanted to spare you from worry."

Stunned, Unanna embraced the limp body. "Oh, Dumuzi, my love," she whispered. "I've lost you forever." She laid her head on his chest and tried to coax the husband who'd always obeyed her wishes. "Don't leave me, dearest. Come back from the netherworld. Come back to help raise our son..."

The physician gently pried Unanna from the limp form. "Lie down for a while," he urged. "You need rest for the baby's sake."

Unanna, still in a state of shock at losing her husband, responded vaguely. "Yes, perhaps I should." The physician left and she staggered to an adjoining bedroom but couldn't sleep. She lay awake on the bed, reproaching herself. What more could she have done to save Dumuzi? It was all her fault for causing Lord Enlil's wrath to fall upon their household. If only she hadn't forced him to switch loyalty to Lord Enki.

ဆာ ၈၃

Unanna gave birth to a sickly girl who couldn't nurse at her mother's breasts due to insufficient milk. After delivering her own baby, a healthy boy, Majeena nursed both children. She marveled that her son bore the same birthmark on a shoulder: a brownish fig shape, as had Tiras, his father.

Unanna took no interest in her offspring. "My slave bears a handsome son while I bear an ugly girl," she told Majeena in the courtyard. "Look at those squinty eyes! Those wispy curls! How can I love her?"

"I'm truly sorry, mistress," Majeena said. She bowed her head over the babies cuddled against her large breasts. "I'll care for your daughter as if she were my own."

"See that you do, slave woman," Unanna said. "In sympathy with your condition, I've allowed you to call your son, Abram, after Tiras's tribe. But understand that Abram will grow up in slavery. Uneducated. As ignorant as his detestable father who took advantage of an innocent girl."

"Yes, mistress," Majeena said placidly, hiding her emotions.

Unanna scowled. "And no father to guide Abram. I'm sure Tiras will never return."

"He will return," Majeena replied, clinging to hope.

"Never!" Unanna shot back. "But even if he does, I wouldn't allow him inside my father's house. I despise him for betraying adda's trust." She paused to calm herself. "Instead of the slave quarters, sleep in the upstairs nursery. So you can hear the babies' crying at night. You have full charge of rearing both children."

"Yes, Mistress," Majeena said and smiled at the two small bodies hugged against her breasts.

Unanna looked with contempt at her tiny daughter in Majeena's arms. A bad luck omen that brought misfortune, she thought. It caused the loss of her beloved Dumuzi. If she hadn't been pregnant, demanding so much attention, she would have noticed her husband's weakening condition and perhaps saved him. "You're dismissed," Unanna said and returned to her bedroom to rest.

৪০ ৫৪

Since Unanna had no interest in her daughter, even refusing to name her, Majeena called the child, Nammu, after the goddess of sweet waters and mother of Lord Enki. Caring for both children, she watched them grow side by side, playing in the nursery and courtyard while she spun wool, tottering about in the garden while she picked flowers for the balcony urns, and whispering secrets in the kitchen while she supervised the cooking. Although Unanna didn't allow her daughter to play with the other slaves, Nammu and Abram were together since birth due to her care. Running through the house, they played hide and seek, tag, or wrestled.

By age seven, Abram knew he was a slave, inferior to Nammu who someday would become his mistress. Majeena trained him to be respectful toward her. "Remember, Nammu isn't as strong as you. She's frail, has poor eyesight, and might fall. Be careful not to harm her when you play. And let her win all the games. Understand?"

He scratched at his genitals under the loincloth and asked his mother, "Ama, why am I a slave and Nammu isn't?"

Majeena stopped cutting up a lamb carcass on the brick table. She wiped her perspiring brow with her robed elbow. "That's the way Lord Enki made us. I'm sure the blessed god had a good reason, just as there's a reason for animal sacrifice." She wagged a finger. "Stop scratching your zibbinu. Our mistress wouldn't like that in front of Nammu. You must always try to please her."

Abram nodded; his hands dropped to his side. "Why do you call it a zibbinu? That doesn't sound Sumerian."

Majeena sighed. "It's from your Bedu father."

"Where is he? Why isn't he here?"

Majeena's brow knotted. She knew this question would arise as Abram grew older. "Tiras had to return to his tribe in the desert, but he'll come back."

"When?"

"That I don't know. Just have faith, like me."

Abram watched his mother quarter the lamb with a sharp knife. "What's Lord Enki's reason for making us slaves?"

She shook her head. "Nobody knows the gods' purposes. We're here to serve their needs. As slaves serve their masters."

"Ama, I don't like being a slave. I want to be free like Nammu to do whatever I like."

Majeena sighed. "Every day you seem more and more like your father. Even your birthmark is like your father's. Abram, you must accept the truth. As long as you live in Sumer you're a slave unless you buy your freedom. But for a slave, shekels are hard to come by."

"Suppose I find a way to earn them? I could buy my freedom then. And find my father."

She continued chopping the lamb for stew. "That's a big dream, son. I still miss Tiras after all these years. But we must accept whatever Lord Enki sends us. Why burn with ambition for a life we aren't destined to have?

Abram silently disagreed. It wasn't his fault he'd been born into slavery. Why should he be satisfied with nothing? Lord Enki was unfair. There must be a way to free himself.

In the courtyard Nammu called out, "Abram, where are you? Let's play hide and seek."

Majeena wiped her hands. She hugged Abram and kissed his downy cheek. "Go to her, son." She pushed him playfully toward the kitchen entrance.

He nodded, sulking, and left to join Nammu, but soon they ran about upstairs: Nammu to hide and Abram to find her. She crouched behind a balcony urn.

"I found you," he said, squatting beside her.

"You always find me, Abram. How do you know where I hide?"

He laughed. "You always choose the same place!"

"Well, tomorrow, I'll hide somewhere else." She looked up at him. "Will you always find me, Abram? No matter where I hide? Will you always look for me? Please promise you will."

"I promise, Nammu."

Her thin lips widened into a smile. Her gaunt face lit up. Her squinty eyes shone. "I love you."

"I love you, too," he said solemnly.

"Then give me a hug."

He embraced the little girl in her tufted gown. She laid her head on his bare shoulder. "Ama never hugs me," Nammu whispered. "She only talks to me when she wants me to do something. I wish Majeena were my mother."

"Me, too," he said. He felt saddened by Unanna's neglect.

"Promise you'll never leave me."

"I promise," he said and turned away with a frown. A mistress could do whatever she pleased. Not slaves. But Nammu seemed so alone except for Majeena and himself. Nammu needed him.

৪০ ৪৩

Having no other playmates, the children became inseparable. Whenever Nammu became ill, Abram stayed by her bedside. He held her hand and encouraged her to get well. He visited the small chapel beneath the balcony stairs and asked Lord Enki to cure her. Whenever she became burdened by her mother's demands, and hated herself after Unanna called her an ugly cow, Nammu turned to Abram for comfort.

"You're not ugly," he reassured her. "I love you. So how can you be ugly?"

"You always make me feel better, dear Abram." She kissed his hand. "I pray to Lord Enki to keep you safe."

"And I pray to Lord Enki to keep you well," he responded.

Consequently, when reaching thirteen, Nammu refused to consider the young suitor selected by her mother. Instead, she planned to marry Abram someday and run off without Unanna's blessing. She schemed how to approach him about marriage.

৪০ ৪৩

Abram, however, didn't return Nammu's passion, only brotherly affection. Lying on his bed in the slave quarters, his head propped on his arms, he pondered his destiny. He wanted to free himself and his mother from bondage and then search for his father in the desert. But then, he'd have to explain his plans to Nammu, and feared that moment. Will she still love me, he wondered? Will she let me go?

CHAPTER 18

October, 3496 B.C., Arabiyah
(Al-Nefud Desert in northern Saudi Arabia)

WHEN TIRAS'S YOUNGER SON, RIMUSH, had turned ten, Na'amah caught him planning to run away as an adventure in the dangerous Nefud Desert. She'd rolled over beside Tiras when she heard whispering and thumping. She lifted her portion of the rug, careful not to awaken him as he slept soundly from exhaustion. Curly-haired Rimush and his eleven-year-old brother, Canah, the son of Abada, were dragging stuffed goatskin sacks toward the opened tent flap.

"What!" Na'amah exclaimed. She grabbed her son by his sheepskin cloak. "In the middle of the night you sneak off with Canah," she whispered to avoid awakening her husband. She shook a finger at the older boy, who stood by the flap. "Always getting into trouble, Canah. Now you make trouble for my son. Your mother will punish you for this! She shouldn't abide such behavior."

Canah stuck out his tongue in impudence and ran off with his sack to Abada's tent where he lived.

Na'amah bit her lip in exasperation. She persuaded Rimush to return to his rug and sleep. To spare Tiras additional concern, she kept silent about the incident.

Early the next morning, Tiras's former second wife, Abada, arrived at Na'amah's tent. She frowned as she paused with her son. At the outdoor hearth, Na'amah used a wooden stick to stir a kettle of rice for breakfast. When she looked up, Abada said, "You should learn to forgive a child's foolish pranks. You know how children are. Or maybe you were too righteous to be a child," she added, glancing at Rimush staring at her.

As Abada's frown deepened, the mole beside her nose seemed to darken; her heavy eyelids drooped lower, shielding the bleary pupils.

"You're an ugly wife who didn't deserve Tiras!" Na'amah exclaimed. Rising, she wiped her hands on her robe and spat on the sand. "You'd better warn Canah to leave my Rimush alone. Or there'll be trouble you can't handle."

"Trouble? Huh!" Abada spat on the sand. "We'll just see who can't handle it!" She reached over and pulled Na'amah's thick braid.

"Kara!" Na'amah yelled and jumped up. She pulled off Abada's shawl and grabbed the thin hair spreading over her shoulders.

The boys rushed to their mothers' defense.

"Leave my oomah alone!" Canah yelled, pulling at Na'amah's arms.

Rimush started pummeling Abada's back. "Baba will punish you for hurting my oomah!"

Finally awakened, Tiras rushed from Na'amah's tent. "I demand peace between you!" he said, glaring at the two women wrestling with each other. They sprang apart. The boys, tired, dropped to the sand.

"Abada, since you divorced me, I have no obligation to you," Tiras said sternly. "Go back to your tent. Take care of our Canah."

He turned to Na'amah. "You must stop fighting and causing a commotion." He took Rimush's hand. "Come, son," he said gently and led him inside.

Rimush turned to grin at Canah. The boy, walking with his mother toward her tent, swiveled to scowl at Rimush.

                        ೲ ೞ

Tiras resolved to end the rivalry between Na'amah and Abada. He pondered the problem the following night as he sauntered past the young married men gathered as usual before a tent belonging to one of their wives. They drank fermented date wine and gossiped about the latest divorces, marriages, and births while their wives and children rested inside their tents. Tiras smiled at them, although his day had been exhausting. He'd helped to tend a sick ewe whose stomach swelled with her unborn lamb. Then, he'd prepared in his mind more sermons, and now he was worried about his wives and their squabbling.

A tribesman shouted behind Tiras, "You still won't sit with us?"

Tiras turned toward the young men with their flowing braids and straggly beards. They sat on the sand with legs outstretched and held cups of wine. "My head is heavy with important thoughts. Perhaps the next time."

"Perhaps you dream of another wife?" one man said. "A beauty who can settle your family's arguments." He laughed before refilling his cup from a terracotta jug.

Tiras sighed. "I've separated from two and still can't keep them content."

Another man called out, "Keep Na'amah happy. The others will find ways to pleasure themselves with their new husbands."

The men howled with laughter.

When they quieted and drank more wine, the first one added with remorse, "Please forgive us, Tiras. You're our great priest who brought us good fortune but we make fun at your expense. You see us acting silly from too much wine. No offense."

Tiras smiled. "Forgiveness granted." He continued walking. "Salaam, 'alaykum," he called out as the men resumed talking.

"'Alaykum, salaam," the men responded. One of the men added, "Stay well and prosper. We're looking forward to your joining us again."

Tiras nodded and continued toward Na'amah's tent, still

preoccupied with keeping peace among his wives and children. As a respite from his troubles, he returned to preparing a sermon for the weekly ceremony. The story should illustrate a moral in obeying El's commands: perhaps how El created man in His Bedouin image and so expected worthy behavior. Or, how the Abram tribe had been especially chosen by El to follow Him. Or the enormous flood that El sent to punish the wicked, except for pious No'amah and his family. There were so many to choose from.

At Na'amah's tent, he squatted outside to think. Despite Abu-Summu's threats, the tribe had flourished. Their children were healthy. Their animals grazed at lush pastures from plentiful rain. The Abram owed a great deal to El for their prosperity. But what about the covenant?

As always when ending a sermon, Tiras urged his tribesmen, "Don't forget about the covenant and El's great reward of our own land if we obey His commands."

"But when will the covenant arrive?" a tribesman had finally asked at the last sermon, echoing Tiras's growing concern.

Another said, "Yes, please ask El when we might receive the covenant."

Tiras sighed. "Be patient, my kinsmen. El will send it at the right time. Only He knows what's best for us."

Since the former priest's banishment, Tiras had continually warned the tribesmen to obey El to gain their promised land. Despite his reassurances, they still questioned when the covenant would arrive. In addition, he worried that the war raging between his two wives, Na'amah and Abada, might infect his sons.

༄༅

Suddenly, Tiras's fears about his children exploded into reality. Strong, husky Canah attacked slim Rimush. He'd caught Rimush alone behind Na'amah's tent while she collected firewood with the other women at a sand dune. Rimush was patting the donkey, Na'al, and whispering secrets into his bristled ears. Canah, smiling, approached Rimush and punched him in the nose while the donkey brayed in alarm. "You'd better not tell or I'll beat you harder!" Canah warned, and left the weaker boy bloody and running to Na'amah in tears.

Rimush blamed it on an accident, dreading more of Canah's attacks if he told the truth. "I ran into an abal bush," he blubbered.

Na'amah stopped gathering the dry, shallow roots of shrubs from a sand dune's base and anxiously examined the wound. Then, sighing, she balanced the sack of firewood on her head and took his hand. "Come, son. I'll take care of it."

They returned to her tent where she unloaded the firewood outside. From a goatskin sack hanging against a tent wall, she dripped a few precious drops of water on her son's wound and with a cloth wiped off the blood.

"Be careful, Rimush," she said. "Watch where you're going. Water is too precious to waste on carelessness."

"I'm sorry, oomah," he said. "I'll be careful."

The next day, after Canah and Rimush finished helping with the sheep shearing, Rimush headed toward Na'amah's tent. Canah approached his younger brother and spewed insults. "You're a weakling! A coward! Unworthy of being the son of a great priest!"

A few days later, Canah caught Rimush alone while heading toward the pasture. Rimush began to run but Canah was faster. He grabbed his younger brother and pummeled his back. "I'm Tiras's eldest!" he exclaimed. "You'd better follow my orders or be sorry!"

"I won't!" Rimush protested. Whimpering from the pain, he rubbed his aching back and fell to his knees. He looked up at his smirking older brother and said, "I'll tell baba. He'll punish you!"

"Yes, go and tell," Canah jeered. "The tribe will have to dig up the Nefud to find you!"

Frightened, Rimush kept silent about the encounters. He mumbled excuses to his exasperated mother. He fell. He bumped into a tree. A swarm of bees stung him. Finally, unable to bear the pain anymore, he waited one evening until Tiras left for the weekly sermon. Rimush watched his mother busy weaving, and burst out, "It's Canah's fault. He keeps beating me and insulting me."

Na'amah turned scarlet with rage. She jumped up from the carpet and embraced her son. "Baba and I will keep him from hurting you."

That night when Tiras returned to Na'amah's tent after worship, he found her clenching her hands in agitation, her cheeks glistening with tears. "Canah is beating our son," she told Tiras. "He's full of bruises. He kept blaming it on accidents. Tonight, he finally told the truth." She turned to Rimush cowering in a corner. "Come here. Show your father."

Rimush walked slowly to Tiras who examined his son's face. His chin had purpled. "Show more," Tiras said. Rimush opened his robe and pushed up the sleeves. His chest and arms were laced with reddened wounds. Tiras grew angry, not only at Canah but also at himself for missing what had been plainly happening in front of him.

He bent toward his son who trembled. "Did your brother do this?"

Rimush nodded. "But Canah said if I told you, he'd make it worse." He paused. "Baba, I'm afraid."

Tiras grimaced. "He beat you and then threatened you! I'll wait until he's fully awake tomorrow so he can pay close attention." He bent to embrace his son and hold him close. "Go to bed, Rimush. Don't worry. I promise he won't hurt you anymore."

The following morning after breakfast, Tiras strode to Abada's tent and saw Canah playing outside. The boy had slipped a pebble in his slingshot and was about to shoot at a bustard flying over a tamarisk tree when Tiras appeared, glaring at his son. Canah dropped the slingshot.

Tiras gripped his sturdy son's shoulders. "No more hurting your brother!" he warned. "Otherwise, you'll be severely punished. Do you understand?"

Canah bowed his head and mumbled, "Yes, baba."

That seemed to resolve the matter. After Tiras's warning, Canah

Bernadette Miller

no longer fought with Rimush. The brothers avoided each other but spoke politely at greetings to satisfy their father. When Canah reached fourteen, he wed a young girl from the Abram tribe and lived in her tent, as was the custom. When Rimush, the younger brother, reached fourteen, he wed Zillah, a petite girl from another tribe, but they stayed with the Abram.

Then, a year after his wedding, Rimush began growing a hump on his back—as if El wished to prove that Canah was right—the eldest son was the strongest and deserved to be Tiras's favorite. The hump had grown slowly. It started as a small ball of fat nestling against Rimush's narrow back. At first, his parents hadn't noticed. Since Rimush's wedding, they didn't see him as frequently.

One evening, Tiras shared supper with Rimush in Zillah's tent. He spotted the strange bloom atop his son's back. While Zillah was busy at the outside hearth, Rimush leaned over for a slice of goat cheese. His father cried out with alarm, "My son, what is that basket you're carrying on your back?"

Rimush had shrugged. "A blessing of extra flesh. I'm used to it." He laughed to mask his self-consciousness at his disfigurement, concerned that he would lose favor in his father's heart.

Tiras set down his bowl of stew. He leaned over and felt the lump. Rising, he ordered Rimush to remove his robes. There in plain sight a fleshy ball had grown between his son's shoulders. He touched the soft mound. "Does that hurt?"

"No, baba."

So, even from flaming Jahannam, Tiras thought, vicious Martu cursed his son with a deformity. His final revenge for being displaced by El, but his God must have a reason for all that happens. Tiras gazed into his son's pale brown eyes. "Rimush, never question El's purpose. He'll often test our faithfulness." He grasped the thin shoulders. "Obey His instructions and you'll always find peace."

"Baba, I'll never abandon El. I believe in Him with all my heart."

Tiras smiled, satisfied, and the men finished their supper.

৵ের

Rimush's troubles with his brother Canah hadn't ended. Although Canah loved his wife who soon became pregnant, he grew increasingly resentful toward Rimush. It seemed unfair that his father showed greater love for the younger son, rather than following the custom of granting it to the eldest. He schemed how to get revenge on Rimush and become their father's favorite.

CHAPTER 19

May, 3485 B.C., Sumer

O N HIS FOURTEENTH BIRTHDAY, ABRAM spent the night tossing on his straw mattress in the slave quarters. He pondered how to free himself and his mother from slavery so he could seek his father, Tiras, in the desert. Sumerian slaves could buy their freedom, but how could he accumulate enough shekels? The problem seemed insurmountable.

One afternoon, Abram visited Ur's bazaar, seeking herbs for his mistress's bath. Forced to wear his hated loincloth that identified him as a slave, he wound his way around rugs heaped with merchandise and stopped before a stall featuring cinnamon cakes with their intoxicating aroma. He fingered the coins in his palm. Occasionally his mother treated him to sweets after their mistress's dinner parties.

"Can you pay?" the vendor asked Abram. "If not, don't linger here." He came outside with a reed whisk and shooed Abram away. "Slave boys hanging around without shekels invite thieves!"

Someday, Abram promised himself, he'll be free and enjoy all the sweets he wanted, but for now, a cylinder of herbs required all his coins.

Nearby, an old woman whom he'd seen many times, sat on a rug, her legs stuck out. Tendrils of gray hair peeped out from under a shawl. In her lap, she wove flat reeds to form a basket. She looked up and smiled with toothless gums. "So, young man," she said, lisping. "Would you like to learn basket making?"

He nodded shyly. "Sit beside me," she said. "My name is Ashnan. What are you called?"

"Abram."

Ashnan nodded. "I'll make another one. My little son died many years ago. Sometimes I get lonely."

He squatted on the rug with his clay cylinders of herbs and watched her.

She picked up some marsh reeds. "First, form the basket base. Taper an end of some flat reeds, like this. Next, split a side piece and weave it among the others to form a flat square. Notice how I bent all the reeds along the outside so they stand up? Those are the spokes."

Abram, fascinated, watched her knobby hands swiftly weave the outer spokes forming the basket's sides. She tucked the top ends down into the basket and tugged at corner spokes so that the basket would rest nicely on its "feet" when placed on a table. She completed the basket handle.

"Basket making is satisfying work," she said as he admired it. "You can earn lots of shekels. I never tire of it."

He stared at her. *Earn lots of shekels!* "If I come back tomorrow," he said eagerly, "will you let me make one?"

"You're a nice boy. I'll teach you."

He thanked her and rushed home. Perhaps selling baskets could earn enough shekels to buy his and ama's freedom.

Three days later, after scrubbing Unanna's courtyard walls, he dashed to the bazaar and joined Ashnan, named after the grain goddess, who taught him to make baskets. After that, whenever the opportunity arose to purchase something at the bazaar, Abram volunteered so he could learn basket making and earn shekels. Ashnan corrected him when his basket base didn't form perfect little squares.

"You can't sell crooked baskets, my young friend," she said.

Abram shook his head in disgust at his stupidity.

Ashnan added, "You need patience. Learning is hard. But someday it will satisfy your desires."

"I'm anxious to learn. I ache to leave Ur and find my father."

"Ah, just as I suspected. You're ambitious. Well, let's work and see how fast your freedom comes."

For several weeks, the pair sat side by side making baskets and selling them to passing customers. Ashnan gave him food and a shekel for every twenty baskets he made and sold. At first, escaping to the bazaar twice a week, Abram could make only one good basket each day. Ashnan offered to increase payment as his skill improved and he sold more. He asked how much it would cost to buy his freedom.

"Ten shekels," she replied. "About the price of a donkey."

Abram began calculating. Ten shekels for himself. Ten for Ama. That makes twenty. Plus, a guide to find his father, and donkeys to carry the travelers and supplies. At least two hundred shekels. A huge sum! Maybe, after a few more years, he might have enough.

৳৹঄

Abram visited the bazaar as often as possible, improving his skills and earning more shekels. He stashed the coins in leather pouches beneath his bed in the slave quarters overlooking the back yard.

His mother finally questioned him about his absences while he mopped the kitchen floor. Where do you disappear to?" she asked, opening the beehive oven in the kitchen. "I hardly see you. If our mistress finds out that you're shirking your duties, she'll punish you. I won't be able to protect you."

"I'm trying to develop a business to earn money," he finally confessed to her. "Making baskets at the bazaar. An addub is teaching me. Ama, please don't tell anyone," he whispered. "Not even Nammu. I'd be punished."

Majeena frowned as she shoved platters of bread dough in the oven. "I don't like betraying my mistress's trust after she forgave me—" She broke off, then added, "She's arrogant, but good to us. She's given us food and shelter all these years. Never demanded more than we could accomplish." She sighed heavily. "All right, Abram, make your baskets. Save your shekels. Perhaps someday you'll be free."

"You, too, ama."

Majeena gazed toward the doorway. "No, I'll...stay here. Tiras might return." She paused as their mistress entered.

Unanna, now middle-aged and gray-haired like Majeena, resembled a heavy-set matron. Her cheeks were creased with wrinkles. Her former youthful beauty had vanished. Following the latest fashion, she wore a tufted gown with one shoulder bare. Majeena had parted her mistress's gray hair in the middle, brushed it into a long ponytail, and wrapped it about her head. Unanna had stopped wearing a headdress.

She turned to Majeena. "Prepare for a banquet in two days. We need to plan the menu. Abram may purchase the items at the bazaar."

"Gladly, mistress," Abram said, smiling.

Unanna glanced at him and turned to Majeena. "Good. But it might take him a while."

Abram's heart thumped with excitement. "Yes, mistress. I'll go as soon as the menu's decided."

Unanna looked at him sharply. "You're a bright little lad. Unlike my Nammu—" She turned abruptly and left.

When Abram returned to the bazaar the following day, he couldn't find the old woman, Ashnan. Perhaps she'd abandoned her business. Depressed, he bought the items ordered by Unanna. For a couple of weeks, Ashnan remained absent from the bazaar. Then, one afternoon when Abram had nearly lost hope, she reappeared on her rug. He rushed over and squatted beside her. His brows wrinkled with concern at her thin body, reddened face, and her left eye nearly shut.

"I'm sick," she said. "I can't continue making baskets." She pointed to a pile of reeds. "There are plenty. Collect more. The marsh Arabi don't mind. Use my bazaar rug and take over my business."

"Ashnan, I don't want to replace you. Please..."

"No, Abram, you're a good soul. Favored by Lord Enki."

"Lord Enlil," he corrected her. He'd adopted Dumuzi's personal god. Ama had often mentioned her former master's kind heart. "Thank you, Ashnan, for all you've taught me. I owe you much."

"Well, I'll leave you here. I need rest. Make your baskets, Abram, and earn your freedom." She rose with effort, grasping a wooden staff for balance, and tottered toward the exit.

He shook his head at his preoccupation with ambition. He'd never noticed her growing illness. He stared after her. Then, for two hours, he wove and sold baskets. Reluctantly he rolled up the rug containing leftover reeds and baskets. He stored the filled rug behind a thicket far from the road and carefully covered the mound with spiny brambles, hidden from curious eyes.

Seeing her son's contentment, Majeena allowed his business to continue despite her silent disapproval. Unimpeded, Abram developed his skills and acquired regular customers. The pouches under his bed became stuffed with shekels.

Nammu, however, refused to accept Majeena's feeble excuses for Abram's absences. At fourteen, Nammu was scrawny, her eyesight so poor she constantly squinted. Her small head was matted with wispy, black curls. During childhood, her devotion to Abram had increased to an obsession.

Finally, Unanna forbade her daughter to enter the slave's bedroom without her permission. "You're at a marriageable age with an excellent suitor waiting. I won't allow you to visit a boy in his room, particularly a slave." She waved a hand at her daughter's objections. "You've become a woman. Your playtime with Abram has ended. Have nothing more to do with him except as his mistress."

Nammu's cheeks scrunched up; her eyes welled with tears. "Mother, I can't—"

"You can and will!" Unanna interrupted. "Our discussion has ended." She paused. "And have Majeena do something with that horrible hair."

Nammu disobeyed her mother. The next day, she spotted Abram in the courtyard and ran to catch him as he hurried toward the balcony steps with a bucket and scrub brush. She touched his bare arm and whispered, "Abram, you seem to run every time I approach you. Why can't we chat like before?"

"I'm busy fulfilling chores and buying necessary items at the bazaar," he said, hoping to discourage her. "I'm much older now and don't have time to chat." He ran upstairs to prevent his mistress from discovering them together.

Then, another day, Nammu secretly sought Abram in the garden while her mother was attending a dinner. "Abram, what should I do about the suitor Mother provided?" she asked as he dumped a bucket of soil onto a flower bed. "I don't love him. I want to be with you."

He looked up and shook his head. "Nammu, I'm only a slave. I have no right to interfere with your mother's plans."

Her eyes filled with tears. "You've always guided me since our childhood. Who else can I turn to?"

"There's nothing I can do," he said and knelt with his spade to overturn the soil. He hated hurting her, but he had to stop her dependence on him. Unanna, enraged, might punish his mother as well as himself.

Nammu couldn't understand his rejection of her. The final blow came one evening after he'd returned from the bazaar and was resting in his room. She suddenly swept aside the doorway curtains.

Abram looked up, startled, his brows furrowed with worry. She shouldn't visit him here. If Unanna found out, she'd be furious and punish her daughter. And probably him, too.

Nammu rushed to his bed. She grasped his arm. "Abram, my feelings are so intense," she pleaded. "Surely you must reciprocate. How can you deny your passion?" Her body quivered.

"I do love you, Nammu," he replied gently. "But as a sister. Not a lover or wife." He stroked her face to calm her. "You told me you've been forbidden to visit the slave quarters. Your mother will be angry."

"Oh, so that's why you deny your true feelings. Because you're a slave and I'm your future mistress. Isn't that so?"

"No."

Outside, a copper pail clunked in the garden. He jumped up and jerked aside the doorway curtains. The garden was empty except for two birds overturning the pail. He closed the curtains, relieved at not being caught in his bedroom with his mistress's daughter. He sat on his bed. How could he convince her? She seemed destined for tragedy, like her parents. Her father, Dumuzi, died before she was born. Her grief-stricken mother had aged beyond her years. The midwife's daughter, herself a midwife, often treated Unanna for various ailments.

Abram turned to Nammu, "You must accept my feelings. You're still young. You'll fall in love again."

"Not with the man I want to spend my life with," she said and stared at the curtained doorway. "Maybe you prefer another. And that's why you reject me. Well, I'll leave you in peace, Abram. I don't want to be a burden." She hurried outside before he could protest.

The truth, though, was that he did like someone. He'd met the young woman at the bazaar. Nights, lying on his bed, he enjoyed chanting her name, like an incantation: Nisinna, Nisinna, Nisinna. It seemed miraculous. The very utterance of her name caused her to appear in his imagination.

She had dropped by one afternoon at the bazaar to buy a basket. "Did Ashnan teach you?" she asked, examining his basket's workmanship.

"Yes," he said, surprised. "Did you know her?"

Nisinna surprised him with her faulty grammar. "Mother and her were slaves for Master Balulum. He treated them good until he drinks too much. Then his real bad temper made their lives miserable." She paused. "My aunt bought our freedom. I help out at her meat stall."

They continued chatting. Abram silently thanked Nammu for teaching him to speak correctly. Despite Nisinna's low-class manner, he admired her large, firm breasts, tiny waist, and ample hips under the tufted gown. She eyed him boldly, making him think that she wouldn't shrink from a man's touch. He especially liked her walk, the way she swung herself from side to side as if still surprised by her fourteen-year-old body. He agreed to visit her the following week.

Nisinna and her aunt lived in Ur's poor section. Narrow, irregular streets, unpaved and undrained, wound among high, mud-brick walls. The stench of garbage lining the streets nauseated Abram. He would have turned back but his desire to have her made him keep the appointment. The only traffic consisted of infrequent pedestrians with laden, braying donkeys.

The evening surpassed Abram's expectations. When he arrived, Nisinna pulled him into her room at the rear. She began kissing him while tugging off her dress. Returning her passion, he unwrapped his loincloth and they lay together on her wooden bed that occupied most of the room. Their lovemaking pounded the old bed. The headboard with its faded flower design creaked and whined.

They rested a few minutes. "Where's your aunt?" he whispered.

"Don't worry," Nisinna said, giggling. "She's helping a friend." Nisinna snuggled close to him.

They chatted some more. She was soon ready again. She arched her body against him and purred like a cat. Several times they made love. Abram wondered if he could satisfy her. Despite his experience the past year with several slave girls, Nisinna was unique. She couldn't seem to get enough. He finally lay back, panting.

Bernadette Miller

"Let's rest a while," he gasped.

"Did I wear you out?" she teased.

"Men are different from women. My zibbinu needs to regain strength."

"Zibbinu? That's not Sumerian."

He pointed to his flaccid penis. His face flushed. "My Bedouin father's expression."

"Bedouin? Oh, you must love him a lot to quote him."

"I...never knew him. My mother told me all about him. But someday I'm going to find him in the desert. I'm saving shekels for the journey."

"Enough shekels has to take years," Nisinna said, leaning on an elbow.

"I have a plan." He rose, his jaw thrust forward.

She watched him wrap his loincloth about his hips. "When you coming back?"

He tied the loincloth's loose ends. "Next week." He leaned over to kiss her before leaving.

When Abram returned home, he discovered Nammu weeping in the courtyard. Concerned, he placed his arm about her shoulders. "What happened?"

"My mother died while you were gone." She wiped away tears with a cloth. "Slaves are in the tomb preparing the burial." Sobbing into the cloth, she blubbered, "Now I'm an orphan with no other living relatives. Except for Majeena and you. But you no longer care about me."

His stomach heaved in sympathy. "Nammu, I'm only a slave. We're not on equal footing."

"You know we mean more to each other than that."

"You mean a great deal to me. But that doesn't change our status."

Looking tired, her eyes puffy, she rose. "I must see to my mother's funeral. We'll talk afterward."

He bowed. "As you wish."

Agitated over the news that Nammu was his new mistress, Abram strode to his bedroom and groped for the stuffed pouches under his bed. He'd saved almost enough shekels for his and Ama's freedom, but not enough to find his father, Tiras. That might take another year. Then, again, perhaps buying his freedom now would solve his financial problem by providing extra hours to sell more baskets.

He waited until Unanna had been buried and Nammu sufficiently recovered to approach her with his request. One afternoon in the garden, he revealed his plans except for Nisinna. "I want to buy my freedom," he said. "I have enough shekels."

She squinted at him and asked, "Where did you obtain so many?"

"Selling baskets at the bazaar," he replied honestly.

"I see." Nammu sat down and indicated he sit beside her on the bench. After he sat, she observed him for a while and said, "Abram, I can't sell you your freedom. You mean too much to me. Although," she added at seeing his crestfallen face, "according to Sumerian law, if you marry a free woman, you become free if the woman grants it. We could sign a contract and marry for two years. After that if you're still unhappy, I'll grant a divorce, give you your freedom, and enough shekels to pursue your dreams.'"

"Nammu, you know I don't want to marry you."

"Am I so ugly that you can't bear the thought of marrying me? Even for a short time?" She turned away.

He placed a hand on her shoulder to comfort her. "I've told you repeatedly, I do love you. But not as a husband."

"If you loved me, you would marry me. Marriage is the natural outcome of love." She turned toward him. "The suitor my mother found years ago persists in courting me but he's growing weary of my protests. He's probably just interested in my huge dowry. My mother's inheritance from Mah Ummia, plus half of Balulum's property after he murdered my poor grandfather. I don't love the suitor but I don't want to remain a maid. He gave me two days to respond." She touched Abram's hand on her shoulder. "Please let me know before then. I pray it will be yes."

"Nammu, I'll always love you. Whether I marry you or not."

She gazed at the floor. "I can see why you'd refuse. Why marry someone as ugly as I?" She looked up, her cheeks wet. "But couldn't you endure it for just two years?"

He smiled to calm her. "Your offer is tempting. I'll give it serious consideration."

Encouraged, she smiled back with her crooked teeth. "I'll eagerly await your answer, but please make it fast."

He returned to his room, his forehead furrowed in thought. He hadn't anticipated such a quandary. Unlike his father's people, the Sumerians were monogamous. He had enjoyed his trysts with Nisinna. He didn't want them to end. Nor did he long to be stuck with homely Nammu for whom he had no sexual desire, only childhood affection. Still, after two years of marriage, he'd be a free citizen and could follow his destiny instead of meaningless toil as a slave. What should he do? He must carefully weigh the consequences before deciding.

CHAPTER 20

May, 3485 B.C., Sumer

ABRAM CELEBRATED HIS WEDDING DAY but not as he might have hoped. He scanned the courtyard. Majeena had described Unanna's wedding. Then, like now, balcony urns of anastatica and hawthorn had perfumed the air. Musicians seated against the wall played lively tunes on lyres, reed flutes, and tambourines. The courtyard filled with admiring guests eager to witness the beautiful Unanna marry her handsome Dumuzi. Now, snickers emanated from the few guests awaiting Abram's unappealing bride.

He wondered again if he should marry Nammu. The previous night in his bedroom, his final one as a slave, Abram had prayed to Lord Enlil that despite the unwelcome marriage he would try to forget Nammu's ugliness and treat her kindly. He shouldn't hurt his best friend on their wedding night.

In the courtyard, he watched the guests whispering, perhaps about his lowly status. He stroked his sprouting beard and reminded himself that after marrying a free Sumerian woman, he must behave as a proper citizen, respected by Ur's townspeople, his former life forgotten. To mask his self-consciousness, he straightened his ankle-length pleated skirt and smoothed Nammu's woven shawl adorning his left shoulder. Finally, he no longer wore his hated loin cloth: a symbol of derision, proclaiming his lowly slave status. To his surprise, he missed it. The garment had been wonderfully comfortable, allowing unrestricted movement. Uncomfortable clothing, he reminded himself, was a small price to pay for his new life as a free Sumerian citizen.

He looked up, startled from his reverie. The guests applauded listlessly as Nammu entered. Her slender body seemed shrunken behind the white tufted robe. The netted veil mercifully concealed her face. She probably ignored the guests' snickers and smiled at achieving her heart's desire by forcing her childhood friend and former slave to marry her, hoping he'd remain married to her beyond their two-year contract. Following the custom, she strolled about the room so the guests could admire her ensemble. She stumbled. They tittered. Resentment welled up inside Abram. Two years of marriage to the homeliest and clumsiest woman in Ur. Would freedom be worth the cost?

Nammu stood before him and waited a few moments. Finally, she extended her arms, her face still hidden behind the veil. "Husband, you haven't asked me to dance."

He rose and bowed, feeling constrained by the long skirt. "I'm sorry, Nammu. I was deep in thought." He placed his hands on her shoulders. They followed the traditional wedding dance. They slid their feet sideways, then forward, and backward. He grimaced as Nammu tripped in her sandals when they turned. He caught her before she fell.

"Abram, please forgive my awkwardness," she whispered. "You know my difficulty in maneuvering because of faulty eyesight. I'll depend on you to guide me."

He nodded and continued struggling with her. After a few moments, he said, "Nammu, you must be tired. Let's sit and enjoy our wedding."

She shook her head. "I'm not tired at all. Please let's continue dancing. I so enjoy having your arms about me."

He frowned and led her about the room. The guests ate and drank and continued whispering among themselves.

Even Nammu could sense she was being ignored at her own wedding. "All right, Abram, let's sit a while."

Majeena, wearing her usual black dress, approached the couple. She glowed at Abram's new status in Sumerian society. Her lowly son, born a slave, would soar in stature by wedding a Sumerian woman from a prominent family and gaining his freedom in two years.

She said, "I wish you both great happiness in your life together."

Nammu squeezed her slave's hand. "Thank you, Majeena."

"Yes, thank you," Abram repeated with a forced smile. He was unable to publicly call her mother. The woman who had borne him had become his slave as well as his wife's. He hadn't revealed his burden to his mother: marrying against his will to obtain their eventual freedom. Despite nagging suspicions that the marriage wasn't his desire, she still filled with pride at his apparent achievement.

It was time to lift Nammu's veil. More titters erupted from the guests as Nammu squinted up at Abram. Wispy curls escaped from under her shiny wig. "My bride," he said as warmly as possible, holding her about the waist.

"My adored Abram," she whispered back. Smiling, she rested her head against his shoulder.

The musicians played a solemn march. The couple again danced. After several hours the guests emptied the room. Abram dismissed the musicians. Slaves carried leftover food to the kitchen.

Nammu bit her lip from disappointment. "Majeena said that my mother's wedding lasted several days."

Abram took her hand. "Their rudeness doesn't matter. We're married. Your dream has been satisfied."

"At last." She beamed at his reminder and turned toward the balcony. "Come, let's rest now as husband and wife."

He stifled a groan at picturing her lying under him. Forcing a smile, he led her upstairs to their bedroom. The frescoed walls

Bernadette Miller

gleamed with pearl-paneled scenes of worshippers kneeling with large, staring eyes. In Unanna's former bedroom, he picked up Nammu and placed her on the bed's wool coverlet, her wedding robe trailing to the floor.

She covered his hand with hers. "Please, sit beside me while I calm myself. I'm so agitated by our wedding. I'm afraid I'll disappoint you in our lovemaking."

"You won't," he said, still in the habit of comforting her as when they were children. He ignored his reluctance to make love with her, stripped off his skirt, and tossed it on the rug. He lay atop her. Her response to his kiss surprised him. She was not passionate, like Nisinna, but tender and affectionate.

Her lips lingered on his. "Oh, Abram, if only you knew how much I love you." Her slender arms entwined about his neck. She looked up at him with shiny eyes. "You're the light of my life. My constant source of joy. From the moment Utu shines through my window and awakens me, until Nanna lulls me to sleep with his moonlight, you bring such happiness. Simply by your presence. My only wish is to bring you the same happiness. "

"Nammu," he whispered. "I don't want to hurt you but you know I didn't ask for this marriage..." He paused as her eyes filled with tears. "Please don't cry. I can't bear it." He bent to embrace her. He kissed her wet cheeks and moist lips. She hugged him back. Their tongues explored each other's mouths. Surprised at his zibbinu rising, he began undressing her and flung her robe onto the floor. He caressed her body and kissed her tiny, nearly flat breasts. Then he arched her body toward him. He took her hands and gently placed it around his zibbinu, stroking it until it swelled.

"What do you want me to do?" she whispered. "I just want to please you." Her wispy black curls spread across the coverlet like underbrush.

"Don't worry," he replied, caressing her thin body. "I'll guide you so we can both enjoy the experience."

She nodded. Slowly he thrust his zibbinu inside her. They rocked back and forth for several minutes. Panting, he continued caressing her. They both moaned in unison as his seed sprayed inside her womb. Nammu was no longer a maid. Blood droplets dotted the mattress. They repeated the effort several times. Tired, Abram rested while his bride lay beside him. She propped herself on an elbow. Her free hand ruffled the dark curls adorning his chest. She gazed, as if in disbelief, at her husband.

"Did you have an experience?" he gasped.

"Oh, that explains it," she said. Her eyes widened in wonder. She smiled at her new knowledge. "Several times," she confessed.

Utu began fading outside their window. Nammu's appearance softened in the twilight. Abram could see only her face's outline, her smile and the dark eyes staring at him with love.

"Are you hungry?" Nammu asked finally, sitting up.

"Yes!" Grinning, he leaned over to kiss her. He delighted in her soft lips on his. She was incredibly sweet, far more so than he would have imagined.

Downstairs, they enjoyed their first meal together as husband and wife. Ravenous, Abram devoured the roast beef and rice prepared by Majeena. His bride ate some soup, her attention focused on her husband being properly fed. When they made love that night, Abram was again surprised by her eagerness to please.

"Abram, is it more exciting for you if I arch my back toward you? Or would you rather I just lie here? Then you can place me in the position most enjoyable for you."

Abram smiled with amusement. He whispered, "Most enjoyable is watching your enjoyment."

She stroked his face. "Have no doubt that being with you is the most enjoyment I'll ever know."

They made love for several hours and fell asleep in each other's arms.

ೞಜ

Bernadette Miller

As days turned into weeks, then months, and the months into years, Abram's life with Nammu passed pleasantly. He marveled at her tender kisses and determination to grant his every wish. She planned the menus to tempt his palate and ordered slaves to supply clean coverlets daily. They were commanded to pile the straw mattress at least a foot high under the coverlets, which he preferred, and carefully tuck the ends into the bed frame. On late afternoons, she greeted Abram with a warm smile after his return from the Edubba where he was learning to read and write. She embraced his shoulders while he rested in a high-backed chair. He had grown accustomed to wearing the ankle-length, white skirt in place of a loincloth.

One afternoon in the courtyard, he looked up as she pushed aside his shawl to kiss his neck. "You look tired," she said. "Are you studying too hard? You spend so much time at the Edubba, struggling to become educated. I worry about your health failing."

"No, I'm well and content," he said, fondling her arm. "But I want Sumerian gentlemen to accept me as a legitimate citizen, not a former slave. I want them to greet me respectfully as they do with each other. Chatting about the weather and inquiring about my health. To accomplish this, I need the education I missed as a boy. I must speak correctly, imitate their manner of politeness, and never show emotions publicly. I'll always be grateful to you for teaching me."

"You always were ambitious to improve yourself. But I never could see any fault in you."

Abram laughed. "I have too many. Especially compared with you, my devoted wife."

"Then you're glad we married?" She gazed at him with impudence. Her headdress had tilted to one side.

Abram grinned. "You know the answer." He rose to kiss her. He held her tightly against him.

"I'll always love you, Abram." She trembled against him despite their many hours of intimacy. "You've made me so happy. If only I could bear your child."

"You've given me all the happiness I could ever want." They kissed again. Her trembling increased. He led her upstairs, their arms linked.

හ⟨ය

Gradually—he couldn't remember exactly when—Abram realized he had developed an overwhelming love and passion for his wife. Her exquisitely affectionate nature more than overcame her homely face and gaunt figure. One night as they rested in bed after lovemaking, he held her in his arms and whispered, "Nammu, I love you. I'll never seek a divorce."

He was rewarded with her kiss and hug. "My dearest Abram," she murmured. "You know I'll always love you. No matter what you do."

හ⟨ය

Despite her intense happiness with her new husband, Nammu yearned for a child but the midwife could find nothing wrong with her. One evening, Nammu finally told Abram, "Let's buy a baby at the bazaar. "I need to hold him against my breasts. Unlike Unanna, I yearn to experience motherhood. I would love him so much. Especially a little boy. Comfort him when he's sick. Stroke his cheek to calm his anger. Of course, he'll grow up to become your personal slave. But until he reaches manhood, I'll enjoy raising the child I couldn't conceive for you. "

"All right, my love," Abram said, eager to please her as she pleased him.

හ⟨ය

At the bazaar, snuggled in a blanket, the baby boy stared at Nammu. His hazel eyes, unusual for Sumer, adorned a narrow face with thin lips and soft cheekbones. Even more surprising: he had downy blond hair.

Bernadette Miller

"Elamite," the agent said at the couple's startled gaze. "They're mostly blond or redheaded. Bought him from a Sumerian warrior. He killed the parents during a mission and grabbed the boy along with their valuables."

"Oh, look at those big hazel eyes," Nammu said. She removed the baby from the basket and cuddled him in her arms. "And that yellow hair! Very special." She turned to Abram. "I want this one."

Abram nodded and grasped a tiny finger. The baby had a lean chest and limbs, but then he smiled, gurgling his pleasure, and reached out both hands. Abram couldn't help returning the smile. "We'll call him Aradmu," he told his wife. She nodded. Her gaze never left the wrapped bundle in her arms.

Despite the child's future slave status, Abram and Nammu lavished attention on Aradmu. They played with him, bouncing him on their knees. Abram let the boy ride on his back as if he were a donkey. They gave him toys and whispered endearments.

"Who's the most enchanting child in the world?" Nammu would croon in the nursery. "You, my darling."

The boy would clap his hands and reach up to kiss her cheek.

Finally, on Aradmu's sixth birthday, Abram forced himself to tell the truth. "We bought you at the bazaar to be our slave," he said reluctantly. "You're not our natural son, though we love you as if you were. But you need to understand that you'll grow up to wait on us at our pleasure."

Aradmu looked up, nodding and smiling, as if he didn't understand.

Abram patted the boy's wavy blond hair. "Well, go eat. Nammu has a special birthday gift for you." The child ran eagerly to the kitchen. Abram shook his head. He had done his best not to mislead the boy but how could he hurt someone so young who trusted him and for whom he felt deep affection? He would wait until Aradmu was old enough to understand that in Sumerian society, babies were often purchased to become future slaves.

Despite his contentment with his family, Abram hadn't abandoned his hope of seeking Tiras, his father. He hesitated reminding Nammu. Instead, he first approached his mother.

In the kitchen, Majeena begged him not to go. "Please don't leave me. You're all I have left of your father."

"But I won't stay there forever. Just a visit. And I'll take you with me. You could see Tiras again!"

"Abram, I'm already in my thirties. I don't want to leave the only home I've ever known. Please wait until I've gone to the netherworld."

"Ama, he's never coming back. But we might find him if we look." He paused as his mother shook her head, wiped at her tearing eyes, and opened the beehive oven.

"Much as I long to see him again, I can't go." She removed a meat tray from the oven drawer and set it on the brick table. "I'm too old to wander about in the desert." She smoothed her graying hair. "Son, please wait. I couldn't bear to lose you after losing Tiras."

"All right, I'll wait," he said, surprised at her finally admitting that her lover would never return, having abandoned her. Perhaps it was better for her to accept the truth rather than live a lie.

"You're my love," Majeena whispered, hugging him.

He smiled and returned her hug but the familiar kitchen seemed like a tomb, trapping him in Sumer.

ಶಿ ಅ

Yet when Majeena died soon after, Abram wondered how he could endure such a loss, despite Nammu comforting him. Watching his mother's funeral, he couldn't repress his tears before the slaves. He remembered her loving nature, her hugs and kisses, and her pride at his marrying a free Sumerian citizen. She'd been his only link to his father. He would miss her stories about Tiras, how the tribe worshipped a bull-god that terrorized them, and how Tiras yearned

Bernadette Miller

to free himself from that god, just as Abram had yearned to free himself from slavery.

In the small chapel beneath the stairway, Abram watched slaves carry his mother wrapped in matting down the ladder and into the tomb below. His dearest blood relative was gone. But his father and other family members remained, unaware of his existence. Although he loved Nammu, it was time for the desert journey he'd dreamed of all his life. It would help divert his sorrow from losing his mother.

He approached Nammu with his intention after they finished dinner and sipped wine. "I've decided to finally seek my father in the desert," he said, putting down his wine goblet. "Something I've always wanted. I won't be gone more than a couple of months."

She burst into sobs. "I thought you were happy with me. Was I so wrong?"

Abram rose to embrace her. "Nammu, I love you more than I ever thought possible." He paused at the tears spilling down her cheeks. "I won't stay permanently with my father. I'll return to Ur. Please believe me."

"If you truly loved me, you wouldn't leave," she interrupted. "You'd continue sharing our wonderful life together."

"I will! But seeking my father has been my cherished goal since childhood."

"Then take me with you," she said, "so we could be together."

He shook his head, reluctant to hurt her, but determined to accomplish his childhood dream before it was too late. "A desert journey would be too strenuous for you. Ama used to describe how harsh my father's life was." He paused as tears continued streaming down her face. How could he cause his dear wife such anguish? "Let me think it over," he said. "I'll give you my answer in a few days."

She embraced him. Her face clouded with doubt. "Abram, please don't abandon me. Don't leave me here, crying from loneliness."

CHAPTER 21

*March, 3468 B.C., Arabiyah
(The Uplands in northern Saudi Arabia)*

TIRAS HAD REACHED HIS FIFTY-FIFTH winter and had grown ill. His adored wife, Na'amah, had perished the previous year from old age. Word spread throughout the camp that he was dying. His kinsmen huddled near the sacred tent where he lay as if mere closeness to their sick priest would continue bringing good health and prosperity. They waited in anxious silence, staring at the tent flap, hoping for Rimush's reassurance. Inside the tent, Rimush obeyed his father's request for his presence. He bent over the elderly, frail man to catch his last words.

Tiras, lying on his rug, gestured for his hump-backed son to bend closer. Rimush's braids brushed his father's face. "You must teach the tribe all that I taught you," he gasped while Rimush studied the deep-set watery eyes and wrinkled cheeks. He clutched Rimush's hand. "Don't be fooled by the other tribes' false gods. Or lying priests."

Rimush's brows furrowed with worry. "Baba, are you sure I can replace you? My will isn't strong, like yours."

Tiras nodded. "I, too, once doubted myself. But I regained my courage." He reached up to press Rimush's shoulder, the one containing the fig-shaped birthmark. "We're so much alike, my son.

You'll find the courage, as I did, by exalting El." He coughed. "It's almost time." He leaned back against the rug.

"No, baba, stay a while longer."

Tiras stared up at his son's glistening eyes. "I forbid you to cry! Much remains to be accomplished. Listen." He reached up to hold Rimush's face in his shaking hands. "Don't let your hot-headed brother Canah become the priest," he muttered, his eyes narrowing. "Or our tribe will be miserable again. Like with Abu-Summu." He tightly grasped Rimush's arm. "Swear by our ancient custom that you'll follow my commands."

Rimush placed his hand between his lean thighs and said solemnly, "I swear that Canah will never become priest. And our tribe will remain faithful to El through future generations."

"Then I bless you, my son, and give you your birthright. Henceforth, follow my example as priest. My work is completed."

"No, please don't leave. I still need you."

Tiras closed his eyes and lay quietly. Rimush bent to hear the heartbeat. Silence. He stared at his dead father and blinked back tears. He must follow Tiras's commands and not show weakness. He paused to regain his composure, lifted the tent flap, and stepped outside. Under the scorching sun, he called to the crowd waiting by the tent. "Baba has started his journey to El in paradise."

"Tiras, our great priest, is dead," the Bedouins wailed in unison. They beat their chests and continued their lamentations.

"Who will lead us on our path to El?"

"Who will explain good and evil?"

"How can we reach the Oasis of Eden without Tiras's guidance?"

They pounded their heads, tore at their robes, and pulled at their hair. "Without our great Tiras, we're lost—like stray sheep."

"Listen, my kinsmen," Rimush said, fighting back tears. "My father left us a legacy. Avoid sinful temptations. Cling only to El. Then we shall meet our dear Tiras in Eden."

"That's true," a tribesman murmured. He wiped his damp eyes. "El promised us this paradise."

"But without Tiras, who will lead us to El?" another moaned, weeping.

The others nodded. They began wailing again.

"Return to your tents," Rimush urged, blinking back tears. He struggled to remain calm for his kinsmen's sake. "We'll find an answer to your worries. Meanwhile, I must prepare baba for burial."

Heads downcast, the tribesmen left. Just before sunset they gathered again behind Tiras's tent to bury the body within twenty-four hours to avoid attracting animals seeking prey. After the burial, Rimush stared at the stones outlining the grave.

"We must honor our great priest's memory," he told the tribesmen. His brows knitted together in earnestness as he motioned for the mourners to gather about. "Baba offered us a treasure that some of you young ones can't appreciate. You hadn't been born during the fearful time of our former bull-god, Martu." He stifled a sob and silently reprimanded himself. He must obey baba's last wishes to guide the tribesmen to El. "Kinsmen, don't listen to lies about false gods. Cling only to El. He will always protect us."

His older brother Canah shouted to the crowd, "Keep upon your breasts our sacred amulet, the six-pointed star! It will remind you of El's power. The importance of obeying Him." He scanned the tribesmen as if to gauge the effect of his speech.

Excited, they chanted, "Yes! We'll wear our sacred amulet. We'll never forsake El. We're His chosen people."

"But I warn you that El can become jealous," Rimush added, worried that his hot-headed brother was trying to assert his authority. "Worship no other god before him."

The tribesmen, calmed, chanted, "We'll worship only El, forsaking all others."

"Someday, as my father preached," Rimush said, wiping away his tears despite his promise to baba, "the Abram tribe will receive El's covenant that proves we're His chosen people. Then, El will heap

Bernadette Miller

blessings upon us in the Promised Land. But we must earn this covenant by following the instructions laid down by our beloved El."

"We'll obey the instructions!" Canah shouted. He waved his muscular arms that bulged beneath his robe. "We'll scorn all other gods. They've become an abomination to us."

"An abomination!" the tribe repeated. "We'll always obey Him! No other shall persuade us!"

꧁꧂

The following night, the tribesmen knelt on their rugs before the blazing bonfire and recounted their history. They silenced when Rimush stood near the Ark. Shivering in the cold, he clutched his cloak about him. He scanned the tribesmen watching him expectantly. He must quiet his quaking heart and follow his father's wishes. Canah cannot become the priest!

He hid his trembling hands and said in a loud voice so all could hear, "Listen, my kinsmen. My father, the great Tiras, has bestowed upon me the birthright of priest. He knew that by nature I am peaceful. I can calm your fears. Inspire you to obey El's commands. Will you accept me to replace the great Tiras?" He was surprised at his confident tone.

"Baba, it is so destined!" shouted his son, Abimah. "Just as my esteemed grandfather wanted."

The tribesmen turned toward one another. They softly debated whether to accept Rimush.

Canah jumped up. "No! I should inherit the role of priest. I'm Tiras's eldest son. The birthright belongs to me!"

"That's true!" a tribesman shouted. "The eldest son should inherit the birthright. Rimush must follow tradition."

Then, Abimah rose, his tiny eyes glaring at Canah. He said with clenched jaws, "Everyone knows that my father was Tiras's favorite.

He was personally selected by him as his replacement. Let my father receive the birthright bequeathed to him."

Canah stared at him. His thick lips curled in contempt beneath his beard. "So, the Abram tribe must break with tradition to grant Rimush a special favor as he has always received in life. And to bring this about, Rimush's weak son, Abimah, tries to persuade us. Throughout our history, the eldest son has inherited the birthright. It's mine by right and I claim it!" He strode to the Ark and held out his brawny arms to include all listeners.

"My kinsmen," he preached, "always we hear the same words from my brother. Submit to El. Follow His instructions to live an ethical life and one day we shall receive the covenant and our own land. Surely our God has grown weary of my brother's half-hearted lectures. Let me arouse a zeal in you for El. Let's convert other tribes to join us! Isn't it better to surround ourselves with worshippers of our own faith rather than enemies? If the tribes resist, no matter. We've grown with enough fighting men to convince our neighbors."

The tribesmen contemplated Canah's urging. They silenced when Rimush stepped forward, frowning with concern. He must keep his promise to baba not to allow belligerent Canah to become the new priest. But how to accomplish this without enraging his brother?

He said gently, "Canah, let me take my place as priest. Baba willed it. The tribe already consented. I alone among his children bear his birthmark."

A tribesman exclaimed, "Rimush should be our new priest. That was Tiras's desire."

The others shouted, "Yes! Rimush should be our priest!"

Finally, Ruach's youngest son, recently elected as sheikh, rose. He said solemnly, "Let it be as our tribe decrees. Rimush is our new priest."

ಬಂ ೞ

Thereafter, Rimush preached nightly before the Ark, that sacred stone altar where Tiras had presented revelations about El. He answered his tribesmen's questions by dreaming the replies or imagining brief conversations with El. At each sermon, Rimush reminded his kinsmen of the future covenant with El and their reward of the Promised Land.

Resentment festered in Canah at being robbed of his birthright. Nights, while one of his wives snored peacefully beside him, Canah stared at the tent wall, remembering baba's return from his long journey to Ur. Which of his children did he hug and kiss first? Rimush! But the eldest always comes first and deserves special attention. Then, during his mock battle with Rimush, using the toy donkeys brought from Ur, his brother brazenly claimed to win the fight. Canah gritted his teeth. If weak Rimush were so intent on winning battles, his sturdy brother would prove his superior strength. He'd ask his kinsmen again: who should be priest? Rimush with his miserable hump? Or the eldest son with his strong body and fearless heart!

Each day while Canah tended his flock, rage coursed through him like a wild river. "*There's still no justice for me as Tiras's eldest son,*" he reminded himself again and again.

೮೦ ೮ೞ

One night, after a sermon, Canah accompanied Rimush to his first wife's tent. Canah lingered at the tent flap. "Rimush, I must speak with you about an urgent matter."

"Yes? Come. Let's discuss over wine whatever troubles you."

Canah followed his brother inside the tent. A copper lantern heated the small space. Canah dropped his cloak on the carpet and settled on a cushion before the qata. He politely ate some figs, washed down with two cups of date wine.

Rimush opened his cloak. "So, my brother, tell me how I can help you."

"It's about my becoming the new priest."

Rimush sighed and refilled Canah's cup. "That's already been decided by our tribe. The sheikh confirmed it. Do you propose overturning their decision?" Rimush studied Canah's glowering eyes. "Ah, I see what feeds your unhappiness. But I can guide our kinsmen toward peace and contentment, whereas you'd lead them toward war, destruction, and death. Baba bequeathed to me his inheritance. In time you'll accept my being the priest."

"You're wrong! I'll never accept it!" Canah snatched at his dagger and thrust it toward his brother. Wiry Rimush swayed to one side and grabbed Canah's wrist, pressing hard against his pulse. Canah, surprised, momentarily dropped the dagger to rub his aching wrist. Within seconds, Rimush swiftly picked up the weapon, prepared to defend himself. Instead, he relived Canah torturing him during childhood and impulsively plunged the dagger inside his brother's chest.

Clutching at his robe, Canah moaned from intense pain and sank onto the carpet. His eyes widened from horror and disbelief that his weakling brother had stabbed him. Blood gushed out and enveloped him in a bright red pool.

"Canah!" Rimush cried out. Fearfully, he bent over his brother. "What have I done?" Gasping with regret, he slowly pulled out the dagger. It was too late. Canah's large body lay crumpled on the rug, his left leg bent under his body, his precious life fluid oozing from his heart. His dark eyes closed.

I've killed my only brother, Rimush thought, and covered his face with his bloody hands. *If only I'd allowed Canah to become the priest since it meant so much to him. Oh, Canah, now I understand why you despised me. I ignored your lifelong anguish at being passed over, and my being our father's favorite. Now, I've destroyed my own flesh and blood.*

Rimush looked up toward the tent roof; tears dripped from his beard. He worried what other evil awaited inside him. He began wailing and beating his chest at his horrible future. *"Please, my god, help me atone for my vile selfishness. I'll be dragged to Be'elzebub's fury in Jahannam and burn there forever!"*

His wife, Zillah, had been gathering ghada twigs outside for the hearth. She heard the commotion but was reluctant to interfere between the two brothers. Then, hearing her husband's loud cries, she jumped up and rushed inside the tent. The petite woman gazed at Canah's body crumpled on the rug. "What happened!" she exclaimed. Her lip, twisted upward from a jackal's attack, gave the impression of sneering.

Rimush was silent. His face was flushed and his eyes looked vacant.

She squatted to feel Canah's heart and clapped a hand over her mouth in shock. "He's dead." She looked at Rimush in horror.

Eyes filled with tears, Rimush blubbered, "Oh, my poor brother. He suffered all his life because of me. Finally he became so angry at not being the tribal priest, he tried to stab me. I struggled to twist the dagger away but ended up killing him." Rimush wiped his face with his sleeve. "My brother was right! I stole his birthright. He should have been the new priest."

Zillah rose with her blood-soaked robe and hugged Rimush. "It wasn't your fault," she said. "Canah drew his dagger. You had to defend yourself." She turned to gaze at the lifeless body drenched in blood. She shook her head. "I'll speak with his wives about this tragedy so they can bury him. Meanwhile, I'll try to clean him. For their sake."

From a storage sack, she removed a goatskin sack of water. She squatted and began cleaning Canah's face. "Go outside, husband. Walk a while in the clear air to ease your spirit."

Rimush nodded. He fastened his sheepskin cloak and left the tent. He grimaced as he walked past tents lit from lanterns, with the families inside probably eating and chatting. If it wasn't his fault, he pondered, why was Canah gone? How could he continue preaching about obeying El's command to lead an ethical life after committing murder? Would El forgive him? Or banish him forever to Jahannam? He shuddered as he passed several tents. He dropped to his knees on the sand and bowed his head.

"*El, I beg you to forgive my sin,*" he prayed silently. "*You know I didn't mean to kill Canah.*"

A sudden wind blew, wrapping Rimush's blood-soaked robe around his body as he knelt on the sand. The moon slid behind a cloud. The acacias waved their branches in fear. Rimush's heart began beating fast. A sign!

From a far distance, he thought he heard a voice whispering in reply, "You must atone, Rimush. Find your way back to me. Only then will you be forgiven."

"*I will find a way to atone,*" Rimush promised. His forehead throbbed at hearing El's instruction. He rose, burdened by his terrible crime. His merciful God had spoken, but how could he atone for such an abominable deed?

CHAPTER 22

July, 3468 B.C., Sumer

ABRAM STILL MOURNED THE LOSS of his beloved wife, who had died three weeks earlier from the same chest pains that took Dumuzi, her father. After seventeen years of marriage with Nammu, whose only desire had been his happiness, Abram felt lonely. His mother had died years ago, leaving no relatives.

In the garden, a lanky male slave approached. He set a platter of honey cakes and cups of apricot juice on a wooden side table. "Master, you've had little nourishment since my mistress's burial."

Abram gazed at his attentive Elamite slave. It seemed only yesterday, that he and Nammu had bought Aradmu and raised him, the closest they'd come to having a child. Nammu continually hugged the lad as if he were her son. She bought him toys and ordered slaves to prepare his favorite dishes. Because of the special attention, Aradmu might have grown up believing that his master and mistress would eventually accept him as their legitimate son.

Instead, Abram had hoped that Nammu could conceive, bearing the fruit of their love. But who wouldn't be proud to have such a son as Aradmu? A fine, handsome lad of fifteen with a beard the color of ripe wheat, high cheekbones, and large hazel eyes that were filled with concern for his master.

"Thank you, but I'm not hungry," Abram said. "You may return later." He paused. "You're like a son to me. Always caring about my health and happiness. I know how much you miss Nammu," he added softly.

"She was my mother..." Aradmu's lips trembled. "Forgive me, master, I know she didn't bear me." He nervously plowed his blond, wavy hair. "Please eat something. I left the food on the table to tempt you."

Abram nodded and watched Aradmu leave. How could he have survived his wife's death without that caring young slave? Aradmu, too, grieved over losing Nammu. Abram gazed up at the garden's palm fronds lacing the sky. If Nammu were still alive, she'd be sitting on his lap, smoothing his brow, and entertaining him with jokes. He shook his head in sorrow. Why did the gods take her away?

೮೦ೞ

Abram's only source of comfort at losing Nammu was his slave, Aradmu. He also spent more time studying the clay tablets at the Edubba, especially his father's Bedouin language. One afternoon he looked about his garden and reproached himself. He shouldn't keep dwelling on Nammu. What happened to his childhood ambition? It was time to seek his father and his people in the desert. He lacked for nothing, having inherited Mah Ummia's large house. Slaves obeyed his every command, and the Edubba had long ago satisfied his hunger for knowledge.

It was time for his journey.

Ama had described what Tiras told her about his desert family's suffering. His inherited wealth could help. He'd be a dutiful son. He'd get to know his father, and then return home.

Excited by the prospect of finally finding his father, Abram hired a guide at the bazaar who'd assured him he was experienced.

"Moiseh, as I told you at the bazaar, I want to find my father,

Bernadette Miller

Tiras, a Bedouin in Arabiyah and a member of the Abram tribe," Abram explained in his courtyard. "How well do you know the desert, and do you speak their language?"

Moiseh, a husky, dark-haired man past thirty in years, set his beer goblet on a side table. "My lord, let me reassure you that having been born in the desert, I'm very experienced. I know many desert dialects. Although I've lived in Sumer most of my life, I've traveled a lot as a guide and know all the migration routes. Yes, I could probably find your father but in the desert there's no certainty."

"Understood," Abram said, pleased. The stocky guide seemed ideal. Although he dressed like a Sumerian man with ankle-length white skirt and shawl and chest-length beard, he had a Bedouin's round, sun-darkened face, but the scar spanning his forehead as if slashed by a dagger looked threatening. Perhaps the guide was a ruffian, secretly planning to rob him once they were alone in the desert.

"How did that scar happen?" Abram asked. He deliberately kept his voice casual so as not to antagonize the guide.

"From fighting a desert bandit," Moiseh replied. "I was lucky to survive. The desert is dangerous. Are you prepared to make such a journey?"

"Yes," Abram said without hesitation.

"There are many dangers," Moiseh continued. "Wild animals. Sudden sandstorms that could bury us. Flash floods in the wadis from unexpected cloudbursts. Great heat and thirst during the day and fierce cold at night. Roaming bandits could rob us and leave us to rot in the sand."

"Enough!" Abram declared. "I can survive." He was surprised that the guide tried to discourage him, but perhaps that was a sign of honesty. He clamped his teeth shut at the challenge. He'd endured a humiliating childhood as a lowly slave who possessed nothing, not even his own body. Surely he could endure the desert.

"Of course, not all those dangers happen all the time," Moiseh added. "The desert is enormous, mostly empty of tribes. We might find your father without a single incident. But if any of the things that I mentioned happen, our lives could be lost."

"I understand the threats," Abram said. "I'm willing to face them and pay you as well." He reached for his beer. Perhaps the guide meant well, sincerely trying to warn him. He gulped the beer and said, "As far back as I can remember, I've longed to find my father. He'd returned to the desert, unaware of me. But the present opportunity might be my last."

They chatted for a while. Abram, embarrassed that he'd been born into slavery, didn't reveal his past. The men agreed on a date and the necessary preparations.

Aradmu bought supplies at the bazaar. He trimmed Abram's chest-length beard to neck length to resemble Bedouins. They wore white robes and had their long hair braided and tucked under their turbans. But despite Abram's efforts, his pale complexion—untouched by the sun goddess since he spent his time indoors—suggested one who lived in the city.

But Moiseh reassured him. "We'll probably go unnoticed, my lord. The turbans and beards reveal only our eyes."

Finally, Aradmu packed the three donkeys and all was ready. In the side yard, Abram said a fond farewell to his personal slave while Moiseh waited outside in the alley.

"Good-bye, Aradmu," Abram said. "I'll miss you and the time I spent teaching you. But I will return."

Aradmu's eyes dampened. "Master, I feel deeply honored you entrusted me with your household. But I fear for your safety. I pray to Lord Enlil to protect you."

Abram, smiling, put his hand on the slender shoulder. "Don't worry. We'll return."

He glanced at Moiseh who gestured they should leave. Abram led his donkey along the pebbled walk, through the metal gate, and onto the alley. Moiseh followed with the other two animals. Their hooves echoed against the cobblestones. Beyond more alleys and the

Bernadette Miller

Ceremonial Boulevard, the travelers passed the bazaar and headed through the bronze double-gate. Abram glanced back at the walled city. He'd been happy in Ur with his wife and mother. He left as a free man with great wealth. Ama had described his father's fierce bull-god, Martu, and its horrifying demands. Lord Enlil, god of the air, had blessed him with much happiness. Surely his father's tribe would welcome a caring religion. He would gladly convert them to Lord Enlil.

Ahead, Moiseh turned and called out, "You might want to visit Shuruppak. The city is famous for King Ziusudra who survived the great flood by building a huge ship and saving the population. Though smaller than Ur, the city is interesting. I lived there for several years."

Abram frowned. "My wife and I visited Shuruppak many years ago as well as other cities. There's no time for sightseeing. My father must be very old now. I pray we aren't too late."

Moiseh, his face expressionless, said, "As you wish, my lord."

Despite his fawning words, Abram noted his guide's cold lingering stare as if annoyed at being ordered about. He reminded himself of his former slavery and how it felt to be given commands. But he paid Moiseh an ample sum for his services: ten shekels a week plus food, lodging, and other expenses. For this generous sum he expected friendly service.

As the travelers headed along the road past fields of emmer, wheat, and barley, Moiseh spoke only when spoken to. Occasionally Abram dismounted from his donkey to walk. He plucked figs from roadside orchards and gazed at the ploughed fields hugging the river. Beyond the fields, the vast mysterious desert stretched toward towering, stony hillsides.

He worried how his father's tribe would react to his arrival. Although he could speak the language well enough from his studies and practice with Moiseh, he'd never lived in the desert. He could neither tend flocks, find his way, nor even prepare food for himself.

To survive, he must rely totally on his family's hospitality when he reached them.

As the pair travelled beside the marshlands, with its arch-shaped reed houses and basket-shaped boats, Abram recounted the numerous obstacles to his quest. Bedouins lived in simple tents while he had a luxurious house with enough water to wash and cook with. They had multiple wives. The Sumerians only one. Suppose his relatives rejected him as a stranger? An outsider whom they considered untrustworthy? He'd read on the clay tablets that the Bedu were crude and uneducated. It must be true. He'd seen a few at the bazaar. They were filthy, spewing a foul odor. He shuddered. Suppose he couldn't adapt to their primitive habits? He reminded himself of their shared blood that could unite them in friendship. He stared at the distant sand dunes and sighed. Only his journey's end could supply the answers.

Bernadette Miller

CHAPTER 23

July, 3468 B.C.
(Al-Nefud Desert in northern Saudi Arabia)

ABRAM AND MOISEH HAD LEFT SUMER and entered the great Nefud Desert in Arabiyah. Abram looked about while riding his donkey, his long legs dangling over the sides. The hard red sand was flat, dotted with vegetation. Sandstone outcroppings outlined the horizon. Moiseh had wisely advised him to wear layered woolen robes as protection. A thick wool turban protected his head, neck, and face. Heavy woven socks warmed his sandaled feet. A belt pouch held a copper dagger. Abram wished he could replace the cumbersome garments with his simple Sumerian skirt and shawl. After several hours, the men stopped to rest. They refilled their goatskin bags at rain-water pools.

Moiseh built a campfire that Abram knew he couldn't have done. Their donkeys nibbled at small bushes, surprisingly damp, and the men moistened their hands before eating rice, dates, and bread. Abram looked about and nodded. There was much to learn about his father's land, but also much to endure. His muscles ached from riding many hours. He hated eating with his fingers. Moiseh had convinced him not to pack utensils and other comforts that would require numerous donkeys. He realized he had to prepare himself for the Bedouins' strenuous life.

He often thought about meeting his father after all these years. What would Tiras say? Ama had described him as small in stature, not tall like Abram. And his mother had said that Abram's narrow face and deep-set dark eyes resembled his father's.

He had so many questions. Why hadn't Tiras returned to Ur for her? Didn't he love her? If he'd known she bore his son, would he have returned to visit?

Abram gazed at the distant horizon. Only his father could answer these important questions.

At night, Abram didn't sleep well. He yearned for his comfortable, wooden bed with the deep straw mattress and soft, woven coverlets. Instead, wearing a sheepskin cloak for warmth, he curled up uneasily in his rug on the hard sand. He never felt warm enough at night, despite the campfire. It didn't seem to bother Moiseh. The guide fell asleep promptly. His whistling snores occasionally awakened Abram. Besides, he kept imagining scorpions and snakes biting him while he slept. Jackals foraged for food, as well. How could he fight one, and especially while sleeping?

Each morning, he pushed aside his robes and examined his body for possible bites.

One morning, while mounting his donkey, Abram asked Moiseh, "Suppose a poisonous viper bit me while I slept. Is there a cure? Would I die?"

Moiseh shook his head. "Many people die in the desert, as I'd warned you, but rarely from snake bites, especially if you stay enclosed in your rug. You might scare it to death by your reaction." He chuckled as he urged his donkey forward. "There are numerous dangers," he called out. "Dying from a snake bite at night is unlikely. Being cold-blooded, they need sunlight to provide energy. He paused. "If it happens, let me know. I can suck out the venom."

Despite the reassurance, Abram remained skeptical. Suppose

Moiseh, sleeping soundly as usual with his loud snores, didn't hear his shouting? It would help if his guide were friendly.

Then, one evening while warming his hands at the campfire, Abram remarked, "That empty valley we just passed looks like good protection from wild animals."

Moiseh, adding more twigs to the campfire, replied, "My lord, never encamp in a wadi. Although rainfall here is infrequent, wadis can quickly form a lake many feet deep. They're treacherous. A nasty death if we become trapped in one."

Abram tried not to picture being caught in a sudden flood. He'd drown while his sour-faced guide managed to scramble onto the bank. Why should Moiseh risk his life to save his employer? The guide was probably jealous and resented working for a wealthy man with leisure time. The guide rarely smiled and spoke only when spoken to.

Abram couldn't help staring at the forehead scar. Fear crept over him. Suppose during the night while he slept, Moiseh decided to rob and kill him, leaving his rotting flesh as a banquet for wild animals? He must trust Moiseh, he reminded himself. No one else could guide him to his father, especially being this far into the desert.

"Our main danger," Moiseh continued, "is from the tribal leader who owns this part of the land. Of course, we might not meet anyone. The desert is enormous with scattered tribes. Much worse are marauding bandits. Fortunately, none have appeared. Otherwise, we could be murdered." He touched his scar self-consciously.

Abram began trembling. He pictured the bandits surrounding the pair. How could he and Moiseh defend themselves with only daggers and Moiseh's bow and arrow worn over his shoulder? They'd surely die. He'd never meet his father. He prayed: *Please, Lord Enlil, keep me safe from bandits and other dangers.* Reassured, he lifted his head and gazed at the desert. Lord Enlil usually answered his prayers.

After several weeks, Abram's face felt as though the sun goddess had set it afire. His clothes felt permanently damp from perspiration. He longed to return to Ur where he could bathe in his own tub.

Moiseh cautioned him to continue wearing several robes and a turban during the day. "Layered clothing protects against intense heat as well as cold. Otherwise, your skin will burn."

Abram nodded. If only he could rip off his clothing and jump into a lake. "When will we reach an oasis?" he asked again.

"Another week or two," Moiseh promised. He looked amused, as if pacifying a child.

Irritated, Abram surveyed the sea of undulating sand patterns, distant dunes, and occasional stony outcroppings.

ℰℭ

As Moiseh had advised, they finally spotted an oasis. The village of adobe houses and shops rose like a mirage under the shimmering heat. Weary Abram walked his donkey through the alleyways' pebbled streets and followed Moiseh leading his two donkeys. The men stopped to buy supplies, and Moiseh rented a bedroom in a modest home. They ate dinner alone in the kitchen. The family respectfully stayed in the small garden. The household's servant waited nearby to serve their guests' needs.

At last, Abram slept in a real bed although he missed his thick straw mattress, and the small room was inferior to his. Two thin straw coverlets hid the bed's hard wooden slats. Gaping holes punctured the plastered walls. He sighed as he lay down, pulled a coverlet over him and fell asleep, despite Moiseh's snores nearby.

During breakfast, he said to his guide, "A swim in the lake would be refreshing."

"My lord, we must push on to find your father," Moiseh said. "We still have a long journey ahead."

Abram nodded and dressed. Of course, they must push on but could he survive the journey? His muscles felt numb from so much hard riding. He and Moiseh occasionally walked to rest the donkeys, and he wasn't used to walking either. He tried to focus on Tiras. That evening, beside the campfire, he asked Moiseh, "How will my family greet me, a stranger?"

His guide nodded gravely. "Please don't anticipate their disapproval. Bedouins are noted for their hospitality, probably because the desert offers few places of refuge. They'll endure hunger to provide enough for their guests. If they accept you as a kinsman, they'll probably celebrate with a feast." He sipped water and added with a grin, "If not, don't worry. Our wits will defend us against a possible attack."

Abram stared at him. Just two against an entire tribe? Offended at Moiseh's seeming lack of concern for their safety, he turned away and again prayed to Lord Enlil for protection. He tried to relax his muscles although his stomach remained knotted.

"Living as a gentleman in Sumer, I'm not used to such hardships," he told Moiseh. Perhaps his stern tone would make his companion realize that the misguided humor was falling on unappreciative ears.

"Well, as I warned you, there are many dangers," Moiseh said, unrolling his rug for sleeping. "I'll do my best to shield you from them."

Abram, curling up in his own rug, mumbled, "Thank you." He wondered if Moiseh spoke truthfully. How far would he go to protect his employer?

৪০ ೮೪

The men traveled for another week. One afternoon, Abram pointed to distant sand dunes ahead. Rising to a thousand feet, they swelled in tandem over the landscape like a woman's breasts. "Must we cross those?" Abram asked in alarm. He felt exhausted.

"Yes, but they're passable," Moiseh replied. "Desert landscapes change with the shifting sand. The land might appear flat for many miles. Then suddenly there are dunes and stony mountains."

"How can you find the proper route?" Abram asked, looking about. "There are no landmarks for guidance. Just endless sand." He turned toward his far left. The ground was flat again with occasional vegetation. To the far right, the smaller sand dunes had been whipped by the wind into long ridges that undulated across the desert like red snakes.

"There are plenty of landmarks if you know how to spot them. Small dunes tend to shift with the wind and are unpredictable. But larger ones stay year after year as well as the outcroppings. By counting the large dunes ahead and keeping those undulation shapes to my right, I can tell how far it is to the next oasis. In this case, three dunes will bring us to our destination."

Impressed, Abram said, "Could I learn such things at my advanced age?"

"Certainly. If you're determined."

Abram silently thanked Lord Enlil for finding him a capable guide, despite his doubts. "Where do you think the Abram tribe is now?"

"Probably in the Al-Dahna Desert. They usually stay at the largest oasis." Moiseh rose and stretched, grunting his satisfaction. "My lord, we'd best be on our way." He picked up his donkey's reins, followed by Abram. "We still have a long journey before reaching the Al-Dahna."

The dunes were surprisingly hard, not soft and slippery as Abram had feared, but the climb caused him to pant beside the lumbering donkeys. The animals brayed loudly, undoubtedly in protest. He sympathized with their misery. At the summit the travelers rested to sip water and survey their surroundings.

Moiseh said unexpectedly, "Though I haven't lived here since boyhood, the desert still fascinates me."

"Why did you stop living in the desert?"

Bernadette Miller

"I could have been a sheikh, a chief, like my father. But when I was young, I fell in love with a pretty girl from Shuruppak. Kirigal couldn't survive in the desert. So, we stayed in Sumer. She died five years ago." Moiseh stared at the dunes, as if seeing a distant time. "I still miss her. But I also miss Bedouin life. The freedom and loyalty." He paused and added, grinning, "On the other hand, I got used to city comforts. Besides, I loved Kirigal. She was a good wife but full of mischief. Never boring." He heaved a deep sigh, then motioned toward the donkeys. "My lord, we should resume our journey. This evening, we'll rest. We can refill our water bags and let our donkeys graze."

It was Moiseh's most revealing speech. Perhaps the guide's attitude was softening toward his wealthy employer. Reluctantly, Abram mounted his donkey. His long legs dangled over the sides. His backside was sore from sitting so long. The oppressive heat hugged him like an unwelcome lover. His hands and exposed face felt gritty from sand. He debated with himself why he'd undertaken such an arduous journey. By now, his father was old, probably too feeble to remember the woman he'd abandoned, unable to acknowledge the son she had borne him. Still, he'd traveled this far to fulfill a youthful dream. He must press on.

For many days, the pair followed the Abram tribe's migration route across the Nefud. After a brief shower, Moiseh stopped to let the donkeys graze on the clumps of vegetation dotted with tiny flowers that perfumed the air. Abram stared, awed by the desert's unexpected beauty. Surprisingly, his perspiration seemed to lessen. His clothes felt dry. He gazed at the landscape. Rodents darted about the vegetation. Several white gazelles appeared from behind a thicket. The graceful animals hesitated, sniffing the air. Moiseh readied his bow and arrow.

"No, don't shoot!" Abram called out. "They're too beautiful." Satisfied, he watched the gentle creatures slip away.

"My lord, we need meat," Moiseh grumbled. That afternoon he

shot a hare instead. He skinned the animal with his dagger, emptied the innards, then stuffed it on a spit and roasted it over a campfire, built up from ghada twigs. Hungry, the men devoured the crispy flesh. They wiped their hands on clean cloths moistened from an abal bush. Blue-black crows and buzzards circled overhead, hoping for a meal. The men packed some meat among their provisions and flung the rest several feet from the campfire. The birds, squawking, swooped down and fought among themselves to peck at the remains.

One night, as Abram lay in his woolen rug, he scanned the immense, glittering domain of Lord An, the sky god. Then he scanned the horizon outlined by stony hills. The distances, seemingly devoid of life, looked overwhelming. He inhaled the pure, clean desert air. A sense of peace engulfed him, as if the present isolation were a welcome change from the bustling streets of Ur. His city of birth seemed as remote as the gods and goddesses twinkling in the sky.

A week later, the travelers turned south and finally entered the Al-Dahna Desert with its enormous limestone cliffs and the reddish dunes opposite. Despite the day's heat, the nights remained cold. They rested near wells scattered among the sandy plateau and refilled their water bags.

In another two weeks, they approached Al-Dahna's largest oasis. Following his guide, Abram led his donkey through the village of whitewashed houses and shops jammed together. The donkeys' hooves clattered against the pebbled streets. At the alley's end, a row of palms shaded a beautiful, clear lake.

Moiseh, turning, said, "My lord, this is the Al-Ubiyah oasis, the favorite of many Bedouins, and the largest in the Al-Dahna."

Al-Ubiyah! Abram, holding his donkey's reins, stared at the houses. He called out to Moiseh ahead of him, "Majeena, my ama, told me a story about this oasis. My uncle Loban was murdered here. The family took revenge by killing all the inhabitants. Is it safe?"

"Yes. Since that blood-feud, some survivors remain and new tribes have settled here. Such feuds can last through several generations. This one ended when your father's people paid the diya, blood money, to the survivors' descendants with sheep and goats."

"How do you know what happened?"

"News travels in the desert. Most guides have visited this oasis many times and heard the story from the survivors' children. The Abram tribe is usually here by now. Probably bartering in the shops or swimming in the lake."

Abram prayed silently. *Thank you, dear Lord Enlil, for leading me to safety.*

An old woman, squatting before a house, motioned to the visitors. She shifted her shawl about her gray head and smiled with missing teeth. She emitted a whistling sound when she spoke. "You need rest and shelter, my lords? I can take care of your donkeys."

Moiseh asked the price. Satisfied at her answer, he agreed to the arrangement. Two boys led the donkeys to a rear shed. Abram and Moiseh ate in the kitchen. Moiseh spoke to the woman in his native tongue. Occasionally he spoke to Abram using the same language. Abram understood he shouldn't speak Sumerian. The old woman might harbor suspicion toward strangers from another land. His former pale skin had darkened enough from the sun to make him look like another Bedouin.

The next day, he and Moiseh joined the men at the lake. Abram scanned the group. One of them could be a relative! The Bedouins stared at him with narrowed eyes. To put them at ease, Abram ignored them. They stripped off their clothes and waded into the water. He was surprised to see their naked skin nearly as pale as his, protected from the sun's burning rays by their layered robes. Unconcerned now with revealing his country's origin, he stripped off his clothes, like the others, and waded into the water.

After scrubbing off the desert grime, he floated on his back and welcomed the warming sun. The palms waved gently in the soft breeze. The men shouted to one another as they splashed in the water. Abram sighed with contentment. On the bank, he dried himself with cloths while slapping at the mosquitoes buzzing near the foliage. He pulled on his robes. Nearby, two bareheaded men also dressed. Their shiny black braids glistened in the sun. Abram overheard some of their chatter.

The younger one, squatting, tucked his braids into his turban. He said, "Baba, it must have been horrible for grandfather to witness what happened when his brother was murdered." His voice dropped to a whisper.

The older, scrawny one had a hump on his back. He squatted beside his companion and joined him at killing mosquitoes. "Yes, Tiras was too young to have seen such a sight."

Tiras! Abram's jaw dropped in astonishment. He turned sharply in their direction.

CHAPTER 24

August, 3468 B.C., Arabiyah
(Al-Dahna Desert in central Saudi Arabia)

THE HUMP-BACKED BEDOUIN SWIVELED TOWARD Abram. "You take a keen interest in our discussion," he said, displaying gaps in his yellow teeth. His brown face was deeply creased. "Are you from the village? I don't recall seeing you before."

Abram struggled to recover his composure. "Excuse my rudeness by interrupting your conversation. Are you a son of Tiras? From the Abram tribe?"

The man jumped up. "None of your business." He fingered his belt dagger.

The younger man jumped up as well. Wiry with tiny eyes, he withdrew his dagger and held it at his side. "You'd better not interfere with us."

The other Bedouins, already dressed, gathered about the hump-backed man and the strangers. "Are you threatening our priest?" one of them asked. "Leave us in peace. Unless you're begging for a fight."

Another man unsheathed his dagger and pointed it at Abram. "Go now! Or you'll regret it!"

Had he made a mistake? Abram scanned the men's scowls and drawn daggers and turned toward Moiseh. Suppose these rough, threatening desert men weren't his relatives? If he persisted, they might harm him. But after so many hardships, he must find out about Tiras.

Ignoring the possible danger, Abram stepped forward then and smiled to show friendliness. "I was named after the Abram tribe," he said. "I'm one of you." He scanned the confused men and added, despite his pounding heart, "I was born to Majeena, a Sumerian woman in Ur, and Tiras from Arabiyah. My guide, Moiseh, and I have traveled many miles seeking my father. If you have no knowledge of Tiras, I'll leave you alone and never bother you again."

The men stared in astonishment at Abram. "The son of Tiras," one said in disbelief.

The hump-back frowned. "Baba never mentioned fathering a child in Ur."

"He didn't know," Abram said. "Although he promised to bring my mother to join his tribe, he never returned." Abram pushed up a sleeve, exposing the brownish fig shape on his shoulder. "My mother said that my birthmark is like my father's."

The Bedouins gazed in surprise. "Look, baba's birthmark!" the hump-back said. He pushed up his sleeve to show a similar mark. "This man might be my brother!"

The others crowded about Abram, wanting to see for themselves.

"Yes, the birthmark looks like Tiras's," one said, surprised. The rest nodded.

"But that alone doesn't prove he's Tiras's son." The young man's hand still rested on his dagger. "Maybe other men have the same birthmark."

The hump-back turned to Abram. "Tell us more about baba."

"Your tribe is called the Abram. You worship a bull named Martu."

"Not anymore," one man replied, scoffing. "Besides, all the tribes know each other's gods from gossip in the oases. Tell us something only baba's son would know."

Bernadette Miller

Abram hesitated. He'd never known Tiras. What could he say? He tried to remember what his mother had told him. "Baba had three wives," he said slowly, "and three children. The favorite wife was Na'amah. But a daughter was sacrificed." He paused, trying to remember more of Majeena's descriptions. "Baba's favorite son was little Rimush when baba came to Ur."

The group stared at Abram in astonishment.

One murmured, "That's all true."

Another said, "He must be Tiras's son."

The younger man countered, "His guide might have told him all this."

"That's right!" another shouted. "Leave us, strangers. Mind your own business. Or you'll be sorry."

Abram's heart beat fast. What could he say to convince them?

"Wait!" The hump-back pushed forward into the circle. "It was my fault I lost a brother. Let me discover if El sent this brother in forgiveness. Or if the stranger is trying to gain our confidence to control our tribe." He turned to Abram. "Tell me something your guide wouldn't know."

Abram thought hard, trying to remember his mother's stories. "After his daughter, Shallah, was sacrificed, Tiras became determined to replace Martu. He wanted to find a more sympathetic god who wouldn't demand your children's blood. He persuaded his father, the sheikh, to allow him to travel to Ur. He stayed in Ur for four moon-cycles because he suffered a severe injury to his leg."

"That's true," the hump-back said. He turned to the others watching with their hands on their daggers. "And the stranger looks like baba. That same narrow face with deep-set eyes. He must be my brother!"

"It is so!" another man shouted.

"A miracle!" others shouted in awe.

The hump-back approached Abram and embraced him. Surprised, Abram kept his hands at his sides. He shouldn't disparage the unmanly behavior. He must become accustomed to the habits of these desert men who were his kin.

The hump-back said softly, "I'm Rimush. The very son you mentioned. I lost my older brother, Canah. Now, our merciful El sends me another. We are indeed your father's people. We welcome you."

When Rimush stepped aside, the younger man with tiny eyes embraced Abram. "I'm Abimah, the son of Rimush. Uncle, we're delighted to meet you."

Abram tried to smile, overcome with joy at finding his family. "I've been wanting this occasion for a very long time, and now... now... we're reunited, at last." He paused. "Where is baba? I long to see him."

Rimush hesitated and turned toward the lake. Others gazed off in the distance. Some stared at their feet.

A shiver crept up Abram's spine. Something was wrong. He felt a sense of dread. "Is he?" He couldn't bear to say the word "dead," something he was afraid of hearing.

Finally, Rimush said softly, "Baba died many moon-cycles ago. We still miss him."

Tears welled up in Abram's eyes. He was too late. Tiras was gone. He'd spent a lifetime being fatherless, hoping for guidance from the most important man he would ever know. Now, after an incredibly difficult journey, he would never meet Tiras. Dead! If only he'd gone when his marriage contract with Nammu expired. She would have welcomed him back. Why didn't he leave? Instead, the answers to his questions died along with his father.

"I had so much to ask him," Abram said. "And so much to tell him." Tears dampened his bearded cheeks. He felt embarrassed at displaying emotion. "Did our father suffer at the end?" he finally asked with faltering voice.

Rimush put his hands on Abram's shoulders. "Baba died quietly of old age. He didn't suffer."

Abram nodded, his face wet. "Did he...ever...mention my mother...?"

Bernadette Miller

Rimush shook his head. "None of us knew until now." He paused. "Perhaps that's why baba stayed so long in Ur."

"My mother loved him very much. He promised to return but never did."

Rimush nodded. "Don't grieve, my brother." His callused fingers wiped away Abram's tears. "Baba lived a long and useful life. He was loved by all the tribe."

"Thank you for your comforting words," Abram whispered, his voice breaking. Tiras was gone. Nothing could bring him back.

Rimush said, "I share your grief. After baba's death, I cried many nights alone in the darkness." He squared his shoulders to summon self-control and turned to his kinsmen. "Tomorrow, let's celebrate the arrival of my new brother with a feast. Our blessed El sent this gift to replace poor Canah."

"We'll celebrate the miracle!" the others shouted.

"I'm delighted to meet you," Abram said, trying to recover his composure.

Rimush smiled. "And we're glad, my brother, to welcome you to our tribe. Baba's spirit has returned by sending us his son."

Abram said, "Moiseh and I must retrieve our donkeys in the village and settle our finances with our hostess. Then we can go with you."

"We'll wait for you at the village entrance," Rimush said, smiling.

Later, Abram and Moiseh saw the Abram tribesmen waiting, as Rimush had promised. Several men led Abram's donkeys while the two brothers walked side by side along the trail. They chatted about their father's life in Ur.

At the camp, Abram scanned the eighty black tents stretched across the sandy plain. The strip of pasture fringing the distant lake contained flocks of grazing sheep and goats. Bedouins guided them with their shepherd's crooks. Near the tents, women cooked at outside hearths. The aromas of saffron and cardamom perfumed the air. Some tribesmen had just returned with donkeys laden from bartering at the oasis.

News spread throughout the camp that a son of Tiras had mysteriously arrived. The visitors became surrounded by kinsmen eager to greet Tiras's son.

"We're so glad to meet you!" one shouted and hugged him.

"How wonderful to meet our great leader's son," another said and kissed his cheek.

Abram smiled despite his uneasiness. Bedouin men were unexpectedly warm and friendly. But their hugging and kissing seemed childish and womanly.

Rimush led Abram and Moiseh to a tent in the heart of the encampment. He pushed aside the flap and waited. Abram stooped and entered a desert tent for the first time. He noted the black, primitive, goat-hair dwelling held upright by poles. The interior was surprisingly cool despite the sun god filtering through the weave.

Rimush called out to his wife outside at the hearth. "Zillah, prepare food and drink for our honored guests. A new brother from a faraway land." On the large carpet covering the sand, he arranged stuffed cushions in a semicircle for the diners.

Abram sank onto a comfortable cushion beside Moiseh. He scanned the bulging storage sacks hanging from side panels and the qata, the dividing curtain with its geometric designs that defined the tribe.

Rimush introduced his petite wife, Zillah, who entered through the open tent flap, balancing on her arms clay bowls of food. She wore a pale blue robe, her black plaits covered with a blue shawl.

"I welcome you," she said, smiling at the strangers. Her mouth, twisted by deformity, curled upward at one corner. "Please, eat." She placed the bowls on the carpet and squatted over a cushion. She turned toward Abram who stared at her mouth that seemed to be sneering.

"One afternoon as I gathered ghada twigs for our hearth," she explained, "a jackal attacked me. Right inside our camp! Luckily my Rimush rushed from my tent with bow and arrow and killed him."

She tried to smile, which deepened the impression of sneering. "We had little to eat at the time. All that meat turned into a feast with our kinsmen! So, the attack was an unforeseen blessing."

"A blessing for me that El spared you," Rimush said. He patted her arm.

Abram nodded, inspired by their optimism about misfortune.

"It's time to enjoy our meal with our treasured guests," Rimush added. He spat on his hands, like the others, and dried them with his soiled sleeve. Then he spat into copper cups and wiped them dry. Zillah poured goat's milk into the cups. With their right hands, the men began eating from communal bowls.

Abram choked back his revulsion, unwilling to annoy his generous hosts. It seemed as if they ate each other's dirt.

Rimush passed a large bowl. Following their example, Abram used his right hand to eat the concoction. It tasted surprisingly good.

"Bustard," Rimush explained, smiling. "A desert bird. It's a delicacy. I'm pleased you like it. The birds were killed just this morning by tribal hunters. They're plucked, cut into pieces, and thrown onto hot ashes. We especially enjoy the bustard's undigested red-haired caterpillars. Zillah's treat."

Abram nearly choked on his food at the horrible description. He covered his cough with a free hand and then tried to swallow the repulsive bits of caterpillar while forcing a smile.

Zillah nodded modestly at her husband's praise. She passed around a bowl of freshly roasted truffles, their rinds splitting from the heat.

Rimush jumped up. "Let's have wine." He poured date wine from a jug into two cleaned cups. Bending to one side, he farted before offering the cups to his guests.

Despite himself, Abram winced. He accepted the wine. He hoped his host hadn't noticed his repugnance at the unwashed cups, repulsive food, and flatulence. Moiseh, he noted, seemed quite at home with the food and drink.

"Tomorrow, we'll show you our flocks," Rimush said. "Do you know how to herd?" Abram shook his head. "Ah, it isn't difficult. You'll learn quickly."

"I don't plan to stay permanently," Abram said, lest Rimush misunderstand his intentions. "I wanted to reunite with my father's family and then return to Ur where my son awaits me."

Rimush leaned back. His hump squashed against the tent wall like ripened fruit. His head nearly rested on his chest. He noisily gulped down date wine and belched. "I see. So, you don't wish to stay with us. Perhaps we're not to your liking. Perhaps we disappoint. We're simple desert people, after all. Not like city dwellers with their critical manner."

"My baba's the tribal priest!" Abimah added. "An important position. He's wise. Chosen by my grandfather himself as his heir! You could do worse than heed his advice."

Abram said, "My decision not to stay permanently has nothing to do with your father. Ur is where my son lives. I promised him I would return. It's my home. I wouldn't live anywhere else."

"Do you think only a big city makes people happy?" Abimah asked, glaring at Abram. "Perhaps a grand city dweller is too soft to live with us and had best return."

"Abimah, you're insulting our guest!" Rimush exclaimed. "You must learn to silence unwelcome thoughts." He turned to Abram. "I deeply apologize for my son's rudeness. You are our honored guest."

"And please forgive me if I appeared impolite," Abram said. His head reeled from the strong wine. "I am very happy to be here. We traveled for many days and nights to meet my family."

"Tell us about Ur," Rimush said suddenly. "Why did baba live there so long? When he returned, a different spirit seemed to rule him."

Abram accepted more wine. Emulating the others, he reclined on an elbow and described Ur. His hosts listened, wide-eyed. Abram's eyes grew misty as he remembered his birthplace. He would postpone

Bernadette Miller

mentioning his Sumerian gods until the next day when he would be refreshed from sleep. After another cup of wine, he leaned back, his tension drained. He finally felt relaxed, less concerned with cleanliness and his supper's contents.

"I think the wine has soothed you, my brother," Rimush said. He slapped Abram on the back.

Abram waited during an awkward silence. "I'm indeed happy to be here," he finally responded, smiling.

The conversation dwindled. Rimush rose, followed by his son. He told Abram and Moiseh, "Sleep in the mag'ad, the visitor's area. I'll spend the night with Zillah behind the qata, so if you need anything, call out. I'll be nearby." He yawned.

Abram forced himself not to frown. Apparently, his relatives proved the Sumerian description that Bedouins lived in crude tents and didn't behave in a civilized manner. He wouldn't be here more than a couple of weeks, he reminded himself. Just long enough to rest for the return journey. Meanwhile, they were kind and seemed overjoyed to meet him.

As Zillah brought out two woolen sleeping rugs, Rimush embraced Abram. "Sleep well, my brother."

"And you, likewise, my brother." Abram tentatively put his arms around Rimush's shoulders, careful not to squeeze the hump while trying to ignore his odor.

The guests, wrapped in warm rugs, slept near the lit copper lantern still exuding heat. Just before falling asleep, Abram relived the day despite his head reeling from the wine. Unexpectedly, his anxiety of being rejected had been replaced by fear of contamination from his own relatives! These were his people, he again reminded himself. They were crude but sincere and hospitable. It was good he found them. Tomorrow, he would teach them about his personal god and protector, blessed Lord Enlil. They'll welcome compassionate Lord Enlil, the opposite of their hateful bull-god, Martu.

CHAPTER 25

August, 3468 B.C., Arabiyah

T HE FOLLOWING EVENING, THE TRIBE celebrated Abram's visit. At dusk, the men began gathering before Zillah's tent. They wore festive clothing: wide, ankle-length shirts; the neckline and cuffs were embroidered with multi-colored threads. Their glistening black braids flowed over their shoulders. Singing, the tribesmen called out to Abram.

"Come out, our honored guest."

"Come out. Share our joy at your arrival."

At his brother's insistence, Abram wore Rimush's best shirt adorned with gold thread. The brothers chuckled at the shirt that reached Abram's calves instead of his ankles. His graying braids framed his bearded face.

Hearing the tribesmen's urging, Abram opened the tent flap. The men cheered and clapped. He smiled at their warm welcome and waited awkwardly, like a young bridegroom, uncertain what to do next. Moiseh waited behind him.

"Go outside, my brother," Rimush said nearby. "So the celebration can begin."

When Abram emerged, the tribesmen gathered about to hug him. "We're so glad to meet you!" they shouted, taking turns pressing his body against theirs.

Abram kept repeating, "Yes, yes, I'm delighted to be here." He hesitated hugging them. Equally unsettling was their strong smell.

Rimush took Abram's hand. "Make way for our guest," he told the crowd. The men parted. He led Abram and Moiseh to the guests seated on rugs that radiated out over the desert in semi-circles. Scattered campfires provided light and heat. The visitors joined Rimush on his rug near Zillah's tent. She sat on a rug with their son, Abimah, and a female Bedouin.

His wife had prepared another special treat: roasted dabbs, spiny, fat-tailed lizards, with yoghurt and almonds. In the flickering shadows, everyone ate communal style from food piled on clay plates. The travelers, still hungry from their long journey, helped themselves to succulent meat, crispy pancakes with wild honey, figs and pomegranates, and cups of date wine from terracotta jugs.

"Eat, my brother, as much as you can," Rimush said, munching meat. "It's all because of you." Yoghurt dripped over his chin, whitening his beard.

Abram winced at his brother's bad manners. He silently reproached himself. For the first time, he sat among his family to enjoy a celebration. He shouldn't allow Sumerian etiquette to spoil it.

Rimush pointed to surrounding rugs. "Those are my other wives and children. And my deceased brother's relatives."

"Who's that lovely woman sitting with Zillah and Abimah?" Abram whispered, hoping that the woman nearby wouldn't overhear his gossiping about her.

Rimush whispered back, "Alcalah. She's the daughter of our cousin, Ruach, who died many seasons ago. A widow too old to marry. Besides, no one eligible remains to marry her. All her brothers-in-law have died." He pointed at the musicians who entered a large clearing amidst the rugs. "There's music and dancing to celebrate your visit." He explained the instruments. "That's the oud being plucked. Others shake tambourines and rattles."

Abram nodded and watched the two musicians drumming on copper pots overturned on a rug.

The tribesmen jumped up to form circles in the clearing and dance. As usual, they clapped their hands above their heads and swayed rhythmically to and fro. In the nearest circle, several held out their arms and gestured for Abram to join them. He rose and tried to imitate their steps. Moiseh joined the dancers. The women, seated on rugs, clapped to the rhythm and sang the verses. Then the children sang with high-pitched voices. The desert reverberated with their exuberant melodies.

When the dancing ended, Abram returned to his rug. Filled with a sense of peace, he leaned back on his elbows and twisted about to gaze at Alcalah, the widow. Her white embroidered robe emphasized her smooth skin. Kohl outlined her almond-shaped dark eyes. Silver bangles tinkled on her wrists. She wore long silver earrings and a carved wooden donkey suspended on a beaded chain about her neck. At the nape of her neck, a silver comb fastened two graying plaits. Though plump, she sat upright with good posture.

She turned toward Abram. He smiled at her. She smiled demurely and turned to nod at Zillah who continued chatting.

Surprised by his pulse quickening, his heart beating faster, Abram stared at the stunning woman. It seemed inconceivable that having loved Nammu so deeply he could be drawn to another woman. But the attraction seemed mutual as if a golden thread linked them together.

Feeling his gaze upon her, the widow turned again in his direction. She started to smile, caught herself, and turned away sharply, as if she didn't want others to share their intimacy.

Abram turned back to Rimush who had been chatting with relatives nearby.

"So, my brother, why are you interested in Alcalah?" Rimush whispered, grinning with amusement. "There are plenty of widows here eager for marriage, if you change your mind and decide to stay with us. I can arrange a meeting. But consider someone younger. Alcalah has no children and is too old to bear any."

"Only Alcalah holds my interest," Abram said, surprised by his admission.

"Should I arrange a meeting?"

"As soon as possible." Abram gulped more wine.

Rimush laughed. "A beautiful woman is still beautiful, no matter how old, eh, my brother?"

৪০ ৫৪

The next morning after breakfast of leftover pancakes with honey, Abram and Moiseh inspected the tribal flocks near the oasis lake. The animals grazed in the lush grass while juveniles played and younger ones nursed.

"These are mine," Rimush said proudly, pointing to several flocks at the herd's perimeter.

His sons circled their flocks with their shepherds' crooks. They waved. Rimush and Abram waved back.

Abram turned to Rimush in bewilderment. "How do you know which are yours?"

"Come, I'll show you." Rimush led him to his flock. "I raised them all from birth. He approached a sheep and lifted back its ear. "See that dyed black mark in the shape of a six-pointed star? That symbol has belonged to the Abram tribe for many generations. The three dots and circle beneath the star indicate my flocks. I'll teach you all I know."

"I owe you a great deal," Abram responded, impressed by his family's generosity.

"No," Rimush said, beaming. "Our tribe owes you for bringing back the spirit of our beloved baba." They wandered about, examining the other flocks. Finally, Rimush said, "Let's return to Zillah's tent for our midday meal."

For several hours, the men stuffed themselves with food and drink. The Bedouins belched and farted. Abram smothered his disgust. These were his people, he reminded himself again. Their ancestors had survived the desert's harsh wilderness, gaining great knowledge from the experience. Despite all those Edubba tablets he'd studied, he had much to learn about his family. He should focus on learning rather than criticizing.

While the sun god bathed the diners in his warm glow, the men chatted and watched Zillah outside, chopping a pile of branches. The earthy aroma of freshly-cut twigs filled the tent, a welcome relief for Abram.

Reaching for a fig, Abram said, "My brother, you don't have slaves to help with the work?"

Rimush set down his cup of goat's milk and gazed through the tent flap at the sand stretching toward the distant horizon. "Only Bedouins are free. We would never own slaves."

"Well, what about servants?"

Rimush shook his head and turned toward Abram. "I'm afraid you misunderstand. We can't afford servants. Our tribe is rich in tradition, loyalty, and heart. But our flocks are our only source of wealth."

"How can you endure with just animals?"

"They give us everything!" Rimush exclaimed. "Milk, cheese, butter, wool, hair, even their skin." He ate a fig and picked at his teeth for bits that stuck. "Depending on the season," he continued, "we migrate with our herds through the deserts, seeking good pastureland. But we must pay a tribute with part of our herds to the tribes claiming the land."

"Why not settle down, like Moiseh, in a village?" Abram urged. "Build a solid house. Cultivate land. Plant a garden. Isn't that more appealing than your struggle?"

Rimush stroked his beard a while. "Yes, that must seem sensible to city dwellers. But we love our independence." He gazed through

Bernadette Miller

the tent flap at the sand stretching toward the horizon. "Only people like us are truly free," he said. "Here we seek pastureland wherever we please, as long as we pay a tribute. But city dwellers must answer to their king who holds their life in his hands. They're always worried about being accused of a foul deed."

Rimush leaned over and patted Abram's shoulder. "My brother, in time you'll learn to appreciate the desert. Its unexpected beauty. Raising animals instead of grunting over plowed fields. Security and friendship from living with a loving family." He paused, gazed into the distance, and sighed. "But someday we'll roam over our own desert land," he said softly, as if speaking to himself. "Other tribes will pay us tribute. Someday, the Promised Land. Something we've always wanted."

His voice trailed off. Turning toward Abram, he withdrew from his robe a silver six-pointed star on a beaded chain. "Wear this. Zillah made it for you. Our tribal symbol has also become the symbol of our new God. It reminds us that our tribe now belongs to El."

Abram's eyebrows lifted in surprise. What happened to their bull-god, Martu, the one that ama had told him about? "New god, my brother?"

"As revealed by our beloved baba. This evening, you'll learn about it. For now, rest."

They embraced. Abram, curious about El, hung the amulet about his neck. He gazed down at it in wonder. The amulet signified his acceptance by the tribe: an extended family of over eighty households. Each person committed to helping the others. Although he was a stranger, his kinsmen trusted him.

After Rimush left to tend to his herd, Abram turned to Moiseh who'd remained silent during the discussion. Despite his lingering doubts about his guide, Abram felt the need to confide in someone and discuss his ambivalent feelings about his family. He spoke frankly, relieved that Zillah had left with a sack to dig up roots for the outside hearth.

"My kinsmen are sincere," Abram said. "I want to be at peace with them. But how can I overlook their distasteful manners? Despite my best intentions I often feel disgust."

Moiseh leaned back on his cushion, propped on an elbow. He nodded as if he understood Abram's confusion. "My feelings, too, were mixed," Moiseh said. "I tried to adapt to living in Sumer after my Bedouin boyhood. As you know, Sumerians are extremely polite. They disapprove of so many things, no matter how slight. I solved the problem by dividing my time between the two. Summers, I live in Shuruppak where it's cooler. Winters, I'm back in the desert where it's warmer. Well, over time I came to appreciate both the Sumerians and the Bedouins. These past few months are the longest I've seen the desert for many years. I'm not sorry. Your kinsmen are kind and generous. Worth knowing." He reached for a bowl of dates on the carpet and offered it to Abram.

"Thank you, but my hunger is elsewhere," Abram said. He hesitated, grateful for Moiseh finally speaking to him with frankness. Encouraged, he yearned to be honest with his guide. In a large city like Ur, he and Nammu could conceal his lowly birth from newly-acquired friends. He'd educated himself, carefully observed gentlemen's behavior, and developed a sense of refinement. Everyone accepted his lie of being the son of a highly-respected family that had moved to another country.

Abram flushed now with shame at having deceived his Sumerian countrymen. His entire adult life in Sumer had been built on lies, abetted by his wife. Perhaps his proper place was with his desert kinsmen. Although they were crude, uneducated, and lacking even basic manners, they nevertheless valued high moral standards, like honesty and sincerity. He could trust their word, especially when danger threatened. Impulsively, he decided to confess to Moiseh who looked sympathetic.

Abram took a deep breath and whispered, "Although I've been a Sumerian gentleman for many years, my mother, Majeena, was a

Bernadette Miller

slave. So, I was born into slavery. My owners' only child, Nammu, and I grew up together. After her parents died, we married. That's how I became a free citizen. When my wife died, I inherited all of her family's possessions. Our friends didn't know that I was born a slave."

Moiseh stared at him with tilted face. "My lord, I had no idea. Forgive me if I seem improper—"

"Not at all," Abram reassured him. "Your surprise is understandable. Married to a wealthy woman all those years, I didn't walk around Sumer, bragging about my lowly childhood. On the contrary, I worked hard to better myself. I reasoned that if I behaved like a Sumerian gentleman, I could convince myself and others that I was indeed one." Abram paused, his gaze downcast. "Perhaps my wealth also helped. But despite seventeen years of marriage as a free citizen, I still remember my birth. "

He looked up and smiled at Moiseh's astonished look. "Well, maybe the free spirit of desert living is prompting this confession. Or, maybe it's because we've been together a long time through numerous hardships. And you brought me safely to my family. I'd like to regard you as a friend rather than a guide."

"My lord, I'd be honored to be your friend."

"Then consider it as such. Although I'll continue paying your salary. But please call me Abram. Not lord."

Moiseh smiled broadly. "As you wish...my friend."

Abram smiled back, pleased at their new friendship.

That evening, they joined the male tribesmen with their older sons. They spread their borrowed prayer rugs near the crackling bonfire and knelt like the others. Rimush stood at the stone altar they called the Ark. He opened his arms wide beneath his multi-colored cloak as if embracing his listeners.

"Let's give thanks to El for bringing our kinsman, Abram, into our tribe. We bow in submission to El's will." The men, except for the visitors, rapidly bent their heads back and forth in agreement. When they raised their heads, Rimush added, "Now, let's recall our blessed ancestors whose roots gave us life." The tribesmen recounted their history.

Rimush paused again and said, "Time to chant our praises to El, as to a loving father. For just as we are shepherds to our flocks, so our glorious Lord is our shepherd. With His love we will never lack for anything. He heals our wounds. Delivers us from evil. Overflows our cups of wine. And guides us to lush pastures beside clear oasis lakes."

The tribesmen shouted "Yes!" in unison. They began chanting and nodding, rapidly bending their heads backward and forward. When they stopped, Rimush said, "Let's repeat the stories about our beloved El, starting with paradise, the Oasis of Eden. How El pitied Adham who felt lonely. So, El fashioned a woman from one of Adham's ribs. He called her Evewah, Lady Who Brings Life, because she could bear children. But then Evewah ate fruit from the forbidden Tree of Knowledge in paradise and enticed Adham to eat as well."

He continued the story, so familiar to his tribesmen but astonishing Abram who recognized parts based on the Sumerian tales about Dilmun, a paradise created by the goddess Nin-Kursag as a sanctuary for deities. Lord Enki ate a forbidden plant and Nin-Kursag punished him with severe indigestion. As he lay near death, Nin-Kursag felt pity and summoned Nin-ti, Lady of the Ribs, also called "Lady Who Brings Life. Nin-ti saved Lord Enki by replacing his ribs.

Rimush concluded, "Listen, my kinsmen. Woe to those who stray, like errant sheep, from our Shepherd's guidance. They'll remain forever in Jahannam. There, the Satan, Be'elsebub, aided by his servants, the jinns and shetans, remains supreme to torture them."

"Yes!" shouted the tribesmen, nodding rapidly.

Abram's amazement grew. His Bedouin father had infused the Sumerian stories, such as those about the netherworld, with significance and fervor. The new way offered much. A god like

Bernadette Miller

a loving father, one he'd never known, and unlike the Sumerian gods who could seem distant and aloof. And El preached goodness. Surely a man would want to live honorably. Abram stared at the Ark. Although he'd never abandon blessed Lord Enlil, it would be interesting to compare the Bedouins' stories about El with the Sumerian religion. He would discover how much Tiras had changed.

When the ceremony ended, Abram rolled up his rug and left with Moiseh. They spent the night in Zillah's tent, in the mag'ad.

୫୦ ୯୪

Several days later, Rimush introduced Alcalah to Abram while Moiseh inspected the herd. Her head held high, a smooth hand sweeping aside the tent flap, Alcalah bent to enter Zillah's tent. Wearing her white embroidered robe with the carved donkey necklace, she folded gracefully onto a cushion, her long, silver earrings swaying, her silver bracelets tinkling on her arms. Abram followed and sat cross-legged nearby. Her genteel manner delighted him, as well as the fragrance of thyme and chamomile, concealing the musky odor.

Rimush called out to Zillah behind the qata, "Bring food and drink for our guests." He turned to the couple smiling at each other. "Well, I'll attend to my flocks," he said and left them alone.

Zillah set down communal bowls of baked bread and cheese and cups of goat's milk. She disappeared behind the qata.

Abram noticed that Alcalah wiped her hands on a cloth before eating. Her elegance surprised him. "I've been admiring your jewelry," he told her.

"Thank you," she said. "The silver comes from the oases, delivered by caravan merchants. The jewelry..." She paused. Her eyes suddenly filled with tears. She turned away and daubed at her cheeks. "My dear mother made it. She died several seasons ago."

"I'm sorry to hear about your mother," Abram said gently. "I, too, lost my beloved mother. And, of course, you know about my father, Tiras." He swallowed hard to relieve his pain and dawdled over goat's milk to give himself and Alcalah time to recover. Then he said, "Please tell me about the carved donkey. It's unusual."

She fingered the necklace. "It has an interesting story."

"Please tell me."

"The great Tiras gave carved donkeys to his children after returning from his long journey to Ur. Many seasons later, I married a cousin who inherited it from Rimush's nephew. My poor husband gave me the donkey on our wedding night but died soon afterward from a lion's attack. I later married another cousin. He died while hunting jackals in the Nefud."

"I'm so sorry to hear of your losses." Abram paused. "You never remarried after your second husband's death?"

"No."

"How surprising to hear that!" Abram exclaimed. "You're so beautiful..." He paused, his voice trailing off, embarrassed by his outburst.

She smiled at him. "You're very polite. Paying me compliments I don't deserve."

"I never pay compliments I don't mean," Abram said, meeting her eyes until she turned away.

She nervously fingered her necklace. "Well, then, thank you." She gazed toward the qata. "According to our customs, I should marry a brother of my husbands. But they're all dead."

Abram leaned forward. "Alcalah, is it possible to marry someone other than a tribesman?"

Startled, she stared at him. "I'll speak boldly with you, Abram. As you can plainly see, I'm no longer young and vigorous. I couldn't bear children to help in old age. I've nothing to offer a man."

Abram gazed at her flawless skin and dark eyes with their serene and alert gaze. "You offer more than you realize," he whispered.

Alcalah blushed, her tanned cheeks tinted a lovely pink. He also

Bernadette Miller

blushed, as if he had forgotten in his advancing years what it felt like to fall in love. They fell silent. Finally, Alcalah rose, the pink still tinting her cheeks. "Well, I shouldn't delay you. Rimush is probably expecting you to visit his flocks."

He jumped up. "I already have." He paused. "I'd like to see your flocks. Who's tending them?"

"Rimush's sons kindly volunteered."

"Perhaps you could guide me there?"

She hesitated but finally nodded.

"Then, come, Alcalah. Let's walk to the pasture."

Outside, he grasped her hand, surprisingly soft for a woman who must live a hard life. She didn't withdraw it. Holding hands, they crossed the sand and entered the pasture carpeted with lush grass and wild flowers. Alcalah pointed to her small flock grazing near the lake. Abimah, the oldest son of Rimush, waved at them with his shepherd's crook. Smiles were exchanged.

"When my husbands were alive, our flocks were larger," Alcalah explained, looking up at Abram. "I'm not as good with them. Poor Abimah is busy helping to tend his father's flock as well."

"But I understand that tending a flock is man's work," Abram said, bending toward her. "You probably excel at women's work. Cooking and weaving."

She pursed her lips. "Abram, you must stop paying me so many compliments. I don't wish to become vain and spoiled."

"I'm merely telling the truth," he whispered and squeezed her hand.

They gazed at each other. Perhaps, he thought, she felt as he did. Perhaps her heart swelled like his from so much happiness. How could this desirable woman remain without a husband?

They chatted some more. He escorted her to her tent. "May I visit tomorrow?"

"Yes," she said. Her cheeks tinted pink again.

They exchanged smiles and he returned to Zillah's tent. He found himself whistling a newly-learned Bedouin tune.

CHAPTER 26

August, 3468 B.C., Arabiyah

THAT EVENING, ABRAM AND MOISEH joined the worshippers near the bonfire. Rimush stood before the stone altar, the Ark, and pleaded with the tribesmen to remain faithful to El. Then, he pointed at Abram. "Look, our new kinsman from Sumer joins us in praising El. Isn't that so, my brother?"

Abram rose, embarrassed because he intended to cling to Lord Enlil. He didn't want to upset the tribe so he pondered an appropriate response. Finally, he said, "I'm new to your ways, my brother. Please tell me more about your god so that my path might be clearer."

"El warned us against pursuing evil. Don't you agree?"

Abram scanned the tribesmen sitting on their rugs. "Yes. But equally important are laws."

"Uncle, please explain laws," Abimah said nearby.

Abram turned toward his nephew. "Sumerians seek justice in a courtroom, supervised by judges who have studied our laws and can apply them fairly. Without justice, a man might be stripped of the sole thing remaining to him."

"But we have our own justice," Rimush explained. "It's called bisha'a. The accused walks through a ring of fire. If he's unhurt, then El has revealed his innocence. If he burns, he's guilty. As punishment, we distribute part of his flock to his accuser."

"So, you expect your god to settle disputes," Abram said. "Sumerians settle them with laws and appropriate punishment. Here, your tribe has perhaps eighty households. But Ur has over thirty thousand citizens. Laws are needed to avoid chaos. It takes years to study all of them."

The tribe, gazing at Abram, leaned forward, fascinated.

Rimush said, "You have many gods. The Abram tribe only one. Yet our god is so powerful we dare not utter His true name. By worshipping El, you, too, could be guided by Him."

"Your god sounds powerful," Abram replied. "But why should I abandon my Sumerian god who always protected me? During my desert journey, I might have experienced many dangers. Overflowing wadis. Wild animals. Marauding bandits. Thanks to my blessed god, I arrived here safely. How could I be so ungrateful by abandoning dear Lord Enlil in favor of your El?"

"Baba, tell him about El's miracles!" Abimah shouted.

Rimush nodded. "For many generations, Martu, our former bull-god, terrified our people. When baba returned from Sumer, he persuaded us to accept El Who conquered Martu. No longer must we sacrifice our children. A miracle!"

Another man shouted, "Our Tiras was able to talk with El. He got commands directly from Him. Another miracle!"

A tribesman added, "And what about El curing Tiras's oldest boy? After being poisoned by our former priest and near death. More miracles!"

Abram said gravely to appease them, "Well, I'll give your El serious thought."

Rimush held out his arms to his new brother. He felt a dagger in his heart at remembering how he'd killed his older brother, Canah. "Would you like to stand by my side at the Ark?" he asked and took a deep breath. "I don't want to deprive you of sharing your thoughts with our kinsmen."

Abram, unwilling to usurp Rimush's position, shook his head. "I know nothing about your god. Only the Sumerian."

Rimush looked at him. "Would you like me to teach you?"

Abram had no intention of switching his faith, but Rimush seemed eager to convince him. How could he disappoint his brother in front of the others? "All right," Abram agreed reluctantly.

"Good! We'll start tomorrow. But now, my kinsmen, it's time to rest. Before the moon touches the horizon and awakens the dawn."

The men silently picked up their rugs. They walked back to their tents in small groups based on close kinship and friendships. Abram walked with Rimush and Moiseh. Others followed. Shivering in the cold, Abram clutched his cloak about his robes and strode across the sand. Silently he begged Lord Enlil not to turn from him. He must temporarily pacify his kinsmen, especially his brother Rimush who has shown him such kindness.

At Zillah's tent, Rimush laid a hand on Abram's arm. "Sleep well, my brother."

"And I wish you the same, brother," Abram responded and caught himself in a yawn as they exchanged an embrace. Abram reprimanded himself for not yawning privately. He was not so tired as to become crude like the Bedouins. These people are his family, he again reminded himself. They accepted him wholeheartedly. He watched Rimush sweep aside the qata and enter the maharama, the women's section, to spend the night with Zillah. Then he turned toward Moiseh who sat with drooping eyelids.

Moiseh mumbled, "A good night to you, my lord...uh, my friend,"

Abram smiled and thought about Alcalah. He felt the need to share his longing with his new friend starting to unroll his sleeping rug.

"I...I'm interested in a woman here," Abram confessed, whispering so that Rimush and Zillah wouldn't overhear.

Moiseh bolted upright. "Yes? Who?"

"Alcalah."

"She's lovely," Moiseh said, also whispering. "Good choice." He plopped down on his rug and stuck out his legs beneath his robes.

"Do you think Rimush would approve? That is, if I wanted more than friendship with her?"

Moiseh stared at his employer. "You want to marry her?"

"Well...maybe. Yes!"

"Bedouin marriages are arranged," Moiseh said. "Strangers aren't usually permitted to join the tribe. But since you're Tiras's son, the sheikh would probably make an exception."

Abram grinned. "Think so?"

"Of course," Moiseh said, smiling. He paused. "Well, good night, my friend. We'll speak more in the morning." He rolled up in his rug. As usual, he promptly fell asleep, snoring loudly.

Abram thought about the tribe. They seemed content despite their hardships. After all, what makes men happy? Did wealth make him happy? Or was it Nammu who filled his days with love? He felt so lost after she died, but now in his advancing years he's happy again simply thinking about Alcalah. Suppose the sheikh wouldn't allow them to wed?

Abram snuggled down into a warm, woolen rug. He rested his head on an outstretched arm. Soon, he reminded himself, he'll return to Ur, hopefully with Alcalah whether the sheikh permits the marriage or not. So, why worry? Besides, he had no intention of abandoning his personal god to worship a different one because of convenience. He gazed at the dividing curtain, then closed his eyes, and thought, *Blessed Lord Enlil, my heart always belongs to you. Please don't abandon me. Let Alcalah become my wife.*

∞ CB

While his sons tended his flock, Rimush began teaching Abram and Moiseh about the tribe's new God. Zillah set out food and drink and retired behind the qata.

Abram thoughtfully spooned honey onto a bread-cake. "Why is El your only god?" he asked.

"Because he conquered all the others," Rimush replied.

"Why can't I see him?" Abram asked, finishing his bread-cake.

Rimush pushed the bowl of dates toward Abram, who ate several. "El is too powerful to be seen. Baba was the only one allowed to see him. But if others did, they would be blinded by El's brilliant light. I've never seen him, but I've been blessed to talk with Him."

"You've talked with Him!" Abram exclaimed in amazement.

"If I may be so bold as to join the conversation," Moiseh said. He put down his goat's milk and looked quizzically at Abram.

"Please don't hesitate," Abram replied. "I'm sure my brother would welcome converts."

Rimush said, "Yes, Moiseh. Continue."

Moiseh leaned toward Rimush. "Worshipping a lone god isn't new. My cousin told me about some people in Amrata who started worshipping only the sun god. Of course, the Per-ao doesn't know this." He looked at Abram. "Per-ao is Amrati for Great House of the King. It translates into our tongue as Pharaoh."

"Ah, but El isn't anything like the Amrati sun god!" Rimush cried out, his hump looming as he leaned toward Abram. "El is mightier than all those other gods. Don't you see, my brother? It's more beneficial to worship one rather than spreading devotion among many."

"That sounds reasonable," Abram replied gravely. "But Lord Enlil always helped my family. He might take revenge for my desertion. I can't take that risk."

Rimush sighed and poured milk into Abram's empty cup. "Since baba convinced us to worship El, sickness has abated. Sometimes, if we've done something foolish that might displease El, we confess our sins into the ears of a goat. We send it out into the desert to appease El and show our obedience. We're always rewarded for our piety."

Rimush paused and shouted toward the dividing curtain. "Zillah, bring more bread-cakes and dates for our guests!" He turned

Bernadette Miller

toward the men waiting for his explanation. "Winged humans bring El tidings of Earth," he continued. "Upon a good man's death, these gentle creatures flap their giant wings and carry his soul up to the Oasis of Eden, our paradise. But woe to the wicked! They bear his soul down to Jahannam, the fiery netherworld, for eternal punishment."

Like the Sumerians' Annunaki, children of Lord An, Abram thought. To punish their sins, Lord An forced the Annunaki to sprout wings like birds and fly the dead to the netherworld. He kept silent to avoid upsetting his brother and watched Zillah set down filled bowls.

"Besides," Rimush added, "El proclaimed us as His chosen people. We alone shall enter paradise if we've obeyed His commandments and lived a good life."

Abram nodded as if in agreement while marveling again at how the simple tribesmen had transformed Sumerian ideas. The Sumerian gods created a paradise for themselves, not man. But why shouldn't man have a paradise? The Sumerians were first to claim they were their gods' chosen people. Well, why can't the Bedouins make the same claim if it makes them happy?

Still, Abram kept silent. He didn't want to upset Rimush by explaining how the tribesman, influenced by Tiras, had copied parts of the Sumerian religion to fashion a new one, and thus possibly angering the Sumerian gods. Still, Rimush seemed content, utterly convinced that El had been the sole source of Tiras's inspiration. Abram hesitated at confusing Rimush and possibly causing a loss of faith in El.

"Baba once asked El His name," Rimush said, leaning back. "Our God replied, 'I am that I am.'" Perhaps our mind would burst with knowledge that's beyond our power to understand." He sipped goat's milk, and added, "El is more powerful than the Sumerian gods. They're concerned mostly with their own comfort. Our God is concerned mostly with ours."

"A good point," Abram admitted. "I'll consider it." He rose. "But now I must leave. I promised Alcalah I'd visit."

"So, even as we debate these important matters, your attention is elsewhere."

Abram laughed. "I am, after all, but a man with the usual desires."

"I'll see to my flock," Rimush said, rising. He embraced his brother.

Abram avoided the hump by hugging Rimush about the neck. He enjoyed the warmth of comradeship. Since Nammu's death, he'd nearly forgotten what it felt like to share another's affection. Besides, he thought ruefully, by not bathing, he was growing accustomed to everyone's odors, and by this time, he probably had his own odor.

When they separated, Rimush paused at the tent flap. "I'll join you and Moiseh for supper. Until then, my brother, "salaam 'alaykum."

"'Alaykum salaam," Abram and Moiseh replied.

Outside the tent, Abram watched Rimush head toward the pasture. He turned to Moiseh. "Have you somewhere to go while I visit Alcalah?"

Moiseh stared at the tension poles holding the tent to the sand. "I met a maiden who interests me."

"I see," Abram said, smiling. "So we both have men's business to attend to."

At Alcalah's tent, the third beyond Rimush's, Abram paused at entering the home of an unmarried, single woman, although his meeting with her had been arranged by Rimush. While he stood debating, Alcalah, wearing her white embroidered robe, opened the tent flap.

"Come in," she said.

He followed her to the mag'ad where he glanced about, admiring her beautifully-woven dividing curtain, cushions, and storage sacks.

"Please sit and share some bread-cakes with dates," she said.

He smiled and sat on a cushion, his long legs stretched out, his robes curled about him.

She set before him a cup of goat's milk flavored with honey, a jug of milk, and a bowl of bread-cakes. Then she sat gracefully on a nearby cushion, her white robe flowing about her, the silver bracelets tinkling.

Although full, he drank the milk and ate two cakes, not wishing to appear rude.

"Tell me about your life in Ur," she said, carefully setting down her cup on the carpet.

"I'd rather talk about you."

She sighed. "So many compliments." She leaned forward and filled his cup with more goat's milk from the jug. "Abram, there's little to add to what I've already told you about myself. Your distant city seems...like a magical place. Please tell me about Ur and your life there."

He sipped milk. Should he tell her about his slave birth? Her gaze seemed so direct and sympathetic, she might understand even if the tribes didn't have slaves. "My mother, Majeena, was born as a slave to a Sumerian man who cured Tiras's injury. The Sumerian man didn't know that my mother had lain with Tiras. His daughter, my mistress, forgave Majeena for bearing me, the child of a Bedouin. So, I grew up a slave."

Alcalah listened intently, her eyes glistening at hearing such honesty from a man she'd just met.

"A slave has no freedom?"

"None."

Alcalah mused over this description. Her expression was one of pure beauty, he thought.

"I hated being a slave," he continued. "I finally gained my freedom by marrying Nammu, my childhood playmate. If it weren't for Nammu, I don't know how I could have endured a life of servitude. Her death nearly overcame me with grief. But all my life, I longed to find my father, Tiras. So, after Nammu's death, I finally hired Moiseh, a desert guide. Then, fortunately, I met Rimush and the others and learned that my father had died." His voice trailed off at his sense of loss. "And now I'm here with you," he finished.

She continued gazing at him, her head tilted to one side as if examining his heart. She touched his arm. "Abram, I share your grief at losing your loved ones. Do you have kinsmen in Ur?"

He savored the touch of her hand. "No. They're all here in the desert." He paused. "Well, except for a slave that I raised like a son."

They chatted some more and fell silent. Abram gazed into her dark eyes.

Finally, Alcalah said, "Well, Rimush must be eager to see you. I don't want him to feel that you've abandoned him because of me."

"You can't imagine how I enjoy being with you," Abram said.

Alcalah blushed. "Me, too."

She's adorable, Abram thought. He reached over and kissed her soft hand. "Tomorrow?"

Alcalah nodded and escorted him outside. He turned once, then twice, to look back at her. She'd remained standing outside her tent to gaze at him before stepping inside.

୫୦୦୫

During the following weeks of spending time with Alcalah, Abram thought of little except her. He decided to propose. She seemed to care about him. The tender way she looked at him, the way she listened so intently. Would the tribe approve and, if so, would she marry a foreigner whose life had been so different than what she was accustomed to? How should he approach her?

Finally, one afternoon, after eating and chatting, he burst out impetuously, "Would you consider marrying again?"

Startled, her eyes widened, she said, "Perhaps. But no tribesman is available. At least none who's appealing."

"Suppose the man isn't a tribesman..." Abram's voice trailed off. He hadn't intended proposing so bluntly but didn't regret it.

"Are you asking...me to marry you?" She stared at him in disbelief. "All our marriages are arranged by kinsmen."

"Yes...well...this might seem sudden..." He set down his cup and leaned toward her. "Alcalah, as you can see, I'm no longer young and vigorous. Having a wife such as you would fill my remaining time with much happiness. That is, if you could feel as I do."

"Abram, we must discuss practical matters. I live alone in my tent. It's hard for a woman to be without male help. I have no children to tend my flock. And yet..."

"And yet?" he coaxed.

"I have only a few sheep and goats. A small dowry."

"In Sumer I'm wealthy. A large house with slaves and many shekels. You'll live like a queen, lacking nothing." Her frown worried him. "You wouldn't want to live in Ur?"

"I'm a daughter of the desert. This is my home. My family's here. Why not join our tribe? They love you like a kinsman. As you said, you have no family in Ur, only a son you could bring here. Who else cares about you? Wouldn't you rather live with an affectionate family?"

He stared at the rug's intricate patterns, and then looked up. He savored her mature beauty with a new-found admiration "Alcalah, as you wisely reminded me, my kinsmen have shown me much affection. We could stay here in the desert. Among your family and mine. And I could bring my son here."

Smiling, she said, "Are you certain you want this?"

"Yes," he replied, gazing into her dark eyes. "But I need to settle my affairs in Sumer, and return with Aradmu. Would you accept him as our son?"

"Gladly," she said. She refilled his cup. "There's another matter." She hesitated.

He pressed her hand. "Please confide in me, Alcalah."

"For us to marry, you must accept El, the one true god. El chose the Abram tribe as His special people. I could never marry a disbeliever. You've worshipped Sumerian gods all your life. How can I expect you to forsake them in favor of mine?"

Abram withdrew his hand. He stroked his beard, thinking.

Their god tempted him with the desire for an ethical life. A worthy cause, but if he accepted El, what calamities might befall him after abandoning Lord Enlil, his personal protector? Mighty Lord Enlil might become enraged at a Sumerian worshipping an unknown god with whom he had no prior relationship and hence bore no deep feeling. Perhaps, in retribution, Lord Enlil would curse the tribe with sickness and death, a risk he wasn't prepared to chance.

"I understand," Alcalah said, turning away to hide her disappointment. "I can't ask for such a sacrifice."

Abram rose. She accompanied him to the tent flap. He turned toward her. "Much as I long to marry you, Alcalah, I must study your El before deserting Lord Enlil. I'll give you my answer soon," he said and kissed her hand. "May I visit again tomorrow?"

She nodded, her eyes shiny. "If you still want to."

"I haven't become discouraged from seeing you, but I need to consider your requirements for marriage."

"I'm also patient. I'll wait for your answer, Abram."

He smiled. Nammu had said something similar when they were young. A good omen.

That night, Abram tossed restlessly beneath his rug. Unable to sleep, he watched the woven walls shimmer in the breeze blowing gently against the tent. The tiny area compared with his house in Ur seemed to close in about him, suffocating him. He thought about Alcalah and his heart seemed to swell again with happiness. Then he remembered his sworn devotion to Lord Enlil. His personal god wouldn't appreciate his worshipper switching devotion and dedication. Abram rose in the mag'ad, opened the tent flap, and gazed upward at the sky with its twinkling star goddesses and the Bedouins' god, El. Was the answer there, as Rimush had described in his sermons?

Lord Enlil, he prayed silently, *please forgive me if I pretend to accept El. I'll always adore you. Deep in my heart where no one will know.*

Nearby, Moiseh slept peacefully. His snores, gentle for once, washed over Abram like a lullaby.

Bernadette Miller

Suddenly a brisk breeze whistled through the tent. A sign! Fear struck at Abram. He held up his arms toward the tent ceiling, worried by the ill omen. *Please, Lord Enlil, I beg you not to be angry with me.* He shuddered, trying not to picture Lord Enlil's possible revenge at being replaced. Sickness might come, or worse, he would lose Alcalah. *Please help me capture Alcalah for my own. I'll be lost without her love.*

The breeze outside faded. Peace and quiet reigned. Abram nodded, recognizing Lord Enlil's response. The forgiving God had allowed him to accept El under pretense and marry Alcalah. What other meaning could there be?

During his next visit, Abram assured Alcalah he was eagerly learning about El. "Thanks to Rimush's patience," he lied, "I'm beginning to believe that your god might be greater than mine. El's miracles are impressive." He paused, worried about his deceit. Was it right to lie to someone he loved? The truth, though, would hurt her.

He decided to take a middle path. "But I still have questions," he said, smiling. "Why should I pray to an unseen god who shows no proof of his existence? No statues or carvings. How do I know your El is the true god, above all others?"

Alcalah placed her hand on his arm. "Abram, the creator of everything we see can't be trapped in a piece of wood or stone. Like a loving father, El knows the evil that tempts us. He persuades us to follow a moral life to avoid catastrophes." She dropped her gaze. "I learned this from Rimush who learned it from Tiras. Rimush struggles to answer many questions. Some he receives after experiencing deep emotion; El appears to him then. Others arrive in dreams. Rimush tells the tribesmen and they repeat the stories for future generations."

Although he disliked lying, Abram nodded as if eager to hear more.

&⊃CB

As the tribe migrated through the Nefud Desert, the couple

began meeting daily in her tent. Two weeks passed. One evening, after answering more questions, she pushed the bowl of bread-cakes toward her guest. "You're not eating."

"I'd rather look at you because you're so beautiful."

She blushed. "You know I'm too old for such compliments."

He reached for her smooth hand and admired her clean fingernails. He whispered, "My Alcalah, you'll always be beautiful to me. I'm willing to accept your god if you'll become my wife."

"Abram, I wish you would accept El because you realize His greatness. Instead, you regard Him simply as a requirement to marry me."

"But it is a requirement. You told me so. Now that I'm willing to accept it, you're still unsatisfied."

She bit her lip and gazed toward the tent ceiling as if seeking El to resolve this dilemma.

He pressed her hand against his heart. "I love you. I want to be with you for the rest of my life."

She turned toward him, her eyes brimming with tears. "Oh, Abram, I do return your love. I'm happy you accept El, no matter how you arrived at that decision."

Abram rose and helped Alcalah to rise. He put his arms about her and sought her lips against his, his beard brushing her cheeks.

She didn't refuse him. "I'll tell Rimush about your decision to convert," she whispered when they separated.

"My love," Abram murmured. "I'll do everything possible to make you happy." They kissed again. "I need to settle my affairs in Sumer," he added, and bring back my son, Aradmu."

"Would your son be happy here after growing up in a city?"

"He'll be happy as long as I'm with him, the only father he's ever known."

She nodded. "I'll regard him as my son as well." She looked at him, her eyes luminous. "I'm sure the sheikh will grant permission for our marriage since you're Rimush's brother."

Bernadette Miller

"Then, come, my Alcalah. Let's tell Rimush."

She rested her head against his chest. "You've made me happier than you could ever imagine. My only regret is that I'm too old to bear a child."

"It's unimportant as long as we're together," he said, holding her close.

She smiled up at him and they left the tent. Abram's pulse raced with excitement at being united with his beloved Alcalah.

The couple, holding hands, walked across the sand to the pasture. Rimush, bent over a calf, looked up and smiled.

"Alcalah has agreed to be my wife," Abram said. "I will convert and swear allegiance to your El."

Rimush beamed and waved his shepherd's crook at the tribesmen. "Come closer!" he shouted. "Important news!" The men ran across the grassy strip filled with grazing animals. "Listen, my kinsmen," Rimush called out, "My brother Abram will wed the widow Alcalah and accept El as the only true God. Let's embrace our new tribal brother."

The tribesmen gathered about Abram and Alcalah. "Congratulations!" they shouted and hugged the couple. Abram hugged them back, welcoming their affection. Then, he and Alcalah strolled back to her tent to discuss wedding plans. Still holding her hand, he tried to overcome his guilt that her sweetness seemed to surpass Nammu's.

That night, Abram lay awake beneath his rug. He pondered his recent decision. His past no longer mattered. His future lay with Alcalah and the Abram tribe, but would El accept a Sumerian among His chosen people, knowing the supposed convert lied about his devotion? Would He reject Abram and possibly harm him?

CHAPTER 27

MOISEH HAD MET RAKEL WHILE exploring the Abram camp on his own. One evening, he had wandered about the pasture, skirting the grazing flocks. A pretty young woman ran about, waving her shepherd's crook and whistling to keep her animals restricted within a half-acre of grass. Surprised she didn't have a husband for this chore, Moiseh approached her. He was also surprised that she didn't resemble a Bedouin. Her hair was auburn, not black, and twisted in shiny curls past her shoulders. Although she wore desert robes, her fair skin was reddened rather than brown like an almond from the sun god.

"Why do you stare at me?" she called out to Moiseh, who lingered near her. "Are you following me?"

"I'm visiting your tribe," he said. He admired her small uplifted chin. He gazed in surprise at her flashing eyes. They were deep blue. Only once he had seen such eyes: fair-skinned foreigners with blond hair visiting Shuruppak, seeking a desert guide.

"Where are you from?" he asked when she stopped to confront him.

"None of your business. I don't speak with strangers. If you're indeed visiting. Which I'm beginning to doubt because of your rudeness. Then you should be with your host, not interfering with my work." She turned in dismay as a ram wandered off. "Oh, see what you've done. Leave me alone!" She ran after the ram and guided him back to the flock with her shepherd's crook. The flock bleated at the noise and confusion.

He panted to keep up with her. "I'm visiting Rimush," he called out. "The son of Tiras." Maybe that would impress her enough to allow conversation, he thought.

She stopped. "Tiras, the great priest?"

"The same." He smiled. "May I help? I used to have a flock."

"No. You're still a stranger. Besides, I don't require a man's help." She ran after another wandering ram.

"So you're quite independent," he called out, admiring her spirit as he pursued her. "You're not Bedouin by birth? Who were your people?"

She guided the ram back to the flock. "I don't have time for conversation. Can't you see how busy I am? Oh, there's another one leaving."

"I'll catch him," Moiseh said. He chased after the ram. Whistling, he grabbed the horns and gently pulled him back to the flock while the ram snorted his displeasure.

She laughed. "I'm surprised Bilba didn't bite you. Usually he's not so polite."

"I told you I know my way around a flock," Moiseh said. He watched her head toward another runaway. "Let me help."

"Go away. I don't need help."

He continued chasing her as she ran back and forth. "You have a gorgeous face," he shouted. "Why aren't you married?"

"Because I can't stand stupid men like you!"

"I know far more than you imagine! I'm from Sumer, a land far, far away."

She stopped again and smiled. He noticed her charming dimples. "Now you have my attention," she said, pointing her shepherd's crook at him. "I'd like to know more about Sumer. I'm Rakel."

"Moiseh," he said, reaching for her free hand. She pulled it away.

"We can't talk here because you're busy," he said, "although I'd gladly help if you'd let me. May I meet with you in your tent?"

"Certainly not! I don't want the tribe to assume I'm no longer a maid. I'll meet you near the pasture this evening."

"I'm eager to see you again," Moiseh said.

"We'll discuss Sumer—nothing else."

"As you wish." He felt blood pounding in his ears. How many years had passed since his wife died? Too many.

That evening, Moiseh mumbled an excuse to Abram about exploring the camp, and slipped out of the tent. He headed toward the pasture but didn't see Rakel. Disappointed, he wandered among the herdsmen, asking for her. Finally, a Bedouin boy pointed toward the distant well. Moiseh hurried in that direction and saw Rakel carrying a lamb, a newborn.

She looked up. Tears wet her face. "Poor thing. Lost its mother. I hope to raise it."

"We need to find a surrogate mother," he said. "Or the baby will die."

She shook her head. "None will accept it."

Moiseh thought for a moment. From his belt he untied a goatskin filled with milk. "Let's try this. It might work." He sat beside her on a flat rock and offered the milk to the lamb. It could barely open its eyes. Moiseh guided the tiny mouth to the milk. The baby sucked it noisily.

"Oh, you do know your way around animals," she said. "You must have been a Bedouin."

"Among other things." He forced himself to concentrate on the lamb. "You didn't tell me where your people were from."

"My foster father who recently died found me in the desert. I was wrapped in a rug and left beneath a tamarisk tree. I'd been abandoned. He raised me."

"Who was he?"

"Jethro. A Midianite from Cana'an. He'd married a woman from the Abram tribe. Decided to stay with her people. We don't know where my original parents came from. Maybe farther east. I've lived my entire life with the Abram tribe, but I never met anyone else with blue eyes. Are they very ugly?"

The lamb had stopped sucking and closed its eyes to sleep. Moiseh reached over to pat the tiny head. Rakel reached over as well. She withdrew her hand when he touched her. Her hand was smooth from patting sheep with their oily wool.

"Your eyes are beautiful. So why didn't you marry?" he asked gently.

She shrugged. "I enjoy my freedom. I don't like anyone giving me orders, not even my foster father although we loved each other. He finally gave me my own tent to have peace between us. No man would be happy with me."

"I would," Moiseh whispered.

She stared at him. "You're too old. I'm seventeen."

"Yes, I'm older. Past thirty. But my heart's young."

"And I don't like that ugly scar on your forehead."

"That's a sign of my manhood. I defeated a desert bandit. My scar is misleading. It doesn't necessarily mean someone is bad. I could take care of you. If you'd let me."

She shook her head and gazed down at the lamb sleeping in her arms. "I'll carry him to my tent, poor little thing."

He accompanied her and paused outside the tent flap. "May I visit you tomorrow, Rakel?"

"All right. But don't expect anything to come from it." She turned abruptly and entered her tent. She soothed the lamb who'd awakened and begun bleating.

Moiseh bent and shoved the goatskin of milk through the open tent flap. "I'll bring more tomorrow."

"Tomorrow you may help if you wish," Rakel said from inside.

Moiseh agreed and headed back toward Rimush's tent. His arms swung by his side as he strode over the clumps of vegetation, his body as weightless as air. He hadn't felt this young in years, not since he'd met Kirigal, his deceased wife. A Sumerian related to the royal family, Kirigal had ordered him about as if she were a princess and he were her loyal subject. He smiled at the memory of their meeting.

୫ ୪

The young woman had waited by her mansion entrance, in a driving wind, while a slave rushed to open the heavy oak door. She clutched the door handle for support. Her other hand grabbed her headdress threatening to topple over. Moiseh braced himself against the wall, removed his shawl, and held it around her headdress, shielding it from the wind.

"Excuse my impertinence," he said politely, "but I believe you need this." Her stare chilled and excited him. He determined then and there to win her affection.

She scanned his hairy chest and grimy tufted skirt and said coldly, "Who are you to be so bold with royalty? A commoner from the very lowest class."

"Yes, I'm a humble desert guide," he replied, grinning. "But I could make you very happy."

"Humph! I don't admire your rudeness." The door swung open. She swept past him into the great hall, her head held high, and turned toward him. "Desert guide? You're rash as well as a fool."

Her disdain didn't discourage his determination. He unearthed her habits. She had several lovers, but nobody special. She would meet them secretly in a café in a nearby city. Other nights she enjoyed meeting with her women friends, sitting on the grass outside her mansion, drinking wine. One night he sneezed and was thus discovered behind the bushes. His presence embarrassed and outraged her.

"How dare you follow me!" she exclaimed. "I never want to see you again."

He bowed and left but looking back he noticed her dark eyes watching his retreat. "I won't give up!" he had shouted at her.

He sighed. It took two years for her to yield. A delicious and rewarding wait! Now, as he walked back to Zillah's tent, he savored the memory of his wedding night. Kirigal had abandoned her family and wealth to marry him. She'd agreed to live in a modest house near an irrigation canal, only to die from illness five years later. He'd wept ceaselessly, blaming himself for not providing healthier surroundings. In despair, he considered ending his life. Instead, he returned to work, his only consolation. His travels throughout the desert kept him busy. After ten endless years, he finally stopped mourning Kirigal. Instead, he would now dream about Rakel.

⟐⟐

Several days after meeting her, he disappeared from Rimush's tent while Rimush taught Abram about El. Abram assumed that Moiseh, being a guide, enjoyed exploring. But Moiseh's only exploring was in helping Rakel with her flock and the orphaned lamb.

"Don't expect anything beyond friendship," she warned him repeatedly. "I have no desire to lose my freedom."

"I can assure you that if you were my wife, you'd gain my protection while keeping your freedom. Besides, I'd spoil you with love."

"Would you really spoil me?" she teased while serving dates.

He nodded, delighted that their friendship had progressed so that he could visit inside her tent. "Tell me what you want," he whispered. "I'll give it to you. No matter what."

"A kind, understanding man," she said and tossed her head, her curls flying.

"I'm that man!" Moiseh exclaimed. He leaned over to kiss her lips.

She jumped up from her cushion. "No, you're not. You assume

too much." She set out cups. "Let's have goat's milk. I saved some for the lamb. In a corner of the tent, the lamb bleated and wobbled toward Rakel, who caught it in her arms. "Come to oomah, little one."

"You need a real baby to hold," Moiseh said.

Her skin flushed as brightly as a pomegranate. "I'm not ready."

"But soon." Moiseh reached out to pet the lamb who snuggled against him.

"He likes you! You're wonderful with animals."

"Thank you." Moiseh continued petting the lamb.

After several weeks, Moiseh wondered if indeed anything would spring from their friendship. Rakel was unlike most women. He preferred excitement, the reason he'd been attracted to his demanding wife. Rakel wouldn't commit herself to marriage.

"No, I'm too young, especially for you," she kept saying.

After seeing each other every day and watching him work with her flock, she softened toward him, enough one evening to allow him to kiss her lips.

"Ah, shepherdess of my heart," Moiseh murmured. He bent toward her and embraced her. The kiss was not as he'd expected. She was surprisingly gentle, as with the lamb. "Is this the first time you've kissed a man?" he asked. She blushed. "Then I'm glad you chose me." He kissed her again.

She put her arms about him but turned her head to one side.

"Can't make up your mind about me, eh, Rakel? But I'll convince you." He kissed the nape of her neck as tenderly as possible, his beard brushing her skin.

When they separated, she said, "Moiseh, you're most persuasive. Come to see me. Help me with my flock. Maybe one day I'll yield."

"I'll obey your commands," he said and stroked her hand. "Until tomorrow."

"Tomorrow," she murmured and turned her back on him.

He left to rejoin Abram in Rimush's tent. The men earnestly discussed El.

Bernadette Miller

"So, my tent companion finally appears," Abram said, glancing up as Moiseh entered and sat cross-legged on a cushion. Abram and Rimush smiled at their visitor who helped himself to baked bread with liquid butter. "Moiseh, you're welcome to join our discussion," Abram said. "We missed your contributions."

"But I don't know much about the gods," Moiseh replied, his gaze fastened upon his meal. "I've never been interested in such things."

"Never interested in the gods?" Rimush stared, his brows lifted in surprise. "Would you convert if I could prove El's value?"

Moiseh hesitated. He busied himself with chewing bread.

Abram grinned. "Perhaps your new friend might persuade you?"

Rimush looked from one man to the other and focused on Abram. "My brother, is something happening with Moiseh that I don't know about?"

"I like a young Bedouin woman," Moiseh said, gazing at the carpet. "But she won't consider marriage. Certainly not with me." His lips squeezed together.

Startled, Rimush asked, "Who is she?"

Moiseh sighed. "Rakel."

The men fell silent for a moment, contemplating what to say.

Rimush shook his head. "Rakel is unruly. She's been of marriageable age for several seasons. No man wants her. She's like a wild animal. She disregards our customs and taunts the tribesmen at every opportunity. Several young men pursued her. She laughed at them. In fact, she challenged one to a wrestling match. She won because he feared hurting her. He walked away, humiliated. Why would you crave such a woman?"

"Because she's pretty and feisty. The kind that charms me. I'll persuade her to be my wife."

"Then let's make it a double wedding," Abram said. "I'll wed my Alcalah the day you wed your Rakel."

While ABram learned how to care for flocks-shearing sheep, slaughtering, helping with birth, and treating the old and sick- Moiseh pursued his desire which seemed destined for defeat.

Hoping to end the impasse, Alcalah talked with Rakel. "You'll never know love, as I have," she said in Rakel's tent one afternoon while the women squatted on the carpet and spun wool. "You'll never experience a man's passion and dreams. Never ease his fears. Never share the companionship of a life together."

Rakel stared stubbornly at the spindle that she twirled with her right hand while her left hand guided the wool streaming onto it. "I like Moiseh because he's persistent. He refuses to give up like the others. I even like the scar because it shows his manliness. But he's too old for me—"

"But that's exactly what you need," Alcalah interrupted. She shifted the branch of twisted wool under her left arm, and leaned forward. "Moiseh in gratitude will give you whatever you ask. A younger husband might demand more as you grow older. Lose interest and prefer a younger woman."

"Oh, I don't know…" Rakel's voice trailed off. She focused on the wool-gathering spindle twirling on the carpet. "I suppose if Moiseh truly loves me." She pursed her lips. "I'd hate to relinquish my freedom to become some man's servant."

Alcalah laughed. "Poor Moiseh will be the servant!"

Rakel joined her laughter. "Well, he is kind and understanding. He certainly knows how to care for animals." She paused. "I'll consider it and give Moiseh my answer."

"I hope you'll agree soon." Alcalah gathered up her spindle and wool that she placed in a basket. At the tent flap, she turned toward Rakel. "Abram wants a double wedding."

Rakel's eyes narrowed. "So that's the reason you visited me."

"But not the only one," Alcalah responded, hoping she was

persuasive. "As you yourself said, Moiseh's kind. He'll obey your every wish. You'll be happy with him."

Many days passed while Rakel pondered Moiseh's proposal. Although he helped with her flock and shared a mid-day meal in her tent, he had waited before broaching the subject again to avoid seeming like a pest. Each time she demurred, offering excuses.

"I'm too young," she said one afternoon. Squatting on her carpet, she handed him a bread-cake from the bowl.

"No, you're just the right age," Moiseh replied seated beside her. He put down the food and leaned over to kiss her lips. "A young tribesman wouldn't understand you."

She nodded but still refused his offer.

The following week, she protested, "I'm too independent."

"But that's exactly what I like about you," Moiseh said, grinning. "Just like my first wife." Rakel's lips curved in a slight frown; her lovely blue eyes narrowed. Did she reveal a hint of jealousy? A good sign! "Not many men appreciate feisty women," he reminded her and was rewarded with a smile.

The following week she confessed, "I'm too nervous about marriage. I'm worried we wouldn't get along and I'll be unhappy."

"Ah, but you already know me," he said. "Wouldn't you feel more comfortable with someone you know well? Rather than a kinsman you've hardly spoken with."

"That's true," Rakel said. She gazed thoughtfully at the bowl of uneaten honey cakes beside the cups of goat milk. "Let me think about it."

"Don't wait until both of us are in our graves," Moiseh said, rising from his cushion. "It won't be any fun then. Well, I should join Abram and Rimush who's teaching us about El."

The next week, Rakel asked, "Would you agree to worship only El?" She stared at him fixedly.

"Yes," he assured her. "Your wish is my command."

"Then, maybe, just maybe. Nothing definite. As I said, maybe, I'd consider marriage with you."

"Ah, shepherdess of my heart," Moiseh murmured and embraced her for a kiss.

"I said, maybe," she reminded him after their kiss. "Nothing definite."

"Yes, yes, maybe," he said and they kissed again.

"Well, maybe more than maybe," she said moving closer to him on the carpet. They kissed again. Her blue eyes were shiny. "All right," she whispered in his arms. She sighed deeply. "Let's marry."

Delighted, he hugged her, they kissed once more, and he returned to Zillah's tent, swinging his arms and grinning from ear to ear. Renewed energy flowed through him, as if El had lifted twenty years from his body to return his vigorous youth.

"She agreed to marry me!" Moiseh exclaimed while opening the tent flap.

"Congratulations!" Rimush said, shifting on his cushion. "We'll welcome you into our tribe."

Abram, beaming at the news, repeated, "Yes, congratulations!" At last Alcalah would be his. He still felt uneasy about accepting the Bedouin god, El. It's only pretense, he reminded himself. He still worshipped Lord Enlil in his heart, like any pious Sumerian. But would Lord Enlil agree to the pretense? Both gods might punish him.

CHAPTER 28

October, 3468 B.C., Arabiyah
(Al-Nefud Desert in northern Saudi Arabia)

THE NIGHT BEFORE HIS RITUAL acceptance of El, Abram tossed about and finally donned his cloak and walked outside in the moonlight spraying the desert. At the oasis lake, he squatted on the grassy bank and gazed at the rippling water. *Dear Lord Enlil, please forgive me if I seem to worship another. Tomorrow, I'll stand before Rimush and pledge my loyalty to El. But you'll always be my heart's choice. Alcalah and my family mean so much to me. I can't join them unless I pretend to accept El.*

He inhaled the pure, clean air, the realm of Lord Enlil, and glanced about for a sign from his personal god. *I'll learn the tribe's rituals, Lord Enlil. I'll assure my beloved family of my devotion to El. But I'll never forget you. Never!* He sat rigid with expectation. *Please, dear Lord Enlil, send me a sign. Let me know that you agree with my decision.*

After all, Abram reasoned, hadn't the tribesmen adopted some of the Sumerian religion? He shook his head. They hadn't adopted his gods, like Lord Enlil. He glanced about the desert, his brows furrowed with worry. A hare emerged from its burrow, sniffed the air, and scurried away. *Lord Enlil, you're commanding me to abandon you?*

Unsure of Lord Enlil's intent, Abram gazed at the star-filled sky. Was that El's paradise? His body shifted with uneasiness. El promised a great deal to His worshippers. Was it possible to worship both gods without inviting their anger?

The following evening, he stood before Rimush at the altar. Near the bonfire's sparks, Abram took the sacred oath. He placed his hand between his thighs and promised to worship only El. Afterward, his elated kinsmen crowded about. They hugged him and thumped his back in excitement.

"Now you're one of us!" one shouted.

"You belong to the Abram tribe!" another shouted.

Abram smiled shyly, knowing he lied. "I am one of you," he agreed and gazed upward toward El's shining home as his kinsmen continued hugging him. He tried not to shudder at the fear of both gods punishing him.

Several days later, determined to forget his false conversion, Abram celebrated the double wedding. Moiseh and Rakel joined him and Alcalah at her tent flap. Each bridegroom shared a cup of wine with his bride. The brides drank and stomped on their cups, as was the custom. As the pieces flew about, the tribe applauded and shouted congratulations.

For the grand feast, hunters had shot several hyenas. The animals had been skinned, drained of blood as an offering to El, and cooked whole in hearths. Copper lanterns lit the rugs piled with food that radiated out from Alcalah's tent. The guests enjoyed roasted meat with saffron and cardamom, pancakes slathered with wild honey, and sweet pomegranates, figs, and dates washed down with date wine or goat's milk. Musicians played. Tribesmen jumped up to dance. Others ate, drank, and chatted.

Abram sat with Alcalah on her rug. His heart nearly burst with happiness. They held hands, like young newlyweds, and beamed at their kinsmen. Rakel had spread her rug so that she and her brand-new husband Moiseh could sit nearby. Jokes sailed back and forth.

Bernadette Miller

The festivity with food-laden rugs and joyful singing and dancing lasted two days.

Moiseh, happily married to Rakel, no longer wished to return to Sumer. The tribe had welcomed him as a member since he, too, had performed the ritual to worship only El and had wed one of their maidens.

The next evening, after the weekly worship, Abram told Moiseh, "I'm delighted you'll remain with us. I consider you a good friend." From a robe pocket, he extended two shekels to Moiseh.

"I had to remain with a dear friend," Moiseh said. The two men hugged. He added, "But don't keep paying me. I'm your friend now. Not your hired guide."

Abram flushed. He should have been more sensitive to Moiseh's feelings. "I'm sorry," he said and pocketed the shekels. "I truly honor your friendship. You're a man worth knowing."

"And I honor yours," Moiseh said and they hugged again. "We'll always be close friends," he added before heading to his tent nearby.

₯Ↄ

The new converts to the Abram tribe proudly wore the six-pointed star against their robes. It confirmed their belonging to the tribe as well as devotion to El, although Abram secretly clung to Lord Enlil. Weekly, they knelt on their prayer rugs near the blazing bonfire and heard their tribe's history until they knew the stories by heart.

One evening, as Rimush finished his sermon, a tribesman called out, "What about the covenant with El that proves we're His chosen people?"

Another said, "Rimush, please ask El how much longer must we wait."

"Be patient, my kinsmen," Rimush replied, distressed at not knowing the answer. "We'll receive the blessed covenant just as He promised Tiras. We will have our own fertile land. Meanwhile, let us chant our thanks for the plentiful pastures and good health."

"Yes," the tribesmen murmured in unison.

Abram tried to ignore Lord Enlil's possible revenge for the conversion. Many nights he looked up at the sky and begged Lord Enlil for mercy. Lord Enlil remained silent. Perhaps the god excused his deceit.

৪৩ ৫৩

Gradually, Abram adopted the Bedouins' way of life. At dawn he rose to tend his flock. Ten sheep and five goats were Alcalah's. Another five sheep had been given by Rimush as a wedding gift. On late afternoons, he returned with his flock and enjoyed a meal with Alcalah. Once weekly, he joined his tribesmen for Rimush's sermon. After the sermon, he returned to Alcalah's tent where they made love and fell asleep in each other's arms. Together they planned to migrate with the tribe, celebrate weddings and births, and attend funerals of close kinsmen. Abram also planned to visit Ur, settle his affairs there, and return with Aradmu. He waited until the tribe encamped once again at the Al-Mawf Oasis.

"If only I could bear your child," Alcalah said during a meal. "I would feel complete."

"My darling wife," Abram replied. "I'd welcome a child." He put down his bowl of rice with goat cheese. "But you know that a woman in her thirties can't bear children. You're pleading for the impossible."

"With El's help, anything is possible."

Abram nodded but remained skeptical. Even El couldn't supply such a gift. He still feared Lord Enlil's revenge. An unforgiving god could send a disaster at any time—just when he'd never felt happier—and wipe out everything he held dear.

Then, just as Abram had feared, Alcalah became sick. One

morning she vomited her breakfast and complained that her breasts felt sore, as if she were pregnant, though she knew that was impossible. She was way past her childbearing years. Abram tried to reassure her. "El will cure you," he said. He held her against him and stroked her hair. "Have faith. You'll get better."

Later, Abram stared past his flock at the distant dunes, certain that Lord Enlil was finally punishing him. *I'm sorry. What can I do to atone? Please, Lord Enlil, send me a sign.* He waited. No sign came, not from the clouds nor the distant dunes. The tamarisks stood stiffly in the windless air. Apparently, Lord Enlil's anger couldn't be appeased. Abram trembled to think he might lose Alcalah. *I'll do anything you want. Please, don't take her from me.*

⁝⁞

When Alcalah first experienced sickness, she feared a dreaded disease, perhaps the same that had killed Tiras's mother. One afternoon while digging for firewood, she discussed her illness with Zillah, who startled her by saying, "You're probably pregnant." Alcalah shook her head. "Your belly has swollen," her diminutive sister-in-law reminded her.

Using a wooden stick, Zillah dug into a sand dune's base and dragged out dry, shallow roots of shrubs for the outside hearth. Grunting, she added them to a goatskin sack. "Remember how you'd stopped bleeding? Then your bleeding started again after the marriage. A miracle!" She looked up and smiled, her injured lip, as usual, twisting in a sneer. "And you said your breasts are swollen."

Alcalah straightened. Her breasts still felt sensitive to her touch. She protested the misguided advice. "Nevertheless, I'm too old! No one my age has borne children. I must be sick." She paused. "I fear for my Abram. He loves me deeply. How will he endure without me?" She bent awkwardly to lift her sack of roots.

Zillah sighed and said impatiently, "Did your monthly bleeding stop again?"

"Yes, but—"

"Congratulations," Zillah interrupted. "You're pregnant!" She grinned and balanced her filled sack on her head.

Incredulous about her pregnancy, Alcalah told her husband after dinner, her eyes widened in excitement. "Good news, I'm not sick. I'm carrying your child! I just found out this afternoon."

Abram put down his cup to rise and hug his wife. He stared down at her as if unable to believe his ears. "So that's why we celebrate with date wine."

Alcalah laughed jubilantly in his arms. "Imagine: a child at our age!" She gazed up at him. "A miracle!"

He kissed her cheek. "You prayed to our powerful El for a child," he said, catching his breath in awe. "Even though we knew it was hopeless. Now He has sent one."

"If a daughter, I'll name her Sarah."

"And if a son?"

"Then you can name him."

"Gladly," Abram said and they embraced with joy.

That night when the tribesmen gathered before the altar for the weekly ceremony, Rimush called out, "Kinsmen, hear my remarkable news! Despite her age, Abram's wife carries a child." He scanned the awestruck men. "Let's thank our glorious El for this miracle."

The tribesmen shouted in unison, "Yes!" and rapidly bent their heads back and forth to show agreement.

Rimush continued. "It's surely an omen that soon we'll receive the covenant, the agreement that promises our loyalty to El who will then lead us to our promised land."

When the worship ended and Rimush left with the others, Abram lingered. He gazed at the bonfire's remaining sparks. Gracious Lord Enlil must have understood his need for love and family. Lord Enlil had sent no revenge, no disapproval, only silence. But El had sent a miracle! Granting an older couple the birth of a desired child as if to prove that His power surpassed Lord Enlil's.

In the cold night air, Abram clutched his sheepskin cloak about him. The Bedouins' powerful tribal god had reigned supreme. Not even Lord Enlil could have produced such a wonder. El bestowed many gifts. A loving wife. A future child. His family's affection. He owed El and the tribe a great debt.

A hawk circled over a burrow. It nosedived. A loud squeal erupted. In the moonlight, Abram stared at the hawk. It lifted a dead rabbit in its claws and flew away. The bird had found its meal, a treasure. The tribe also hungered for their treasure—the sacred covenant. How could he help them?

⁎ ⁎

The following January, the Al-Gaffah Oasis lake in the Nefud had again dried up. As before, the tribe encamped much farther east near the Al-Mawf Oasis so that the tribesmen could barter their goods in the Sumerian city or Ur, reachable within half a moon-cycle. Moiseh guided the large group, joined by his wife, Rakel, along with Abram and his wife, Alcalah, who held in her arms their baby daughter, Sarah, born six moon-cycles past. Alcalah had wanted to see the marvelous city that Abram had described. He planned to sell his possessions in Ur, buy a large flock of sheep and goats to divide among his kinsmen, and persuade Aradmu to join the tribe as his son, freed from slavery.

The group had packed donkeys with supplies and wool for bartering. Along the way, the two couples shared a campfire during mealtime. The desert lit up with the campfires of their kinsmen who had joined their journey. At Abram's campfire, the once-quiet desert reverberated with chatter as the travelers warmed their hands and shared their supper of roasted rabbit shot by hunters, and bread-cakes with liquid butter. After supper, the two couples discussed the day's events. Abram again described Ur to Alcalah and Rakel. Moiseh added an occasional comment.

That first evening, Rakel listened intently. She leaned forward, her auburn curls glowing in the firelight. Moiseh squeezed her hand. They smiled at each other. "I can't wait to see Ur," Rakel said. She snuggled closer to Moiseh, who put his arms around her.

Alcalah, cuddling baby Sarah in her arms, said tentatively, "I'm also... eager...to see it."

Abram knew she hoped that he wouldn't change his mind about staying in the desert once he was back in Ur. He patted her arm. "My birth city is truly wonderful as I've told you. I'll be happy to be there again. But it can't compare to being with you."

Alcalah sighed. "Oh, Abram, you're still pouring compliments on me. I couldn't possibly deserve so many."

Before Abram could reply, Rakel turned to Moiseh and asked, pouting, "Why don't you talk to me that way?"

Moiseh laughed. "My love, I'll pay as many compliments as you wish. But you're so wonderful, my tongue fails me."

Rakel grinned. "Well, I hope you'll always feel that way. Even when I'm old with wrinkles—" She stopped abruptly and clapped her hand over her mouth. Then she whispered to Alcalah, "I'm so sorry...I forgot...I didn't mean to insult you."

"Young people might see older ones that way," Alcalah said, frowning. She touched the tiny wrinkles in her cheeks. "But I can't be as old as my mother claimed. Otherwise, I wouldn't be cradling my darling child."

"You'll always be beautiful," Abram said.

"And I'll always love you," Alcalah replied, returning his tender smile.

The next morning, the travelers continued their journey, alternately riding their donkeys or walking them past gigantic dunes, and trading comments with other tribesmen surrounding them. In the distance, ridges undulated toward the horizon. Occasionally,

Bernadette Miller

the travelers stopped near a well to rest, eat, and refill their goatskin bags. After supper shared at their campfire, the two couples chatted for a while before sleeping.

Alcalah sighed. "Our kinsmen seem so far away."

Abram stroked her hand. "We'll be home soon. Meanwhile, Ur has marvelous sights. You won't be disappointed." He paused and exclaimed enthusiastically, "I've missed my birth place. Ur is unlike any other city. Filled with interesting shops and a huge bazaar offering merchandise from everywhere. Some buildings—temples and royal palaces—are tall enough to touch the sky. The grand houses with gardens offer every comfort. So much to enjoy."

She nodded, but not with enthusiasm, Abram noted. *Well, why not?* he thought. *Everyone they loved lived in the desert. How could he bring about the covenant his kinsmen yearned for?*

A week later, they approached Sumer's marshes with its islands of reed houses and basket-shaped boats. Farther along the road, Alcalah caught her first glimpse of Ur with its high mud-brick wall and the huge, bronze double-gate. Gasping with surprise, she stared at the immensity, unable to comprehend a city that big. What wonders it must contain, she thought. The travelers paused with their donkeys outside the gate amidst the crowd of merchants with their laden animals.

"Look at that!" Rakel exclaimed. "Biggest place I've ever seen."

"In all your eighteen seasons," Moiseh teased his wife.

She wrinkled her nose. "Careful. Or you'll pay for that."

The others stifled their laughter as the gate suddenly swung open. The travelers entered the city and led their donkeys toward the bazaar bustling with shoppers. Rakel gawked at rugs heaped with huge alabaster urns, copper cooking pots and platters, strange silver utensils, spouted tea kettles with dainty mugs, carved animals made of precious stones, and musical instruments.

"I must explore it," she told Moiseh.

"On the way back," he replied.

"Promise?"

He nodded and kissed her cheek.

She hugged him. "You're a good husband."

"Thanks to El, you finally noticed."

The couples, grinning, scanned the broad avenue with its tall, graceful palms. "This is the Ceremonial Boulevard," Abram said proudly, guiding his donkey whose hooves echoed against the paved street. "Here, we celebrate feast days, led by our renowned king."

Alcalah and Rakel nodded and stared at the odd-looking Sumerians' clothing: the men's ankle-length tufted or pleated skirts, their bare chests partially exposed beneath shawls, and the women's elaborate headdresses above the black wigs. The Sumerians ignored them or glanced at them with disdain.

"They don't like us!" Rakel said.

Moiseh grinned. "They're very fussy, my love. Sumerians prefer other Sumerians. Not outsiders. They especially dislike Bedouins, although we're welcome in the bazaar. Sumerians consider themselves superior in every way, especially their religion."

Abram chuckled. "Yes, but that's because the Sumerians are superior! They invented amazing things for their people's comfort." Without realizing it, he spoke enthusiastically in the Sumerian language while the group stared at him, uncomprehending. "An organized army instead of citizens gathering like an unruly mob with daggers and switches. City-states, games, sailboats, glue..."

He paused, embarrassed by his ranting. "Well, too many to recite here," he said, reverting to their desert tongue.

Alcalah looked at him with alarm. "Are you regretting that you came to live with us?"

He patted her hand. "Of course not, dear one. I've been happy and content with you and our tribe." To distract her and lift her spirits, he began explaining the sights to the two women while they approached the Sacred Way. He pointed at the immense tower soaring toward the sky. "There's our ziggurat. It contains the king's palace and splendid temples where Sumerians worship their gods." He then turned their attention across the street. "Those mansions are where the richest live," he said, nodding toward the gleaming white-washed houses soaring above the mud-brick walls. "Sumerians work hard to acquire wealth so they can possess beautiful things which they deeply appreciate. They make the finest hand-crafted items."

As the group passed along narrow, winding alleys lined with numerous shops, Abram added, "Anything you could possibly want is right here in Ur. The greatest city in the world! I'd almost forgotten what it's like."

Alcalah, overwhelmed, nodded and scanned the passersby hurrying past the travelers. Did Abram give up all this for her?

Among the maze of alleys radiating out from the Sacred Way, Abram guided them along the Alley of Sweetness. "Named because of the bakery," he explained. Near the bakery, at the end of the alley, he paused before a metallic garden gate.

"This is my house," he announced.

Alcalah watched him and heard his sigh, as if deeply regretting his desert move. Troubled, she gazed up at him. How could she persuade him to stay with his family?

CHAPTER 29

January, 3466 B.C., Sumer

ABRAM GLANCED FROM ALCALAH TO his former home. He took a deep breath. He was home—but it felt more like a distant memory. Here he'd been born a slave. Now he returned as a Bedouin with a wife and baby as well as a loving family. The Bedouins' wise religion and earthy values had taught him the importance of an ethical life, rather than pursuing wealth and success. The house now seemed strange, as if it belonged to another.

Alcalah, standing beside him, shifted baby Sarah's sack about her neck and shoulder to get a clearer view. He smiled as she stared up in awe at the two-story, whitewashed house and glimpsed, through the opened door, the balcony overlooking a spacious courtyard.

A slender blond man then opened the garden gate that creaked on its hinges. Wearing his loincloth, he greeted the visitors with widened eyes, his jaw slack with surprise. His hazel eyes glowed. Smiling, he bowed deeply and unlatched the gate.

"Master, you're most welcome! I'm so glad and relieved to see you!"

Replying in Sumerian, Abram said softly, "I told you that I'd never abandon you." He turned to introduce each family member. "Aradmu, this is my wife, Alcalah." She smiled with questioning eyebrows at the young man, as if wondering who he was and his importance to her husband. Abram turned to Moiseh. "And this is my good friend Moiseh and his wife Rakel." He turned to his family and spoke in their familiar tongue. "The young man greeting us so warmly is my son, Aradmu, who's in charge of my household."

Smiles were used to exchange greetings since they spoke in different languages.

"Come," Abram said, "let's refresh ourselves and eat and drink. We're weary after our long journey. I'll explain later about Aradmu."

He motioned to Aradmu who led them through the spacious courtyard and into the large kitchen where Alcalah and Rakel stared with eyes widened in wonder at the beehive oven on its high brick base, the long oak table and benches, the copper pots hanging from wall hooks, and the overhead shelves of copper bowls, platters, and golden goblets. While waiting to eat, the family chatted among themselves, exclaiming at the luxurious surroundings, unimagined despite Abram's descriptions.

Two female slaves served roasted lamb with vegetables, fruit, and baked bread. While the slaves began removing the emptied platters, Abram told them that he wished to speak to Aradmu.

Soon, Aradmu entered and bowed to Abram. "You sent for me, master?"

The guests glanced in surprise from Aradmu to Abram, wondering about their relationship until Abram motioned Aradmu closer and took his hands.

Abram spoke in Sumerian, further bewildering his guests. "Dear Aradmu," he said, "I plan to convert all of my possessions into flocks of sheep and goats and return to the desert with my family. I give you your freedom. But I ask you to join us. Not as a slave but as a free man. I'll free all my slaves."

Aradmu beamed. "I'm most grateful, master."

"Not master," Abram said to the young man bowing low. "Henceforth, you will be known as my son. Don't bow. Embrace me as a loving son."

Abram rose. Aradmu tentatively put his arms around his adopted father. His eyes widened in astonishment when Abram hugged him. Fighting tears, he stammered, "Then, mas...adda...I'll help prepare for our desert journey."

Abram studied his son. "I'd like to rename you in my new tongue." He paused for a moment. "Would Lot suit you? Or would you prefer another name?"

"I'd be proud to bear any name you choose," the former slave said, smiling. "Now, I must prepare for our journey."

"You don't want to live in Ur as a free citizen?" Abram gave his son a questioning look to make sure his decision was firm. "With enough shekels to live comfortably?"

"I'd rather stay with you, adda." Lot wiped his eyes. "Where I've always been in my heart."

Abram beamed and kissed Lot's cheek. He turned to his guests and spoke in their tongue. "This is Aradmu, my adopted son whom I raised since he was a baby. Now he will become a free man and with the new name of Lot. He will travel with us back to Arabiyah." He turned to Lot. "Now, Lot, greet my wife Alcalah as a loving son for she shall be your mother. And our baby, Sarah, will be your sister."

"Gladly," Lot said.

Alcalah rose, smiling, and the two embraced.

Abram, too, smiled at his wife and son. "My happiness is nearly complete."

ঙ০৪

The next day, with Lot's help, Abram hired an agent at the bazaar to sell his house and land in exchange for sheep and goats. With the numerous remaining shekels, he hired shepherds to help tend the large flock outside Ur until the family could return to Arabiyah. Abram also bought donkeys for transporting household items. He freed his slaves and paid them to do chores until his departure with his family. Then, aided by Lot, he sought employment for them as paid servants in wealthy households.

At first, Alcalah and Rakel kept busy, examining Abram's house and garden. A former slave girl gratefully tended baby Sarah. Rakel rushed through the house with loud comments: "Oh, look at that splendid kitchen." And: "Do they need all those rooms? I'd be lost here."

Finally alone, Alcalah sat on the garden bench. She inhaled the heady anastatica and hawthorn adorning the flower beds lining the wooden fence. Overhead, birds twittered in the palm fronds. Despite the hustle and bustle outside, the garden seemed as peaceful as El's paradise, the opposite of the desert's potential disasters. Her home held close ties of kinship, Alcalah reminded herself. She would suffer in Ur, an unfamiliar city crowded with strangers and unknown customs.

She rose and walked indoors. The freed slaves hurried about, cleaning and dusting. They glanced with curiosity as Alcalah inspected the rooms surrounding the courtyard. Rakel was right about the kitchen with its indoor conveniences, she thought. What comfort! Unable to believe her eyes, she gazed again at the beehive oven with its tempting aroma of roasting pig for supper. An oven inside a wife's house! No need to break her back building an outdoor hearth. And enough platters, bowls, goblets, and pots to supply several oases shops!

Leaving the incredible kitchen, she smiled at the freed slave girl washing the table. The girl hesitated but then gave her a bashful smile in surprise before returning to her chore.

Alcalah walked through the courtyard's rear archway and climbed the balcony steps. She stroked a smooth alabaster urn of flowers against the wooden railing. Inside a bedroom, she stared at the soft straw mattress with coverlets and the bed frame decorated with Sumerian scenes. She studied the peculiar wall frescoes: the chiseled ivory figures staring with enlarged dark eyes. She shook her head in reproach. Was she wrong to persuade Abram to give up all this comfort for her? She bowed her head and prayed. *Oh, compassionate El, please don't let him change his mind."*

She finally questioned Abram one night when they were alone in a balcony bedroom. "I'm concerned that perhaps you regret leaving Ur and a comfortable life. You tossed aside your education and everything you valued to live a harsh desert life without all these luxuries."

Abram reassured her. "I'm selling everything so I can be with you. The desert will be my new home." He pressed her hand. "I wouldn't want to live anywhere else without you. Surely you know that."

She smiled with relief but tentatively as if still uncertain. She watched him gaze wistfully through the upstairs window as if he didn't miss the desert at all.

The following day, while Abram arranged his transactions, Alcalah joined Rakel and Moiseh touring the city of Ur. It was a distraction from her concern about her husband remaining there. The trio soon paused before the bazaar with its tempting wares.

"I want to explore it," Rakel pleaded with Moiseh. "Come back for me."

"You need shekels," Moiseh said. He tugged inside his robe. "You're lucky I brought some. I had a feeling... Here." He put several coins into her outstretched hand. "Be careful. Or they won't last long. Tomorrow we'll barter our wool."

She tossed her head. "I can take care of myself." She rushed toward a merchant smiling beside his rug heaped with merchandise. Her loud complaints echoed to the street. "Why can't you speak my language? With so many Bedouins bartering here, you can't learn a few words?"

Moiseh laughed and turned to walk with Alcalah. She shaded her eyes and looked up in wonder at the soaring tower and its gate called Bab-El. "My husband abandoned so much for me," she told

Moiseh as they headed toward the tower. "For the rest of his life, he'll confront hardships. Perhaps even the death of our precious child. Am I selfish to demand he stay in the desert?"

"It was his decision as well as yours," Moiseh replied, guiding her across the Ceremonial Boulevard. "His happiness begins and ends with you."

"For that reason, I must help him fulfill his dreams. Let Abram lead! Sarah and I will follow."

Moiseh said gravely, "At first, I mistook his haughty demeanor as a wealthy, spoiled Sumerian gentleman. Then I learned about his humiliating childhood as a slave. How he prizes his desert family. He's an honorable man worth following."

They ended their walk at the ziggurat where they climbed to the top terrace. Alcalah gasped at the extraordinary city far below her. Miraculous Ur must guard all the world's surprises! But Abram kept repeating that he'd gladly given it up for her. What could she offer in exchange besides her love? She smiled, remembering how he enjoyed playing with baby Sarah. He laughed like a child himself when Sarah held out her arms to him. Sarah was El's greatest blessing.

Back at the bazaar, they found Rakel at a rear stall. Filled baskets exuded the aroma of cinnamon and sesame. She rolled her eyes at them. "Oh, they have the best Al-Halwa I ever ate." She wiped her fingers on her robe and held out the sticky bar to Moiseh, who shook his head. She munched the bar and then stopped and looked at Alcalah. "Here, take some. I don't want to be greedy."

Alcalah shook her head.

"Please."

"Rakel, she doesn't want it," Moiseh interrupted softly. He paused. "Now that you've fed your belly would you like to explore the city?"

"Yes!" Rakel said.

"You two go on without me," Alcalah said. "I'll return to Abram's house."

In the desert she was used to observing landmarks to avoid getting lost. Besides, Rakel tried hard to be nice, but she was so very young and sometimes aggravating. Alcalah approached The Alley of Sweetness, and stopped short. Someday, she reflected, Sarah will be Rakel's age. She and Abram might then be with El in His Oasis of Eden. Who will care for Sarah then? Who will comfort her when she's sad? Laugh with her when she's joyful? It would be wise to welcome Rakel's friendship. Sarah might need her.

The following days, while Alcalah rejoined Moiseh and Rakel touring Ur's grandeur, Abram settled his finances. Night after night, he lay with open eyes beside his wife sleeping peacefully on the straw mattress. Exhausted, he shifted his share of the coverlet, thinking how he owed all his contentment to his desert kinsmen. How could he bring about the covenant and thus repay his enormous debt?

Early one morning, while he lay in bed, he finally fell asleep and dreamed that El appeared, wrapped in a cloud. The God pointed a finger at him. "Assure your people I have chosen them. To seal our covenant, they must prove their faithfulness by worshipping only me, not false gods."

Abram whispered, "Yes," his heart pounding from excitement.

"Tell the tribe to leave Arabiyah. Their offspring shall cover a fertile land that I have bequeathed to them. I shall bless and preserve them for untold generations. They shall be fruitful and multiply. Ask Moiseh to guide my children to this land. It's called Cana'an."

Abram said, breathless with awe, "Forgive me, but how do I know if this is real?"

"Look out the window," El said and disappeared before Abram could question Him further.

Opening his eyes, Abram gazed about the room as if dumbstruck. He felt unable to grasp what he had just witnessed in his dream. Jumping up, he rushed to the window. A shimmering rainbow spanned the sky. Surely a sign from El! After months of wondering how to bring about the covenant, he had finally seen El in a dream! Trembling, Abram awakened Alcalah.

"I dreamed that El spoke to me," he said, shaking as he bent over her. "We will have the covenant and our promised land. It lies in Cana'an. Moiseh will guide us there."

"Oh, Abram," she said, also trembling. "El has chosen you to confirm the covenant. The blessing of our own promised land—something we've always yearned for."

He sank onto the bed, shocked by the morning's events, and said haltingly, "When I reveal this second miracle, our tribe will marvel at El's power. Future generations will never doubt Him." He struggled to his feet, his face suffused with wonder.

She touched his forehead. "You're flushed. You look ill. Perhaps you should rest until you can recover from such a miraculous vision."

"No...I...have much to accomplish before we leave."

"Come then, you need food." She took his hand and led him downstairs to the kitchen where Lot was preparing roasted barley with milk, pomegranates, and freshly-baked bread. Rakel sat at the table with Moiseh.

Abram turned to his son. "Lot, there's no need for you to do such work. Our servants who are still here can take care of things."

Lot shook his head. "Adda, I've been preparing your breakfast most of my life. I wouldn't want anyone else to do it."

Abram embraced his loving son, who embraced him in return. "I insist you join us for breakfast," he said. His son nodded and placed platters of food on the long, wooden table.

While the group began eating, Abram related his experience with El. "Last night," he began and trembled at the importance of his message. "El spoke to me in a dream. We'll have our covenant and our Promised Land. It lies in Cana'an. El sent a rainbow as a sign."

Rakel sat with jaw agape. For once her tongue lacked words. She turned toward her husband for guidance.

Moiseh jumped up and bowed to Abram. "Revered one," he whispered.

"Revered one," Rakel echoed, bowing beside her husband.

"No, no, don't bow to me." Abram motioned for them to sit. "We have only one God. I'm merely a vessel through which our great Lord has spoken. El has commanded that you, Moiseh, will lead our tribe to Cana'an."

Moiseh blushed at being entrusted with such an important mission. "I'm honored," he said. "I know Cana'an well. It's vast and inhabited mostly by Amorites, Phoenicians, Ugarites, Eblaites, and some smaller tribes. But there's plenty of wilderness near Amrata, along the coast of the Great Sea, where we could live." He paused, stroking his beard. "Where exactly is the Promised Land?"

"With El's help we'll find it," Abram replied, "Our God will send more signs. Like the rainbow at my window this morning."

Excited at the prospect of finally having their own land, the group prepared to return to the Al-Mawf Oasis in Arabiyah. They stuffed their belongings into woven storage sacks and packed the caravan of donkeys. The morning of their journey, Moiseh and Rakel waited with their donkeys in the alleyway for Abram and Alcalah who paused before the garden gate.

For the last time, Abram observed the Sumerian house of Mah Ummia. This same house where he'd been born and raised and married Nammu. Although he'd found happiness here, he had no regrets that he'd never see it again. His new life stretched before him with Alcalah and Sarah, his kinsmen, and the Promised Land in Cana'an. He glanced down at El's symbol glittering against his robe, the six-pointed star, and then looked at Alcalah. He returned her serene smile.

Today, Abram thought, they would travel back to Arabiyah and join their kinsmen with a great gift. Beyond Ur's mud-brick wall, newly-bought flocks of sheep and goats tended by hired shepherds awaited the journey. Afterwards, the tribe would undertake their long

Bernadette Miller

journey to Cana'an. He closed his eyes and imagined that wondrous land promised by El. He saw the sparkling lakes surrounded by lush pasturelands filled with date palms and wild honeycombs. An Oasis of Eden where the tribe would flourish with their growing flocks. There, in the Promised Land, the tribe would bring forth their future children and their children's children for countless moon-cycles. Each would relate the tribe's stories until they spread throughout the earth, cultivating the seeds that Tiras had planted long ago.

--The End--

GLOSSARY OF ARABIC WORDS AND PHRASES

'Alaykum salaam: return greeting.

Al-Dahna: desert in central Saudi Arabia, linking Al-Nefud in the north to the southern desert.

Al-Halwa: ancient confection made of sesame butter and honey.

Al-Lat: pre-Islamic sun goddess.

Al-Qais: pre-Islamic wind god.

Al-Nefud: desert in northern Saudi Arabia.

Al-Uzza: pre-Islamic dawn goddess.

Amrata: possible name for ancient Egypt.

Amorites: Arabic tribe in ancient northwest Syria.

Arabs: people who speak a Semitic group of languages, mainly in the Middle East.

Arabiyah: fictitious name for ancient Saudi Arabia, possibly used by ancient Persians.

Arameans: Arabic tribe in ancient Syria.

baba: father.

Bab-el: Translated from the Sumerian, Babu-ilu, meaning Gate of God, at their ziggurat; probable source of biblical Tower of Babel.

Bab-Ilim, ancient Arabic city in northern Iraq; probable source of biblical Babylon.

badawi: desert dweller

baram: forbidden, as eating animal blood that belongs to a god; possible source of biblical kosher.

bayt: tent.

Bedouins: Arab desert tribes migrating seasonally with their flocks of sheep and goats.

Be'elsebub: Probably from Ba'al Zbl, Ugaritic storm god in ancient Syria; biblical Satan.

Ca'adus: god of good health. (His staff is used as a modern medical symbol).

Cana'an: Large land mass comprising Israel, Syria, Lebanon, and Jordan; probable source of biblical Canaan.

clan: group of Bedouin blood relatives migrating together.

Council of Elders: group of rulers elected by a Bedouin tribe and led by the sheikh.

dakhil: formal procedure showing homage to another tribe's god.

dar: group of blood relatives, including in-laws, migrating together, often away from the tribe.

dirah: land owned by a particular tribe.

diyah: blood money. Sheep and/or goats paid to recompense an atrocious deed.

Eblaites: tribe in ancient Syrian city of Ebla.

El: Semitic name for god, a generic term used throughout the Middle East.

Ghata: Fictional Bedouin tribe claiming rights to the Uplands.

gully: dry ditch created by formerly flowing water.

Ibn haram: bastard!

Il-lah: pre-Islamic moon god.

Jahannam: underworld, hell.

kara: Ass! (slang)

kelbeh: Goat Bitch! (slang)

kisich: vagina (pussy, slang).

mag'ad: tent's front area for male visitors and entertaining guests.

maharama: tent's back area for a woman's privacy.

Al-Manat: pre-Islamic goddess of fate.

Martu: imaginary bull-god worshipped by the Abram tribe.

Midianites: tribe in northwestern Arabiyah.

Moloch: Cananite god of fire.

Nile: the main river in Egypt. Ancient Egyptian name: Iteru.

oomah: mama, mother.

Phoenicians: ancient Arabic tribe in Lebanon.

qata: woven curtain inside a Bedouin tent, separating front & back areas.

Rub'Al-Khali: aka Empty Quarter. Mostly uninhabitable desert in southern Saudi Arabia.

Salaam 'alaykum: greeting; hello.

Semites: people who speak an ethnic group of languages, mainly in the Middle East.

Sharmata: Daughter of the Wind! Whore!

sheikh: Bedouin leader, elected by Council of Elders, makes all final decisions except religious.

shlicke: shit (slang)

Shumeru: Arabic name for Sumer.

Sydyk: Cananite god of justice.

Tribe: group of Bedouin clans migrating together.

Ugarit: ancient city-state in northern Syria.

Uplands: fertile area in Saudi Arabia, north of the Nefud Desert.

Wadi: dry river bed that can instantly become a deep pool from a heavy storm.

Walla: Fictitious Bedouin tribe claiming all rights to the Nefud Desert.

Yam: Cananite god of the river.

Yarikh: Cananite moon god.

Zibbinu: penis (dick, slang)

Glossary of Hebrew Words and Phrases

Evewah: Goddess Who Brings Life; possibly from Hebrew Hawwah, Eve, first woman.

Biblical Words and Phrases

Shinar: shene neharot ("two rivers"), probably Sumer, a land between the Tigris and Euphrates rivers.

Yahweh: biblical god of Israel. Possible from Iah, Egyptian moon god, and Weh, a derivative of Wah, Canaanite storm god.

Glossary of Sumerian Words and Phrases

ab: water.

Adamu: First man, created by Nin-Kursag and Nin-ti, possible source of biblical Adam.

adda: daddy, father.

addub: basket maker

ama: mama, mother.

an: Heavens, Heavenly One.

Annunaki: Lord An's children. Winged humans, possible source of biblical angels.

Arabi: Arabs.

arad: slave.

Ashnan: goddess of grain.

ba: house

Babu-Ilu: Sumerian: Gate of God, at their ziggurat. Translated into Bedouin language as Bab-El, probable source of biblical Tower of Babel.

bedu: an Arab desert dweller who migrates with his tribe and their flocks of animals.

demon galas: evil ghosts of the unburied dead.

Euphrates: river in ancient and modern Iraq. Called Buranuna in Sumerian.

cuneiform: a form of Sumerian writing on clay, pictographs using a wedge-shaped object.

Dilmun: mythical paradise for the gods; possibly referring to Bahrain, an island in the Persian Gulf; probable source for story of Garden of Eden.

dub: clay tablet.

dubsar: scribe, writer (on clay tablets).

Dublal-makh: courthouse in the Sacred Way for trials and legal document preparation.

dumu: unmarried.

e: of

Ebla: ancient city in Syria.

eden: meadow

Edubba: House of Tablets, school.

Elam: non-Arabic country in southwestern Iran, probably Indo-European. biblical Elamites.

Ensi: righteous ruler, governor of a province.

gal: big, great.

Ga-makh: great storehouse in the Sacred Way where donations were made to the temple.

Indo-Europeans: people speaking a European group of languages.

Ki-en-gir: Land of the Civilized Lords; Sumerian name for their country.

Lady Inanna: goddess of love.

Lady Nammu: goddess of the primeval sea, mother of Lord Enki.

Lady Nanshe: goddess of ethics and morals.

Lady Nin-ti: rib goddess, and birth goddess.

Lady Ninisinna: goddess of medicine and healing.

Lord An, sky god, father of the gods.

Lord Dumuzi: god of vegetation.

Lord Enki: god of wisdom. First man, Adamu, created in his image. Mah Ummia's personal god.

Lord Enlil: god of the air.

Lord Nanna: moon god.

Lord Utu: sun god.

lu: man.

luabgal: male erection (fictional slang).

Mah Ummia: great teacher.

mashkim: legal arbitrator similar to a bailiff

Meluhha: ancient Indus Valley; India.

minna: coin, equivalent to 60 shekels, 15 pounds of silver.

mu: seed, ship

munus: woman.

Netherworld: underground. Place to which the dead are flown by the winged Annunaki.

Nin: lady

Nin-Kursag: Lady of the Mountain, mother of the gods. Co-creator of Adamu, the first man.

Per-ao: (ancient Egyptian). Literally: Great House of the King. Translation: pharaoh.

Sanga: high priest.

Sag gigga: black heads; how Sumerians called themselves.

sar: to write (on baked clay tablets).

shekels: currency in coins equivalent to weight of silver.

Sumerians: non-Arabs occupying ancient southern Iraq; probably Indo-Europeans and possibly emigrated from ancient Turkey or Elam (Southwest Iran).

Sydyk: Canaanite god of justice.

The Chosen People: How Sumerians regarded themselves, based on their technical advances. Adopted later by ancient Israelites.

The Divine Word: How Sumerian gods created the world by simply stating their commands.

The Sacred Way: huge complex containing the ziggurat, King's palace, temples, etc.

Tigris: river in ancient and modern Iraq. Called Idigna in Sumerian.

Ur: major city-state in Sumer, ancient Iraq; probable source of biblical city of Abraham.

Wah: Aramean storm god.

Yam: Canaanite river god.

ziggurat: huge complex in Ur containing the main temple, courthouse, Great Storehouse, etc.

BIBLIOGRAPHY:
SAUDI ARABIA AND IRAQ

NOTES:

1. The prehistoric language spoken in Saudi Arabia and throughout much of the Middle East was proto-Semitic. It led to ancient Arabic followed by ancient Hebrew. Although modern Hebrew predates modern Arabic, the latter was used because it more closely resembles the proto-Semitic.

2. Tribal histories handed down from father to son evolved over generations until writing reached Canaan (location of Israel, Jordan, Lebanon, and Syria) about 1,000 B.C. Before printing was invented, the stories still evolved due to tiny mistakes by scribes laboriously copying manuscripts by hand.

3. With no Jewish Hasidism nor Muslim Sharia law, ancient Bedouin women were free to own their own tents, dress as they wished, leave their husbands, and say pretty much whatever they pleased.

4. The surprising Sumerians in Southern Iraq were not Semites but probably Indo-Europeans. Although they seemed to have claimed southwestern Iran as their homeland, their language is unrelated to any other, including Iran's. The closest is Turanian, an ancient Turkish language. Surprisingly, Turkish archaeology

reveals similarity in the strange and unique headdresses worn by ancient Turkish and Sumerian women.

5. Most of the authors listed below are archaeologists, explorers, university professors, or professional photographers. Details in *A House in the Land of Shinar* are based on information from the following sources:

Saudi Arabia: Books

Al-Asnam, Kitab. *The Book of Idols.* (Written during the 1400s A.D., and discovered by Ahmed Zaki, Syria, 1912. Pre-Islamic deities.)

Albright, William Foxwell. *Yahweh and the Gods of Canaan.* Indiana, reprint, 1994.

Broberg, Catherine. *Saudi Arabia in Pictures,* 2003

Burckhardt, John Lewis. *Notes on Bedouins and Wahabys,* 1831.

—————, *Travels in Arabia,* 1829.

Cole, Donald P. *Nomads of the Nomads:* Aldine Publishing Corp., 1975.

—————, *The Al-Murrah Bedouins of the Empty Quarter.* Aldine Pub., 1975. (British explorer. Lived among the Al-Murrah tribe of Southern Arabia during the 1950's.)

Dickson, Harold Richard P. *The Arab of the Desert.* George Allen & Unwin Ltd., 1949.

Doughty, Charles. *Travels in Arabia Deserta.* Philip Lee Warner Publisher, 1921.

Eastep, Wayne. *Bedouin.* Stacey International, London, 1985 (Photographer).

Hart, George. *A Dictionary of Egyptian Gods and Goddesses.* Routledge, 1986.

Hitti, Philip F. *History of the Arabs.* New York: St. Martin's Press, 1955.

Hoyland, Robert G. *Arabia and the Arabs.* Routledge, 2001.

Ibn-al-Kalbi. *The Book of Idols.* Nabih Amin Faris, 1952 (Pre-Islamic deities).

Ibrahim, Said E., and Donald P. Cole. *Saudi Arabian Bedouin,* 1978.

Lancaster, William. *The Rwala Bedouin Today.* Cambridge Univ. Press, 1981. (Customs of a North Saudi Arabia tribe.)

Lawrence, T.E. *Seven Pillars of Wisdom,* 1991.

Mauger, Thierry. *In the Shadow of the Black Tents.* Tihama Press, Jeddah, 1986.

_____, *The Bedouins of Arabia*. Souffles, Paris, 1988 (Photographer).

Moscati, Sabatino. *Ancient Semitic Civilizations*. Capricorn Books, 1960.

Musil, Alois. *Arabia Deserta*, 1927

_____, *Manners and Customs of the Rwala Bedouins*. Natl. Geographic Society, 1928.

_____, *Black Tents of Arabia*. Creative Age Press, 1947.

Pritchard, James B. *The Ancient Near East*. Princeton University Press, 1971.

Raswan, Carl R. *Black Tents of Arabia*. Hungry Mind Press reprint paperback, 1998. (German explorer. Lived among the Rwala Bedouins of N. Arabia for over 23 years, starting around 1900. Excellent description of life among these Bedouins.)

Thesiger, Wilfred. Arabian Sands. Penguin Books Paperback, 1971.

_____, *Across the Empty Quarter*. Penguin paperback, 2007. (British explorer. First to travel across the Rub'al-Khali desert, Southern Arabia.)

Saudi Arabia: Internet (Also see books for specific topics)

Arabian Cuisine:

Numerous dishes explained and alphabetized. http://www.arab.net.

Saudi Arabian recipes and cuisine. www.nestle-family.com/English/Saudi-recipes.aspx

Ancient confections, Al-Halwa or Al-Halva: types and how prepared. www.wikipedia.com.

Bedouin Culture:

Arabian Bedouins, photos and descriptions. www.canadian-arabcommunity.com.

Bedouins of the Sinai. National Geographic Society. www.geographia.com/egypt/sinai

Bedouin tribes, traditional culture, *Wikipedia*. www.wikipedia.org.

Clothing, jewelry. www.wikipedia.org & www.canadian-arabcommunity.com.

Egyptian Bedouins, Tour Egypt, photos and descriptions, www.touregypt.com

Desert Plants & Animals:

Acacia trees. *Wikipedia*, www.wikipedia.org.

Tamarisk trees. *Wikipedia,* www.wikipedia.org.

Caravan trails. Saudi-Aramco World, July-August, 1969, www.saudiaramco.org.

Desert animals. Saudi-Aramco World, Jan-Feb, 1970, www.saudiaramco.org.

Donkeys. The American Donkey & Mule Society. www.lovelongears.org.

Donkeys, photographs and types. *Wikipedia, www.wikipedia.org.*

Herding sheep & goats. *Wikipedia, www.wikipedia.org.*

Onagers (Asian Wild Ass). *Wikipedia, www.wikipedia.org.*

Deserts, Descriptions and/or Photographs

Arabian deserts, photos, descriptions, www.wikipedia.org.

Arabian Peninsula, description. *Britannica Online Encyclopedia.* www.britannica.com

Desert Dunes. Central Intelligence Agency, http://www.ciaworldfactbook,us/index.html

Desert Dunes, types. U.S. Government publications. http://pubs.usgs.gov/deserts/dunes/

Deserts, Library of Congress: https://loc.gov//photos/?q=deserts

Desert topography. *Saudi Arabia: A Country Study,* Helen Chapin Metz. Washington GPO for

The Library of Congress, 1992. www.countrystudies.us.

Modern Egyptian Sinai Bedouins. www.geographia.com/egypt/sinai.

Modern Egyptian Sinai Bedouins by Bernadette Miller. Author's unpublished photographs.

Saudi Arabia, Al-Dahna Desert, Tuwaiq Escarpment, photos, limestone cliffs. http://dunwich.mine.nu/saoudi/album.

Saudi Arabia, Al-Dahna Desert, Tuwaiq Escarpment, photos, limestone cliffs. www.splendidarabia.com.

Saudi Arabia deserts, Lonely Planet World Guide, descriptions and photos. http://www.lonelyplanet.com/destinations/middle_east/saudi_arabia/facts.htm.

Saudi Arabia, Nefud Desert. Description and photos. www.encyclopedia.com.

Saudi Arabia, Nefud Desert. *National Geographic.* www.nationalgeographic.com.

History: (See also Saudi Arabia: Books)

History of Al-Murrah tribe, Rub'Al-Khali Desert (Southern Saudi Arabia). *www.Wikipedia.org*

Music and Musical Instruments:
Arabic music and instruments.www.canadian-arabcommunity.com
Live Bedouin music and dance, video. www.geographia.com/egypt/sinai.
Pre-Islamic musical instruments. http://en.wikipedia.org.

Oases: Al-Hasa, Saudi Arabia
Britannica. www.britannica.com/place/Al-Hasa-region-Saudi-Arabia
Flickr (photos of the oasis and streets, District of Hofuf). www.flickr.com.
Nikola Gruen, photographer. www.pbase.com.

Pre-Islamic Pagan Deities
Index of Pagan Deities, ancient Canaanite & Phoenician religions. *Looklex Encyclopedia,* www.lexicorient.com.
Photos of pagan gods & goddesses. Instone Brewer. www.instonebrewer.com.
Pre-Islamic Arabian Gods, alphabetized. www.wikipedia.org.
Religions of the ancient Near East. Wikipedia. www.wikipedia.org.

Saudi Arabian Tribes:
Ancient Amorite Tribe. *Wikipedia,* www.wikipedia.com.

Semitic Languages:
Ancient North Arabian Arabic. *Wikipedia.* www.wikipedia.org.
Proto-Semitic and Semitic Languages. *Wikipedia.* www.wikipedia.org.

Weaving and Crafts: (See also Saudi Arabia: Books.)
Ancient weaving in Saudi Arabia, *Warps, Wefts & Wadis.* Virginia McConnell Simmons, Saudi-Aramco World, Sept-Oct. 1981, www.saudiaramco.com

Basket Weaving. www.basketweaving101.net.
Bedouin Weaving and Tent Making. Joy May Hilden. www.beduinweaving.com.
Bows and Arrows, how to make. *Wikipedia.* www.wikipedia.org.
Tent making. www.canadian-arabcommunity.com.

Iraq (Sumer): Books

Algaze, Guillermo. *Ancient Mesopotamia at the Dawn of Civilization.* 2008.

Bibby, Geoffrey. *Looking for Dilmun.* Pelican Books Reprint, 1972. (Ancient Bahrain believed to be the original site of the Garden of Eden.)

Bottero, Jean. *Everyday Life in Ancient Mesopotamia.* Johns Hopkins University Press, 2001.

Crawford, Harriet. *Sumer and Sumerians.* 1991.

Childe, V. Gordon. *New Light on the Most Ancient East.* W.W. Norton paperback, 1953.

Galpin, W. *The Sumerian Harp of Ur.* Music and Letters, 1929.

Kramer, Samuel Noah. *The Sumerians.* Univ. of Chicago Press, 1963. (Professor and Sumerologist. Spent 30 years translating the clay tablets)

_____, *History Begins at Sumer, 39 Firsts in Recorded History.* 1981.

Lloyd, Seton. *Archaeology of Mesopotamia.* Thames and Hudson, London, 1978.

Mallowan, M.E.L. *Early Mesopotamia and Iran.* McGraw Hill paperback, 1971.

Mellaart, James. *Earliest Civilizations of the Near East.* Mc-Graw Hill reprint, 1970.

Parrot, Andre. *Nineveh and the Old Testament.* Philosophical Library, 1955.

Polin, C.C.J. *Music of the Ancient Near East.* New York, 1954, 1969.

Pritchard, James B. *Archaeology and the Old Testament.* Princeton, 1958.

_____, *Earliest Civilizations of the Near East.* McGraw Hill paperback, 1970.

Roux, Georges. *Ancient Iraq.* Penguin Books paperback, 1964 (Most complete description).

Saggs, H.W.F. *The Greatness that was Babylon.* Hawthorne Books paperback, 1962.

Salim, S.M. *Marsh Dwellers of the Euphrates Delta,* 1962.

Thesiger, Wilfred. *The Marsh Arabs.* (South of Sumer, near the Persian Gulf), Penguin Books paperback, 2007.

Wellesz, E., Ed. *Ancient and Oriental Music.* Oxford, 1957, pp. 228–254.

_____, *The New Oxford History of Music,* vol. 1. London, 1957.

Wolkstein, Diane, and Kramer, S.N. *Inanna, Queen of Heaven and Earth.* Harper & Row, 1983. (Stories and hymns from Sumer.)

Woolley, Sir Leonard. *The Sumerians.* W.W. Norton & Co. paperback reprint, 1965. (British archaeologist. Original discoverer of Sumerian graves. Excellent account. Includes photographs of Sumerian women's headdresses and jewelry from archaeological sites.)

Black, J,A., Cunningham, G., Robson, E., Zolymi, G., *The Marriage of Martu.* Electronic Text, *Corpus of Sumerian Literature.* Oxford, 1998.

Iraq (Sumer): Internet

Archaeology (See also Books)
Artifacts. *Looklex Encyclopedia.* www.looklex.com/e.o/sumer.htm.
Description of Ur, Ziggurat, etc. Wikipedia. www.wikipedia.org

Culture
Clothing, food, jewelry, photos. Univ. of Chicago. http://mesopotamia.lib.uchicago.edu
Clothing, lifestyle. www.ancientneareast.tripod.com/sumer.htl.
Clothing, lifestyle. www.fsmitha.com, www.wikipedia.org, www.historyguide.org.

Video Lecture. http://study.com. (Click on Search: Sumerians. Click on "ancient Sumerians: history, civilization & culture" icon. Click on video icon.)

History
History of Sumer plus photographs. http://history-world.org.
Lifestyle. :www.ancientneareast.tripod.com/sumer.htl.
Macro history of the Sumerians. www.fsmitha.com/index.html.
Sumer. www.answers.com
Sumerian King List. http://crystallinks.com/sumergods.html

Sumerian Inventions (See also Books: S.N. Kramer, L. Woolley)
Wikipedia. www.wikipedia.org.

LITERATURE (See also Books: S.N. Kramer)

Ancient History Encyclopedia. www.orient.eu/article/750

Ancient Sumerian scripts: www.ancientscripts.com/sumerian.html

Cuneiform writing: www.penn.museum/games/cuneiform.shtml

Poems, lamentations, epics, stories about gods and goddesses: https://slewsgranger.word/press.com

Music & Musical Instruments (See Also Books-Sumer)

Musical instruments. http://ww.searchaol.com/aol/video (Search: Sumerian musical instruments)

Musical video. http://www.searchaol.com/aol/video. (Search: Sumerian music)

Mythology (See also Books)

Complete list of Sumerian deities. https://wikipedia.org/WikiList-of-Mesopotamian-deities

General mythology. www.home.comcast.net/~chris.s/sumer_faq.html.

Images of Sumerian gods. http://oracc.museum.upenn.edu/amqq/list of deities/enki/

Sumerian gods and goddesses. http://www.History-world.org.

Photographs

Ancient Sumerian cities and artifacts. *Search America Online*, http://www.searchaol.com/aol/image?q=sumeriancivilization.

Artifacts,clothing. ziggurat: www.bing.com/images

Artifacts, Sumerian life. ziggurat. www.123rf.com/stock-photo/Sumerian.html

City of Ur, photos of excavation at site. *Wikipedia.* http://en.wikipedia.org. www.crystalgraphics.com/powerpictures/images.photos.asp?ss=sumerian

Euphrates River. https://www.britannica.com/place/Euphrates/river

Iraq topography. *The Photo Encyclopedia.* www.fotopedia.com.

Lyres and Sumerian musicians. *Wikipedia.* www.wikipedia.com.

Plaques, deities, writing, musical instruments. http://www.shakespeare.com/106901.html

Reconstructed Sumerian cities. www.earthlink.net/~valis2/sumer.html.

Tigris River. http://www.searchaol.com/aol/image

Ziggurat of Ur & Sumerian chariots. *Wikipedia.* www.wikipedia.com.

Proverbs (See Also Books: S.N. Kramer)

Ancient History Sourcebook: www.fordham.edu/halsall/ancient/2000sumer proverbs.html, halsall@murray.fordham.edu.

Made in the USA
Las Vegas, NV
01 February 2024

85205820R00201